DRAGON DANCE

PETER TASKER

KODANSHA INTERNATIONAL
Tokyo • New York • London

FOR FELIX

Distributed in the United States by Kodansha America, Inc., 575 Lexington
Avenue, New York, NY 10022, and in the United Kingdom and continental
Europe by Kodansha Europe Ltd., 95 Aldwych, London WC2B 4JF. Published
by Kodansha International Ltd., 17–14 Otowa 1-chome, Bunkyo-ku,
Tokyo 112–8652, and by Kodansha America, Inc.

Library of Congress Cataloging-in-Publication Data
Tasker, Peter
Dragon dance / Peter Tasker.
p. cm.
ISBN 4770029489
1. Women journalists—Fiction. 2. Political parties—Fiction.
3. International relations—Fiction. 4. Tokyo (Japan)—Fiction. I. Title.
PR6070.A65 D7 2003
823'.914—dc21
2002030175

www.thejapanpage.com

PROLOGUE

In a dull, featureless room in a dull, featureless building in Zhongnanhai, the heavily guarded area of Beijing that is home to the Communist party elite, two men sat facing each other across a table. They had been waiting half an hour already, and neither of them had said a word. The surface of the table was cold and black and gleamed like a mirror.

Peng Yuan watched the other man out of the corner of his eye. He wondered who he was and why he had been chosen and whether he could be trusted.

Not long ago, attending a meeting like this would have meant risking your life. Now he was only risking his career, apartment, pension, party membership, everything that made life bearable. That was why he chose to remain silent. You could never be sure of people you didn't know well. In fact you couldn't always be sure of people you did know well. You couldn't always be sure of yourself.

Peng Yuan had been a Red Guard in the 1960s. He had been among the thousands who had congregated in Tienanmen Square, waving their red books and chanting adulation to Chairman Mao. He had seen loyal party workers, men and women who had dedicated their lives to the Chinese people, dragged from their offices and beaten to death on the street. He had played his part, screaming abuse at the "drowning dogs," rejoicing as the "red fountains" gushed into the air. He had acted as a man lost in a crazy nightmare. In those days the whole of China had been lost in a crazy nightmare. Nobody could be certain that the nightmare would not happen again someday.

The door at the end of the room slid open, and a shrunken figure in a wheelchair glided over to the table, his head nodding in a metal brace. Another man came in behind him, but Peng Yuan's eyes were fixed on the old man in the wheelchair.

For the first time in his life, Peng Yuan was in the presence of one of the great heroes of the Chinese nation. The drive against the Japanese in the winter of 1943, the smashing of Chiang's nationalists at Tianjin in 1947, the brilliant surprise assault on the Americans in Korea—these were glorious deeds that had been replayed over and over again in movies and novels, and drummed into the heads of every schoolchild in the country. Peng Yuan could hardly believe they were breathing the same air. And yet this living legend had summoned him, Peng Yuan, to a secret meeting. At first he had thought it was a joke, or a trap set by his enemies at the institute. But being here today was no joke. It was the riskiest thing he had ever done.

Disappointingly the old general looked nothing like the handsome figure in the movie posters. He was much smaller and frailer than Peng Yuan had expected. Strangely enough, though, the man in uniform behind the wheelchair did resemble the general in the old pictures. Then Peng Yuan realized that the younger man must be the general's son—a senior general himself and the leader of a powerful military clique that controlled a network of arms factories, import-export monopolies, and overseas investment funds.

Peng Yuan stood up to introduce himself.

"I am Peng Yuan, research officer at the Institute of Foreign Relations."

The younger man signaled that he should sit down again.

"Comrade Peng Yuan is too modest," he said, leaning over his father's wheelchair. "Two years ago he was the deputy director of the institute itself, and widely recognized as one of the finest young scholars in his field. Then suddenly he was demoted to a position unworthy of his talents."

Peng Yuan smiled weakly. "Young scholar" hardly fitted him these days, though compared to the man in the wheelchair even old Deng Xiaoping was a spring chicken.

"Comrade Peng Yuan, please explain the circumstances of your unfortunate position."

Peng Yuan spoke slowly, haltingly. It was still painful to recall what had happened—all the lies and treachery, the anonymous attacks on his character, the gradual removal of his privileges.

The general's son nodded sympathetically. "And what made you so unpopular with the senior ideologues at the institute?"

"My critique of evolutionism, naturally. It was a direct challenge to China's current geopolitical strategy and all the vested interests that support it. My enemies were unable to undermine my theoretical work, so they decided to undermine me instead."

The old man frowned. He had the face of a mournful tortoise, gray and wizened.

"Evolutionism?" he rasped in the desiccated whisper that was all that remained of his voice. "That is an intellectual word that tells me nothing! You must learn to use plainer words."

"I'm sorry. I will try to speak more clearly."

"Go on!"

"What I mean by evolutionism is the current optimistic tendency in geopolitical thinking. It maintains that changes in the relative power of nations automatically lead to changes in the structure of relations between them."

The old man's frown deepened. Peng Yuan gave a nervous cough and pressed on.

"To be more specific—the international system nowadays is hostile to China's emergence as a great power, seeking to constrain us at every turn through military alliances and ideological assaults concerning human rights, environmental issues, and other such hypocrisies. The evolutionists believe that as China becomes richer and stronger, the international system will develop in a way more favorable to our interests. All we Chinese need to do is to be patient and make money and ingratiate ourselves with the foreigners."

The old general raised a shaky finger in the air. The skin was mottled by eight decades of heavy nicotine use. "And you don't accept this?"

Peng Yuan's heart swelled with pride. "I have exposed it as a complete fantasy."

He went on to describe, in as simple terms as possible, his computer simulation of relations between China, Taiwan, the US, and Japan. It was the most advanced model of its type, combining the latest developments in game theory with the classic principles of Chinese military strategy. The results were so sensational that no one had yet dared to publish them.

Using this model, Peng Yuan had shown that the US–Japan alliance was an insurmountable barrier to China's long-term strategic goals. Despite all the economic leverage China could exert on the United States and Japan separately, despite all the resources that might be expended in playing one off against the other, the chances of the alliance falling apart naturally were close to zero. It was too beneficial to both sides, and as China's influence grew the benefits would only increase. Rather than weakening the alliance, China's rise would actually strengthen it!

The implications were shattering. It didn't matter how much time passed. It didn't matter how long the Chinese people waited or what further humiliations they endured. As long as the alliance remained intact, China would remain impotent. Unification with Taiwan, the dream of every Chinese leader since the revolution, would never happen. And without supremacy in Asia, the long-term goal of challenging America's global hegemony was nothing but a pipe dream.

When Peng Yuan had finished speaking, the old general sat staring at the wall, apparently lost in thought. His skin was slack and gray, but his eyes were bright. Those eyes, thought Peng Yuan, had seen great things—from the Long March, when the general had been a dashing young revolutionary, to the launch of China's first long-range ballistic missile. He was one of the few heroes to emerge unscathed from the turmoil of the 1960s and the wrenching changes of the 1970s and 1980s. Time and time again Deng's reformists had attempted to marginalize him, but his power base amongst the military had proved too strong. Now, at the close of his life, he symbolized opposition to the slow poison of democracy and the invasion of decadent Western thought.

The general's son broke the silence. "And what if the Japan–US alliance were to collapse? What would happen then?"

Peng Yuan hesitated before answering. That kind of jump in logic was outside his area of expertise. "Well, in that case the world would be a completely different place. Anything could happen."

"Thank you, Comrade Peng Yuan. Now let us hear a less theoretical approach to the subject."

The man sitting opposite Peng Yuan stood up and saluted.

"I am Zhu Gao," he said in a strong Shanghai accent. "I am deputy professor at the Central Military Academy. My specialty is Japanese security policy."

Peng Yuan leaned back in his chair, glowing with self-satisfaction. At last his ideas were being taken seriously. At last there was a chance they would be put into practice.

ONE

The music was so loud that Jackson could hardly think straight. It was some kind of Japanese techno-boogie, with a guy screaming out the words like his ass was on fire.

Davis leaned back against the bar, fingers in his belt, trying to look like some big-city gangster when in reality he was just an eighteen-year-old country boy, no different from Jackson.

"Hey, Kong, I think I like this place already."

Jackson said nothing, took a pull on his beer bottle. He didn't like being called Kong. It made him feel like a freak. Still, Davis was his best friend on the ship, his only friend really.

"These Japanese bitches are hot, man. Even you gonna get your dick wet tonight."

Davis was gazing over at the dance floor, where half a dozen women in hot pants and halter tops were freaking to the rhythm. The beat was pounding away like a sledgehammer. It vibrated Jackson's guts and rattled his bones.

Hooper stuck his head between Davis and Jackson, his eyes mock-solemn like some TV comic.

"Don't know if them girls be capable of accommodating a man of the Kong's dimensions. Maybe they gonna demand risk money."

Davis gave a yuk-yuk laugh. Jackson looked away. This kind of dirty talk made him uneasy. His mother had never allowed it, not from him nor from any of his brothers.

"You think they're ho's?"

"No, Kong, they trainee nuns."

This got a high-pitched giggle from Davis. He was all cranked up on some powder he'd bought at the base, but Jackson stuck to beer, as he always did.

And being the size he was, getting drunk was a financial impossibility.

"Hey, lookee here," said Hooper, nodding over at the entrance. A group of white sailors had just come in and were staring at the dance floor with big, stupid grins on their faces. One of them, a skinhead called Oakley, was bellowing something at the top of his voice, his eyes squeezed shut with the effort, his mouth a great wet hole. You couldn't hear a word he was saying, but you knew it had to be obscene. Oakley couldn't tell you the time of day without making it filthy.

"Let's go get some sushi, before it walk out the door."

Davis sauntered over to the dance floor, using the slow rolling gait that he figured made him look cool and mean. In fact he looked more like Mickey Mouse's doggy friend.

"Come on, Kong—it's sookie-sookie time."

"Not for me, man. You go ahead."

Hooper shook his head in disgust. "What's the matter? You think Jesus won't love you no more?"

Jackson said nothing. He still prayed every night before going to sleep, and for some reason Hooper thought that was funny.

Jackson stayed at the bar, ordered another beer, and drank it as the white guys walked past pretending not to see him. Davis stepped onto the dance floor, started going through his crazy-legs routine. Hooper's approach was more basic: he just took one of the girls by the wrist, and pulled her toward the bar. She was yelling and shaking her head, but not resisting much. That was good. For all his funny guy act, Hooper had a mean temper, especially with women.

The techno-boogie was getting louder and faster, seemed like it was shaking his brain loose. Jackson liked music, but not this crazy stuff. What he liked was the kind that made him feel calm and strong, like the sound of the trumpet, soaring high and pure. He remembered the way his daddy used to play the trumpet in the yard, any song he heard on the radio he could just pick up that trumpet and play it straight off. After his daddy went away, Jackson had never heard trumpet-playing like that again.

"What's the matter, big guy? You look lonesome."

Jackson turned around. A woman was standing beside him, smiling as if she knew him. She had frizzed-out hair and wasn't wearing a halter top or a micro-mini or hot pants, but was dressed normally, in jeans and a white T-shirt. And she was a great looker, in a witchy kind of way. She had high cheekbones and catlike eyes that caught your gaze and held on, made it difficult to look away again.

"You from the big ship—right?"

"How come you know that?"

"You look like you been—on the water too long."

Most women Jackson had met were scared of him at first. When they realized he wasn't so scary, they laughed. But this woman wasn't scared at all.

"It's plenty of fun—on that big ship?"

"Ain't fun exactly, but I kinda like it."

"Yeah? Why you like it so much?"

Jackson paused to consider. It was a serious question, and it deserved a serious answer.

"Well, it's kind of hard to explain. This ship, it's doing important work, defending regional security and stuff. That's a big responsibility, gives you something to think about when you wake up in the morning."

"Hey, you sounding like—such a heavy guy!" She had a strange way of speaking English, fast and slurred, but with sudden pauses as if she'd forgotten how the sentence was supposed to end.

Jackson frowned. "Miss, this is a heavy time for the world. Everywhere you look democratic values are under threat."

Jackson always tried to keep himself informed. He didn't read so well, but he watched the news programs carefully. Davis and the others chuckled when he started talking about the Indonesian crisis or the Middle East peace conference. But the state of the world was no laughing matter. That was why they were all here.

"This your first time—off base?"

"Yeah, we got in a couple days back."

The first night there had been a curfew because of the big anti-US demonstration. Jackson had watched the flotilla of tiny boats bobbing around the shoreline and the noisy crowds surging along the street, the Buddhist priests chanting and banging drums. It had looked harmless enough, but apparently there had been trouble afterward. Cars had been trashed, and a couple of the base workers beaten with steel pipes.

She was staring at him, her eyes as hard and bright as a cat's. "So—how you like Japan?"

"Ain't seen much of it yet."

She nodded. "Then I gonna show you. Got some friends—having a party—just round the corner."

"Huh?"

"Come, I show you—real Japan."

Jackson looked around. Strobe lights were sweeping the dance floor, breaking up the women's bodies into a collage of flashing images—arms thrown in the air, frizzy hair across pouting lips, a jeweled navel, shiny thighs, nipples straining against thin cotton. Oakley and the other white guys were standing at the edge of the floor, grinning and gawking and swigging beer. Hooper and Davis were nowhere to be seen. They must have chosen their women and gone, abandoning him to the loud music and this weird woman.

"Let's go, big guy."

Jackson stared down at her. She had about a third of his body mass, and her eyes were level with his chest, yet somehow he didn't have the power to refuse. Those big black eyes were locked on to him.

"Okay," he muttered.

She looped her arm around his and they walked toward the entrance. Oakley and his friends didn't even look up, neither did the barman. Jackson stared at the ground, said nothing. He felt guilty, although what about he wasn't exactly sure.

Out on the street the air was warm, filled with exhaust fumes and the roar of traffic. Crowds of people rushed past, nobody looking at anyone. Neon signs were everywhere, flashing with that crazy chicken-feather writing. Jackson felt like a child, following the woman as she turned into a side street, then again into an alley barely wide enough for them to walk side by side.

She took a cellphone from her bag, and started speaking in a low urgent voice.

"Who you talking to?" asked Jackson. He couldn't understand a word, but it didn't sound much like a party conversation.

"Talking my friends—waiting eagerly for you to come."

"That's nice." Jackson had heard the Japanese were real polite, but this was amazing. Some folks he'd never even met were keen to meet him!

The alley was quiet, empty. On one side was a high wall topped with broken glass, on the other the backs of some shabby-looking office buildings, not a light anywhere. As they passed under a ramshackle fire escape, there was a faint rustling sound just above Jackson's head and he glanced up just in time to catch a dark shape scooting up to the next floor. It was the skinniest cat he had ever seen, little more than a shadow with fur.

"What happened to his tail?" said Jackson. "Did someone chop it off?"

"Not necessary. Japanese people like no tail cat. Tails cause trouble, knock stuff over in narrow house. No tail cat—much better."

"But don't cats need their tails for balancing?"

The woman didn't answer. Once more she was talking into the phone, so low this time she was practically whispering.

They carried on down the alley, her arm locked around his. Jackson felt the heat of her body, the tingle of her hair brushing his arm.

What kind of people were they going to meet? How was Jackson supposed to behave? He tried to recall what they had been told in the "cultural sensitivity program" the other night. Take your shoes off in somebody's house. Don't leave your chopsticks in your food. Don't piss in the bath. They were ambassadors for their country, the instructor had said. With political tensions so high, they had to be extra careful not to offend anyone. Davis and Hooper didn't pay any attention, just sat there yawning and scratching. Jackson had listened carefully though, and had even asked some questions at the end. This stuff was important, part of the purpose of the big ship plowing through the ocean.

At the end of the alley was a gate with a rusty latch. The woman pushed it open and they stepped into a patch of waste ground containing the skeleton of a building, all girders and struts and wooden boards. Behind it was the highway, cars zooming.

"Here we are," said the woman.

Jackson narrowly avoided stepping into a long trench, several feet deep, containing a pipe that glinted in the moonlight like a long metal sausage. He gazed up at the scaffolding, the crane silhouetted in the moonlight, the blue plastic sheets flapping gently in the breeze.

"Your friends are here?" he asked incredulously.

"Yeah. They eagerly waiting—other side."

She took him by the wrist and together they walked over the ridged mud toward the gaping hole between the boards that marked the doorway. Jackson was getting more and more confused. What would her friends be doing having a party in a half-made building?

Jackson passed through the hole in the boards to the inside of the structure. It was sticky underfoot, and there was the smell of paint thinner in the air. It took his eyes a couple of seconds to adjust to the gloom, then he made out the outline of a shovel, a cement bag, and a pair of rubber boots half hidden behind a plastic sheet. The boots suddenly took a step backward and disappeared from sight.

"What's going on?" said Jackson, glancing over his shoulder. But the woman hadn't followed him inside, and that was when Jackson got a prickly feeling in the back of his scalp. This was all wrong, he suddenly realized. He shouldn't be here, had to get out fast. He turned in the squelching mud, lost his balance, and was vaguely aware of a figure coming out of the shadows, something swishing through the air toward him. There was an explosion of pain at the back of his knee, and suddenly Jackson was lying on his stomach, face down in the mud.

Someone stepped forward and poked him in the side with a metal pole. Jackson twisted around, grabbed the pole, then froze with shock. The face staring down at him was like a dog's, with slits for eyes and a black plastic snout. Jackson yanked at the pole with all his strength and had just grappled it free when another pole smashed against his hand. He gave a yelp of pain and let go.

A second dog face appeared behind the first, gazing down at him and nodding. A gloved hand thrust something into his face, a thin rubber tube that made a faint hissing sound. Jackson tried to twist away and bellowed for help, but the only sound that came out was a choking rattle. The muscles of his face felt totally rigid, as if they'd turned to iron. Then suddenly the world was rushing away from him, high into the sky, getting smaller and smaller until it was just a pinprick of light.

And then the pinprick disappeared.

It was six-thirty in the morning when the open-backed truck arrived at the building site and the group of laborers jumped out. Ahmed was the only non-Japanese on this job, but after three years of illegal work all over eastern Japan he had a good understanding of the Japanese language and customs. In fact he was starting to feel at home in Japan. He had learned how to play mah-jongg and sing traditional ballads, and had even developed an interest in baseball.

Every morning at five o'clock, Ahmed went to a small square around the back of the station near his lodging house and waited for the yakuza to come in their trucks. There were usually twice as many men as jobs, but Ahmed almost always got picked. The yakuza knew he was tough and hardworking.

One of the best things about Japan was the yakuza, he thought. There were many gangsters in Ahmed's country, but they were unreliable idlers and bullies who double-crossed you at the first chance. These Japanese gangsters weren't like that at all. They were hard workers themselves, always rushing from job to job. And they always paid the promised money at the promised time. You didn't need to count it.

The men pulled the tools out of the back of the truck, then stood in line while Tanaka, the foreman, gave his usual morning speech. The content of it didn't matter; what was important was the serious way he intoned it and the way everybody listened respectfully, bowing and shouting "Hai" at the right moments. Ahmed liked this too. In his own country, the foremen were almost as bad as the gangsters. They would often take some of the building materials away and sell them, and the workers rarely had helmets or proper tools.

When Tanaka had finished his speech, the workers picked up their tools. Ahmed took his handsaw and drill and was the first man to reach the building. He pulled up the plastic sheet, ducked inside, then froze in his tracks and let out a startled cry.

Ahmed had witnessed many horrors before in his life, but this was the most shocking: a monster of a man lying asleep on the ground, his huge chest rising and falling. And next to him a girl's half-naked body, face down in the mud, arms sticking out at unnatural angles. There was blood everywhere—a huge dark stain on the ground, spattered on the wooden boards, streaking the man's shirt and trousers. The girl was young, no more than twelve or thirteen. And Ahmed had seen enough to know she was beyond help. This building was going to be bad, he thought. Nobody should live in it, nobody should work on it any more.

He backed out as quietly as he could and went to get Tanaka.

"Look at him," growled the taxi driver, glancing at the liquid crystal screen mounted in the dashboard. "He's garbage, that guy."

The taxi suddenly swerved to avoid a truck turning left. Martine bounced back in her seat, one hand grabbing for the safety strap. On the flickering screen she saw a close-up of Jackson being hustled down a flight of steps by two uniformed policemen, his eyes big and scared.

"A twelve-year-old girl—he cut her up like sashimi!"

"It certainly is terrible," said Martine, glancing at the traffic.

The taxi driver shook his head. "It's time to kick the Americans out of this country and build up our own military. According to Nozawa-sensei, it would be good for the economy too. The unemployment problem would be cured within months."

He accelerated toward the next set of traffic lights, which were showing amber. Martine took a firmer grip on the safety strap.

"You sound like a big fan of Nozawa."

The lights turned red. The taxi shot through, then squealed to a halt at the next tailback.

"Of course I am! He's the only man with the guts to stand up for Japanese culture. The old politicians are just fools, nobody even understands what they're saying. It's no wonder all the foreigners are laughing at us."

Martine made sympathetic noises. This was the fifth taxi driver she had met this week who was an enthusiastic supporter of Nozawa. Using taxi drivers as symbols of public opinion was a journalistic cliché, but like all clichés it had some value. The conventional wisdom amongst Japan-watchers—diplomats, financial analysts, and think tankers—was that Nozawa was a political joke, a flaky showbiz character who would never attract serious mainstream support. But Martine had a feeling that the Japan-watchers were getting it all wrong. Again.

The taxi spluttered forward a couple of yards, then eased to a halt. It was complete gridlock this time.

On the TV screen a line of police were pushing back the crowd, clearing a way for Jackson to reach the black van. Martine made out the shape of a rightist in combat fatigues yelling into a megaphone. There was shoving and bellowing and women's voices screaming and a few objects being hurled through the air. Jackson held up a brawny arm to shield his eyes, but something caught him on the back of the head. The taxi driver gave a snort of derision.

"That thug deserves the death penalty. This idea of handing him over to the Americans for trial—it's ridiculous. They've got so many lawyers over there, if you pay them enough money you can get away with anything, right?"

"Well, in fact it's a bit more..."

But the taxi driver was in full flow. "There are too many foreigners in Japan these days, they call us yellow monkeys and walk around like they own the whole country. The women are just as bad..."

The taxi driver stopped in mid-sentence. Martine saw his eyes blinking warily at her in the rearview mirror.

"I'm sorry if I was rude," he muttered. "I said some bad things. It's just that you speak Japanese so fluently. Somehow I forgot..."

"Don't worry," said Martine sweetly. "Tell me more about Nozawa. Do you think he can really make an impact politically?"

The taxi driver was happy to change the subject. He starting talking about Nozawa's down-to-earth opinions, the fact that he was as tall as most foreigners, how his songs were so moving, his voice so strong and manly...

Martine kept one eye on the TV screen. There was a close-up of Jackson sitting in the van, staring ahead blankly, his lips moving. Martine realized that Jackson was actually saying something, articulating the same word over and over again. It was not hard to make out. "Mama," Jackson was saying. "Mama, mama, mama..."

On the never-ending tickertape of daily news, amongst all the manmade and natural disasters, the plane crashes and car bombings and floods and massacres, a few events stand out as stories in the true sense. They have a narrative. They change the way people look at the world, which is to say that they change the world itself.

The killing of little Mari Yamada would be one of those events, Martine had sensed immediately. At the time the story broke she had been over at Makoto's apartment. Makoto was cooking linguine in a stainless-steel pot he had mail-ordered from Italy. Martine was sitting on the tatami floor, staring disconsolately at the *shogi* board. She had been taught the game by a fourth-grade master and prided herself on her skill, but somehow Makoto had beaten her again. For such a straightforward kind of guy, he could be incredibly sneaky sometimes.

17

She glanced at the clock and considered whether or not to turn on the TV. She hadn't heard the news since early afternoon, and these days that made her nervous as too much was happening, none of it good. And since Charlie, the bureau chief, spoke hardly any Japanese, it was up to Martine to make sure they didn't miss anything important.

On the other hand, it was Sunday night and the first time she and Makoto had been alone together for weeks. Martine had been busy covering the latest twists and turns in the crisis, chasing down contacts, filing three or four stories a day. And Makoto had been absorbed in his own problems at the brewery, talking to lawyers and bankers. Now at last everything was right—the atmosphere, the food, the fact that Makoto's son was away on a school trip and his mother had gone to soak her aged bones in a hot spring in the Japan Alps. Martine had the feeling that if she pressed the button on the remote control, the intimate evening they had both been looking forward to would disappear like a mirage.

She pressed it anyway, keeping the volume down low. And as soon as she saw the newsreader's face—the agitation in his eyes, the suppressed anger in his mouth—she knew that she was right. Out in the world something big had happened. She turned up the sound, and pulled out her notebook.

"Hoi!" called Makoto from the kitchen. "What's going on in there?"

"Quiet!" hissed Martine. "I'm trying to hear what the guy's saying."

"Huh?"

She hardly heard him. In her mind's eye, the story was already forming neat columns, upper left on page five.

Martine's instincts proved to be correct. Mari-chan's murder by an American sailor caused outrage throughout the population. Almost immediately the internet chat rooms were overflowing with angry messages. The tabloids and weekly magazines responded with savage glee, splashing the story over their front pages in huge blood-red characters. On every channel the morning gossip "wide shows" made it their lead feature. Regular programs were interrupted to show press conferences with Mari-chan's grief-stricken parents. Japanese TV crews descended on the small Alabama town where Jackson's mother lived alone, and interviewed everyone from the local cops to the barber who used to cut his hair.

Crowds stood silently in the streets of Ginza and Shibuya, following the events on giant video screens. Two images were shown over and over again. The first, obviously leaked by the police, was of Mari-chan's naked body half covered by a blood-soaked sheet. The second showed Jackson being pulled from the house by the police, his teeth bared in what looked like a maniacal grin. Only from the angle at which his arms were being levered up could you deduce that it was actually a grimace of pain.

It was as if Japan had been waiting for something like this to happen. The economic crisis had been going on for too long now and people were angry, frustrated, bewildered by the slow collapse of everything they held dear. The first politician to seize the opportunity was Nozawa. He was bitterly critical of the prime minister, the American military, and the lack of morals in modern society. He even visited Mari-chan's house to offer his condolences, and organized a demonstration outside the US Embassy.

Nozawa's poll ratings rocketed. After just two years as a member of the Upper House, he was now by far the most popular politician in Japan. Of course the competition was weak, since most of the political establishment was despised for its incompetence, lack of integrity, poor leadership, and inability to understand ordinary people. Nevertheless it was remarkable that a middle-aged rock singer with cranky opinions could have such an impact on the national political scene.

In recent decades, drafting celebrities into the Diet had become common practice. In the last election, seats had been won by, amongst others, a faith healer, a transvestite comedian, a TV chef, and a bronze-medal-winning synchronized swimmer. These minor celebrities were not expected to have any real political influence, nor did they. In fact no sooner did they enter the political world than their own popularity generally began to slump dramatically.

Nozawa was proving to be the exception. He was a major star, and was burning brighter than ever, using the political stage as skillfully as he used the stage at the Budokan.

The serious Japan-watchers were confident that the Nozawa phenomenon was strictly temporary, an aberration that had cropped up while the establishment was paralyzed by the UNG scandal. After the sudden collapse of the United Nippon Group, Japan's largest bank, dozens of senior politicians were under investigation for corrupt dealings. Even so, it was unthinkable that Nozawa would have a lasting effect on domestic politics, let alone on international relations. After all, Japan was a highly controlled, stability-obsessed society. There couldn't possibly be a place in the power structure for a man who had been dismissed by one of the *Tribune*'s star columnists as "a cross between Bruce Springsteen and Benito Mussolini."

But the problem with serious Japan-watchers was that they spent too much time in conferences and seminars, and not enough time talking to taxi drivers. And they underestimated the power of a story, the way it can develop its own momentum, converging with other stories into a churning, tumbling tide that sweeps away everything in its path.

Martine's taxi continued its crawling odyssey through the traffic. Even in the pre-crisis days, getting around had needed a lot of patience. Now with the roadblocks and random searches, it could take as much as an hour to get the four or five miles from Otemachi to Shinjuku. The trains weren't much better either. However long you thought it was going to take to get somewhere, it always took longer.

Martine took out her palmtop computer and sat back in her seat. Two messages had appeared. One was from Charlie, asking her to get back to the office as soon as possible. Apparently there was something urgent to discuss. Martine gave a sigh of annoyance. In all likelihood this "urgent" discussion was a pretext for checking up on Martine's activities.

The other message was a strange one. It was brief, with no title and no signature.

> Blond goddess,
> You are looking so beautiful with your new hairstyle. But please stay away from Chiba City tonight. There may be a regrettable event at eleven o'clock. Incidentally I like the shape of your lips. What you could do with them makes me very excited.

Martine gazed at it in distaste. She had indeed changed her hairstyle a month ago, going for a simple summer look with bangs that framed her face like a bracket. This weirdo must have noticed it on the video-clip that had just been uploaded to the *Tribune*'s website. As for that last comment, it was beneath contempt.

The *Tribune*'s former CEO had a lot to answer for. Six years ago he had launched the "E-growth" strategy, designed to transform the stodgy conglomerate into a leading player in the new economy. That CEO, like the new economy he championed, was long gone now—golden parachute, Caribbean island, twenty-two-year-old aerobics instructor—but the legacy remained. Even now journalists were still required to offer "dynamic interactivity," which meant answering questions live on the internet and fielding e-mails from readers all over the world. The problem was that the men who wanted to get interactive with Martine—and they were always men—were rarely interested in her stories.

Martine deleted the message and closed the mailbox. The taxi driver turned around, his big shiny face creasing into a smile.

"Hey—would you like to sing one of the sensei's songs?"

"Excuse me?"

"I mean, we could do a duet. Look—there's a karaoke built into the radio."

He pulled a bulky microphone from under the dashboard and thrust it at her. Martine smiled and shook her head.

"Thanks, but I don't have the right voice for this kind of music."

Which was true. Nozawa's songs weren't difficult to sing—if they were, they wouldn't have been in such demand at karaoke boxes all over the country—but there was a certain lilt to them that Martine couldn't carry off. Most of his recent hits were based on the quavering melodies of traditional *enka* music, cleverly blended with elements of blues, country-and-western, reggae, techno, and rap. It was a formula that had revolutionized the Japanese music industry, appealing simultaneously to all segments of the market—from housewives to high school kids, from trendy office girls to shaven-headed judoka.

"Are you sure? Your voice sounds very nice to me."

"But not as nice as yours," retorted Martine.

The taxi driver's smile widened, revealing a chunky gold tooth. He took a CD case and pulled out the disc.

"This is my favorite," he said, waving the plastic case at Martine's face. "It's called 'Wind of the Gods.'"

Martine glanced at the CD case. The picture on the cover showed Nozawa in an old-fashioned pilot's helmet, leather flaps down over his ears. He was smiling sardonically at the camera, a small white cup of saké in his hand. Behind him was the outline of a warship, its deck covered in flames and columns of black smoke billowing into a blood-red sky.

Martine winced. The original "wind of the gods" was the providential storm that had saved Japan from invasion by Kublai Khan in the thirteenth century. It was also the nickname of the Japanese suicide pilots who had attempted in vain to halt the advance of the American fleet in the last months of the Pacific War. Martine had researched the subject for an article and had even managed to interview one of the surviving pilots, a man who had been on standby to fly when the surrender was announced. He had gone on to become a schoolteacher, and at the age of eighty-five he was one of the sanest people she had ever met.

The taxi slid forward a couple of yards before coming to a halt again. The taxi driver pushed the disc into the CD player, and fiddled with the controls.

"Are you sure you don't want to do a duet?"

"Positive," said Martine.

"All right, which one shall I sing for you? How about 'The Pilot's Last Words to His Sweetheart'? That's a very sad song. Last week I sang it with a customer I was taking to Kawasaki. He'd been drinking quite a bit, and he started crying in the middle."

Martine shook her head and glanced at the CD case. "Hmmm—how about the next one—'Dried-up Rice Fields of My Heart'? Do you know it?"

"No problem," said the taxi driver happily. "I know the words to every single song. I could sing it in my sleep!"

He slid the microphone into a special holder mounted on top of the dashboard. The music started with the thump of a taiko drum and a slow descending riff on the shamisen. He hunched his shoulders slightly and started to croon:

The hometown is broken down, the schoolroom is empty,
The train line is covered with weeds…

It was a surprisingly accurate rendition, capturing the swaggering melodrama of Nozawa's delivery, from the quavering high notes to the earthy growls between the verses. Martine caught a few pedestrians glancing into the taxi as they hurried past. They could probably hear the muffled beat of the drums. They could certainly see the taxi driver leaning forward into the microphone, and the blond woman in the back nodding her head and clapping along with the rhythm.

It was just past six when the taxi pulled into the hotel forecourt. The sun was setting over the western skyline, bathing the concrete and glass in a blood-red glow. This was the time of day when beer gardens on top of department stores and office buildings would switch on their signs, ready to serve hordes of thirsty office workers. The number of beer gardens, like every other kind of business, was steadily declining from year to year, but up there on the roof, with the warm breeze ruffling your hair and an ice-cold glass of beer in your hand, you could travel back in time, back through the years of crisis, past the decade of stagnation that preceded it, into the bygone era of growth when the whole country was brimming with energy and resolve and the future excited hope, not despair.

The taxi driver turned to hand Martine her change.

"I know your face from somewhere," he said suddenly. "Didn't I see you on TV a couple of weeks ago?"

Martine shrugged. In fact she had appeared on a late-night TV panel discussion on the collapse of the yen.

"Weren't you in that drama series, the one about the high school teacher who moonlights in a Ginza hostess club?"

"I'm not an actress," said Martine, slipping the change into her purse. "Sorry to disappoint you."

The taxi driver grinned. "Really? Well, you should be. You've certainly got the looks for it. Those long legs, and your neck is beautiful."

"My neck?" Martine resisted the temptation to scratch her left ear, which had started itching madly.

The grin got wider, revealing a couple of glinting teeth. "You're here on a date, I suppose."

"I'm here for work, actually," said Martine.

"You do your work in this hotel? Hah! Now I understand—you must be Russian."

There was a time when Martine would have been outraged by the implication. She would have said something sarcastic and flounced out of the taxi, seething with rage. Now she didn't even pause as she stepped smoothly out. One thing she had learned from Makoto was that there was no point in taking offense when no harm was intended. Much better to save your energy for when it was.

"I'll wait here if you want," said the taxi driver merrily. "Afterward I can show you some interesting places, like a noodle restaurant where the noodles come shooting down a bamboo slide, or a bar with a shark in a tank."

Martine didn't look around. He wasn't expecting her to agree. He probably wouldn't have known what to do if she had.

Martine called Nozawa's suite from the hotel lobby, then took the elevator to the thirtieth floor. When the doors opened she was confronted by two square-headed, square-shouldered men in black kimonos. They were members of Nozawa's security team, what he called his "ministry of defense."

"Meyer-san?" asked the first.

"At your command," said Martine with well-practiced meekness.

"Before meeting the sensei, there are certain security procedures. Are you willing to accept a body search?"

"A body search! What, by you?"

The bodyguard stared at a spot on the carpet in front of him. "Of course not," he said tightly. "One of our female staff is waiting for you in the next room."

Martine noted with amusement that the man was actually blushing.

They led her down the corridor and into one of the guest rooms, where she was greeted by a tall young woman dressed in the same kind of dark kimono. According to the plastic badge on her chest, her name was Kawamoto.

"I'm sorry to put you to this inconvenience," she said with a bow. "But you can understand how it is, there are so many crazy people around these days."

"That's for sure," said Martine dryly.

"We're getting so many threats. So many people want to harm the sensei—it's very disturbing."

Kawamoto gave a little shudder. Like most of Nozawa's female disciples, she looked as if she had been chosen for qualities other than sincerity and diligence. She had large liquid eyes, a full, rather mischievous mouth, and thick glossy hair—"black as a raven's wing," as one of Nozawa's lyrics went—cascaded over her shoulders. Martine guessed that she had started off as a devoted fan, the kind who hung around hotels and concert venues waiting for a chance to snatch a photo or, better still, to get invited to a private party. In other words, a groupie.

Kawamoto emptied Martine's bag onto the bed. Martine perched herself on the desk by the window and watched as her notebook, wallet, and lipstick were each scrutinized in turn.

"It must be fun working for Nozawa-sensei," prompted Martine, swinging her feet back and forth.

The girl's smooth forehead was creased by a frown. "Fun? This isn't some kind of game, you know. We're working to restore Japan's social, economic, and spiritual health—to cure the three cancers."

Martine nodded sympathetically. Japanese people seemed to have an affinity for sets of three—the three finest gardens, the three great generals, and so on. Now Nozawa had contributed the three cancers, as well as the three viruses (speculation, wastefulness, and individualism) and the three pillars of the economy (heavy manufacturing, rice farming, and nuclear energy).

Kawamoto seemed eager to talk. Martine encouraged her with a friendly smile.

"And you think you can restore economic health by refusing to buy imported goods?"

"That's a symbolic matter, a chance for people to show their patriotism. People everywhere should have pride in their own country's products, don't you think?"

Martine said nothing. Being half Scots and half Swedish, born in Africa and educated in Oxford, Washington, and Paris, with her father now living in Sydney and her mother in Tuscany, she found the question impossible to answer.

"So have you destroyed your passport yet?"

"Of course," said Kawamoto. "I did it on New Year's Day. It gave me such a feeling of freedom."

This had started as a one-off publicity gimmick and had turned into a social phenomenon. Every few months, crowds of Nozawa's supporters would congregate outside an office of the Japan Tourist Board or Japan Airlines and sing songs and set fire to their passports one by one.

"Freedom? What kind of freedom is it when you can't travel wherever you want?"

Kawamoto shook her head. "You wouldn't understand. For such a long time we Japanese have been enslaved by a certain idea of foreign culture and foreign countries. In order to restore the health of our national culture, we have to release ourselves from this slavery."

"So what happens if you want to spend your honeymoon in Guam?"

Martine's attempt at a joke fell flat. Kawamoto seemed positively insulted.

"I would never marry a man who would even consider such a stupid idea! Can't you see why I burned my passport? I made a commitment to be in Japan every day for the rest of my life. I will breathe only Japanese air, and my feet will touch only Japanese soil."

She sounded sincere, but that last phrase wasn't her own. It was a direct quotation from "I don't wanna go to Narita," the opening song on Nozawa's last album.

"That's one good thing about this crisis," went on Kawamoto hotly. "It has made us understand what we've lost. The Japanese people have become weak and selfish, and greedy for money. We must restore national pride and respect for our ancestors."

"And how are you going to do that?"

"Wait and see," said Kawamoto, her large eyes shining with missionary zeal. "Nozawa-sensei is leading us forward. The world will be forced to take notice of Japan again!"

"Ah."

"I would like to discuss this more with you, Meyer-san. I'd like to make you understand why Japanese people are supporting Nozawa-sensei so strongly. Unfortunately there isn't enough time now, but please call me in the near future. It is important that the world should see the situation correctly."

Now Martine got it. Kawamoto was a plant, the equivalent of one of those Soviet-era Russian interpreters who were so eager to make friends with foreign journalists. Still, the offer was worth considering. The central mystery of the Nozawa phenomenon was how someone like Kawamoto—an ordinary young woman, no different from the fun-loving "office ladies" who stream through the boutiques of Shibuya and nightclubs of Roppongi—had developed the mindset of a reactionary. Understand that, and you would understand everything.

"Thank you. I'll be in touch."

Kawamoto opened a black attaché case and took out a metal detector.

"Good. Now please take off your necklace and wristwatch. This won't take long."

Martine did as she was told, then slipped off the desk and held her arms in the air.

Five minutes later the two male guards led Martine to a room at the end of the corridor. There was no number on the door, just the characters for "Shogun" embossed in ornate gold script. One of the guards rang the bell then moved aside, eyes glued to the carpet. It was as if glimpsing the interior of the room would be an act of lese majesty. The door swung open, and Martine stepped inside.

The room was buzzing with activity. There were around twenty people present, among them senior guards in kimonos, earnest-looking researchers murmuring into cellphones and tapping away at laptop computers, and political operatives in dark suits with slicked-back hair. Martine glanced around. Nozawa was not present, but she did recognize the three people sitting at the table by the window.

25

On the left was Eiji Yamazaki, the godfather of Japanese pop music and producer of Nozawa's last ten albums. With his round face, androgynous features, and blank expression, Yamazaki looked rather like a space alien who had come to earth to study the behavior of the natives. Back in the seventies he had been a member of the Silver Robot Dance Band, the legendary pioneer of computer-generated music. From there Yamazaki had gone from strength to strength, winning Oscars for his movie scores, performing duets with Pavarotti and Sting, staging multimedia extravaganzas—complete with lasers, giant holograms, and thousands of extras—in Venice, Kyoto, and in front of the Egyptian pyramids.

It was Yamazaki who had masterminded Nozawa's rise to superstar status. Before he took over as producer, Nozawa's career had been in the doldrums. The fresh-faced young folksinger had been reduced to a mere purveyor of sentimental ballads, indistinguishable from dozens of other has-beens on late-night TV. Yamazaki had positioned him at the leading edge of musical fashion, blending musical influences so seamlessly that it was impossible to tell what came from where.

Yamazaki seemed to sense Martine's presence. His eyes flicked over in her direction, held her gaze for a brief moment, then returned to the screen of his laptop computer. It was like being scanned by an insect.

The man in the middle was Professor Suzuki, an academic from Tokyo University who served as Nozawa's economic adviser. He had made his name by developing the "endogenous social capital model," a controversial theory that, if taken to extremes, could be used to justify trade barriers, government control of wages and prices, and the closure of financial markets. His most recent proposal was the "Social Protection Program," by which companies that kept to the traditional Japanese system of lifetime employment, seniority pay, and obedience to the bureaucracy would be rewarded with subsidies. These would be financed by special taxes on companies guilty of selling at "unfairly low prices" or making exorbitant profits.

But at least Suzuki was a genuine expert, a man whose work had been widely debated in academic circles all over the world. The man sitting next to him was something else entirely. Jiro Yasutani was, in Martine's opinion, little more than an opportunist with a talent for self-promotion. Originally a writer of manga comics, he had scored a huge success with *Sacrifice*, the tale of a patriotic raccoon dog set in the closing days of the Second World War. Nozawa wrote the theme song for the movie version, which was repeated on TV almost every month.

These days Yasutani's smirking face was everywhere. He was on commercials for everything from saké and soy sauce to five-year bank deposits that carried an interest rate of 0.1%. His most popular forum was a Sunday night

TV show that featured bizarre conspiracy theories and paranormal phenomena, such as UFOs, poltergeists, and continents under the sea, all described without a hint of skepticism.

Yasutani's latest interest was paleontology. The TV cameras had followed him to the mountains of central Kyushu where, trowel and chisel in hand, he had made a series of sensational finds. The shards of stone he uncovered proved that Japan had been populated hundreds of thousands of years earlier than previously thought. The conclusion was obvious: the Japanese were not merely a distinct race, but originated from a different, earlier branch of Homo *sapiens*. According to Yasutani, Homo *nipponicus* was highly cultured, peaceful and cooperative, and communicated through a form of telepathy that still existed, though in much weaker form, amongst Japan's modern inhabitants. Forget about Lucy from East Africa; the common ancestor of the Japanese was Keiko from Kumamoto Prefecture.

The whole thing was preposterous, of course, but strangely not a single dissenting voice was to be heard. A couple of senior academics had even commented that Yasutani's theories were "worthy of consideration." As Makoto had pointed out, the universities were restructuring too, coping with the decline in the student population. A few well-aimed donations from Yasutani's production company would go a long way.

"Meyer-san, you look as pretty as ever!"

Martine turned to face a tall man with a smooth oval face and slicked-back hair that curled around his ears and onto his collar. He was wearing a gray silk suit, an open-necked shirt, and tasseled loafers. He leaned forward, clearly intending to give her a peck on the cheek. Martine headed him off by thrusting out her hand.

"Good to see you again, Shimizu-san. And thanks for setting this up."

Yasuo Shimizu was Nozawa's chief adviser, the mastermind of his public relations strategy. The senior secretaries of most politicians were long-serving party hacks steeped in "Nagata-cho logic," the way of thinking found in the insular world of Japan's political district and nowhere else on earth. Shimizu was a different type entirely. For many years he had been head of the Japanese operations of Byrne & Company, one of the largest management consultancies in the world. He had a global reputation as a marketing guru and had published dozens of books on the IT revolution. Martine found him charming, sophisticated, and as slippery as a piece of overboiled tofu.

"I really appreciate your help. An exclusive interview with Nozawa-sensei is a rare event these days."

That was true enough. Nozawa was not keen on submitting himself to detailed questioning by journalists. He preferred to communicate with the public directly through his phone-in radio show and his website, now one of the most popular destinations in Japanese cyberspace.

Shimizu grinned. "This is no ordinary interview, Meyer-san. We're giving you a major scoop, one of the biggest stories of the year."

"I'm honored, of course. But why me?"

"Because people don't trust the Japanese press any more. If they see a story in the *Asahi* or the *Nikkei*, they assume it's been planted by one of the political factions and they just yawn and turn the page. But if the same story appears in your paper first, splashed across headlines seen all over the world—that's a different message entirely. It proves that foreigners are sitting up and taking notice."

Martine smiled. Nozawa was intensely conscious of what foreigners thought and said. This was a common trait among nationalistic Japanese.

"I can't guarantee the headlines, I'm afraid. That's for the editor to decide."

"Sure. I know how you people work. But this is something special, Meyer-san. It's the kind of story that could make a journalist's career."

"Tell me more," said Martine, intrigued.

Shimizu shook his head and held up a well-manicured hand. He gestured in the direction of the master bedroom. "Go ahead. He's in there waiting for you."

Martine knocked lightly at the door. There was no answer, so she turned to Shimizu, who gave a nod of encouragement. She pushed open the door and stepped inside.

A man was standing at the big picture window which framed the neon-splattered Shinjuku skyline. He turned and gazed at Martine, arms folded across his chest. He was wearing black jeans and a white T-shirt cut high to show off his bulging biceps, the product of his enthusiasm for bodybuilding.

"Welcome," he said, with a nod of the head.

Martine bowed low and felt her hair brush down over her cheeks.

"I'm honored to have the privilege of meeting you," she said in her softest, most feminine voice.

28

Martine had met many showbiz celebrities over the years, from movie directors to pop stars to talk-show hosts. When you saw them on the stage or the screen, they all seemed like a special breed of human being, lit up with energy and purpose. But face-to-face, with no script, no makeup, no special effects, and no well-rehearsed studio audience, they usually looked shrunken and drained, ordinary even.

Nozawa was different. For a start he was taller than she had expected, lean with long legs and narrow hips. Some of his original fans were probably grandparents by now, but he looked hardly older than Martine herself. He was an exceptionally handsome man. With his deep-set eyes and curling smile, he could have been Irish or Basque or Lebanese. And the way he moved lithely toward her, head slightly cocked to one side, reminded her of the time she had spent in Italy.

"Come and sit down. It's a great pleasure to meet such a distinguished journalist."

Nozawa's voice was the same as in the recordings, deep and slightly hoarse. He gestured her over to a table by the window. There was a bottle of saké on the table, and a shiny black guitar propped up against the wall.

"Thanks for coming here this evening, Meyer-san. It's important that my message goes out not just to the Japanese people, but to the whole world, including our enemies and rivals."

Normally when meeting Japanese men Martine felt in control from the start. They were either reticent and unsure of themselves, or clumsily eager to impress. Nozawa was neither. He was cool, amused, and totally at ease. Martine had the unfamiliar feeling that in the game of sexual dynamics she was on the defensive. That hadn't happened since she first met Makoto.

"Enemies and rivals?" she repeated. "Who do you have in mind?"

"Any countries that are plotting to weaken our financial system. Any countries attempting to destroy our culture. Any countries that think they can use us as a colony, exporting drugs and crime and murder."

He paused before the word "murder," to make sure she got the reference.

"Some people say I'm anti-Western, but that's not true. I'm not anti-Western, I'm pro-Japanese. Ordinary people have been suffering here, losing their jobs, and watching their children turn into monsters in front of their eyes. Meanwhile the government does nothing except run up enormous deficits and turn Japan into a whore for foreign countries. All this needs to be changed."

"And you're going to change it?" asked Martine, pen zipping across the page of her notebook.

Nozawa glanced over her shoulder at Shimizu, who had slipped quietly into the room while they were talking. He was leaning against the wall next to the door, arms crossed over his chest. For a moment their eyes met and some sort of signal was exchanged.

"We are about to establish a new party," Nozawa said. "One that answers the needs of ordinary people, one that will make them proud to have been born Japanese."

Martine nodded politely. This was hardly what the world wanted to read about—yet another Japanese political grouping. In the past few years dozens of factions and "study groups" and miniparties had been formed, as the jockeying for power intensified and the old configurations dissolved. None of them had made any real impact. But then again none of them had boasted a charismatic figurehead like Nozawa.

"You said 'we.' Who else is joining you in this project?"

"Already I have the support of sixty other politicians. All are under forty-five years old and all are excellent men, sincere and patriotic. I can't give you their names yet, but several members of the opposition parties are included."

Sixty Diet members—that would be quite a force. But how would they be able to fight an election? The kind of resources necessary would be way beyond the grasp of junior politicians, no matter how intelligent and well-meaning. In Japanese politics, it was only after winning four elections that you became a serious figure, and only after winning eight did the big money come rolling in.

"This sounds like a major project," said Martine. "Where are the financial resources going to come from?"

Nozawa glanced over her shoulder at Shimizu, who was still leaning against the wall, arms crossed.

"It won't be expensive," Shimizu interjected smoothly. "That's the whole beauty of the idea."

"Not expensive? But no politician can make any impact in this country without spending billions of yen."

"Correct, Martine-san, and that's a powerful barrier. But what actually causes the high cost of politics? Just think about the economics of the issue."

"Go on," said Martine, trying to disguise her impatience. Nozawa was the story, not Shimizu. But Shimizu wasn't going to shut up until he'd had his say.

"It's the cost of communication. Building up a support base, nurturing it, expanding it, mobilizing it—that needs a sophisticated organization with a huge budget. And that's where the problems start. The only way politicians can get their hands on the kind of money they need is from corporate donations. Naturally, corporations don't give out money unless they get something in return. So you have the recipe for constant scandal and public distrust.

"Anyway, you can see the big picture. If the problems of Japanese politics are caused by high communication costs, then the solution must be lower communication costs. Right?"

Martine nodded. Shimizu plowed onward.

"And that's where we have an overwhelming advantage. Nozawa-sensei has his own direct communication system already in place, and it's more powerful than any politician could ever dream of. Eighty percent of all Japanese households own at least one of his CDs. His Sunday night show is the highest-rated program on TV. There are three million members in his fan club, who get a newsletter every week and buy the sensei's T-shirts and jackets and headbands. Three million people! Just think about that, Martine-san. Ichizo Ogawa has the biggest support base in Japanese politics, and he only has fifty thousand members!"

Shimizu seemed genuinely excited by what he was describing. Martine listened to him prattling on about synergies, platforms, and franchises. Could this whole project have been dreamed up by Shimizu himself? Martine considered the idea, then rejected it. Shimizu was no visionary. He was a hired gun, the kind of guy the visionaries would need to make sure everything went smoothly. So who was behind it? Surely not Nozawa himself, but who?

"So when are you going to announce this to the world officially?"

"Very soon," said Nozawa. "The optimum time will be at the start of the next nationwide tour, to coincide with the release of my new CD. It's a concept album, called 'National Regeneration Songs.'"

"A concept album?"

Nozawa had used the English word, pronouncing it with the heavy, semi-ironic emphasis that he often used with foreign words.

"Yes. In the past there used to be lots of concept albums, produced by such excellent groups as the Beatles and Pink Floyd. I have always been a big fan of the Beatles, especially John Lennon."

Martine blinked with surprise. "Lennon? But he campaigned for world peace. That's rather the opposite of your approach, isn't it?"

31

"It isn't important what he campaigned for. The important thing is that he campaigned with all his spirit and no fear of the consequences. He was ready to risk his life at any moment. I am the same. I'm ready to risk my life at any moment."

Nozawa gazed into space, as if entranced by a vision of Lennon's ghost.

"The Beatles came to Japan only once. At the time I was a junior high school student and had never even been outside my hometown. But when I heard about the Beatles, I knew everything was going to change. They would change Japan. They would change me. I had to go and see them, it was a matter of destiny. Do you believe in destiny, Meyer-san?"

"Yes, I do," said Martine, without hesitation.

"Getting to Tokyo wasn't easy in those days. I had to ride in the back of a truck filled with pumpkins, a twelve-hour journey. I was sick the whole way. Even now I can't stand the smell of pumpkins. As for the money I borrowed, I had to work in the rice fields every Sunday for half a year to pay it back. But I succeeded in seeing the Beatles. And I was right. Four young men burning with hope and sincerity—they changed everything."

Nozawa picked up the guitar that was leaning against the wall and started strumming chords. Martine watched his fingers shifting over the fretboard. The look of a man's hands had always been important to her. Makoto's were strong, square, dependable. Nozawa's were long and surprisingly pale.

"Once there was a way," he crooned softly in English. "Get back, John! Get back to where you once belonged..."

It was an uncannily accurate imitation, catching every flattened Liverpudlian vowel.

Shimizu stepped forward and tapped his watch.

"I don't want to rush you, but we have to end this interview in five minutes."

"Five minutes?"

"Yes, the sensei is starting rehearsals for the tour this evening. It's the most important tour of his life."

Martine suppressed her annoyance. She had been hoping to get more information about Nozawa's controversial policy ideas, of which there had been many recently. He was proposing "moral guidance classes" in local shrines, for adolescents to attend at six o'clock every Saturday and Sunday morning. He wanted a special tax on foreign banks and financial institutions. As part of his "Population Revival Program" he was targeting a twenty-percent increase in the birth rate. There would be lotteries open to couples with three or more children, financed by a "bachelor tax" on unmarried men over the age of thirty-five. But those were subjects that would have to wait for another day. Right now there was one topic that dwarfed all others in importance.

"Sensei, my readers are especially interested in your views on security issues. What do you mean by a 'fully independent defense policy'?"

Nozawa leaned back with a smile on his face. He had obviously been expecting the question. "The meaning is clear, I think. Japan has money and technology, but it will never be taken seriously until it defends itself with its own blood. Look at the British. They have no money and no technology, but they've spilled their blood all over the world. That's the reason they are taken seriously, the only reason in fact."

"What about the US–Japan Security Treaty?" pressed Martine. "Does it still have a useful role?"

"Useful for who? It's not useful for us, and never has been. The role of that treaty is to keep the Japanese totally dependent on the Americans, like good little children who do whatever daddy says."

"So you would favor terminating it?"

"Of course! Japan is a nation under occupation. General MacArthur's army is still here, sixty years after the end of the Pacific War."

That was a catchy quotation. Martine could see it as a subheading, or maybe a lead-in to the opening paragraph. But then Nozawa came up with so many quotable comments. Compared to the usual cliché-mumbling Japanese politician, he was a journalist's dream.

"Are you calling for negotiations on the future of the US bases?"

"Calling for negotiations?" snorted Nozawa. "That's old-style political thinking! The Americans aren't wanted here on Japanese soil. They must leave when we say so."

"But what about the leases? They still have many years to run."

"Those leases were signed under duress. We can pass a law any time, and the bases will come back to Japanese ownership. If the Americans refuse to accept the decision of the Japanese people, then we'll withdraw all financial and logistical support. No water, no electricity, no food, no fuel, and no civilian workforce. If they still want to make a fuss, we'll sell our national holdings of US treasury bonds, dump them like foul-smelling garbage."

Nozawa chuckled. It was obviously a prospect that intrigued and delighted him. Martine led him back to reality.

"This is a period of escalating tension throughout Asia. Isn't there a risk you're going to destabilize what is already a dangerous situation?"

"And who made the situation so dangerous? The IMF, the World Bank, the meddling of the US and Europe. If you white people had left Asia to the Asians, none of this would have happened!"

That was a sentiment that Martine was coming across with increasing frequency. In fact many of Nozawa's views were widely held by Japanese politicians, bureaucrats, and intellectuals. Except that they held these views fatalistically, almost shamefacedly. Nozawa held them passionately, with a clear understanding of where they would lead. In that sense he was a true politician, perhaps the only one left in Japan.

Shimizu cleared his throat. "I'm afraid we have to stop there, Meyer-san. We look forward to seeing a nice article on the front page of your excellent international newspaper."

"I'll see what I can do."

Nozawa got to his feet, the black guitar still cradled in his arms. "By the way, I'm hoping you will attend my next concert."

"When is that going to be?" said Martine, putting away her notebook.

"Next Sunday evening. It's an open-air concert in support of the anti-US bases movement. There'll be places for our all good friends at the front. Here, take this."

Shimizu held out an envelope emblazoned with an ink drawing of Nozawa and the characters "National Regeneration."

"Inside are two tickets," Nozawa said. "One for you, and one for the man of your destiny."

Martine gave a little bow and said contritely: "I'm honored by the invitation, but we're not allowed to accept gifts—it's a company rule."

"Company rule! You don't look like the sort of woman who cares much about rules."

Nozawa was staring at her with a sardonic smile on his face. It looked as if he was going to say something else, but he just stared at her, as if trying to read her mind.

"Maybe not, but I do care about my professional reputation. Please don't get me wrong, I'm very keen to attend the concert. In fact, I'll pay you for the tickets right now."

She fumbled in her handbag, while Nozawa carried on staring at her, arms folded across his chest.

"You're *paying* me for them? That's a very Western way of behaving, very dry and logical. In Japan we like things to be wet. You've been in Japan long enough, Martine-san. A woman like you should understand when to be dry and when to be wet."

For the first time in years Martine felt acutely embarrassed. Why was this happening? She was furious with herself. More times than she cared to remember she had listened to men being lewd, obscene, gross, saying the things about women they said when no women were around. She had been disgusted, puzzled, bored, and even occasionally amused. *Never* had she been embarrassed.

Nozawa put the guitar down on the table and moved purposefully toward her. For a moment Martine had the bizarre idea he was going to lean forward and kiss her. Instead he thrust out a hand and they shook hands. His grip was warm, strong, rough. She could still feel the imprint when she was walking down the corridor toward the elevator.

Early evening, and Narita Airport was still seething with people. In the north wing security room, Deputy Manager Hasegawa sat staring at the flat-screen video display that covered the entire wall. Halfway through his shift, his head was aching and his eyes were slipping in and out of focus. The screen in front of him was split into twenty squares, each with a picture that changed every minute. Crowds of salarymen, elderly tourists hauling huge suitcases, school kids carrying tennis rackets, flight attendants pushing their cabin bags—a constant flow of human traffic poured into the departure lounge, swarming through the duty-free shops and blocking the escalators from top to bottom.

Hasegawa sipped at a cup of green tea while his tired eyes flicked from screen to screen.

The new software system had just been installed, and he wasn't used to it yet. What was supposed to happen was that if you saw someone suspicious, you zoomed in and froze the screen. Immediately a duplicate image with a blank face would appear next to the subject. Then you clicked again and chose from the menu of possibilities—male or female, young or old, yakuza or religious fanatic or swindler on the run. In seconds the program would find the closest facial match from the police and Interpol databases and fit it into the blank space. One last click, and you got a drop-down text summarizing the subject's personal history, criminal record, and known associates.

According to the supplier, the program "ushered in a new era in computerized identification systems." Hasegawa had his doubts about it, though. Already it had managed to fit the body of a top-ranking yakuza with the face of a flight attendant caught with a few grams of marijuana. In Hasegawa's opinion, it would be a long time before computers could beat the judgment of experienced professionals such as himself.

His gaze lingered on Screen 5, where a stunningly attractive woman was just walking through the X-ray machine. She was tall, with frizzed-out hair, catlike eyes, and a "brain-killer" figure. She was wearing round sunglasses propped on the top of her head, which made Hasegawa think she was maybe a model. One of the guys at the checkpoint, a youngster called Kato, tapped her on the shoulder. He was doing a routine follow-up, so Hasegawa zoomed in to get a better look.

The strange thing was the woman's reaction. Her eyes widened and she started glancing around nervously, as if looking for someone to come to her aid. When Kato started to question her—as he always liked to do with a good-looking woman—her face froze and her fingers knotted tightly together.

Hasegawa broadened the field a little and tracked the direction of her glances. Twenty yards away stood a middle-aged woman with short gray hair and baggy trousers, who looked rather like a housewife off on a shopping trip to Europe. She nodded at the younger woman and made a quick hand signal that Hasegawa interpreted to mean "Don't worry, it won't take long." Then she turned and disappeared into the duty-free shopping area.

Hasegawa shifted back to the younger woman. The check had finished now, and she scooped up her handbag and walked away, her face still pale and taut. Surprisingly, she marched straight past the duty-free area, not even bothering to glance inside. Now Hasegawa's professional curiosity was fully engaged. A woman put into a state of panic by a routine security check. Two people pretending that they didn't know each other. This was just the kind of problem that the new software was supposed to solve. Hasegawa zoomed in, froze her and clicked. When the menu appeared, he clicked "all female" and waited for the computer to find the best match.

For almost half a minute the space where her face had been was filled with a blinking question mark. For some reason the program was taking an unusually long time to run through the database. Hasegawa was about to click "Cancel" when suddenly the question mark was replaced by a female face. Hasegawa gazed at it with rising excitement. The hairstyle was different, but the eyes, the jut of the lips, the shape of the nose—they were too close to be a coincidence. Hasegawa clicked again, and this time his spirits fell. The program was trying to tell him that this woman was Reiko Matsubara, Japan's most notorious terrorist, wanted for murder, hijacking, and bank robbery. The only problem was that Matsubara had committed these crimes over thirty years ago, well before the woman in the Narita Airport departure lounge had been born.

Hasegawa gave a grunt of irritation and clicked on "Cancel." This "epoch-making" software was next to useless, just as he had thought. On the next screen, he watched the woman take the moving walkway to Gate 15, where the flight for Hong Kong had started boarding. So she was an ordinary tourist, off on a sightseeing trip with a family friend. Just imagine if he had rushed down there and accused her of being a terrorist! He would have been the laughing stock of the department.

Hasegawa's gaze shifted to the next screen. Two large black men were just coming through the checkpoint, grinning and swinging their bags as if they hadn't a care in the world. Hasegawa felt a surge of anger. After what he'd seen on TV recently, he would never look at these people the same way again. He grabbed for the mouse, zoomed in, and froze.

F O U R

Martine emerged from the hotel lobby to find Shinjuku filled with throbbing red lights and the hysterical wail of sirens. The plump, middle-aged doorman was standing at the curb gazing at a long line of empty taxis. Martine placed him as an ex-section chief from some old blue-chip company that had collapsed earlier in the crisis. He would be one of the lucky ones who had found a job.

"Has something happened?" said Martine.

"Another bomb threat. The whole area has been sealed off."

"So where's the bomb supposed to be?"

The doorman shrugged. "There's no information. It could be anywhere."

Beyond the hotel forecourt, an ambulance was trying to force its way down a street that was blocked solid. A medic was leaning out of the window screaming through a megaphone, his words lost in the noise of the siren and the revving of engines.

Martine hurried to the nearest subway station. She was going to be late for the meeting with Charlie, which meant she was going to be late getting to Makoto's place, which meant they would only have a few hours together before he left on a long business trip.

This plague of security alerts was becoming a real problem, shutting the city down for hours at a time. The police were overreacting, but that was inevitable given the pressure they were under. So far they had made no progress in tracking down the mysterious Okinawa Liberation Army that had regularly claimed responsibility. Some said they weren't really trying, that the OLA had become a useful distraction from all the political scandals. But that was too cynical, Martine felt. After all, the OLA had been responsible for so much mayhem. In the past couple of months movie theaters had been set ablaze, express trains derailed, teenagers trampled underfoot by panic-stricken

37

crowds at sports events and festivals. Advance warnings had been sent to newspapers and TV stations, but they were too cryptic to be of any use. Martine believed that the police were doing their best. The problem was that their best was no good at all.

Also, the police were being hampered by a familiar problem. Whenever a crime was given sensational coverage by the Japanese media—a woman poisoning her husband for insurance money, a homeless man buried alive by a motorbike gang, a high school girl decapitated by bullies—you could bet there would soon be dozens of copycat incidents, and this was no exception. Over the past few months there had been bomb attacks all over Japan. Bomb-making instructions were freely available on the internet—anyone could do it, and anyone did. And it wasn't just the usual thugs and petty extortionists, but also housewives with grudges against sarcastic shopkeepers, middle-aged bachelors living alone with their parents, school kids scorned by their teachers, teachers scorned by their pupils.

So the police were getting nowhere, and the security alerts were becoming a regular occurrence, costing hundreds of billions of yen in lost GDP. At first it had been a shock, but now it was just another aspect of the crisis that people were learning to live with.

There was a long wait at the subway station as staff checked passengers' bags and ran metal detectors over their bodies. Security on this line was particularly tight since the two incidents last month. First an unemployed salaryman had run amok with a sword, killing three people and wounding ten others before jumping in front of an oncoming train. Then there was the assassination of a credit analyst from a major bank, shot down during rush hour by a teenage hitman.

Martine recalled that even just a few years ago Tokyo had been considered one of the safest cities in the world. Nobody said that any more, just as nobody talked about wise, benevolent bureaucrats, selfless business leaders, or obedient wives who thought only of their husbands' needs. All that had gone—if it had ever really existed. The crisis had exploded the myths a whole society had grown up with, and there was nothing to fill the space.

The platform was seething with people, and it wasn't until the third train arrived that Martine managed to squeeze aboard. As usual the train was packed but silent. Martine scanned the tabloid she had bought, aware that several pairs of eyes were scanning her at the same time. Papers like this were not meant for women, let alone foreign women. Their role was to provide stress relief for salarymen, which they did through pornographic stories and mindless abuse of unpopular celebrities. Occasionally, though, they carried snippets of political gossip and scandal that the regular newspapers, all members of the official press clubs, would never touch. About a third of the gossip was fabricated by the editors, another third was disinformation fed to them by the political factions, and another third was more or less accurate. The skill was in knowing which was which.

The front page was taken up by the Mari-chan story. On the right was a photo of the poor girl staring at the camera with shy, melancholy eyes. On the left was a photo of Jackson, apparently glancing across the page at Mari-chan with a gleeful smile on his face. It had clearly been touched up, the pupils of his eyes made bigger, the lips thicker. There was nothing new in the text, just a couple of unsourced quotations from the police. "He claims he can't remember anything that happened." "He's not normal, sometimes screaming like a beast, sometimes crying like a baby." Then came some comments from the owner of the shop where Mari-chan used to go to buy candy with her pocket money.

Predictable stuff, put together by desperate journalists facing a deadline with nothing new to say. Martine turned the page and moved on to the political column. "Cabinet of Crooks About to Fall!" screamed the headline. Underneath was a hazy account of a new plot to oust the prime minister. It wasn't much of a story. There was always a plot to oust the prime minister. Japan had been though fifteen prime ministers in the past twelve years, and each of them had been removed not by an election, but by the scheming of rival factions. There was just one detail in the story that caught Martine's attention. "With the international situation threatening Japan's survival, patriotic young politicians are calling for a radical new approach to national regeneration." "National Regeneration Songs" was the title of Nozawa's new CD. That was either an incredible coincidence, or proof that Shimizu's "delivery system" was doing its work.

The only other story of interest concerned the murder of the Japanese ambassador to the United States. One night last month Ambassador Ohara had been found shot dead in the parking lot of a hotel in downtown Washington. The official explanation was that he had been mugged on his way to a social engagement, but not many people were taking that at face value. For one thing, he had gone without his chauffeur and bodyguard. For another, what kind of social engagement took place at two o'clock in the morning in a hotel used mainly by transvestite prostitutes?

The tabloid dealt with the story from a different angle. Apparently the Japanese embassy had been receiving death threats for months from a white supremacist group called the "Defenders of Aryan America." Just before Ohara's death, dozens of messages had been posted to internet discussion groups claiming that "a big yellow rat" was about to be "exterminated." In one of the messages the exact date had been mentioned. So far that was all that was known. The "Defenders of Aryan America" appeared to be a newly formed group, and the sender of the messages had used advanced conceal-ment techniques to cover his trail.

True or not true? Martine suspected a leak from the Foreign Ministry, attempting to divert attention from the embarrassing details.

The next story was all about soccer. Martine rapidly turned the page. She hated the game—the noise, the empty passion, the gracelessness and stupid-ity of everyone involved, from the players themselves to the pathetic charac-ters who wrote about it in the press. At an early age she had decided she would have nothing to do with any man who made a fuss about soccer. Now, though, she found herself involved with a man whose favorite pastime was fishing. At least soccer fans didn't keep buckets of writhing worms in their bathrooms or proudly present you with a freshly caught trout, expecting you to gut and cook it.

The thought of Makoto reminded her that she had to get the meeting with Charlie over with as soon as possible. Tonight she had promised to help Makoto's fifteen-year-old son with his homework. Exams were coming up, and the devoted father was getting concerned. She would never have expected Makoto to take these exams so seriously. But then he took everything about Ichiro seriously. Ichiro was the most important thing in his life. The brewery came second, and there was no third.

How well did Martine really know Makoto? After eighteen months, she sometimes felt that she hardly knew him at all. For example, he sometimes bought this tabloid to read on the train. When he skimmed through the pages, what went through his mind? He saw the same images as she was look-ing at now—naked women lying spread-eagled, hog-tied, ready to submit to any humiliation. He saw the pornographic cartoons, the reviews of strip clubs and "soaplands." Was he amused, or bored, or even secretly titillated? The lat-ter was hard to believe. Makoto was always so restrained, so gentlemanly. But he was a man, and men were very basic. It wasn't a question of culture. It was the same everywhere, the way they were designed.

The strange thing about Makoto was that Martine had nothing in common with him, and yet she felt completely relaxed in his presence. Most of her relationships had been with men she had plenty in common with—lawyers, journalists, writers, manipulators of information—and not one had lasted more than two years. There seemed to be a time limit in operation. Two years, and that was it. They went away, or she went away, and they never asked her to come back. They were so insecure, these men, so absurdly keen to impress. And when they saw that she wasn't impressed, it disturbed them, scared them even. Makoto was different. He wasn't trying to compete. And he certainly wasn't scared.

They had been together for almost two years now, and Martine could sense that a turning point was at hand. She did her best not to think about it. She wasn't going to say anything. She wasn't going to do anything. But starting again with someone else was out of the question.

Peng Yuan sat alone at the window, gazing out at the throbbing heart of Beijing. The changes of the past decade never ceased to astound him. There were splendid new buildings and flashing neon everywhere, and giant cranes dotted the skyline, indicating that further marvels were under construction. The roads were clogged with expensive cars where once there had been just hordes of bicycles. The shops were filled with the finest goods, the kind that had once been available only to top party officials. And the people, bright-eyed and strong, surged forward with the invisible tide of history.

For a man of Peng Yuan's generation, it was a dreamlike vision. Sometimes he thought he would wake up and find himself back in the old days. He shuddered at the thought of the rough blue tunics, the big communal toilets, men and women together, the daily scrabble for meat and soap, the ever-present fear that something dangerous was happening behind your back.

China had changed, and Peng Yuan had changed too. He looked down at his feet and saw good leather shoes that didn't blister his heels and cramp his toes. He relished the cool smoothness of the shirt against his neck, the pleasant scent of the imported deodorant he used daily.

Now he had everything he'd ever wanted. He lived in a luxurious apartment, large enough to accommodate his wife and child and his aging parents from the countryside. He kept five mistresses in small apartments around the city. Most important of all, he had a secure position at the new institute, with a big budget and a group of assistants devoted to his work. And at the old institute, his enemies had long gone, their corruption and incompetence exposed. Peng Yuan had become a man of influence, the kind you didn't want to cross.

"Come this way, Comrade. The committee are ready for your report."

Peng Yuan followed the svelte shape of the secretary into the familiar room with the long oblong table that gleamed like a sheet of black ice. He had been coming to this room every three months for around ten years now. In that time the committee had grown. Once it had been the old man and his son and some trusted aides. Now there were usually at least twenty of them, including security people, political people, and a few who never gave their names. The old man was still there, though, as bright and alert as ever. If anything, he looked younger each time, his face smoother and chubbier.

How did he manage it? According to the rumors, there was a top-secret medical facility that provided him with experimental treatment involving human placenta, the pituitary glands of pre-adolescent boys, and the organs of a giant clam that lived for one hundred and fifty years. But those rumors were put about by rival factions. Peng Yuan's theory was simpler. The old man from Nanjing was determined to stay alive until he had his revenge on the Japanese for the mayhem they had wreaked all those years ago.

"Welcome, Comrade. We are looking forward to your latest report with the greatest anticipation."

Those were the words of the old man's son, now established as one of the leading figures among the anti-Western group. Sometimes Peng Yuan would read speeches the man had given and recognize some of his own ideas. That always gave him a deep thrill of pride.

Peng Yuan flipped open the laptop computer he had brought and booted the program. Three amoebalike blobs appeared on the screen, twisting and pulsing and shimmering with different colors. The smaller one was attached to the largest by a thin umbilical cord, which contracted and stretched as the two amoebas danced closer to each other and then drew away again.

"Once again I am honored to have the opportunity of discussing my humble research work. For those members who were not present last time, let me summarize how the system works. These strange creatures you see on the screen are topological simulations of political entities responding to a random barrage of internal and external stimuli. You may call the large one the United States, the small one Japan, and the medium-sized one China. Now, according to the principles of turbulence theory..."

It was his usual introduction, dry and theoretical, but the listeners were paying close attention. They had confidence in him, as they should. Over the years his work had proved its value time and again. His conclusions had become more specific, his predictions more detailed and accurate. Thanks to the new resources at his disposal, he had massively increased the power of his model. Hundreds of variables were fed in every week, tens of thousands of matrices generated, and millions of probabilities sifted and sorted. This was the cutting edge of metabolic strategic analysis. Rand Corporation, the Moscow Institute, the new Clausewitz Center in Berlin—none of them had even come close to matching his achievements.

Peng Yuan spoke for twenty minutes, summarizing the key developments since the last meeting, and using the shapes on the screen to show how the stresses within the international political system were rising to a climax.

"We are now approaching the flux point," he concluded. "That is the point of maximum instability, when minor events can trigger sudden reconfigurations."

He turned and tapped in an instruction. The smaller blob flashed blue and purple, and suddenly the umbilical cord snapped and shriveled away to nothing. The larger blob grew another cord which snaked toward the medium blob and attached itself to its belly. At the same time the medium blob grew a pincerlike limb which began to tear away pieces of the smaller blob, which shivered as if in pain, then its color drained away and its movements grew weaker. The medium blob carried on expanding until it overtook the largest in size. It was now almost three times as big as the smallest blob, which was white and completely immobile.

The old man's small round face creased into a smile. "This is the shape of the future. Japan withers and dies, while China grows and grows until it becomes the center of the world system."

Peng Yuan nodded. "It is one possible future. As I said, the coming year has the maximum potential for dynamic change. But if the current system manages to survive this period, it will become unshakable."

"What would happen then?" asked one of the new members of the committee, a fat-bellied Cantonese who was considered the leader of the post-pragmatist ideologists.

Peng Yuan hesitated.

"Show him," croaked the old man.

Peng Yuan bowed. His fingers tapped at the keyboard, and the screen reverted to its former state.

"This is a much simplified version," he explained. "The full process takes many hours."

He tapped in another command, and the blobs started to move. The smallest and the largest blobs danced closer together, until the umbilical cord linking their two bellies fattened out into a bridge. At that they twitched and rippled with color and started growing rapidly. The medium blob circled warily, grew a claw, and tried to tear pieces off the other two. Its movements became more agitated as each attack was foiled, until finally it shook like jelly, turned purple, blue, and green in rapid succession, then exploded into dozens of tiny blobs, each of which grew claws and started attacking each other.

This was not the first time Peng Yuan had showed that sequence. The effect was always the same—heavy silence, interrupted only by the rasp of the old man's breath.

The first to speak was the cold-eyed man from Shanghai. Peng Yuan tensed at the sound of his voice. They had been invited into the old man's circle at the same time, and Peng Yuan clearly remembered that afternoon ten years ago when they had sat staring at each other across the shiny black table. Since then their rivalry had burgeoned, ripened, and soured.

"What about alternative scenarios? Surely there must be a way for the system to return to stability."

"Yes, there is," admitted Peng Yuan, setting up the program again. This time the three blobs kept their distance from each other. Occasionally two of them would link with umbilical cords, but they soon drifted apart again until the cord snapped. More often, two of them would make alliances and tear chunks out of the third with their pincers. These alliances didn't last long, however, and when the sequence ended all three blobs were roughly the same size and color as at the beginning.

"That's interesting," said the man from Shanghai. "What's the probability of such an outcome?"

Peng Yuan smiled. "Very low. In a dynamic system you get stability only if a number of random events lock together to form a feedback circuit. That's about as probable as a man bumping into three of his mistresses in Tienanmen Square on the same afternoon."

The man from Shanghai registered not the trace of a smile. "And what about the other two scenarios?"

"They both have rather high probabilities."

"Are you unable to calculate which is higher?"

Peng Yuan noted the provocation. It was important to remain calm: the man from Shanghai was a master at laying traps for the unsuspecting. He cleared his throat. "Perhaps I should explain my methodology again. You see, this has nothing to do with the old style of probability analysis. What I have created are complex strategic systems which respond organically to random stimuli."

"Can't you give a simple answer?" sneered the other man. "We haven't come here to listen to a lecture."

"Wait a moment," said Peng Yuan testily. "I haven't finished the explanation yet. You can't understand the conclusions until you understand the methods. That's what I always tell my dullest students."

The man from Shanghai shot a sideways glance at the old man's son, who pursed his lips and gave a slight nod before looking away. It was inevitable, he thought. Peng Yuan had been useful to them, more useful than he would ever know, but his role was over now. The flux point was indeed approaching. And there was nothing random about the stimuli that would be applied.

The problem with Peng Yuan was that he had changed so much. Ten years ago he had been an obscure researcher, flattered to have his work taken seriously, and careful to follow every instruction he was given. He had been scared, which meant that he could be trusted. Now Peng Yuan was no longer scared. He was spending too much money, drinking too much, and talking too much. According to the girls they had arranged for him, he had started to boast about his connections in high places, even mentioning the old man by name. The man from Shanghai had warned them many times about Peng Yuan, and he had been right. The situation had become intolerable.

F I V E

When Martine arrived at the office, Charlie was sprawled in his chair, feet up on the desk, watching the sumo highlights on the big flat-screen TV. They were showing the main bout of the evening, and the grand champion crashed to the ground just as Martine walked in.

"I love these fat guys," grinned Charlie. "Especially when their bellies smack together. What a great noise that is!"

The grin was unconvincing. Charlie rarely had a pleasant word for Martine these days. The atmosphere between them had been frosty since she'd confronted him with stealing one of her stories and getting most of the details wrong.

"WHAP!" he said, thumping fist into palm. "Do you think I could grow my belly big enough to make that noise?"

"You'd have to be a lot stricter about your diet," said Martine, pulling up a chair opposite.

"Stricter! You don't need to be strict to get fat, for God's sake."

"Yes, you do. Sumo wrestlers only have two meals a day, and it's always the same stuff. No fancy restaurants, no fine wine—just rice, fish, and vegetables, twice a day, every day."

"You know absolutely everything, don't you! Next you'll be telling me you dated one of those guys."

He was still grinning, but the edge of hostility was unmistakable.

"As a matter of fact, I did."

Charlie acknowledged the joke with a little snort. Except that it wasn't a joke. The man Martine was referring to had retired from sumo with a smashed knee at the age of twenty-one and had then spent ten years studying to be a lawyer.

"So has anything important been going on?" asked Martine casually.

There was no point in being too direct, Charlie would get to the point when he was ready.

"Not really. The peace talks are stalled, the trade talks are stalled, ethnic cleansing in Malaysia continues unabated, an earthquake has flattened some place nobody can pronounce. Oh—and another story that particularly caught my eye. The new government in Algeria is banning women from learning to read and write. I was thinking they might be onto something there..."

"Ha, ha," muttered Martine, refusing to rise to a jibe that was crass even by Charlie's standards.

Charlie's chair was leaning so far back that he was at serious risk of toppling over. His hands were locked behind the back of his head, and his eyes were closed. They had been working together for almost a year now, and it had been a difficult relationship from the start. Charlie was the son of a wealthy stockbroker and a Yale graduate. The way Martine saw it, he had gone into financial journalism because it was a little off the mainstream, but not so far that you couldn't take holidays in Maui or have a live-in maid to take care of your kids. By the age of thirty-two he was a star reporter on Wall Street and author of a well-reviewed book on insider trading. Then he was given the Tokyo bureau, and suddenly he was like a fish out of water, unable to speak the language and without the contacts. Instead he took on the role of an old-style bureau chief, hanging out at cocktail parties, entertaining useless flacks from the ministries, and, worst of all, sticking his nose into Martine's stories.

"The usual stuff, huh?"

"That's right," said Charlie, his smile gone.

"Nothing else?"

"Nothing important. I've just lost my job, that's all."

His voice weakened to a croak, as if the words had got stuck somewhere below his tonsils.

"Lost your job? What are you talking about?"

"Two hours ago I got a call from the deputy editor. He said the paper needs a different approach here, something in tune with the group's new strategic direction."

Martine reached across the table and gave him a squeeze on the shoulder. "I'm sorry," she said quietly.

"Not as sorry as I am! For God's sake—what am I going to tell my wife and kids?"

"Tell them the truth. It can't be helped, can it?"

"It can't be helped" was a phrase that usually drew a snort of amused contempt from Makoto, together with the comment that she had been in Japan too long. Martine was rather surprised with herself for using it. But some things really couldn't be helped, and this was surely one of them. The paper had changed out of all recognition since being acquired by InfoCorp last year. The rationale behind the deal had been made clear from the start—the "cross-platform synergies" that would come from slotting a famous newspaper into an information and entertainment empire that spanned the world. InfoCorp had drafted in new management, and within weeks the entire editorial team had gone. The next step would be to target areas of high cost and low productivity—such as Charlie, with his huge expat apartment, club memberships, and two kids in private school. That stuff about strategic direction was just a euphemism for squeezing costs.

Charlie took a deep breath and blew out his cheeks. "So you finally got what you wanted, Martine. I'm out of your hair for good."

"That's not what I wanted," said Martine.

"Come on—you've been working against me right from the start. I don't blame you, of course. In your position I'd have done the same."

Martine frowned. "What are you talking about?"

He smiled a bitter little smile that she hadn't seen before. "You've been doing your damnedest to make me look bad. You monopolized the good stories, and kept me away from all the good sources. God knows what you've been saying to the editorial guys behind my back."

"I've said nothing."

"Oh yeah? What about that e-mail you sent trashing my story about the banking crisis?"

"You've been monitoring my e-mails?" said Martine, astonished.

"Damn right! I was wondering why my stories kept getting spiked. So I took a little peek in your computer and it was like a Zen moment of instant enlightenment."

"Listen, they just asked me for some numbers. I had no idea it had anything to do with your story until afterward."

"Oh yeah, sure. Whatever."

Martine gaped at him in amazement. The sympathy she had been feeling for him had evaporated completely. Why couldn't he take it like a man? Didn't he have any sense of dignity? And why couldn't he get his numbers right in the first place? Angry thoughts crowded her mind, but she dismissed them. It really wasn't worth the effort.

"Charlie, I need to be somewhere else. Why don't you go home and talk to your wife?"

"Whatever you say, boss."

It was no good. He was determined not to be appeased. Martine gave a little shrug and turned for the door. On the TV they were showing a slow-motion replay of the sumo grand champion rolling over the edge of the ring, arms and feet in the air, as helpless as a giant baby.

Three-quarters of an hour later Martine was sitting in Makoto's apartment, sipping a glass of plum wine and staring at the dummy exam paper on the table. Ichiro was sitting beside her, his sharp features tight with concentration. The sliding door eased open, and Makoto stuck his head into the room. He was on his way back from the bath, wet hair flopping over his forehead, his face flushed and shining from the scalding hot water.

"Not finished yet?" he growled. "You're heading for failure, I think—bottom marks!"

If you didn't know him, it would have been frightening. Makoto rarely smiled when he was joking. There was just a hint of a crinkle at the edge of his eyes.

"Be a bit more patient, Dad," said Ichiro, without even looking up. "This stuff is crazy, even Martine says so."

It was hard to believe he was only fifteen. That lazy, calm way of speaking was the exact copy of his father's. He had the same quizzical way of looking at you too, with head tilted and eyes twinkling. In a few years' time he was going to be irresistible.

Makoto turned to Martine. "Crazy? Didn't you say history was your favorite subject?"

"Second favorite," corrected Martine. "My favorite was Latin. And anyway, this exam has got nothing to do with understanding history."

"Meaning what?"

"Meaning it's nothing more than a perverse quiz, totally pointless. You could answer ten thousand of these questions and still know nothing worth knowing."

Makoto shook his head in mock outrage. "Ah, you foreigners criticize the Japanese educational system, which has enabled our GNP to become so dramatically huge. What insolence!"

"I'm serious," said Martine. "Too much of this stuff could damage your mental health."

"And too little of this stuff could damage the boy's future! Study isn't supposed to be fun. It's supposed to be hard and horrible."

Even Martine couldn't tell whether he was joking now. There was a slight crinkle around his eyes, but she knew that Makoto had a low opinion of "fun." This was a man who had taught himself French in order to read Camus in the original, who had never played pachinko in his life, and who spent a month meditating at a remote Zen temple once every five years.

"But neither is it supposed to be a gigantic bore."

"Oh yes it is! A gigantic bore—that's exactly what we need for programming dull-brained workers and arrogant bureaucrats. Without them, the country would be in an even worse state."

This time he did smile, leaning further into the room, one hand on the door frame. His light summer kimono was open almost to his waist, and his smooth chest was blood red in the glow of the lamp. Martine suddenly imagined his body pressing against hers, the heat of his skin, the hardness of his muscles. She shifted in her seat, trying to concentrate on the exam sheet.

"What about this one?" said Ichiro, rapping the paper with a long slim finger. Martine took another sip of plum wine, aware that both of them were watching her closely. The question was bafflingly pointless, requiring the death of five European kings to be set in chronological order. A long series of teasing challenges to common sense—that's what the education system was like in this country. But that's what the system of writing was like with its thousands of characters, most of which had multiple meanings and multiple pronunciations. It was what the political system was like, the financial system, the legal system, the system of etiquette. It was what life was like. You could never master it, but rather had to keep negotiating, keep improvising. You needed to be able to read things upside down, back to front, and inside out. You needed to know how to play the game, and how not to play the game. That, Martine supposed, was what Makoto wanted for his son.

It took another half an hour to go through the remaining questions. Ichiro was sharp, quick to see how different pieces of information fitted together. She had asked him once if he had thought about becoming a journalist. He had laughed at the idea, rather too loudly for Martine's liking. Only later had she found out that Ichiro already had a clear ambition: he was utterly determined to become a doctor. His mother had died of breast cancer just before his tenth birthday. You didn't need to be a psychoanalyst to see the connection. Already there was a toughness about him, the same hard core of certainty that his father had.

When they had finished, Martine went back to the living room. Makoto emerged from the kitchen, his hands wrapped around three large bottles. "Beer," he said.

It wasn't a question—in fact, it was more like a command, and Martine knew better than to argue. After all, this amber liquid, with its swirls of froth and spectrum of flavors from the bitter to the honey-sweet—this was Makoto's pride and joy. Not just the liquid itself, but also the shape and color of the bottle, the design of the label, the little gasping sound when you eased off the wire-framed cap, the trickling sound as the beer flowed over the heavy glass lip —all had been meticulously planned. This particular brand, the premium brew, was based on a recipe developed by Belgian monks in the fourteenth century. Makoto had spent months scouring Europe for exactly the right ingredients. The launch was due next month, and these bottles were from a test batch.

Martine tilted her glass to the correct angle. Makoto poured for her, then for his mother and himself. The color was good—warm and golden, gleaming with thousands of tiny bubbles. They clinked glasses and drank. Martine let the full, rich taste flood her mouth and felt it tingle against the sides of her tongue. Eight-percent proof—no wonder those monks always looked so jolly.

Makoto was watching her keenly. A word of disapproval and he would be crushed—though of course he would rather die than show it.

"Excellent," said Martine, smacking her lips. And she meant it. The stuff produced by the big Japanese breweries all tasted the same, looked the same, and cost the same. Makoto's beer was in a class of its own. Martine had never been much of a beer drinker—she preferred good champagne—but the quality of Makoto's product was unmistakable.

Makoto's mother had prepared dinner and now they all sat down to eat together. For Martine, this was an ambivalent experience. The food—suki-yaki with soft, creamy tofu, shirataki noodles, and Kobe beef sliced so thin you could almost see through it—was excellent, but the amount she was expected to eat was daunting. Makoto's mother kept loading her bowl with mountains of meat and vegetables.

"You must eat more tofu," she said sweetly. "You have too much stress at work. Tofu is exactly what you need to clear up your complexion."

"You're very kind."

"I expect you have constipation too. I did when I was your age."

"Really?"

"Yes, really. Too much sitting down in the *seiza* position. But don't worry—I've prepared fresh persimmons, the very best thing for constipation."

"Thank you very much," said Martine. Makoto was staring into the middle of his bowl, but the sides of his eyes were crinkled up.

"And for vitality nothing is better than a raw egg. Please take another one."

The little basket of eggs was extended. Martine hesitated, but there was no choice really. She couldn't refuse the egg, any more than she could refuse the plates of baked clams, noodles, and grilled prawns that were sitting waiting on the side table.

"That's right," said Makoto's mother, eyeing Martine as she broke the egg into her bowl. "Two raw eggs every day and you'll soon be feeling young and healthy again!"

Martine nodded politely as she chewed.

Makoto's mother had moved in with her son five years ago, shortly after his wife died. She was seventy-five years old, but with her alert eyes and strong posture she looked fifteen years younger. Every day she cycled to the sports center, where she swam a few slow and stately lengths in the public pool, her spectacles perched on her nose, her hair tied back in a bun. She went to the cinema once or twice every week, and knew more about movies—from obscure European art-films to Hollywood blockbusters—than the *Tribune's* main reviewer. For decades she had headed her own school of tea ceremony, which, according to Makoto, had been in constant and bitter dispute with schools of other styles. Even now she still gave lessons to a few favored pupils.

"Have some more miso soup. The seaweed will make your hair stronger and take away some of that grease."

"Thank you," said Martine with a smile. From the first time they met— over a year ago now—she had realized that she was going to be tested. Makoto's mother was unfailingly warm and friendly, but she had yet to reconcile herself to the presence of this strange foreign woman. Sometimes Martine wondered whether her son had, either.

After dinner Makoto and Ichiro cleared the table, and Martine and the old lady washed the dishes. That was the usual division of labor. Makoto's mother was from an old samurai family in Kyushu, and she had been brought up to believe that men should never enter the kitchen. Martine didn't mind playing along. In fact it was fun in a strange kind of way—just as long as it was understood that playing along was what she was doing.

Ichiro lugged in the sukiyaki pan, his biceps straining under his T-shirt. He set it down on top of a wooden stool.

"Not there," snorted the old lady. "Haven't you got any common sense? It'll leave a mark."

Ichiro muttered an apology, shifted it onto the kitchen table, and scurried out again. Makoto, in his usual hurry to be finished, dropped a fistful of cutlery onto the table. A ceramic scoop rolled off and clattered to the ground.

"Watch what you're doing," said Martine sharply. "Those things chip easily, you know."

She was aware of the old lady giving a firm nod of approval. Makoto got down on his hands and knees to retrieve the scoop from under the table. Martine made sure that nobody was watching, then gave him a dig in the buttocks with the side of her foot.

After they were finished, Martine took a tray of tangerines and rice crackers into the main room. As she sat down, she caught Ichiro stealing a glance up her skirt. She stared at him furiously and he looked away at once, his complexion a little darker than usual.

Martine sat and munched her cracker, one leg crossed over the other. Having a relationship with Makoto meant having a relationship with his mother and son—she had known that from the start. Still, she hadn't realized all the implications. Usually Ichiro treated her as a big sister, the kind of person who would help him with his homework. Occasionally, when he came home late from school and saw her chatting and laughing with his father, he looked at her as if she were an intruder, his eyes blazing and his jaw set hard. And then again, sometimes he looked at her as a woman: Martine found that the hardest to deal with.

Makoto was very sensitive about the situation, which was why the number of times they had spent the whole night together could be counted on one hand. Makoto would never consider sleeping over at Martine's place. It might be well past midnight, he might have a train to catch at seven the next morning—it didn't matter. He insisted on waking up in his own apartment and seeing his son's face before he went off to school. And for Martine to stay at Makoto's apartment, to sleep in the big bedroom with his dead wife's photo staring at her out of the black frame, to waltz off to the shower in the morning with a towel wrapped around her waist—well, nobody was ready for that either.

So the relationship had its frustrations, which had to be negotiated with tact and patience. But it had its excitements too.

Makoto sat down, cradling another glass of premium beer in his hands. Martine listened as he described the difficulties of getting his products onto the shelves of the major supermarkets. Apparently the big beer companies were putting pressure on retailers, threatening to remove their discounts if they stocked any micro-beers. It was a familiar story. Ever since Makoto had set the company up, the beer companies had been trying to run him out of business. They got the banks to shut down credit lines without any warning. They got the Ministry of Agriculture to quarantine his imported hops and barley, the Ministry of Health to make unplanned hygiene checks, the Ministry of Finance to conduct lengthy investigations into his tax affairs. They had even offered him money to close down operations, but Makoto had sailed through it all with steely determination.

The old lady was flicking through a movie magazine, pretending not to listen to their conversation. Ichiro was sitting at the table trying to fix a radio-controlled helicopter, one of his most prized possessions. With his hair hanging over his eyes and lips pursed in concentration, he had reverted to boyishness again.

Makoto finished his tale of intrigue. "So what about you? Have you dug up any good scandals or financial disasters?"

Martine took another mouthful of beer. It was good stuff. The more you drank, the more you wanted to drink. "Not this week, not yet anyway. But I did manage to interview a Japanese national hero."

"Impossible. There aren't any national heroes these days, only national villains."

"Well, this one considers himself a national hero, that's for sure, and so do his fans. I'm talking about the singing politician."

"Nozawa?"

"That's right. He's launching a political party to help promote his new CD. Or he's launching a CD to help promote his new political party. It's hard to know which."

Both Ichiro and the old lady looked up from what they were doing. Nozawa's name was enough to attract their attention.

"Tell me," said Martine. "What is so fascinating about this guy? Even people who oppose everything he stands for actually seem to like him. Why is that?"

There was a moment of silence. Makoto looked, uncharacteristically, as if he were struggling for an answer. It was the old lady who spoke first.

"Nozawa is a kind of genius, I think."

Martine glanced at her in surprise. "A genius? Really? But I was talking to him just a couple of hours ago, and he seemed totally ordinary."

"That's the point," said the old lady, her face slightly flushed from the beer. "He's a genius at appearing ordinary. He knows how ordinary people feel, and he knows how to communicate with them. Ronald Reagan was the same. I saw his movies when they were first released—awful, all of them. But he had a way of talking that was so clear and friendly. Afterward all you remember is that friendly face, not the silly story made by the scriptwriters."

There was a glint in her eye, as if she wanted to goad Martine into an argument.

"And you call that genius?"

"It's an instinct. Every entertainer wants to do something like that, but hardly any of them can. All these big movie stars today—you put them in a stupid movie and they just look stupid. You don't remember anything."

Makoto broke in. "My view is slightly different. I think Nozawa is more like Eva Peron. What he does is give us stress relief. For so many decades we were diligent and hardworking, intent on catching up with the West, smiling and bowing, trying to be respectable, all that boring stuff. Now we're showing that we can be as crazy as anyone. And if you look at history, you can see that's much more natural. We've always been crazy. We like taking things past the limit, everyone together—nationalism, pacifism, industrialism, disco dancing, Italian food, whatever comes into fashion."

Martine nodded. It was rare for her to ask Makoto's opinion on a subject related to her work, and even rarer for him to give a straight answer. He had little interest in current affairs, and an even contempt for modern politicians of all affiliations and all nationalities. His personal heroes were Churchill,

Lincoln, and the sixteenth-century military commander Oda Nobunaga. He never spoke about them, but Martine had noticed that together they occupied a six-foot-high bookcase in his study.

"And what about the songs?"

Makoto gave a snort of contempt. "These days they're terrible—pompous, sentimental, crude, full of idiotic slogans. I really can't bear to listen to such rubbish!"

Another surprise. Makoto, usually so cool and ironic, sounded agitated, almost angry.

"These days? You mean, there was a time when you actually liked them?"

Makoto looked at her oddly and hesitated before speaking. "Well, yes. In the old days his music was very different. It was fresh and honest and full of hope. Of course we were young then too."

"We"—that was also uncharacteristic. Martine though about letting it rest, but her journalistic instinct got the better of her.

"Tell me more," she said gently.

The old lady was watching them like a bird, head twitching from side to side. Ichiro seemed to be totally absorbed in his repair work, but, checking his hands, Martine felt sure he was busily unscrewing a rotor he'd only just screwed in.

Makoto poured himself another beer, and held it up to the light to examine the consistency of the head.

"It was a different world then," he muttered, gazing at the cascading bubbles. "Japan was full of energy, everything moving forward. When Nozawa's first album came out, we were in our final year at university. Sachiko gave it to me as a birthday present. We even went to see him play in a tiny theater in Ikebukuro. He performed for nearly three hours, just with guitar and harmonica—the whole audience was spellbound."

Martine didn't say anything. The idea was somehow difficult to grasp. Makoto always seemed so tough-minded and mature, so detached from the fads and enthusiasms of the zeitgeist. It was hard to grasp that he had once been an idealistic young student, the type that would take his girlfriend to a folk club. But of course he had, and he had gone on to marry that girl. He had also joined one of Japan's most prestigious trading companies, a natural destination for elite students burning with patriotic ambition.

"I still have that album somewhere. I'll get it for you, if you want."

Now it was Martine's turn to flush. "No, that's all right. I mean, please don't take the trouble..."

But Makoto was already on his feet. "It's no trouble. Actually I want you to see it."

He disappeared into his study, leaving a strained silence behind him. The old lady flicked over a page in her movie magazine. Ichiro was now screwing back the same rotor that he had just unscrewed. Martine refilled Makoto's glass, then the old lady's, then her own. The bubbles danced to the surface, forming a dense and buoyant head.

Two minutes later Makoto was back, holding a dog-eared LP sleeve. It hadn't taken long to find. Martine wondered if he kept it close at hand, perhaps with other precious items that he would take out and gaze at when he was alone in his study. You had to know this man well before you glimpsed the core of sadness within him. Their relationship had been three months old before Martine had even heard about Sachiko. Until then Makoto had never mentioned the subject, and she had assumed he was divorced.

"Take a look," said Makoto, handing her the LP. "It's a souvenir from a country that no longer exists."

The cover photo showed a young couple walking down a Shinjuku backstreet hand in hand. They were looking into each other's eyes and smiling. The girl, stunningly beautiful, was wearing velvet bell-bottoms and a floppy hat with a feather in it. The man had a guitar case hoisted over one shoulder, and was wearing a pair of jeans covered in patches and an Afghan coat that reached down to his ankles. He had long hair flowing over his shoulders, and a soft, feminine face.

"He doesn't look like the same person," said Martine, genuinely surprised.

"He isn't the same. But then none of us are."

The old lady gave a little chuckle. "You know, Makoto used to look just like that. He had the same hairstyle, the same kind of jeans. He even asked me to sew on some patches for him—there were no holes, he just wanted some patches."

Martine glanced at Makoto, who was trying his best to look unembarrassed. "You had hair down to your shoulders?"

"Of course, we all did in those days. I even had one of those coats."

Martine stared at him in amazement. "You mean you used to wear an Afghan coat?"

"Sure."

"Have you still got it somewhere?"

"Of course not. Those things weren't made to last more than a year or so."

That was a pity. Martine would have given a month's salary to see Makoto walking down the street in an Afghan coat. It occurred to her that Makoto was almost exactly the same age as Nozawa, and about the same height and build. In his Afghan and shoulder-length hair, he must have looked much the same as Nozawa did on the album cover. In fact, even now there was something of a resemblance in the set of the jaw and the deep-set eyes, alert and wary.

She handed the album cover back to Makoto. There were coffee rings on the back, and the paper was yellow and faded.

"Thank you," she said. "I'm glad you showed it to me."

Makoto nodded and took it back to his room.

Martine sat back and finished her beer. Something new had happened between them, though she wasn't quite sure what. Anyway, Makoto's premium beer was excellent. She felt the soothing warmth radiating from the pit of her stomach and gently bathing the inside of her skull. The room was strangely bright. She realized that for some reason she was smiling.

It was time to go. Ichiro had already gone to his room. Martine bade a formal good-bye to the old lady—this was absolutely essential—then they walked along the corridor to the elevator, Makoto's wooden sandals going clop-clop on the tiled floor.

Makoto's home was a modest apartment in a modest eight-story block in a modest suburb that had so far withstood the crisis without too much damage. There was no high-tech security system, but the neighbors kept their eyes open and made sure nothing unusual was happening. They kept their ears open too, since the walls were extremely thin.

Once upon a time Makoto had lived in rather more luxury, as befitted an elite executive of one of Japan's largest trading houses. Martine had seen photos of the house in the Bay Area, with the swimming pool and tennis court. But when the trading house collapsed and the family moved back to Japan, he had decided to plow all his personal wealth into his brother's microbrewery. That had been a costly move, but she had never heard him utter a single word of regret.

It was a hot summer's night. In the trees below, the screeching of cicadas drowned out the voices of passersby. Neither of them spoke. Makoto was flying to America the next morning, and Martine had deadline pressure on a twelve-page "infomercial" supplement, one of the pet projects of the new management. It would be weeks before they saw each other again, which was a miserable thought.

Just as the elevator doors were opening, Martine glimpsed something out of the corner of her eye, a flash and an explosion of color.

"Fireworks," said Makoto. "There's a big display down by the river, the last one this summer."

"Shall we go and look?"

Makoto glanced at his watch, a garish Swatch that Ichiro had given him as a birthday present. "It's almost over."

"What a shame!" said Martine emphatically. She was feeling quite light-headed now. Makoto gave her an odd look. They got in the elevator, and he pressed the button. It took her a few seconds to realize that the elevator was going up, not down.

"What's happening?" she asked blankly.

"Come on," said Makoto. "We'll have a good view of the last few fireworks from the roof."

They got out at the eighth floor and went up a flight of concrete steps that led out onto the roof terrace. It was a small area, half the size of a tennis court, strung with washing lines and enclosed by a shoulder-high railing. They picked their way between the flapping shirts and undulating bed sheets.

"I hope it isn't over."

"Look, here they come."

Elbows against the rail, they watched the slow-motion explosions in purple, silver, emerald. They were standing close together, and Martine could feel his heat on her arms, his dark energy drawing her in.

"Hurry up, will you?" she said softly.

"What?"

"You are going to kiss me, aren't you?"

Then his lips were on the back of her neck, making tingly little shapes, and his fingers were caressing her hair. She turned to face him, and he pulled her in. His mouth was warm and rough, his chest as hard as a cherry-wood board. She savored the saltiness of his taste, as fresh and strange as the first time.

"It's been so long," she whispered.

"Too long."

She fumbled at the belt of his kimono and it fell open. She knelt down and captured him in her mouth, just long enough to confirm the delicate weave of his skin, the urgent thrust of his blood. Then she stood up for him to unzip her skirt. There was no pretense, they knew each other too well for that.

His breath was hot in her ear. "Are you sure?"

"I need you."

They moved purposefully, each knowing what the other intended. Makoto lifted her off the ground as easily as if she were a child, and she arched backward, gripped the rail in both hands, and let out her breath in a long, surging sigh. He was harder than usual, stretching her, going deep into the core of her being.

Martine relaxed totally, letting her head fall back until her hair was brushing the ground. Above her, Makoto was silhouetted against the mauve sky, his heavy shoulders glistening in the flare of the fireworks. He was holding her so lightly, moving so smoothly, that she felt as if she were floating in the air. Martine matched herself to the rhythm of his breathing, responded to his responses. They could do this exactly together, all it needed was trust and care.

Through half-closed eyes she watched the giant blooms of color opening with a crump, dissolving into cascades of glittering rain, fading and dying.

The last fireworks of summer—they were the ones that stayed with you forever.

On the other side of Tokyo Bay, in the midst of a bone-white citadel of towers and storage drums, a man in spotlessly clean overalls sat in a bubble of toughened plastic. In front of him was a bank of twitching dials and endlessly scrolling screens. The control panel hummed and bleeped and winked, confirming that Japan's largest, most up-to-date chemical complex was operating smoothly and efficiently.

Koji Murata had been seated in the plastic bubble since four o'clock, hardly moving except to adjust a dial or to tap an instruction into the keyboard. Some might think this was a boring job, spending an entire eight-hour shift alone, but Koji Murata didn't think so. To him, process monitoring was more than being a kind of high-tech security man, a mere passive observer sitting there in case of some unlikely emergency. It meant knowing every step of the process, absorbing yourself in it, becoming one with it. When Murata sat at the control panel, he didn't just see dials and charts and columns of numbers. He saw gases swirling, dark oceans churning and frothing, violent chain reactions such as had marked the creation of the planet earth. This plant contained six thousand miles of piping, and Murata still found it as strangely thrilling as when he first joined the company. Six thousand miles— it was enough to stretch from Tokyo to Moscow!

Murata felt a twinge of regret as he noted that the hands of the big luminescent clock were indicating the end of his shift. Soon he would have to discard his clean-smelling overalls and put on ordinary shabby clothes. Then he would get on his scooter and ride back to the company housing, where he would quietly suck down a bowl of instant noodles before crawling into the futon laid out beside his wife's sleeping body. Early the next morning, when she left for work in the convenience store, it would be his turn to lie prone and unconscious. Sometimes days went by without them having their eyes open at the same time, but Murata didn't mind that at all. He didn't miss the conversation.

It was twelve o'clock now. Endo was standing outside the changing room, fitting his peaked cap onto his balding head. Murata stood up and waved at him. Then he froze. Something was wrong with the screen in the middle of the control panel. It flickered wildly, then went blank. Suddenly a new image appeared, one that Murata had heard about, but hoped that he would never actually see in his life. It was a cartoon figure of a smiley face wearing a cow-boy hat.

"It can't be," he gasped. "There must be a mistake!"

But the cartoon figure shook its head, and the smiley face inverted into a frown. Underneath appeared a line of wavy Japanese script—"Time To Die, You Yellow Bastards."

Murata yanked open the door of the plastic bubble.

"Endo-kun," he screamed. "Get over here quick. It's Hiroshima!"

Endo's grin froze on his face, and he dashed toward the door. On the screen, the smiley face morphed into a mushroom cloud. "BOOM" said the text.

Murata punched the emergency button and tapped in the backup instructions, but he knew it was already too late. Hiroshima was the most advanced and adaptable virus ever created. Originally lodged in the Japanese language version of Doorway, the world's leading operating system, it had a polymorphic ability to customize itself to new environments, to fragment and regroup, to combine with harmless graphics codes and lie dormant for months, maybe years. When it manifested itself like this, the damage was already done. It had disabled the backups and infiltrated logic bombs into all the main command areas.

"Look at No. 3," yelled Endo. The needle on one of the dials was spinning crazily. Above it a red light was flashing.

"Too much fluid is going in there. The tank's already at capacity."

"You'd better shut down the pump."

"I can't. There's no response."

"Get the emergency team down there. Somebody's got to shut that thing off or the tank will burst."

"Don't be stupid. It's made of reinforced concrete, six feet thick."

"Well, something's going to burst."

The two men gazed at each other, panic-stricken. Outside a siren had started whooping.

"The pipes! There'll be backflow."

"Try closing the valves."

"No response!"

Six thousand miles of metal piping, thought Murata dully, enough to stretch from Tokyo to Moscow. Somewhere in that maze of metal there would a weak spot, a place where the pressure would be too much. And with the mapping system down, there was no way they could identify it until it was too late.

"Let's get out of here," said Endo tersely.

"What?"

"There's nothing we can do."

"We can't just walk away."

"You're crazy. If the pipes go, can you imagine what it'll be like? The whole place will be a fireball. If you don't get fried, the fumes will burn out your lungs."

"That's nonsense. This place was built with the workers' safety in mind."

Endo shook his head angrily. "You actually believe that?"

Murata said nothing. He wasn't sure if he believed it or not. All he knew was that if the white citadel no longer existed, if there were to be no more nights in the glass bubble monitoring the mysterious beauty of its processes, if his life was to be just a matter of eating, sleeping, defecating, quarreling with his wife, scrabbling for money—then there really wasn't any point in enduring it.

Endo got up and left the glass bubble. Murata didn't even turn around.

S I X

Warwick Fletcher gazed out of the helicopter at the concrete fortress nestling in the bend of the gleaming Thames River. It was from this distance that you could most appreciate the sheer scale of it, the bold purposefulness of its twin tower design. In comparison, the Tower of London looked hokey, a mere whimsy there to please the tourists.

It was twenty years since the InfoCorp head office had been opened, but even now the sight of it filled Fletcher with satisfaction. It symbolized all that he had achieved despite the overwhelming odds against him. He remembered the pompous blathering of the bankers, the nervousness of his advisers, the angry threats of the trade union leaders when they realized how many jobs were going to be cut.

Nobody had wanted him to succeed, and nobody had believed he would. But Fletcher had believed, and that had been enough. History had been created. By combining newspapers, TV channels, and online financial information, he had opened the way to global media convergence. By withstanding eighteen months of violent picketing, he had broken the British trade union movement. And by pitching his center of operations miles away from any other corporate headquarters, he had shifted the entire center of the city eastward, creating a thriving new commercial district where previously there had been nothing but slums and wasteland.

The world had changed since then, and InfoCorp with it. There had been bids and counterbids, mergers and demergers, spin-offs, asset swaps, acquisitions in countries that hadn't even existed when InfoCorp was born. Movie studios, music labels, cable TV companies, shopping channels, internet portals, radio stations, basketball teams, soccer clubs, lifestyle magazines—Warwick had snapped them up, sure in his instinct that people would hunger for more and more information, more and more entertainment, more and more images to fill their minds and help them forget the tedium of their sad little lives. All that activity had built InfoCorp into a gigantic global enterprise, one of the top ten companies in the world by market capitalization. But in terms of excitement, nothing could match the sense of being ahead of a curve that no one else had even seen. Even now, as Warwick contemplated the masterstroke that would turn InfoCorp into the IBM of the twenty-first century, those concrete towers gleaming in the sunshine gave him more pride than anything else.

The helicopter circled the complex twice, then landed on the roof of the main building. Sandy, the ex-SAS man Fletcher used as his bodyguard on this side of the Atlantic, was the first to get out. He stood arms akimbo, cigarette jutting from his lips, his aquiline features expressionless as he scanned the landing area. This was completely unnecessary of course, but Fletcher always let him do things his own way. Sandy was a professional, with an impressive track record that stretched from Belfast to Belgrade.

Sandy gave a nod, and Fletcher gingerly negotiated his way onto the concrete. His knees and ankles felt stiff and tender, and his prostate had been playing up. Jenny had been telling him not to fly so much, but that was like telling a fish not to swim so much. He needed to fly in order to make deals. He needed to make deals in order to live. Jenny should have worked that out by now.

Warwick walked to the edge of the roof and rested his hands on the aluminum railing. He took a deep breath and looked down at the street below, where tiny figures were pouring from the entrance of the new subway station. Sandy and the others watched in silence. They had seen him do this many times before.

With his right hand Warwick unzipped himself and craned forward slightly. He closed his eyes for a moment, then opened them to watch the golden parabola rising into the air in front of him. He gave a grunt of satisfaction as the parabola danced in the breeze, broke into droplets, and dissolved into a fine mist that descended on the heads of the men and women hurrying to work hundreds of feet below.

Mark Fletcher watched from the other tower as his father walked toward the elevator. The limp was more pronounced than the last time they had met, the face darker and more heavily lined, but he was in impressive shape for a man in his mid-seventies. His immense physical strength was still evident in the bulk of his shoulders and his barrel-like chest.

Mark himself was a hefty six foot two. He had won a blue in rugby as a crash-tackling center three-quarter, and he kept himself ferociously fit with squash, judo, and daily weight training. Nonetheless, in his father's presence he felt like a skinny sixteen-year-old. Everything about the man seemed larger than life, from his thick forearms matted with black hair to his huge head, lantern jaw, and jutting lip. Even in the old days—before Warwick Fletcher had become *the* Warwick Fletcher, when he was just another entrepreneur with wild ideas and a disastrous balance sheet—the impact of his physical presence had been overwhelming.

Mark remembered how rooms would go quiet when his father appeared, how important men smiled in his presence and how he never smiled back. He remembered the incident in Las Vegas, he had been seven or eight at the time, when they found two men waiting for them outside the men's room at the restaurant. One of them had put a hand on his father's shoulder and ordered him to go with them. His father had merely made a sudden movement with his elbow and carried on walking. Looking back over his shoulder, Mark had been astonished to see the man sitting slumped against the wall, spitting blood and pieces of tooth onto the carpet. Then his father had turned to him and made him promise not say anything to his mother. "We wouldn't want to spoil her evening," he said with an enormous wink.

Mark himself had come across some hard men in his time. There had been the Russian oligarch who had backed up a takeover bid for their joint venture with two car bombs. There had been the South African international rugby prop who had chewed off the bottom third of his ear while he lay helpless at the bottom of a ruck. There had been political heavyweights threatening new regulations, high-tech billionaires eager to carve chunks out of the InfoCorp empire, drug barons and arms dealers bringing multimillion-dollar libel suits. But all these people had been pushovers compared to the bearlike figure striding purposefully toward him.

"Good to see you, Dad," Mark said, stepping forward with outstretched hand. "How was the Caribbean?"

His father enclosed his hand in a crushing grip. Not much sign of poor health there, thought Mark.

"It's bloody boring," growled Warwick Fletcher. "If you've seen one island, you've seen 'em all. Same thing everywhere—blue skies, coconut trees, black boys grinning at you. What's there to grin about, for chrissake! No wonder the whole place is in such a mess."

That was typical too. Mark couldn't imagine his father actually enjoying a holiday. Not even Jenny Leung had been able to change that.

"I hear you've been doing some scuba diving?"

Warwick frowned. "How do you know that?"

"Well, we do have the largest news-gathering operation in the world here, Dad. There's not much that goes on that we don't know."

The frown got heavier, the stare narrower. "What the fuck are you talking about? My private life is not news. I thought you understood that."

Mark winced. His father only used obscenities when he was really fuming about something. It was a reaction against his own father, the semiliterate brawler from the Australian outback who had founded the family fortune.

"Of course, Dad. Nobody would dream of putting it in print. It's just that we hear things sometimes, all sorts of things."

Mark knew that he was sounding feeble, no different from the gangling sixteen-year-old quailing in the blast of his father's disapproval. That wouldn't do, not this time. He was going to make his case head-on, no matter how furious the reaction.

"Just remember this—our private life is absolutely off-limits. Anyone who sticks their nose in is going to get it chopped off."

"Sure, Dad."

That was a dead giveaway—"*our* private life." What he really meant was "Jenny is off-limits." But Mark was not going to shut up about Jenny. Jenny Leung was the center of the whole problem.

They went into Mark's office and sat down. Warwick thumped his briefcase down on the floor, pulled out two leather-bound folders, and slid one across the glass tabletop. Mark flipped it open and glanced at the title page.

"Another restructuring plan?"

There had been three already, and Mark hadn't found much to celebrate in any of them. Management control had been progressively shifted from London to Los Angeles, and from the board of directors to a "supervisory committee" made up of Warwick himself, Jenny Leung, and a couple of tame lawyers.

His father fitted on his half-moon reading glasses. "The other plans were just tinkering. This is the crucial one, the last throw of the dice."

He stared over the top of the glasses, fixing Mark with his pale blue eyes. Mark gave a noncommittal nod and turned his gaze to the folder. His father's choice of words had been quite deliberate. He was invoking a family legend, the story of how his own father had started out in business.

Jack Fletcher had been the illegitimate son of a good-time girl in a remote Australian mining town. At the age of twelve he became a miner himself, and gradually accumulated a little cache of gold. When he judged he had enough, he exchanged it for cash, made his way to the biggest gambling den in the state, and staked the equivalent of three years' wages on three rolls of the dice. He won all three, and walked out of there rich enough to buy the local newspaper.

Mark was not a gambler himself. He preferred to be in the position of the house, which was why he had purchased lottery franchises in half-a-dozen countries. Still, he understood the power of the idea in his father's mind. "The last throw of the dice" was something you could never walk away from. It was the test of your manhood. Warwick regularly underwent that test in casinos all over the world, winning or losing as much as fifty million dollars a session.

"Take your time, Mark. You're only the fourth person alive to clap eyes on it."

Fourth? So who were the other three? Warwick himself, Jenny, and probably Nelson Curbley, the high-powered Washington lawyer who was deputy chairman of the supervisory committee. Mark tried to control his mounting anger. He was the chief executive of InfoCorp and should have been consulted right from the start, as he had been with the other three restructuring plans. Presenting him with a fait accompli like this was an insult.

"Lot of asset transfers here," he muttered sullenly. And they were all in one direction—from InfoCorp Global Holdings to InfoCorp Asia.

His father nodded. "I'm not looking at the world as it is now, but what it's going to be like in thirty years' time. All through my career I've based my plans on looking thirty years ahead. This time I won't be around to see them fulfilled, but that makes no difference. This is absolutely the right platform for the next phase of development."

Mark turned to the next page, which outlined the new capital structure. He caught his breath. This was worse than anything he had ever imagined.

"You're cutting off Asia from the rest of the group?"

"Not exactly. What we've decided is a sister company structure. InfoCorp Global and InfoCorp Asia will no longer have any financial or operational relationship, though of course they will both still be controlled by the master company."

"What's the point of that?

"The point is strategic focus. You can't sit here in London staring out over the Thames and understand what's happening in Asia."

Mark felt as if he'd been slapped across the face. "That's bollocks," he snapped. "I know the region as well as anyone, for chrissake. I spent three years in Hong Kong setting up the finest digital satellite operation in the world."

"Listen, I'm not knocking your contribution, I'm just stating a fact. From now on we need a dedicated management style, with a single clearly defined line of command."

"Leading to who? To Jenny, I suppose."

"Watch your mouth, mate. Without Jenny's ideas, our Asian business would be flat on its arse by now."

His father's lower lip gave a little quiver. That was an early warning sign of a gathering storm. Mark ignored it. Nothing could prevent a showdown now and the sooner it came the better. He stabbed a forefinger at the center of the paper.

"And what about this private placement of shares? Was that her idea too?"

"Yeah. As a matter of fact it was."

Mark glanced at the list of investors. They were companies he had never heard of, with bland names such as Asian Capital Management, Dragon Resources, and China Development Corporation.

"I suppose the people behind all this are personal contacts of hers."

"What if they are? We want to be insiders in this region, not big white men with colonialist mindsets. We need strong strategic partners."

"Like who?"

"Like I can't tell you right now. Listen, Mark, this game is being played for bigger stakes than you can ever imagine. We're talking about historical forces here, the fate of nations."

"Bigger stakes"—there was the gambling metaphor again. But what were these historical forces he was referring to? The old man had always had a mystical streak, but some of his recent comments had been almost Napoleonic. Mark sometimes wondered if his father was becoming slightly unhinged. After four decades of stable marriage, and constant harping on the importance of family values, he had suddenly embarked on a relationship with a woman less than half his age. Under Jenny's influence, he had become a vegetarian and junked his Savile Row suits in favor of leather jackets and silk scarves. More troubling to Mark's educated mind, he had started hanging out with movie people and bogus intellectuals, such as the self-realization guru now installed as editorial adviser to the *Tribune*.

"You're intending to sell almost twenty percent of InfoCorp Asia, and you're not even going to say who the buyers are?"

"Not yet. But read the strategy paper at the back of the folder. It'll give you some idea of the background."

There was a six-page document tucked into the inside pocket of the leather folder. Mark pulled it out and browsed the first few paragraphs. It was called "Japan vs China—The Coming Powershift." The author was J. J. Murphy of the Industrial Security Institute in Washington.

"So who is this Murphy?"

"He's quite a guy, the most brilliant of the new generation of Asia experts. You would learn a lot from him, Mark."

"Uh-huh. Where did you come across him, Dad?"

He knew the answer to that question already. Warwick Fletcher was unlikely to bump into "the most brilliant of the new generation of Asia experts" in the normal course of his activities—unless Jenny Leung had something to do with it.

"Look, read what he's got to say. And if you're still not convinced, you can talk to him in person. I've just offered him a job."

"Oh really?"

Mark was about to blurt out something sarcastic, but he restrained himself. There was no point in sweating the trivialities, it was time for the crunch.

Mark had a fleeting vision of that South African prop forward charging straight at him, shaven head thrust out, arms and knees pumping away. Mark hadn't faltered that time. He'd gone in hard, right shoulder thumping against those tree-trunk thighs. Dangerous, but the only approach that had stood a chance of working.

He snapped the leather folder shut and looked his father in the eye.

"All very interesting stuff, Dad. But before you go any further, there are a couple of things I want to bring to your attention."

"Concerning what?"

"Concerning Jenny."

The pale blue eyes narrowed. The lower lip started twitching. "Careful, mate."

"It's very simple, Dad. The woman cannot be trusted."

Mark was expecting an explosion of anger, but the reply that came was unnervingly mild. There was even the ghost of a smile on his father's lips.

"Now what can you possibly mean by that, Mark?"

"I mean that she has often given false information about herself. She didn't edit a student newspaper at Berkeley, nor did she work as a part-time language instructor, nor was she active in the Asian Students' Association. In fact she was hardly present at all."

"Go on," said his father, low and quiet.

"As for the idea that she built up her consultancy firm through years of hard struggle—nothing could be further from the truth. When she first moved to Hong Kong, she rented an office in Central and lived in a luxury apartment in Clearwater Bay—quite an expense for a start-up company with no income."

"Is that all?"

"Not quite. There's the question of how she got her first contract with a major American company. That was Digicom."

"And how did she, Mark? Please tell me." The lower lip was twitching and flexing as if it had a life of its own.

"Well, what happened was that Digicom's counterpart, which was a Chinese state-owned enterprise, put her name forward as being indispensable to the deal. So a thirty-two-year-old American Studies graduate suddenly became indispensable to a multibillion-dollar communications satellite deal."

There was silence while his father sat there staring at him in an oddly abstract way, his fingers locked together under his chin. The large square fingernails had become pale and blotchy. What was that a sign of—bad circulation, liver problems? He would have to remember to ask one of the health editors.

"It sounds like somebody's been doing quite a bit of research. Who is it, Mark? Some investigative journalist trying to make a name for himself?"

"That's not important," said Mark tightly.

Without warning his father shot to his feet, sending his chair crashing to the ground. His face was a mask of rage, his voice loud enough to be heard outside in the heliport.

"You're right it's not important. I'll find out soon enough. And whoever's responsible is going to wish he'd never been born!"

"Cool down, Dad. Let's discuss this rationally."

The huge fist came slamming down on the table, sending the ashtrays skipping into the air.

"Shut your mouth, Mark. I told you this stuff is off-limits. Another word about it and I'll have you fired immediately."

Mark remained in his seat, his voice calm and measured. "You can't do that. I'm the CEO of a public company. The shareholders have just given me a three-year term."

"Hah! You've got no fucking idea what I can and can't do, no fucking idea at all."

The last words were pronounced with a savage glee that Mark found shocking.

It was true that his father's ruthlessness amazed even those who knew him well. This was a man who used a flunky to tell his wife that their forty-year-old marriage was over, who had changed his citizenship three times for business purposes, and who switched his support from right wing to left wing and back again depending on which was offering the better deal.

"So you're not interested in the facts?"

"The facts?" roared Warwick Fletcher. "Bugger the facts! I'm interested in the future."

His eyes were bulging, his face dark with blood. He was like an enormous child, thought Mark. A billionaire child ranting and raving, exulting in the noise of his own tantrum.

"The future?"

"Yes, the future. You think I'm just a horny old fool. That's not it, Mark. I know exactly what I'm doing. And nobody is going to get in my way. Nobody, you hear me?"

"I hear you all right," said Mark, fingering his left ear. He would never forget the fury of that moment fifteen years ago, helpless at the bottom of the ruck while human teeth tore into his flesh. And he would never forget the feeling of triumph when he heard the final whistle and knew the game was won.

Ten minutes later, Warwick Fletcher was retracing his route along the Thames, a sheaf of documents perched on his loglike thighs, his jaw set in an expression of steely determination. When the helicopter was no more than a speck above the London skyline, Mark called his friend at Kroll and explained that he had another job, one that would involve a different style of investigation.

SEVEN

Martine put down the toothbrush and gazed at herself in the mirror. The person she saw looking back at her bore an unnerving resemblance to her mother. Not her mother as she was now—overweight, her complexion mottled with years of heavy drinking—but as she had been when Martine was a child. There was no getting away from it. No matter what Martine did with her hair, no matter what she did with eyeshadow and lipstick, she was gradually morphing into her mother.

When she was younger, she had never imagined that such a thing could happen, but now the resemblance was getting stronger year by year. Her neck was thickening, her skin coarsening, and her body was getting bigger in all the wrong places. The nightmare thought hit her once again: one day she would stand in front of the mirror and a fat middle-aged woman would be staring back at her. And the worst thing about this woman would not be the evaporation of beauty, not the boozing, not the increasingly pathetic love affairs. It would be the look in her eyes—the look in her mother's eyes—of crushing loneliness, of disappointment at what she had become.

Ageing, rejection, despair—was that really what lay ahead? If only she could freeze time and stay as she was now forever, with no wrinkles, no blotches, no cellulite. With a relationship that never ceased to be fresh and exciting, and with work that never ceased to be challenging. Impossible, of course, but that wasn't going to stop her from exerting every fiber of her being in trying.

Martine spat out the toothpaste and turned away from the mirror. This much was true—you couldn't avoid your destiny. But the kind of destiny Martine believed in had nothing to do with inheritance. It was as the ancient Greeks said—destiny is character.

Six-thirty on a weekday morning, and there were thirty students in the dojo. Until a few years ago karate had been the preserve of tough guys, headcases,

70

and cops. Now with the crumbling of law and order, martial arts training had become one of the few boom industries. Ordinary men and women of all ages were rushing to learn karate, kickboxing, tae kwon do, shorinji kempo, ninjitsu and all the variants and new improved systems that were appearing like bamboo shoots in the rainy season.

Martine had started karate at the age of ten, got her black belt at fifteen, and had won a silver medal at the European Student Championship. She was no longer a devoted practitioner, but she tried to get to the dojo at least a couple of times a week. It was a good way of working out, and more fun than aerobics or squash. And the sensei here was one of the best. He only accepted the students he wanted, and treated them like family. From his serious, rather morose appearance, you would never guess he was an ex-yakuza who had left the syndicate after five years in jail for manslaughter. That had been a quarter of a century ago, and he still refused to say a word about it.

This morning there were two new students, a tall Japanese woman and a blond foreigner with a black belt in another karate style. The sensei called them out of the circle of students and they introduced themselves with a bow.

"Saya Miki, detective, Azabu Police Station."

"Fritz Schneider, cultural attaché, German Embassy."

The sensei nodded and clapped his leathery hands. "Well then, newcomers, let's see your form. Hasegawa and Kondo, please."

The sensei's two favorite students stepped into the middle of the circle. Hasegawa, a shaven-headed twenty-five-year-old with a chest like a barrel, was the most enthusiastic student in the dojo. After the others left, he would stay behind bashing his fists against a wooden pillar until his knuckles bled. Kazuko Kondo was a squat, cheerful woman who had recently lost her job as an elevator attendant in one of the big department stores. She was technically strong and very fit, as you would expect from someone who never touched a drop of alcohol and went to bed at nine-thirty surrounded by a menagerie of fluffy animals. When Martine first came to the dojo, she'd been capable of beating Kondo in eight bouts out of ten, but now it was the other way around. Lifestyle —stress, work, diet—had taken its toll.

"All right, match up. Schneider against Kondo, Miki against Hasegawa."

The sensei stood there nonchalantly flexing his shoulders as the German stared at him in amazement.

"What does this mean?" he said in heavily accented Japanese. "You are asking me to fight against a woman?"

The sensei was asking Hasegawa to fight against a woman too, but Hasegawa's chubby face was as expressionless as ever.

"Get ready!" called the sensei.

The German glanced at Martine and shook his head theatrically. "This I don't believe," he said in English.

Martine looked straight through him. She had a strong suspicion that he wouldn't be attending this dojo much longer. The other three were strapping on their chest guards.

"Helmets!"

Schneider scrabbled impatiently with his straps, leaving one of them dangling half-fastened.

"Take positions!"

The two pairs separated, Schneider and Kondo to the sensei's right, Miki and Hasegawa to his left. They bowed, then the sensei clapped his hands again and the bouts began.

Martine kept her eyes on Kondo, admiring the flow of her hips and shoulders as she swayed past Schneider's frantic jabs. The plain, practical woman whose other hobbies were cooking and pachinko had been transformed into something else entirely. With her bright, alert eyes and piercing shrieks, she was more like a wild animal than a human being. Schneider was lost, of course, and the end came quickly when he tried an arching reverse kick, which Kondo swept aside with her forearm. For a moment he lost his balance and Kondo skipped forward and tapped him in the middle of the chest with her foot. Martine had been on the receiving end of that tap once or twice and she wasn't surprised to see Schneider go reeling backward and land on the floor with a loud "Oomph!"

The other bout was a different matter entirely. Hasegawa was fast and strong, with a good repertoire of feints and dodges. He had been attending the dojo since high school, and had learned his lessons well. But the cop was good too. She read most of his tricks, and caught him with a few of her own. The sensei watched them in silent amusement, then clapped his hands and called it a draw.

"Everyone in pairs. Meyer, you go with Miki."

So Martine found herself practicing blocks and jabs with the female cop. She was a startlingly attractive woman, with large round eyes and high cheekbones, just the type that Martine would have gone for if she'd been born a man. Her breasts looked fuller and higher than Martine's own, and she had the creamy complexion and graceful, curving neck that Martine especially envied in Japanese women. Twenty years later, when Martine would be dealing with wrinkles and varicose veins, Saya Miki wouldn't look much different from the way she did now. Martine wondered what Makoto would think of this woman. On basic male instincts, which of them would he choose? The idea unnerved her, making her lose concentration so that she missed a block and Saya Miki's fist crashed into her face guard.

"Sorry, sorry!"

"My fault," said Martine, rubbing her cheekbone. "I was thinking of something else."

"Work?"

"Boyfriend, actually."

"Ah."

"That never happens to you?"

Saya shook her head. "I don't think much about men these days."

"No boyfriend?"

"Not any more. But I just bought a dog. He's very cute—and totally trustworthy."

It wasn't so much what she said as the slow, drawling way she said it. Martine laughed out loud. She realized they were going to be friends. After the practice session was over they sat together in the changing room and chatted. On the spur of the moment, Martine asked her the question she had been asking everyone recently.

"This Nozawa guy—what do you think of him?"

"Can't stand him," said Saya, tugging a comb through her hair with surprising violence. "I think he embodies everything that's gone wrong with this country."

"How do you mean?"

"He's completely empty, just says whatever he thinks people want to hear. There are people like that in every organization. These days they rise to the top, and the good people get left behind."

There was an edge to her voice that made Martine think she was talking from personal experience.

"So you're not eagerly awaiting his next CD?"

"I'd rather listen to a CD of my dog barking. At least he's not faking it."

Martine glanced at her watch. She had a busy day ahead of her, so she hurriedly stuffed her equipment into her sports bag, said good-bye to Saya and the others, and left. Outside, the German guy, Schneider, was standing at the side of the road waiting for a taxi. When he saw Martine, he came toward her and held out his umbrella. She could tell he was planning a move by his too-wide smile and the way he was standing there with his chest pushed out. Martine ducked under the umbrella.

"What happened didn't surprise me," he said. "In fact, I should have expected it. That woman is the local champion, I suppose."

"She certainly has good technique."

In fact there were half-a-dozen women in the dojo who were better than Kondo, but Martine let that rest. Schneider was holding the umbrella in such a way that his forearm was brushing the back of her hair.

"It is regrettable, but Japanese people are basically quite racist. It runs deep within their culture, from distant times right to the present."

"Really?"

"Yes, really. There was an excellent article in the *New York Times* recently. It explained the cultural background, why they always try to keep out imports, why they have never apologized for their actions in the war, and so on."

"I see," said Martine, eyeing his hand out of the corner of her eye. His fingers, thick and knobbly, were actually resting on her shoulder.

"I notice it myself, this mentality. When I take the train, often nobody will sit down in the space beside me. It is almost as if they think I smell."

"Well, maybe they're right."

His eyes widened. "What?"

"You do smell," said Martine sweetly. "Didn't you know? Surely somebody must have told you."

"What are you talking about?"

Martine turned her face toward his armpit and took a couple of sniffs. "It's rather like a mature gorgonzola, quite strong if you're not used to it."

He let the umbrella slide to the ground and stood looking at her in shock. Then a big smile slowly spread over his face. "This is a joke, yes? Now I understand. Now I am laughing! Ha, ha, ha!"

Behind him a taxi slid to a halt, and the back door flicked open. Martine slid inside.

"How about dinner tonight?" Schneider called out as the door swung shut. "What's your phone number? Who are you anyway?"

Martine waved a hand as the taxi swished away from the curb.

Martine got to the office just before nine to find that Charlie's desk had already been cleared. The photo of his wife and kids had gone from the wall, and his tennis holdall had gone from the lobby. Even his decaf had disappeared from the shelf in the kitchen.

"When did this happen?" Martine asked Kyo-san, the office manager.

"Just now. You missed him by a couple of minutes."

That was strange. Charlie hadn't mentioned anything about an early departure. She had assumed he would be staying around for several weeks.

"You mean he's gone, just like that, without saying good-bye?"

"Sure," said Kyo-san in her old-fashioned American drawl, acquired in 1960s Los Angeles. "He said it was a condition of his severance package. The story is that he quit on his own initiative, and was keen to get back to the States as soon as possible."

"Huh? Whose idea was that?"

"Head Office's. It's part of the new personnel policy."

"The *Tribune's* new personnel policy is to lie?"

"You got it, honey."

Martine took a bottle of barley tea from the refrigerator, poured out two glasses, and plopped in a couple of ice cubes. Then she put some oatmeal cookies on a tray and took them over to Kyo-san.

In the long years Kyo-san had been with the *Tribune*, she had seen dozens of bureau chiefs come and go. She had watched them arrive full of big ideas, eager to do the Japan story as it had never been done before, to get behind the surface and find out what really made the place tick. She had seen ambitions blocked, marriages dissolve, enthusiasm turn to bitterness. Most of them she had seen leave, like Charlie was leaving, puzzled and frustrated.

Technically, Martine was Kyo-san's boss. She was deputy bureau chief, and she earned roughly double Kyo-san's salary. But Martine was also much the younger of the two women, and it was a Japanese office so she was the one who served barley tea and rice crackers a couple of times a day.

"So what do you know about this new guy?" inquired Kyo-san, cautiously nibbling at a cookie. Her sweet tooth wasn't as well developed as Martine's.

"New guy? What new guy?"

"The new bureau chief. Didn't they tell you? There's a press release up on the website."

Martine shook her head in vexation. But really she shouldn't have been surprised. The new management regime had already shown that it had no respect for the paper's traditions. Stories unfavorable to major advertisers were being mysteriously spiked, and the editor of the arts page had been fired after penning a lukewarm review of a movie produced by InfoCorp's Hollywood studio. As part of the branding strategy, a line of luxury products had been launched, all emblazoned with the *Tribune*'s logo. You could buy leather wallets and briefcases, electronic knickknacks, baseball caps that sported the slogan "Get Real, Get the *Tribune*," and even boxer shorts decorated with headlines. These were all available to staff at big discounts. Charlie had bought a number of items as part of his doomed attempt to ingratiate himself with the new management. The very thought of Makoto owning any of them— particularly the boxer shorts—made Martine shudder.

After munching through a couple of cookies, Martine switched on her computer and checked the *Tribune*'s homepage. As Kyo-san had said, there was a press release announcing the appointment of a new bureau chief. Surprisingly, Charlie's successor wasn't a journalist at all, but an associate at some Washington think tank. According to the *Tribune*'s PR department, J. J. Murphy was "an acknowledged expert on East Asian economic and security issues, with excellent strategic vision and strong leadership skills." Martine didn't like the sound of that: who were the strong leadership skills going to be exercised on? Reading further, she discovered that Murphy had a doctorate in political science from Berkeley, spoke fluent Mandarin, and enjoyed fine wine, paraskiing, and scuba diving. This thinking man's James Bond had tes-tified many times before the Senate Foreign Relations committee, worked as an adviser to American hedge funds, and was responsible for a number of "provocative" op-eds. Right at the end came a few lines about Charlie, who, the world was told, had left the *Tribune* in order to spend more time with his family.

Martine tracked down half-a-dozen of Murphy's op-ed pages in the archives of the *Wall Street Journal* and the *Washington Post*. They had a common theme: Japan was finished as a serious global player and it was time for the US to switch its allegiance to China, with its huge markets and soaring growth. The Taiwan issue should not be allowed to get in the way, and neither should the massacres in Tibet, the missile sales to fundamentalist regimes, or the breach-ing of trade agreements and patent laws. These were merely the unfortunate but understandable responses of nervous Chinese leaders to "encirclement" by the US–Japan alliance. If the US would only dump Japan, the situation would change completely. China and the US would be able to build a long-lasting partnership encompassing trade, investment, and military cooperation. It would be a perfect win–win relationship. The combination of US technol-ogy and the huge Chinese labor force would usher in a golden era of prosper-ity and peace for Asia, indeed the entire world.

Martine took a deep breath. She had a feeling she was not going to see eye to eye with J. J. Murphy.

"This think tank, the Industrial Security Institute—do you know anything about it?"

Kyo-san didn't. On the spur of the moment Martine picked up the phone and rang an old boyfriend, a specialist in intellectual property working for a Washington law firm. His wife answered the phone, her voice turning icy when Martine gave her name. In the background she could hear a baby crying and someone playing the piano. Finally Michael came to the phone.

"Martine, how on earth did you get my number?"

"You gave it to me, remember?"

"Did I? Hmm, maybe I did."

Michael sounded hesitant, as well he might. It had been eighteen months ago, when they had bumped into each other at a conference in Singapore on the trade crisis and had spent a couple of hours in the bar chatting about old times.

"Well anyway, it's great to hear from you," said Michael, exaggeratedly breezy. "How can I be of assistance?"

"I need some information about trade politics, and who better to ask for an unbiased expert opinion than you?"

"An unbiased expert opinion? There's no such thing, not in this town any-way."

"Well, let's try our best. Have you heard of an organization called the Industrial Security Institute?"

"Yes, I have. It's a new think tank, or rather, a lobbying organization. All of these outfits have an axe to grind, usually one that's being heavily subsidized by some interested party."

"So who's subsidizing this one?"

"A handful of Fortune 500 companies, basically the aerospace and satellite communications guys."

"And how does it rank? Is it reputable, or not?"

Martine could almost hear him grinning at the other end of the phone. "Reputable? My God, Martine, sometimes you sound like the Queen of England. The ISI is extremely well funded, it has smart guys, and people listen to them. In that sense, which is the only sense that counts, yes, it is reputable."

"So it's not some fringe organization?"

"Absolutely not."

"I see," said Martine, feeling vaguely disappointed. "Thanks for your help. I may ask your advice again on this subject, if that's okay."

Michael's voice dropped to a murmur. "Sure, sure—though I'd rather you call my office number. Anyway, what's happening with you these days? We really must catch up next time you come through."

"Yes, we must. I'll give you a call."

When she put the phone down, Kyo-san was staring at her over the top of her glasses. Martine gave a little shrug and turned her attention to the pile of newspapers and magazines on the floor beside her.

All the Japanese dailies were leading with the story of the chemical plant explosion. Martine didn't do disaster stories—the news editors could pull the necessary information off the wire services—so she skimmed through the details without really taking them in. A fireball ... a cloud of toxic gas ... five workers and three residents of a nearby apartment block dead ... deepest regrets ... investigations to determine the cause...

Each of the dailies dealt with the subject the same way, with almost identical wording. That was no surprise. Whereas the tabloid press—with its conspiracy theories and scurrilous rumors—was getting increasingly hysterical, the establishment papers were duller and emptier than ever. Thanks to the system of press clubs, official information had always been tightly controlled. Now the editorial boards of the major papers had agreed to follow a policy of "self-restraint," meaning they would avoid "inappropriate" or "irresponsible" stories until the crisis was over.

Martine had good friends working for the Japanese press. They were intelligent, hardworking, highly knowledgeable about whatever field they were in, and they had been the sources for some of her best stories. But they had to play by the rules, especially in the current economic climate. One mistake, one failure to say the right thing to the right person at the right time, and lifetime employment could become lifetime unemployment.

Martine browsed through the three big dailies, absorbing a day's worth of factory closures, bankruptcies, stock price declines, suicides, rapes, and murders. There was nothing that struck a chord with her, nothing that had the shape of a story. She dropped the last paper onto the pile and glanced at the front page again. There was something about that item on the chemical plant explosion that was nagging at her memory, like a piece of gravel caught in her shoe. Then her eyes were drawn to the middle of the second paragraph: "It is estimated that the explosion took place at eleven o'clock last night."

Eleven in the evening. She suddenly remembered the mysterious message she had received on her palmtop computer.

"Kyo-san, where exactly did this explosion happen?"

"I'm not sure. Somewhere in Chiba, wasn't it?"

"Yes, I know that. But was it inland, or on the bay?"

"On the bay, I guess. That's where most of these places are. They need good access from the sea."

Kyo-san was right, as a quick look at the map on the wall proved. So whoever had sent the message was no ordinary nutcase. He or she had predicted the exact time and place of a major industrial accident. Martine didn't believe in psychic powers, so she was left with two possible explanations. Either the whole thing was an amazing coincidence, or what had happened to the Sumi-kawa Chemical's brand-new multibillion-yen chemical facility was no accident at all.

Martine took her palmtop from her bag and tried to retrieve the deleted message. No good—it had gone, vanished into digital oblivion. She thought for a moment, then called a good contact in the police department.

"Sato-san, I was wondering if you had any comments about the explosion in Chiba last night?"

"Comments? What is there to say about an incident like that? The loss of life is very regrettable, and a thorough investigation into the cause is already underway."

Martine sighed. "Regrettable," "thorough investigation"—the standard phrases that were trotted out whenever anything went wrong. You heard them a lot these days.

"Off the record, what else have you got?"

Sato sounded offended. "Off the record? I don't understand what you mean, Meyer-san. This is an unfortunate accident. We're doing our best to work out how it happened."

"What if I said that I know it wasn't an accident at all?"

There was no reply from the other end of the phone. Martine thought she heard the sound of a pencil hitting the floor.

"Perhaps we should meet for a chat," said Martine sweetly.

"Impossible."

"It would be useful for the article I'm writing."

Now Sato sounded worried. "You shouldn't write about this, it's too sensitive. But tell me—what are you going to say?"

"Cover-up, official incompetence, nobody taking responsibility—you know, the usual thing."

There was another pause, broken by the sound of Sato sucking air through his teeth.

"All right," he muttered dolefully. "How about lunch today?"

"What a nice idea!" said Martine, winking across the room at Kyo-san.

EIGHT

Martine met Sato in a traditional Japanese restaurant famous for its mountain vegetables and homemade bean curd. At the entrance you were greeted by a kimono-clad waitress who led you over a wooden bridge, down a stone pathway, then into a tatami room that looked out onto a charming little garden. It was soothing to sit there, listening to the tinkling of windbells and the creak of the waterwheel, and watching the carp glide through the pond like fleshy orange torpedoes. For a few precious moments it was possible to forget that you were on the eighteenth floor of the Sumikawa Bank building, overlooking one of the most heavily congested intersections in the city.

Today Sato was looking far from soothed. When Martine slid open the door of the tatami room, he shot to his feet and glanced nervously over her shoulder.

"I hope you're on your own, Meyer-san?"

"Of course."

"Please understand—this whole meeting is off the record. Not only that, but nobody should even know about it."

Martine nodded, and they sat down at the low table. While the waitress brought in a tray of dishes, Sato made no attempt at conversation. They sat there in silence until the waitress had gone, then he leaned across the table and fixed Martine in his bloodshot gaze.

"How did you find out about this business?" he muttered sulkily.

"I have a source of information."

"Inside the company?"

"You know I can't disclose that."

"How much did he tell you?"

"I can't disclose that either, just as I can't disclose anything you tell me. But I promise you this—I'm not planning to write an attacking piece. The official view will be given due prominence. *Bon appétit!*"

Martine unsheathed her chopsticks and nibbled at a piece of the famous bean curd. Good for her complexion, that was what Makoto's mother had said the other night. Was her complexion really getting blotchy? Maybe the stress was starting to show.

Sato was frowning at her, probably wondering what line to take. But given the position he was in, there was only one line possible.

"Delicious," said Martine politely. She sliced off a larger piece of bean curd and put it in her mouth.

Sato raised his hands in the air, then let them drop to his lap. "All right then," he sighed. "Let me explain. You know the Hiroshima virus?"

So that was it! The Hiroshima virus had appeared late last year. In a matter of days, it had shut down the Tokyo stock exchange, scrambled decades of data at the tax bureau and the Ministry of Justice, and wreaked havoc in hospitals and banks.

"I thought anti-Hiroshima software had been installed everywhere."

Sato shook his head. "This is a new version, a hundred times more powerful."

"Where did it come from?"

"The same place as the first version, I suppose."

That was rumored to be the computer science department of an American university, though nothing had been proved.

"It's horrendous," said Sato grimly. "People are dying, billions of yen of damage is being done. The Americans should take this more seriously. So far they haven't been at all cooperative."

"Not cooperative? How do you mean?"

"The FBI must know who these vandals are. When their own companies are attacked, they hunt them down soon enough. But when it's the Japanese who are suffering the damage—well that's all a bit of a joke, isn't it?"

Martine blinked in surprise. That comment of Sato's would turn the story from a standard news item into a diplomatic hand grenade. "Japan Blames Chemical Deaths on US Negligence"—she could picture the headline already.

"Is that just a personal opinion?" she asked delicately. "Or is it the view of a highly placed source close to the investigation?"

She was giving Sato a chance to withdraw the comment. He'd been a good source, and she owed him that much.

"It's time they got the message," he growled. "Our patience is wearing thin."

Martine had never heard Sato talk like this before. He was usually so suave and relaxed.

"So it's the view of a highly placed source?"

"Certainly, yes," said Sato, slapping the table with the flat of his hand. The little dishes skipped in the air, and the bean curd wobbled.

Martine watched him glowering with rage. What else did he know, she wondered. How many similar incidents had been covered up? "Accidents"—come to think of it—seemed to have been occurring with unnerving frequency in recent months. The horrific fire at the Universal Studios theme park, blamed on sloppy maintenance procedures. The bullet train crash at Maebashi—eighty people dead, the proud symbol of Japanese engineering prowess lying on its side, twisted and broken. There had been innumerable collisions, leaks, and computer failures all over the country, but had they been random events or deliberate acts of sabotage? One thing was sure, though—Japanese bureaucrats would never reveal the truth voluntarily.

After leaving the restaurant, Martine walked back through Ginza. Once the priciest and most elegant entertainment district in the world, the area was now filled with fast-food joints, discount stores, and sleazy "pink salons" where salarymen lined up on their lunch breaks. Martine had done a story about these places a few months ago. She had interviewed one of the salon women, a bright, well-educated single mother who had spent twelve years working for an insurance company that collapsed early in the crisis. Now instead of an office cubicle she had a curtained booth, and instead of a computer and a phone she was equipped with a box of tissues and a bottle of mouthwash. The schedule was regular—ten customers a day, five days a week, then home in time to make dinner for her ten-year-old son. Sometimes she thought she recognized former clients and colleagues, though it was so dark in the booth that she could never be sure. Strangely, she seemed quite cheerful, even claiming that what she was doing was not so different from her old job. It was about understanding men, she said, about satisfying their needs as efficiently as possible, while all the time your mind was somewhere else.

Martine passed in front of a boarded-up restaurant that had once been favored by Japanese writers and intellectuals, and then turned into a narrow alleyway filled with uncollected rubbish sacks. The jazz club on the corner had long gone, leaving only a few tattered posters of past gigs. A huge crow—glossy-feathered and bright-eyed, with a beak like a steel spike—stared at her from its perch on the metal staircase. These creatures were getting bigger, bolder, and more aggressive. There were reports of them pecking out the eyes of sleeping drunks, clawing hanks of hair from unwary passersby, and even swooping down on picnicking families. On spring mornings the trees near her apartment shook with the violence of their feuding. No question about it—the crows were thriving. This crisis suited them fine.

At the end of the alley was a doorway covered by a faded *noren* cloth. Martine ducked inside. As usual the little antique shop was gloomy, impossibly cluttered, and empty of customers. A young man in a blue serge kimono was sitting at the counter inspecting a battered lacquer bowl through a magnifying glass roughly the same size as his face.

Martine picked up a wooden pestle and tapped it against the verdigris-streaked temple bell hanging from the ceiling.

The young man glanced up, eyes narrowed. When Martine emerged from the shadows of a full-size statue of Kannon, the Buddhist goddess of mercy, his face relaxed.

"I like this piece. It would be just right out on my balcony."

The young man shook his head "It isn't intended for outdoors. Rain and wind would cause damage to the paint."

"Well, anyway—how much would it cost?"

"Hmmm... For you—shall we say, thirty thousand yen."

"Thirty thousand? That's a bit expensive, isn't it?"

"I'm sorry, but we only have five in stock. And the factory that made them went bankrupt last year."

"That's a shame," said Martine. Of course these fake antiques weren't supposed to be on sale. They were just samples of the real works of art—often costing hundreds of millions of yen—that were stored in the high-security area at the back of the shop. It used to be only restaurants that displayed plastic simulacra of their wares, but now it was common practice at antique shops, jewelers, and luxury retailers.

"By the way, Meyer-san—were you looking for my grandfather?"

"I'd just like a quick word, if he's got time."

"No problem—please come through."

Martine slipped off her shoes and stepped into the musty corridor leading to the winding staircase up to the suite of rooms where Ken Shiina lived and worked. Of all the contacts Martine had made since she had been working with the *Tribune*, Shiina was the most precious. He was totally unknown to the public, and few journalists had even heard his name. To all appearances he was an eighty-year-old antique dealer. If you chose to inquire more closely, you might discover that he numbered several of Japan's wealthiest and most influential citizens among his clients, and that some celebrated museum pieces had passed through his hands, sometimes more than once. Also that he had written two well-regarded novels under a pen name, and that in his youth he had been a fervent communist.

Little more than that was in the public domain. The fact that for decades Shiina had been the ultimate insider in Japan's political world, a regular drinking companion of prime ministers and faction leaders, a man whose softly spoken and ever-ambiguous advice had broken apart factions and toppled cabinets—this was a tightly guarded secret. Fifteen years ago, Shiina had handed over the antique business to his son and taken orders as a Buddhist priest. Since then he had severed his ties with the political world and become a detached observer. Or at least, that's what he said.

"Meyer-san, it's good to see you after such a long time."

Martine bowed low before entering the room. "I'm sorry to cause trouble at such a busy time."

Shiina was indeed busy. He was fiddling with the aperture of a large camera mounted on a tripod. Stretched out on the floor in front of him was a scroll of animal drawings, yellowish and cracked.

"Motonobu Kano?" queried Martine.

"That's right," said Shiina. "You've got a good eye for paintings."

"Do you see many of these?"

"This is the first ever. The temple that was keeping it had a sudden need of funds, a problem with the back payment of property taxes."

"Really? That must be quite a back payment."

"Yes, indeed."

Shiina motioned her over to the wooden table and poured out some tea. Martine let him start the conversation his own way.

"The weather has become troubling these days. There are winds blowing from many different directions, hot and cold, hot and cold. A big storm is brewing, I think."

"Can't it be stopped?"

"I don't think so. This storm has been a long time coming. All we can do now is batten down our houses and wait for it to blow over. They always do in the end."

Shiina paused. Martine sipped her tea and waited for him to continue.

"Anyway," he muttered softly. "There is a feeling that maybe this storm is necessary. Maybe it's necessary to be woken up by the noise of the roof breaking up."

"Is this opinion now widely held?"

Martine didn't need to say by who. It was clear that the opinion in question was the common view of the Japanese establishment.

"For the moment, yes."

"But what if the storm doesn't pass? What if it stays in people's hearts?"

Shiina gave a dry chuckle. "All storms pass. That's their nature. If it doesn't pass, it can't be a storm."

Martine understood what he was saying, or at least she grasped the direction of his thoughts. With Shiina's elliptical phraseology, that was the best you could hope for. What he meant was that the establishment had decided on a tactical withdrawal. The crisis was deepening and the powers-that-be, their credibility battered by years of scandal and economic chaos, wanted to avoid further responsibility. They probably figured they could afford to let some inexperienced coalition take over and then retreat to the sidelines and watch it fall apart. And if it didn't fall apart quickly enough, then the necessary pressure would be applied and in due course they would resume their traditional role as guardians of the nation's destiny. But what if they were wrong? What if this wasn't just a spell of bad weather, but an actual change of climate?

"Many new political groups are appearing these days," ventured Martine, gently steering the conversation toward specifics.

Shiina slid a piece of red bean jelly into his mouth and licked the remnants off the wooden fork. "This is natural," he mumbled. "Always in times of uncertainty, a lot of new styles and formations are tried. It is the same in art as in politics."

"One of these groupings will be quite substantial, I hear. It will contain sixty young politicians, coming from all the major parties."

"Yes, yes. This has been spoken of."

"It could be very popular, I think."

Shiina looked puzzled. "Popular? Popular with whom?"

"I mean with ordinary people, the public."

"Ah, yes. The public will like it. The public always delights in entertainment, doesn't it?"

Shiina smiled as if he were discussing the behavior of a wayward child. Whether or not a politician was popular with the public was a trivial question to the power brokers of his generation.

Martine pressed on. "It would be interesting to know which factions are supporting this new grouping."

"All the factions are quiet at the moment. They're supporting nothing, opposing nothing. They're merely watching and waiting."

"But this kind of movement can't happen without strong support from somewhere."

"That's true."

"So where is the support coming from?"

Martine had been forced into asking a direct question, which was a kind of defeat. Shiina gazed at the wall as if he hadn't heard properly, his jaws moving slowly up and down. That piece of bean jelly had been in his mouth for a couple of minutes now, but still he hadn't swallowed it.

"Here is an interesting fact," he said abstractedly. "These eager young politicians who are gathering together—in their backgrounds there is a common theme. All received the same education."

"They all attended the same university?"

"It calls itself a school, a place for training the leaders of the future."

Shiina smiled again. The idea that leaders could be trained in a school was clearly one he found amusing.

"You mean the School of Leadership?"

Shiina didn't answer. He didn't need to. There was only one school of leadership in Japan, the one set up by the founder of Morikawa Electric Industries. It had a reputation for grueling study programs and intense secrecy.

"So now they're putting what they learned into practice?"

Shiina made a sound halfway between a sigh and a groan. "Young people are always foolish. It can't be helped. It's only by being foolish that they discover the meaning of wisdom."

These "young people" he was talking about were men and women in their late thirties and early forties, with many years of political experience behind them. In many countries they would be approaching the summit of their careers. In the Japanese political world they were treated like children.

"Morikawa people are elsewhere too. I hear they're strong in media and finance."

"Ah, you know better than me, Martine-san. I'm just a weak-brained old man at the end of his life. All I have is memories."

He gave a long racking cough that Martine suspected was faked, then turned his attention back to the scroll on the floor. This was Shiina's way of saying that the conversation was over.

Martine padded down the creaky staircase back to the shop. Shiina's grandson was squatting on the floor behind the counter, carefully polishing a statue of Daikoku, the god of prosperity. Martine stopped and stared at the statue's joyous features.

"Now that piece is really well done. How much are you asking for it?"

Young Shiina squinted up at her. "This one? Not decided yet, probably around a million yen."

"A million? Not exactly cheap."

"It's authentic early Meiji, Martine-san. It was the property of a famous saké brewing family, and is supposed to have brought them a hundred years of prosperity."

"And then the prosperity ran out?"

"Not at all. They had too much money to continue living in Japan. Last year they sold everything and moved to Monaco. As you know, that's quite a trend these days."

Martine nodded. With inheritance tax rates rising to eighty-five percent, wealthy Japanese families were dispersing to the four corners of the earth.

"And the saké business?"

"Bought by one of the big food companies. I don't think the taste will be as good as it used to be, though."

Martine examined the statue more closely—the chubby cheeks, the pendulous earlobes, the fingers clutching a bag of rice. The little god's zest for life was infectious. You couldn't look into his face without smiling.

"How about seven hundred thousand?" she said, on the spur of the moment.

Young Shiina blinked with surprise. "Are you really interested?"

"Maybe. It'd be just the right present for someone I know."

The boy sucked air through his teeth, as he had probably seen his grandfather do hundreds of times when negotiating prices. "That's difficult... I really can't go below eight hundred..."

Eight hundred thousand yen was more than Martine had paid for her car, a nifty little coupé she had picked up secondhand. But then a hundred years of prosperity wasn't going to come cheap.

"Okay," she nodded. "It'll take me a while to get the money together. I'll pick it up next time I come through."

Martine opened the sliding door and stepped into the trash-strewn alley. Once again, the old man had gone out of his way to provide her with crucial information. The thought made her slightly uncomfortable. It was only recently that she had found out what lay behind his generosity. In hushed tones a senior politician's aide had told her the story of Shiina's years in Paris as an art student and his passionate affair with a model who bore more than a passing resemblance to Martine.

So that was the secret of her best political stories—she had been exploiting the weakness of a sentimental old man. Still, as a journalist what else was she supposed to do? Time and again Shiina had proved himself a top-quality source. He could be obscure, frustratingly ambiguous, and as hard to pin down as a piece of tofu. But never once had he been wrong.

When Martine got back to the office, Charlie's desk was covered with photos of Nozawa. Romantic Nozawa sniffing a red rose and staring soulfully at the camera. Kimono-clad Nozawa practicing his calligraphy. Rockabilly Nozawa, with greased-back hair and aviator shades. Lounge lizard Nozawa, in tuxedo and frilly shirt. Nozawa in a paddy field scattering rice seeds. Nozawa in a car factory holding an oxyacetylene welder. Nozawa astride a large motorbike, behind him the snowcapped peak of Mount Fuji. Nozawa wearing only loincloth and headband, brandishing a sword.

Martine paused in front of Charlie's desk, momentarily transfixed by the profusion of images and Nozawa's chameleonlike ability to change his appearance.

"Sorry about the mess," said Kyo-san. "I'm in the middle of sorting it out. The amount of publicity material they sent is unbelievable. There are hundreds more in here."

She slapped a stack of bulky envelopes lying flat on her desk.

"Have you decided which one you like best?"

"These photos? I don't like any of them."

It was no surprise that Kyo-san was not a Nozawa fan. Tough, sixty-year-old multiple divorcees were unlikely to be his target audience.

Martine scooped up a couple of photos and dropped them into her desk drawer. They would help focus her mind when she was writing up the interview.

"By the way, I've got a couple of tickets for the concert tomorrow. You don't want to come along, I suppose?"

"Absolutely not. Nozawa gives me the creeps."

"You really don't like him, do you?"

Kyo-san shrugged. "It's not so much the guy himself. I mean his music is okay, I suppose, if you like that kind of crap. What bugs me is how people respond. He really brings out the bad side of Japan."

"Because he's so nationalistic?"

"It's not that. There are nationalists in every country these days. I mean, look at those guys in France and Italy. Compared to them, Nozawa is a pussy-cat. No, what bugs me is the way that nobody criticizes him, people just smile and nod their heads. In this country, when something gets popular beyond a certain point, it's not right to go against it. You have to go with the flow, so you don't stand out or cause any conflict."

"And you think that's the secret of his popularity?"

"Sure. That way everyone agrees, nobody has to think for themselves."

For Kyo-san that was an unusually emotional speech. Normally she was apolitical, viewing the world of current affairs with the detachment of a scientist observing the dynamics of a monkey colony.

"But people are like that everywhere, aren't they?"

Kyo-san shook her head vigorously. "I don't think so. Most Americans are dumb. Believe me—I was married to two of the finest examples. But they're dumb in lots of different ways. When the Japanese get dumb, they all get dumb in exactly the same way."

"What you just described is called clustering," said Martine. "There's an economic theory explaining why it's perfectly rational."

"It's not rational. It's dumb."

Kyo-san snapped her lunchbox shut, signifying that she'd said all that she was going to say. The two ex-husbands only came into Kyo-san's conversation when she was agitated, and then usually as examples of men at their most tiresome, unreliable, and thickheadedly male. So why had she married them in the first place? Martine had to assume that there had once been an unpragmatic, uncynical Kyo-san, a woman capable of falling in love with a penniless English teacher and following him to the other side of the world and then, when that didn't work out, trying again with a sports photographer. That Kyo-san was probably still in there somewhere, ready to emerge when the time was right.

Martine glanced at the world clock on the wall, then switched on her computer screen. She had the afternoon to finish writing up the Nozawa inter-view, then the early evening to do the piece on the Hiroshima virus. She scanned the news headlines, just to be sure that no new disasters had occurred while she was out—no major bankruptcies, no explosions, no crashes.

Checking her mailbox, she found two new messages. The first was from Makoto, sent from Narita Airport. There was one line of text:

> I miss you very much, and I want to hold you again.

Martine smiled. He would never say anything like that to her face—he was too conservative, too shy, basically—but for some reason he didn't mind writing it. She typed in her answer:

> When I close my eyes, I can still see the fireworks. I'm waiting for you to
> come back and hold me and do whatever you want.

Too provocative for his sensibilities? She didn't think so. That was what he was expecting. Martine looked up at Kyo-san, who was staring over the top of her glasses. Martine's eyes returned to the screen, and she pressed "send."

The second message had no header and no address and also contained just one line of text.

> Sexy goddess,
> You look very beautiful these days. But be careful—too much orange juice can
> damage your health.

Martine stared at it in puzzlement. The sender was the same person, she was sure. But orange juice? What on earth was that supposed to mean? Per-haps she was dealing with some kind of lunatic after all.

"Kyo-san—have you heard anything about too much orange juice being bad for your health?"

"Orange juice? Are you kidding? More orange juice is just what you need, Martine. It'd help your complexion."

Her complexion again! Why was everyone suddenly talking about her complexion? Frowning, Martine closed the mailbox. But this time she did not delete the message.

NINE

The young general leaned back in his leather chair, an ivory cigarette holder clamped between his teeth. His office resembled the control center of any powerful business empire, which is exactly what his faction of the People's Liberation Army had become. On the walls were photos of the shopping malls and hotels and housing developments that it controlled. On his desk was an array of stock price terminals, keeping him in touch with its hundred-million-dollar portfolio of global investments. On the shelves were choice examples of antique porcelain.

It had taken a quarter of a century to create this empire. The beginnings had been modest—a couple of factories producing Kalashnikov knockoffs for export to Africa and the Middle East. Then they had moved into bootleg compact discs, flooding the Asian market with millions of pieces every year. Then came computer software and video discs, perfumes, designer brand ties and scarves that appeared in duty-free shops all over the world. By the early 1990s, the business had matured and the bulk of its revenue came from real estate, finance, and the trading of anything from imported cigarettes to kidneys and cornea "donated" by political prisoners.

To the world the young general looked like a successful businessman. To himself he often looked like a successful businessman, too, but he had never felt like a businessman. As far back as he could remember he had yearned to be a warrior like his father, planning military campaigns that would decide the fate of nations. And now he was actually doing it. All the other generals might have become businessmen, but this one was carrying on the legacy of his father, the celebrated national hero.

Today the young general was in a contemplative mood. He sat smoking his favorite Sobranie cigarette and gazing at the TV monitor on his desk. The monitor showed two women waiting for him in the room below.

One was a middle-aged Japanese woman in her late fifties, the kind you see in tour groups rummaging through souvenir stores and flashing peace signs for the camera. From her placid appearance, it was hard to believe that she was the international terrorist Reiko Matsubara, wanted by Mossad, the CIA, the French Sûreté, and the British MI6. The other woman was young and beautiful, with long frizzed-out hair and a bright, piercing gaze that was never at rest. That was the gift of her father, a Palestinian bomb-maker killed by Israeli intelligence shortly after she was born.

The two women were chatting away in Japanese, nodding and smiling at each other like any mother and daughter. The general could have asked a translator to come and explain what they were saying, but there was hardly any point. Professionals like these women would assume their conversation was being monitored and would say nothing out of the ordinary. The general was watching them carefully, absorbing their gestures and tone of voice. "The wise man watches friends like strangers, and strangers like enemies"—that was one of his father's guiding principles. The general took his father's maxims seriously. They had seen him through the long decades of warfare, revolution, and political turmoil, through two disgraces and two triumphant comebacks, then through the twists and turns and shifting alliances of the modern era.

"When the enemy advances, melt like snow; when the enemy gets tired, sting him like a swarm of hornets; when the enemy retreats, drown him like the sea"—another of his father's maxims. This one had been the key to his famous victory in 1946, when three hundred thousand of Chiang's nationalists were cut down in headlong flight. The old general's political strategy was the same as his military strategy. When the pro-Western capitalist roaders had been forging ahead, his forces melted away like the snow. Now that they were tiring, he was stinging them. And when they finally retreated, he would muster all his strength and drown them like the sea. That time was near at hand.

The issue that would send the pro-Westerners scurrying backward would be Taiwan. With the rupturing of the US–Japan security relationship, the duty of the leadership to reclaim the rebel province would be clear to the whole nation. The choice would be simple. Would China continue to prostrate itself before the powers that had plunged it into a century of chaos and humiliation? Or would it stand up and claim its rightful position as the leading power in Asia and, eventually, the world?

The middle-aged Japanese woman on his TV monitor was vital to this process, and thus to the future of China. Did she know this? Probably, but it didn't seem to mean much to her. Her only interest now was directing revolutionary activity within Japan. In the coming period of social and political chaos, she believed, there would be no middle ground, just open warfare between reactionaries and the radical left. If the ruling elite could be provoked into heavy-handed oppression, then the masses would gravitate naturally toward the left.

The young general had already set up a training camp in Iran and a cyber-ops center in Bangkok at her request. He had no interest in her revolutionary ambitions, but it was in China's interest to have a well-equipped paramilitary force causing trouble in Japan. It would weaken the social and economic fabric, and make the country even more inward-looking at a time when its strategic position was collapsing.

Without Auntie—as the young general called the woman, though not to her face—this whole project would never have got off the ground. In the abstract, they had known what was needed from the start. That had been clear from the work of that idiot scholar Peng Yuan. Then others with more detailed knowledge had explained the hidden weaknesses that could be exploited, the fault lines that ran through Japanese systems and institutions. But still there was the basic problem of how to apply pressure quickly and efficiently, in a way that nobody would notice. For that, something else was required, a strategic asset somewhere within the system itself.

It was then that Auntie had appeared, expelled from the Bekaa Valley and no longer welcome in Damascus, but still burning with revolutionary fervor. She contacted some old comrades, who spoke to some of their Korean friends in Pyongyang, who passed word through to the young general. They met for the first time in Hong Kong. Auntie explained her ideas, and the general listened. At first he had thought she was crazy. Her group was so small, so weak in resources, but then she explained her ideas in more detail and suddenly the general's mind lit up. There it was—the strategic asset they had been looking for.

His father had been skeptical. He didn't trust the Japanese, and he didn't trust women. The son pointed out Auntie's track record: the synagogue in Buenos Aires, the Austrian airport, the disco in Rome, the cruise ship in the Mediterranean, the CIA man in Athens blown up while taking his children to school—these were all legendary attacks, carried out with ruthless precision. Not once had she failed. Not once had her group been infiltrated. Not once had a member been captured. Her group was certainly small, but that was its strength. It was tightly knit, experienced, and fanatically loyal to its leader. And it controlled a strategic asset of unparalleled value, a man capable of altering the course of Japanese history.

The old general demanded to meet her. They spoke just a few words, and that was enough. The old soldier said she had the same kind of eyes as his sister, tortured to death by Chiang's secret police seventy years ago. There was no compliment higher than that. So it was decided. The project went ahead with a new shape, a new organization, and a new focus.

On the screen Auntie was still chattering away to her daughter. The young general stubbed out his cigarette half smoked and got to his feet. It was time to forget about business and think like a warrior again.

———

Midnight in Kawasaki. The giant warehouse was silent and still. Inside the security room Kenji Kubota leaned back in his chair and yawned. He was nursing his fifth cup of coffee of the night, and the disc player on the table in front of him was playing one of his favorite songs, "Mama's Miso Soup" by Tsuyoshi Nozawa. Kubota had always been a big Nozawa fan. There was something about the toughness in his voice, the way he looked you straight in the eye. This was the kind of guy Kubota had wanted to be when he was young. He had fallen far short—like everyone else he knew—but there was Nozawa showing them that you should never give up, that even in today's world it was possible for a man to be a man.

Kubota glanced dully at the bank of video screens on the wall. Nothing was moving. It was hard to believe that in five hours the place would be buzzing with activity. There would be a dozen trucks growling in the forecourt, each emblazoned with the blue Starjacks logo. The morning shift workers, all sporting the same logo on the back of their overalls, would be running around, shouting out instructions, making sure that the day's supplies were loaded up inside thirty minutes, as stated in the Starjacks work manual. They looked diligent, fresh, enthusiastic, as befitted the employees of a company that had spread so quickly throughout Japan, indeed throughout the world.

Kubota had joined DaiNippon Machinery from high school and had spent twenty years in one of the finest factories in the world. The government had even awarded them prizes for productivity improvements. But all that was gone now. There had been a few years of losses, then a balance sheet problem that Kubota had never properly understood but which had resulted in the factory closing down. Kubota had counted himself lucky to find another job at his age. Most of his friends were still jobless and some were homeless, living in the sprawling cardboard cities that had sprouted in parks and train stations all over the country. But the security company was a tough employer. Every year they either cut wages or increased the workload. On his last assignment—a shopping mall on the outskirts of Yokohama—Kubota had been beaten up by a gang of high school kids. He spent three weeks in hospital and the company gave him nothing—no sick pay, no compensation, not even any help with his medical expenses. The doctors wanted to operate—they said he might lose the hearing in his left ear—but Kubota couldn't afford it, not with the thugs from the loan company breathing down his neck.

Just two weeks ago one of them barged into his apartment. He was an enormous guy with a nose ring and dyed blond hair.

"We're downgrading your rating to C double minus," he hissed, grabbing Kubota by the neck and slamming him up against the wall.

"What does that mean?"

"It means you pay us more interest."

Kubota licked his lips nervously. "How much more?"

"Two percent!" snarled the blond guy.

"An increase of two percent a year? I can pay that. I promise I'll pay it."

"What are you talking about, cockroach! Not two percent a year—two percent a month, of course!"

"But ... but that's impossible. My salary's much too low."

The blond guy put his face so close that his spittle sprayed Kubota's cheek.

"Forget about your salary. You've got good eyesight, haven't you?"

"Yes, I have. What does that matter?"

"It means we could get a couple of million for a cornea, maybe the same for a kidney. We have our own clinic, you know. The doctors are always ready."

He prodded a finger into Kubota's cheek and made a circle shape around his left eye. The leer on the blond guy's face was unforgettable. "The doctors are always ready"—sometimes Kubota woke up in a sweat with those words echoing in his mind.

The disc came to an end. Kubota walked over to his locker to get another one. He chose an old favorite—"Last Train to Kurashiki." The way Nozawa sang those ballads, he could make you feel every word.

Kubota fitted the disc into the player, then gazed in dismay at the bank of video screens. Two on the left had gone dead. That wasn't supposed to happen. He picked up the phone and called Ueda, the security man stationed at the main gate.

"Kubota here. There seems to be a problem with the video system. Is everything all right down at the gate?"

"Yes, all quiet here. But there was something I wanted to check with you. It's about the cleaners."

"The cleaners? What about them?"

"According to the log, they came in three groups of three people. But they left in two groups of four."

Kubota gave a grunt of annoyance. "Wait a moment. I'll check what it says in my log."

The cleaners came during the afternoon shift and left late in the evening. Most of them were either mentally disabled or well over seventy. They came in and did their work silently, avoiding the eyes of the other workers. From what Kubota had heard, the company that employed them got some kind of subsidy from the government and paid them next to nothing.

Kubota flipped open the logbook and ran his finger down the page. "Let's see … eight people in, eight people out. That first entry must be a mistake."

"I suppose so. But there's a security card missing too."

Ueda was new on the job. He worried too much about the little things.

"That's nothing," scoffed Kubota. "Those people are always forgetting to hand in their security cards. Some of them can't even remember their own names!"

Ueda gave a nervous chuckle. Kubota put down the phone and turned up the music. For a few precious minutes he leaned back in his chair, eyes closed, listening to the last song on Nozawa's CD. He waited until the last tremulous note had faded before he opened his eyes and glanced at his watch. It was time for the first patrol of the night. He pulled on his jacket and gloves and picked up the toolbag. He might be able to fix that camera in Cold Area D. He had spent twenty years working with top precision machinery; he understood how these things worked.

He climbed into the electric car and pressed the start button. Kubota sat with his arms crossed, no need to steer. The car ran along an optoelectronic strip in the floor, negotiating the turns between aisles at the same even speed. When he reached Cold Area B, he stopped the cart and got off. He slid his security card into the reader, spun the lock, and jerked open the heavy door.

The cold air was like a slap in the face. The temperature was several degrees below freezing, optimal for the "hundred-percent fresh and healthy" ingredients that Starjacks boasted about in its ads. Kubota walked between the stacks of crates, occasionally rapping them with his nightstick, knocking off little clouds of frost. This was a habit of his. He liked the sound it made, a muffled thump which echoed around the metal walls of the room. One he hit too hard, and the front board of the crate slid loose. Kubota reached inside and pulled out a cinnamon bun, as hard as a rock. How could people eat this stuff, he wondered, tossing it in his hand. He had never even been inside a Starjacks outlet himself. The menu was incomprehensible, you weren't allowed to smoke, the coffee was overpriced, and the customers were silly fashion-conscious people trying to impress each other with their phoney sophistication.

Kubota stuck the bun back in the crate and whacked the loose board into place.

There was nothing unusual at Areas B and C, but when he got to Cold Area D Kubota was shocked to find that the metal door hadn't been properly closed. He gave a snort of contempt. Those Starjacks workers looked so enthusiastic, but actually they were slack and self-satisfied. They wouldn't have lasted long at DaiNippon Machinery. Kubota went inside and checked the thermostat. Fortunately the temperature was still within the target range. He walked over to the video camera, which was pointing toward him and making little circular motions. Kubota put a metal ladder against the wall and climbed up. As he'd suspected, it was a simple problem: the camera's constant motion had caused one of the wires to work loose from its socket. It had probably been set up carelessly, thought Kubota. Just a little more give in the wire, and it would never have happened. He took out a screwdriver, unscrewed the side panel, and fed out another few millimeters of wire. He had just finished when he heard a faint click behind him. As he swung round on the ladder, the neon lights flickered and then the whole room was plunged into darkness.

Kubota cursed and jumped to the ground. He followed the wall around to the door and slid his security card into the reader. But that was dead too. There must have been some kind of power failure. Kubota hammered his fists on the door until the echo made his ears hurt. It was useless of course. He was alone, locked in a pitch-black refrigerated box.

Or was he? He thought he could hear a rubber sole squeaking on the shiny floor outside.

"Ueda, is that you?"

There was no answer. It couldn't be Ueda anyway, he would never abandon his post at the security gate. Then he remembered the missing security card, and another idea hit him. One of those weak-brained cleaners must be out there, probably wandering around unaware of whether it was day or night.

"Let me out!" yelled Kubota. "Come on! I'll explain how to switch on the backup."

That would be no easy task, even if whoever it was outside had been prepared to stop and listen carefully. But then Kubota heard something that made his stomach churn as if he had just eaten half-a-dozen Starjacks cinnamon buns. He listened in shock as the low hum of his electric cart moved away and turned the corner, heading toward Cold Area E where the huge tanks of fruit juices and iced tea were stored. Maybe it wasn't one of the cleaners out there after all—but who else could it be?

Kubota's mind flashed with anger and panic. There was some lunatic out there, or maybe even a thief, and he could do nothing about it. He had failed in his most important duty—to keep the warehouse secure at all times. If his boss ever found out, he would be fired on the spot. And what would happen then? How would he ever repay his loan? He closed his eyes and pressed his fingers lightly against the lids. Left or right, which one would they choose?

His only chance would be if whoever it was out there didn't make too much mess. Then, if he could somehow sneak out without being seen, maybe the Starjacks people wouldn't even notice, or at least wouldn't blame it on him.

Kubota pulled his collar tight around his neck and shoved his hands in the pockets of his jacket. He started softly humming the words to "Last Train to Kurashiki."

T E N

Martine lies naked on the bed, one arm flung over her face. Her skin tingles to the roughness of the hands cupping her breasts, the heat of his breath on her stomach, moving lower, the silky softness caressing her, teasing her open with the delicacy of a feather. She stretches out a hand and touches his face.

"Makoto," she whispers. "Now, please."

He rises over her body, crushing her with his force, his glistening shoulders looming over her, his dark silent face...

... his face

... something wrong with his face

... it isn't his face

Martine freezes. She wants to yell, but no sound comes. The face gazing down at her, lips sardonically curled, is not Makoto's. It is Nozawa's.

"Stay quiet," he breathes, and slides a hand across her mouth.

Martine shakes her head frantically from side to side. She bucks her hips and thrashes her arms and squirms free and rolls off the bed and sits up on the floor, bathed in sweat, heart pounding, eyes blinking in the shaft of sunlight slanting between the curtains. The bed is empty. The room is empty. The clock tells her it's five o'clock in the morning. Outside the window the cicadas are screaming like a treeful of dentists' drills.

Martine took a shower, then called Makoto's hotel in New York. He wasn't back yet so she left a message on the answering machine, nothing provocative this time, she wasn't in the mood. It would be early evening over there, and she wondered how his first presentation had gone. This was a crucial time for the brewery. Another round of financing was needed to launch the premium beer that Makoto had spent the past year developing, but there were no funds available domestically. The venture capital industry had been wiped out earlier in the crisis, and the banks were only lending to government-approved "strategic industries." Makoto had no choice but to go overseas, yet it would be a hard sell there too. In the wake of the euro crisis, investors everywhere had become intensely averse to risk.

Martine and Makoto—it was a strange combination. At least that was the opinion of Martine's friends, and probably Makoto's too. She was used to the comments by now, even found them amusing.

"Oh—are you two still seeing each other?" "So how's your boyfriend, what's his name again, that guy from the bankrupt trading company?" "You mean he's a widower living with his son and his mother? Doesn't that make things rather difficult, technically speaking?" "He runs a brewery? Wouldn't a vineyard be more your style?"

The general assumption was that Martine was being typically perverse, probably on the rebound from some major love affair, probably looking for a few months of light diversion. But it wasn't like that at all. Martine didn't do light, she only did heavy. And she had known this was going to be heavy right from the start.

She had been looking into the UNG scandal at the time. The United Nippon Group was a megabank formed by the merger of five of the country's most prestigious financial institutions, home to tens of thousands of the country's best and brightest graduates, and it had suddenly gone bust. It turned out that almost the entire establishment was involved in one way or another—arranging bailouts of bankrupt companies, channeling loans to politically sensitive regions, hiding losses, siphoning off profits. The world's largest holding company had turned into the world's largest Ponzi scheme.

The trigger for the collapse of UNG was the collapse of Marumen Corporation, a trading house with a history stretching back to the seventeenth century. Martine was working on a human interest story about Marumen, and someone gave her Makoto's name. "He was on the fast track to the top," she was told. "Head of trading in the US, head of project finance in South East Asia. Interesting guy, but difficult to talk to, not the kind to let his guard down."

It was fair warning. When she called Makoto, the voice at the other end was brusquely matter-of-fact. "That business is all finished now. There's no point in digging it up."

"I understand your feelings," cooed Martine. "But surely you want the world to hear your side of the story."

"What are you saying? People have lost their careers, their pensions, their homes, everything. This isn't some story to entertain newspaper readers, it's the real lives of real people."

With this guy, coaxing obviously wasn't going to work. So Martine went for the direct approach. "That's terrible. Did many people lose their homes?"

"It would be irresponsible to discuss such matters with a journalist."

Martine swallowed hard. In her time in Japan she had got used to responses that were slippery, evasive, ambiguous, and sometimes downright meaningless. What she rarely encountered was unadorned rudeness.

"In my opinion, not discussing such matters is even more irresponsible. If everybody just sits there *enduring*, nothing will ever change in this country. This kind of thing will just keep happening again and again!"

Makoto's voice went icy cold. "Look, these are private matters. Can't you understand that? Don't you have any respect for people's feelings?"

Martine fought back the wave of anger welling up inside her. "Of course I do. My job is to communicate the facts as accurately as possible, and that includes the feelings of the people affected."

"Really? I thought your job was to contribute to the circulation of your newspaper."

The wave surged and broke. "Well, if that's your attitude, there's no point in continuing this conversation!"

Martine slammed down the phone, and that was the last she expected to hear of the allegedly interesting but definitely difficult Makoto Ishikawa. Except that the phone rang twenty minutes later, and the same Makoto Ishikawa was on the line apologizing and offering to meet whenever she liked.

"I thought about what you said and found it made sense. I'm sorry if I offended you."

Martine couldn't believe what she was hearing—a man who was willing to admit that he was wrong!

They met in a yakitori restaurant in Shimbashi. From the voice on the phone, Martine was expecting a sour-faced, self-important businessman in a boring suit. But Makoto didn't look like a businessman at all. He was wearing old jeans, a heavily creased leather jacket, and a watch that couldn't have cost more than a few hundred yen. With his sleepy eyes and rumpled hair, he looked as if he'd just got out of bed. Even more surprisingly, he wasn't at all pompous, but laid-back and amusing in a deadpan kind of way.

They had saké, plenty of it. At the end of the evening Martine realized that they'd been talking a lot more about her than about him, supposedly the subject of the human interest story. Too much alcohol, she thought, as she got up to leave. She'd been unprofessional, given too much away. But it had been fun, and she felt more relaxed than she had in years.

He put her into a taxi, and as she turned to wave good-bye Martine remembered the scarf she'd left in the restaurant, hanging from the coat stand. It was one of her favorites, a present from an Italian screenwriter. For a moment she thought about going back for it. No, the waiters knew Makoto well. They would send the scarf to him, and he would have to bring it to her. That was a much better idea.

The taxi pulled away from the curb. In the mirror Martine saw a waiter appear and hand the scarf to Makoto. Had he known it was there all along? Evidently not, because he stuffed it into the pocket of his leather jacket and started sprinting after the taxi.

"That guy is following us," grunted the taxi driver. "Shall I stop?"

"That won't be necessary," said Martine.

"Are you sure? He's yelling something."

"Doesn't matter. Keep going."

The taxi sped away from the figure in the mirror and crossed a major intersection, before coming to a halt at a red light.

"He's still running. Shall we wait for him?"

Martine shook her head. "I'm in a hurry."

Makoto was within a hundred yards of the taxi when the lights changed. The driver made a clicking noise with his teeth, then accelerated away. The taxi swung left at the next intersection, merging into a line of heavy traffic headed for Roppongi.

"He's back," the taxi driver said suddenly.

"What?"

"Your friend. Not the type to give up easily when he sees something he wants!"

He gave a coarse, gurgling laugh that Martine didn't care for at all. The tiny figure of Makoto had reappeared in the mirror. He was four hundred yards away, but the traffic was only moving in fits and starts.

"Looks like you won't escape this time," gurgled the driver.

Martine ignored him. She waited until Makoto was within fifty yards, then instructed the driver to pull in.

She got out of the taxi and waited, arms crossed. "What on earth do you think you're doing?"

Makoto walked the last few yards, chest heaving, forehead glistening with sweat. He pulled the scarf from his pocket.

"Something left—here—this!"

"My scarf! Thank you very much."

Martine waited, but Makoto was in no condition to say anything else. He squatted down and rested his hands on his knees. From that position he looked up at her, his face glowing with triumph. Just like an adolescent boy, thought Martine. Stubborn. Proud. Extreme.

"Not the type to give up easily"—the taxi driver had been absolutely right about that. Martine smiled, then started laughing, loud enough for people to stop and stare.

"What's the matter?" gasped Makoto between gulps of air.

"Oh nothing. I was expecting you to be such a bore."

"What?"

Martine gazed at him. The taxi door was still hanging open. One of them was going to have to say something sensible, and since Makoto could hardly talk, it was going to have to be her.

"Look, I was supposed to be researching a human interest story. But I haven't got enough material."

"Yes."

"This project is going to need more time."

"Yes."

"I think we should meet again soon."

"Yes."

"Is that a Japanese 'yes' or a Western 'yes'?"

"Yes."

Martine got back in the taxi, leaving him squatting on the pavement. That was two years ago. The story never got started, but the research had been going on ever since.

Martine did half an hour of yoga exercises, then had coffee and toast and marmalade. Only when her head was clear did she switch on the television. As usual, she split the screen so that she could simultaneously watch the international news on INN and the domestic Japanese news on NHK.

The INN news anchor had big hair, big eyes, big cleavage, and big teeth inside a mouth that seemed to stretch to the boundaries of her face. She was wearing the same expression of glazed optimism she wore every morning, no matter what tales of death, disaster, and misery she had to deliver. Martine had to remind herself that this woman was actually a colleague, since InfoCorp News Network was the core trophy in the InfoCorp empire that now included the *Tribune* as a minor appendage.

The lead item on INN was the Romanian war. The correspondent was standing in front of a burned-out building interviewing a huge bearded man in a flak jacket, a member of one of the local militias. Martine tried to remember if his people were the good guys or the bad guys. It was hard to keep track. There had been so many changes of sides, so many botched ceasefires and peace conferences. The next item was about the economic chaos in Greece, accompanied by clips of rioting crowds storming supermarkets, and smoke billowing into the air above the Acropolis. Then came the summary of an INN investigation into Yamada Motor's sports utility vehicles, which apparently had a tendency to roll over when cornering at speed in rainy conditions. There was a clip of a sobbing man whose wife and two children had died in a crash. When this was over, the big-haired woman announced euphorically that the Senate Transportation Committee had scheduled hearings for the coming week.

The other half of the screen was a different world. According to NHK, the most important event of the day was the start of the grape-picking season in Yamanashi Prefecture, with clips of happy families clutching baskets of fruit. The second item was about a kite-flying competition near the Tama River. The third was more weighty—heavy equipment orders were finally on the recovery track, up 5.5 percent year on year. That drew a smile of satisfaction from the newsreader. The government's decision to pour money into its nuclear energy program was having the desired effect.

In the last few years government influence over television had grown much stronger. According to one of Martine's friends who worked in the industry, the TV companies had got together and agreed to bury any unpleasant topics in the middle of the early morning news. That way the morale of the nation's workers would not be damaged ahead of a hard day's labor.

Today was no exception. There had been a shooting in Sendai, a bank employee critically wounded by an unknown assailant. The newsreader gave a little shake of the head, then hurried on to the high school baseball tournament. No explanation was given, no comment from the police or the bank. To Martine's knowledge, over ten bank officials had been killed over the past two years, and many more had been attacked. The Japanese financial system had always been a maze of mirrors, but these days the risks of making a wrong turn seemed far greater than ever before.

Martine switched off the TV and went to get her rollerblades. She was due to meet Kimura's friend later that morning to talk about the strange e-mails she had received. Until then she could spend a few hours in the park with her sketchbook.

Ten minutes later Martine was whizzing down the narrow, winding streets with the warm sun on her back and the chime of windbells in her ears, swerving through clusters of dawdling schoolboys, chirping "Good morning" at the old lady doing tai chi on a balcony, ducking under the railroad crossing gate just as it closed, then racing past the convenience store, the jazz coffee bar, the sushi restaurant with its fat cat sunning himself in the window, the pachinko parlor, the tiny shrine at the corner, the karaoke box, the nail parlor, the kimono shop—the whole higgledy-piggledy mess that needed to be straightened out to make the economy more efficient, but which she hoped would never change.

The park at the top of the little hill was quiet. A middle-aged man sat on a bench, reading a magazine and munching a riceball. He was wearing a clean shirt, with a polka-dot tie. At first glance you wouldn't know that he lived in this park all year around.

"Good morning," he nodded to Martine.

"It's going to be hot today, isn't it?"

"Over thirty degrees, probably."

Martine sat down beside him to pull off her rollerblades. For a few minutes they chatted about world politics, the weather, the sumo tournament, the failure of the police to control the motorbike gangs. Then Martine pulled her sketchbook from her backpack and went to her usual place on the other side of the park. On the bench she left half-a-dozen paperback books and a box of biscuits from Fortnum and Mason.

The measure of the depth of the crisis was not the number of homeless people, but the type. Back in the high growth era, the homeless had matted hair and mud-caked trousers held up with string. They had wandered the streets ranting at the traffic, and everyone had looked through them as if they didn't exist.

Then in the era of stagnation, a different kind of homeless person appeared —sad-eyed middle-aged men who had taken a wrong turn and ended up with nowhere to live and out of work. People looked through them too, but it was getting harder. They weren't so different from everyone else.

Two years into the crisis, and now the homeless were people of all ages and types, men and women. There were university graduates, ex-employees of major companies, young couples who had bought an apartment in the wrong area at the wrong price. You sometimes saw whole families, from grandmothers to toddlers, living in sprawling plastic tents. These were people you couldn't look through, any more than you could ignore your own face in the mirror.

Martine sat cross-legged on the grassy slope overlooking the shopping street. She sketched slowly, carefully—the crooked little station building, the railroad crossing gate hanging in the air, the jumble of signs. She had an image in her mind of lines and surfaces crossing and interlacing, of the hidden geometry that held everything together. On paper it never came out that way, but that didn't stop her from trying.

***

"This is a tricky one," said Kimura's friend, peering into the computer screen. "A lot of thought went into it."

"I'm not surprised," said Martine. "He's an obsessive of some sort."

"A professional, I would say. He's thought of everything."

The three of them were sitting around Martine's desk at the *Tribune*. Kimura's friend was sitting in Martine's chair, with Kimura on his right. He had been tapping at the keyboard for almost two hours, with no result. Kimura was a handsome and witty forty-five-year-old bond market strategist at a foreign investment bank. His friend, about ten years younger, had a pale, angular face and long hair that fell over his eyes. Martine knew only his first name, Yasuo. He was a computer security expert attached to an unnamed part of the government. Kimura had met him in a Shinjuku bar about six months ago. Apparently it was love at first sight.

"So the trail has run cold?" asked Martine.

"That's right, unfortunately."

"Nothing else you can do?"

"Not really. Not here, anyway."

Martine wrinkled her nose in frustration. Yasuo had done his best, but Martine's mysterious admirer had made sure that his trail was covered. The message had passed through the servers of the Tohoku Agricultural Cooperative, the University of Bangkok, a casino in Las Vegas, a bank in Tel Aviv, and a pornographer in Denmark, before looping back through the Tohoku Agricultural Cooperative.

"So what would you advise me to do? I mean, what would your department do in these circumstances?"

Yasuo glanced over at Kimura, who gave a brief nod.

"We would probably try string recognition. That means taking the words used and looking for matches against data passing through the grid."

"I see. And what kind of data is that?"

Kimura gave a thin smile, the first Martine had seen on his face. "What kind of data? Every kind, of course. There is no computer message in this country that doesn't pass through the grid. That's what it was designed for."

He glanced at Kimura and they both chuckled.

"And this would enable you to identify the sender of the message?"

"Theoretically, yes. But access to the data cache is strictly controlled. It should never be misused."

"Of course not," said Martine gravely. She recalled hearing that Kimura's trading team had been astonishingly successful this year, managing to be on the right side of every twist and turn in monetary policy. Now she had an inkling of the reason why.

Martine paused and stared at the screen.

"Tell me, Kimura-san," she said finally. "Didn't you once tell me you wanted to write a regular op-ed column for the *Tribune*?"

"Yes, I did."

"And didn't I tell you that I had already asked the strategist from Silverman Brothers?"

"That's what you said."

Martine gave a bright smile. "Well, I think the situation has changed."

They left in mid-afternoon. Martine saw them off to the elevator, and then spent the next few hours on her own, adding the finishing touches to the Nozawa interview, and scouring the internet for information about the Morikawa School of Leadership.

The official website gave the basic background. The school had been founded thirty years ago by Soichiro Morikawa, the most famous Japanese industrialist of the twentieth century. Its purpose was to offer "British-style elite education," though what was described bore absolutely no resemblance to what Martine had experienced at Oxford.

Only fifty students were accepted every year, usually from the cream of graduates from the nation's top universities. It wasn't enough for them to have outstanding exam results, they also had to be physically tough, have "benevolent instincts," and "a strong pride in the uniqueness of Japanese culture." The course was built around the philosophy of Morikawa himself, which was vague and pompous but, in Martine's judgment, reasonably benign. According to Morikawa, excellent leaders should be men of noble character; they should never forget their obligation to the weaker members of society; they should continue to train their minds and bodies rigorously and not indulge in low pleasures; and their mission was to raise the nation's standing and contribute to the future of the human race.

There were a number of photos of Morikawa, a fierce-looking old man in a dark kimono, together with quotations from his numerous books.

"Profits are unimportant to a true businessman. He should have the mind of a priest and the hands of a warrior."

"My company is my family. I am blessed in having eighty thousand children."

"The role of a bank is to provide money to manufacturers. Bankers should have pure hearts and ask no questions."

Martine scrolled down line after line of worthy cliché. Of the great generation of business leaders who drove Japan's postwar recovery, she had always found Morikawa the flattest and least interesting. The man had no narrative. There were no illegitimate children or frolics with geisha, no battles with disbelieving bureaucrats, no rash bets on new technologies. His only distinctive trait appeared to be his meanness. Right to the end of his life, he offered his guests rice gruel and cold sardines and made his wife and daughters wait at table.

In business the Morikawa strategy was passive—wait for other companies to make breakthroughs, then flood the market with cheaper imitations. Morikawa Industries' key strength was the loyalty and commitment of its workforce. Mass calisthenics three times a day; gray overalls worn by all grades of staff, from senior directors to female receptionists; a company shrine where employees were commemorated after death—these were the abiding images of "the Morikawa way." Still, you couldn't deny the man's achievements. He had left school at the age of twelve to work in a backstreet factory that produced lightbulbs. Today Morikawa Industries was one of the largest industrial companies in the world, with top market share in cameras, TVs, watches, copiers, and washing machines.

Extracts from Morikawa's collected essays were followed by quotations from Buddha, Winston Churchill, Yukichi Fukuzawa, Helen Keller, Confucius, and other people whom Morikawa admired. There was little detail about the school's activities, the faculty, or the nature of the courses.

Martine scanned through the hundreds of other references to the school. These were mostly brief comments naming certain prominent people as alumni of the school. Martine was surprised by the variety. Apart from the politicians, there were writers, businessmen, bureaucrats, academics, and even one well-known movie director. And that was just the tip of the iceberg. If the school produced fifty graduates a year, by now there would be nearly two thousand of them altogether, with the most senior ones being in their late fifties. Compared to the many other networks of influence and mutual obligation that permeated Japanese society, the membership was not large. But that concentration would be its strength—giving it coherence and focus.

Martine sat back and stared out the window. She had always thought of the Morikawa school as a marginal institution, little more than a monument to a successful businessman's slightly naive egoism. In fact it was more formidable than she had expected. But was it strong enough to stage what amounted to a political coup d'état? Not on its own. It had a network of high-quality people, well spread through the strategic areas of Japanese society, but what it did not have was the immense financial resources of the establishment. Even after years of economic mismanagement, even after the UNG scandal had entangled dozens of senior politicians, even with public distrust at an all-time high, no credible opposition had emerged. The iron triangle of bureaucrats, senior politicians, and business leaders remained in control of the commanding heights, as it had for generations. To break it would require something special, a complete change in the rules of the game. Which is why they needed Nozawa.

At that moment Martine glimpsed a movement out of the corner of her eye. There was an advertising blimp slowly drifting across the skyline. On its side was an almost cartoonish picture of Nozawa, wearing his headband and smiling sardonically. Martine remembered her dream and shuddered.

Mark Fletcher was woken by the ringing of the phone downstairs. He had the feeling it had been ringing for a long time already. He rolled onto his back and lay there blinking at the shadows on the ceiling and wondering who on earth would have the nerve to call at this time of night. Nobody who worked for him, or at least nobody who wanted to stay working for him, that was for sure. Few people at InfoCorp even knew where he lived, let alone his private number. And those who did had strict instructions never to call after dinner.

Since his marriage, Mark had been determined to keep his home life insulated from everything else. He owed that much to Natasha and the children. The world was just too dangerous nowadays. In many countries—not just what was once called the developing world, but also places like Italy, Greece, and Spain—car bombs and kidnappings had become ordinary tools of business.

The ringing stopped, and Mark gave a sigh of relief. It must have been a wrong number. He closed his eyes again and lay there listening to the sound of Natasha breathing alongside him. She breathed so softly, almost like a child. On a few occasions he had been gripped by the frightening thought that she had stopped breathing altogether. But then he would lean closer to her face and feel the feathery warmth against his cheek and see the dark contour of her breast rising and falling.

The phone had started ringing again. Mark could hardly believe it. It was four o'clock in the morning! The children wouldn't wake up—they hadn't stirred even when there was an intruder in the garden and the alarms were screaming and the security guys were yelling into their walkie-talkies—but Natasha was a light sleeper. Just a few nights ago he had woken in the middle of the night to find himself alone in bed. He had hurried downstairs and gone through every room, nerves jangling. At last he had found her in the games room, playing the children's electric piano with headphones on. Mark stood in the doorway and watched her fingers flying across the keyboard, her head swaying gently from side to side. She didn't hear him, and he didn't disturb her.

This time the caller wasn't going to give up. Mark slid out of bed, eased open the bedroom door, and moved noiselessly down the corridor, glancing into Liam's room as he passed. The boy was curled up under the blankets, just a mop of tousled hair visible on the pillow. It was black, like his mother's, whereas Julie's hair was the same straw blond as Mark's. A soccer magazine lay open on the floor beside his bed.

Mark padded downstairs and into his study. He sat down at his desk and gazed at the phone. For some reason, he felt a strong resistance to picking it up. Perhaps if he waited a few more seconds it would stop ringing. It didn't. Finally he took a deep breath and snatched at the receiver.

"Yes," he muttered, aware that his hands were clammy with sweat.

"Mark! Thank God I got you."

He knew the voice at once. It was Roger Mance, the longest-serving of his father's American advisers and one of the few to survive the latest management shake-up.

"What's the matter, Roger? What's going on over there?"

"There's bad news. Are you sitting down?"

"Say it!" snapped Mark.

"It's your father. He's just had a stroke, a bad one."

An icy flush ran through Mark's stomach. Deep down he had known it would be something like this.

"How bad is bad?"

"He's unconscious, in an oxygen tent. The doctors aren't saying anything yet. I don't think they know."

His father lying helpless in an oxygen tent, tubes sprouting from his body? The idea was bizarre, a joke almost. Objectively, though, Mark shouldn't have been surprised. After all, his father was well into his seventies and had been suffering from hypertension for years. But he had always seemed so brimming with life force, so indestructible. Somehow Mark had assumed that his father would outlast him, just as he had outmaneuvered him every time they came into conflict.

"When did it happen?"

"A couple of hours ago. He was having dinner with Jenny."

"Who else was with him?"

"Nobody, Mark. It was an intimate occasion. They were celebrating her birthday."

Mark's fingers gripped the phone a little tighter. Another image was flashing through his mind, one that he didn't want to linger over. Why had his father ever got involved with that woman? She had turned him into a different person, breaking up his family and business empire in the process. Now she had destroyed him too.

"Jenny's got such presence of mind," Mance was saying. "If she hadn't been there, your father wouldn't have made it."

Mark would have put it differently—if she hadn't been there, none of this would have happened.

"Really," he said grimly.

"Yes, really. Straightaway she called this specialist she knows, got him to come right over. David Liu's one of the top men in the field. He made all the arrangements, took care of everything personally."

"I see," muttered Mark. "Thanks for filling me in. I appreciate it." The words came out automatically. They sounded unconvincing even to himself.

"It's the least I could do. We'll be putting out a press release tomorrow, trying to put a lid on things for a while. It'll be pretty low-key—'suffering from exhaustion,' 'cutting down on routine duties,' you get the picture."

"I suppose that was Jenny's idea too."

"As a matter of fact it was. But that's the best way, right? We don't want any speculation about the company's future, not at this stage of the game."

Of course not, thought Mark. Much better to let Jenny and her stooges in the supervisory committee do what the hell they liked without anyone being the wiser.

"You can be sure of one thing—your father's in the best possible hands. We have everything under control."

"I'm sure you do, Roger," said Mark evenly. He put down the phone and walked back upstairs. Liam was still curled up under the blankets. Natasha was lying on her side, her lips slightly open. Everything looked the same as before, but that was an illusion. In the few minutes Mark had been downstairs, the world had become a different place. He slid under the sheets, taking care not to disturb Natasha, and lay gazing at the shadows on the ceiling.

He recalled an incident that had happened when he was eight or nine. He'd been out in the bay with his father when suddenly someone shouted "Shark!" and they both started swimming for the beach. His father was a few yards ahead. Suddenly he spun around in the water, gave a bellow of pain, and disappeared beneath the surface. Seconds went by. Young Mark stared in horror at the place where his father had been. Not only had his father gone, but now the shark would be coming for him. Suddenly there was a splashing sound right behind him. Mark wheeled round to see his father surging to the surface like a human submarine. "Fooled you!" he roared. Mark had been fooled a few times after that too—the two heart attacks, the polyps operation. He was used to being fooled, to his father always coming splashing to the surface in the end. This time, though, it was different. There really was a shark, and he was going to have to face it alone.

ELEVEN

Martine arrived at Shinjuku Park at seven, half an hour before Nozawa was due to come on stage, and was confronted by a dizzying sight. Thousands of people were sitting in rows, hardly any space between them, a vast human carpet stretching from the edge of the park to the matchbox-sized stage in the distance.

Martine had been to a pop music festival only once before in her life. At the age of seventeen she had been dragged along by a boyfriend who was writing agitprop plays for an anarchist theater group. It had been a muddy, smelly, thoroughly unpleasant experience, made worse by the ear-splitting cacophony generated by the "musicians." She had exited at the earliest opportunity and refused any further contact with the boyfriend, now a partner of one of the big accountancy firms.

This was a different class of event entirely. It was more like a gigantic, highly organized picnic, fun for all the family. People were sitting on newspapers and plastic sheets eating lunchboxes, slurping cup noodles, sipping green tea from plastic bottles, reading comic books, doing all the normal things that you would do in a park anyway. Hawkers with trays around their necks were selling rice-cakes, yakitori, baked yams, steamed buns, and alcoholic drinks. Martine even noticed a woman pouring beer from a familiar wire-capped bottle. That was a sight that would have pleased Makoto. He was always talking about the importance of the fashionable female consumer.

As Martine picked her way through the crowd, she saw Nozawa's face everywhere—on T-shirts, baseball caps, paper fans, kites, helium balloons, lunchbox lids, even winking at her from the electroluminescent wrist tattoos that had recently become fashionable. The Nozawa logo—a lightning-streak "Z" bracketed by a smaller "n" and "w"—was visible on digicams, disc players, cellphones, palmtop computers, and other electronic gadgets. The power of the Nozawa merchandising operation was legendary. In return for long-term multimedia product endorsement, he demanded a fixed percentage of the retail price. Only Nozawa had the clout to cut that kind of deal. No manufacturer could afford to have him on the other side of its marketing strategy.

Music was booming from the loudspeaker towers that dotted the park, loud enough to drown out any conversation. The warm-up act was a glam-rock group that swaggered around in kabuki gear and sang power ballads about loyalty and filial piety. Unknown a year ago, they were now one of the most popular groups in Japan. You could be sure that in a year's time they would be unknown again. Seen from the edge of the park, they were microscopic figures prancing about on a tiny stage. Some people had binoculars pressed to their eyes, others were watching through holo-spex. Most of the audience showed little interest, however. They had come for Nozawa, who had been a star for longer than many of them had been alive.

Nozawa's media handlers had talked about an audience of twenty thousand. Martine, applying a normal PR discount, had assumed it would be closer to ten thousand. Now she wasn't so sure. It was even possible that the media handlers had made an underestimate. The average age seemed to be around twenty-five—young adults, both male and female. Twenty years ago they would have been contented servants of the Japanese economic miracle, facing a comfortable future of lifetime employment and ever-rising living standards. Now they were listening to Nozawa, letting him express their frustration and emptiness. There were older people too, couples in their forties and fifties. That made Martine think of Makoto and poor Sachiko-san. What if she had lived? Was there any chance that they might be here today, somewhere in the crowd holding hands on the grass? Martine winced at the thought. Hearing that Makoto had once been a fan of Nozawa had come as a shock. It had made her realize how little she understood him. But then whoever really understood any other person? The surprises were what kept you on your toes.

It took Martine almost fifteen minutes to reach the VIP enclosure in front of the stage. A huddle of security people stood around the gate, amongst them Kawamoto. Martine smiled at her, but got no response. Shimizu was standing inside, holding a tray of wine glasses. He was wearing mauve-tinted glasses and a white linen suit that made him look like a middle-aged executive trying desperately to be hip, which is exactly what he was.

Martine flashed her security tag at the optical reader and went in. Inside there were a couple of hundred VIPs lolling in airline-style chairs with side tables for drinks and snacks. Martine took her place near the end of one of the rows and watched the glam-rockers finishing their act. The vocalist, who was dressed in a gaudy kimono, thick white makeup, and a shaggy wig, was belting out the chorus of their latest hit. The guitarist suddenly jumped off the stage and came sailing through the air toward where Martine was seated, all the while grimacing madly and flailing at his guitar. She could just make out the wire attached to the harness on his back, but even so ducked instinctively out of the way. The guitarist swung a couple of yards over her head, looped around in a huge arc, and landed adroitly on his feet in time for the next chorus.

The song ended with the vocalist and the bass player, who was made up as a female *onnagata*, kneeling together in the center of the stage. Amidst a blizzard of cherry blossoms, the vocalist produced a dagger and cut his lover's throat. He watched mournfully as the red stain spread over the front of her kimono, then stabbed himself in the chest and slumped to the ground. The guitar whined feedback, the keyboards sobbed, and the drums thrashed. Then the lights went off to thunderous cheers from the crowd. Seconds later all five members of the group were at the front of the stage, linking hands and grinning and bowing.

Martine clapped politely and glanced around her, instantly spotting several dozen celebrities—actors and actresses, sports people, a top-rated chat show host, a TV comedian who had bluffed the world into taking him seriously as a movie director. Closer to the stage were the politicians—younger members of all the major parties, from the Buddhists to the reformists. Prominent among them was the governor of Tokyo without whose approval the whole event could never have happened.

"Good evening, Meyer-san. We're so happy you could spare the time to come."

It was Shimizu, tapping her on the shoulder, and grinning like a cat in a sushi shop.

"Not at all. It was kind of you to invite me to such a remarkable event."

"Remarkable? I suppose it is. But there'll be many more to come, even bigger than this. Incidentally, we all very much appreciated the profile in yesterday's paper. You have such an excellent way with words."

Martine gave a modest shrug. Actually she had been pleased with the article. It had run next to the editorial column with a cartoon of Nozawa standing over the Diet building, poised to bash it with his guitar. Amazingly the copy editors had left the text more or less as she had sent it—plain and factual, with no attempt to load the dice. Anyone with a brain would see where Nozawa was coming from straightaway.

"But it's unfortunate that your partner couldn't make it. I hope his overseas trip turns out to be successful."

Martine flinched but kept smiling. "How did you find out about that?"

"It's my job to make sure relations with the media run as smoothly as possible."

"You must be a very hard worker."

Shimizu shrugged. "I do my best. But running a small business must be a terrible strain, what with interest rates so high now. You never know—there may be some synergies we can find. Nozawa-sensei has always been keen on good-tasting beer."

He gave a wink and went back to his seat. Martine pondered his last words. "Synergies"—what was that supposed to mean? A product placement in Nozawa's next video? One of those fixed-margin endorsement deals? Whatever he meant, Martine didn't like it. Some kind of encroachment had just taken place, a breaching of a border that she had been carefully protecting.

Suddenly the lights went off all over the park and a siren started wailing. The banks of loudspeakers erupted with the thunder of aircraft engines, then the crump of explosions, women's voices screaming, the rattle of anti-aircraft guns. Powerful searchlights strobed the night sky, as if scanning for the phantom bombers.

"Everyone please stay seated," boomed a familiar male voice. "There is no need to panic. If we work together, we can overcome any disaster. Japan is the land of the gods. I am a god, you are all gods. We Japanese are a hundred million gods. Now I have a question for you. Are you ready for national regeneration?"

At that, the words "National Regeneration" lit up the sky in blazing silver characters three hundred feet high. The roar of approval was twice as loud as for the glam-rockers. But Nozawa evidently wasn't satisfied.

"I can't hear you—what's the matter? You all sound ashamed of being Japanese! Let me ask you again. ARE—YOU—READY—FOR—NATIONAL—REGENERATION?"

This time the response was loud enough to be heard halfway to Yokohama.

"One more time please!"

Around thirty thousand voices blurred into a single roar of approval. Even the VIPs joined in, cupping their mouths and howling at the stage. Martine wondered if she was the only person in the audience with her lips shut.

"All right, then. Come on—LET'S DO IT!"

A single spotlight lit up Nozawa sitting on a wooden stool in the center of the stage. He was dressed in a variation on the traditional construction-worker's outfit—headband, bellyband, baggy trousers, and split-toed sandals. Around his neck hung a shamisen.

"This song is for my father," he muttered. "And for your father too."

He plucked at the strings, and a simple five-note riff twanged from the bank of loudspeakers. Nozawa paused as if to listen, then played the riff again. This time a whomping drumbeat came in behind him, followed by bass and electric piano. There was a slow roar of recognition from the crowd. Nozawa played the riff a third time, and the stage lights came on, revealing the full band with brass section, taiko drums, Hawaiian guitar, and four female backing singers in miniskirts and halter tops, jigging to the beat and waving rising sun flags.

Nozawa jumped off the stool and walked to the front of the stage where he struck a pose, legs planted wide apart, the shamisen thrusting from his hip. Even before he started singing, he had the audience in his pocket.

> *Two hours every morning on a jam-packed train*
> *Working all my life for the same company*
> *Living in a shack that costs fifty million yen*
> *When the earthquake comes it'll crash to the ground*
> *Crash! Crash! Crash!*

The backing singers gave little yelps of panic and staggered from side to side, covering their heads with their hands. Nozawa punched a fist in the air, and the whole park joined in on the chorus.

> *Born in Japan, born in Japan,*
> *I'm a throwaway samurai*
> *Born in Japan*

The governor of Tokyo was singing. The world judo champion was singing. The woman who read the news on DaiNippon TV was singing. The park was a sea of rising sun flags.

A gigantic hologram of Mount Fuji appeared above the stage. Martine watched Nozawa pirouetting at the front, clapping his hands above his head, directing the crowd to sing louder. It was hard to believe he was the same person she had met in the Shinjuku hotel. He looked taller, more handsome. Makoto's mother had claimed he was some kind of genius. That was ridiculous of course, but the man definitely had talent. He was a natural actor, playing with absolute conviction a role that he had created for himself.

Nozawa whooped and crooned and whispered. He sang slow, tear-jerking ballads and thumping rockers. He danced a festival jig with the backup singers and blew a funky solo on a conch shell. He pulled off his bellyband and threw it to the crowd, where it was caught by the female newscaster. The taiko drums pounded, the saxes honked, the backing singers oohed and aahed and jiggled their fronts and wiggled their rears.

Martine recognized about half the songs. There were early hits like "Hey Ryu," "Shinjuku Sunset," and "Year of the Snake." From the heavy Zen phase came "Every Grain of Rice" and "Dharma on Fire," and from the latest CD came "Stolen Islands," "Black Ships in the Bay," and "Japanese Skin." Each had a rapturous reception. Martine seemed to be the only person in the park who didn't know the words to every song.

Finally the last song finished, the lights went down, and the whole audience was on its feet, yelling for an encore. Martine watched the governor of Tokyo put his fingers in his mouth and produce a whistle as piercing as a factory siren. A couple of minutes passed, then Nozawa appeared at the front of the stage. He had traded in his construction-worker gear for jeans and a white T-shirt. On the front of the T-shirt was a girl's face. Martine didn't recognize her until the same image appeared as a gigantic hologram stretching up into the sky.

Nozawa raised his hands in the air and the crowd fell silent.

"One new song," he said. "One song for a girl I never met. One song for a death that must not be in vain. It's called 'The Lonely Death of Mari-chan.'"

The song was performed in Nozawa's early singer-songwriter style, with a bare accompaniment of acoustic guitar and harmonica. It was a powerful work, Martine had to admit. Each verse described Mari-chan's death from the viewpoint of a different person—her father, Jackson, an American politician, a Japanese politician, a salaryman reading about it in the newspaper, then Nozawa himself.

> *Nobody can say who's to blame*
> *Nobody's bad and nobody's good*
> *MacArthur's army defends democracy*
> *MacArthur's army defends capitalism*
> *MacArthur's army brings us movies and burgers*
> *MacArthur's army is here forever*

The song ended with a long, mournful harmonica solo and then a flourish on the guitar. There was a moment of silence, as if the audience couldn't make up its mind whether to cheer or weep. But that was a decision that didn't have to be made because the rest of the band ran on stage and launched into "Hopeful Morning," a karaoke favorite of millions of salarymen. Like a true professional, Nozawa was going to leave them on an emotional high, baying for more.

> *Everybody sing together*
> *Everybody dream together*
> *The sun will rise again*
> *The storm may be strong, the rain may be cold*
> *But tomorrow is coming, a hopeful morning*

Nozawa leaned forward, cupping his hand around his ear. The crowd roared out the next line of the song.

> *And the sun will rise again!*

116

Even the VIPs were on their feet now, swaying from side to side, punching their fists in the air. Nozawa gazed down from the edge of the stage. For an instant Martine had the impression he was staring right at her. He wagged a finger in the air, as if scolding her for not singing.

In this world only one thing is certain

Nozawa stopped again to let the crowd bellow the chorus. This time Martine joined in, adding her voice to the tsunami of sound.

THE SUN WILL RISE AGAIN!

The words floated into the night sky, echoed amongst the skyscrapers, slipped through the tunnels and neon-splattered alleys of Shinjuku, and faded into the roar of the traffic and the thunder of the trains.

The event was brought to an efficient, orderly close. The crowd filed out of the park one row at a time, following the instructions that boomed from the loudspeakers.

"Please be careful not to leave anything behind."

"Please remain seated until your section is called."

"Thank you very much for your attendance. Please put any litter in the bags provided."

It was the same soothing Big Sister voice you heard everywhere in Japan, in subway stations, in government offices, in museums and shrines and sports stadiums. People sat patiently, waiting their turn. And when it came there was no shoving, no shouting, and not a trace of litter left behind.

The VIPs were led to a marquee behind the stage, where a buffet had been prepared. There were long sushi bars, handmade noodles, haunches of finely marbled Kobe beef, salvers bearing huge crayfish still wriggling their antennae long after their flesh had been carved into slices. The members of the band were already there, flushed with the energy of performing. Nozawa had yet to appear. Martine made polite conversation with a software entrepreneur, a Japanese astronaut, and a Buddhist priest who appeared on TV quiz shows. Finally she was buttonholed by a junior politician, a man who had just succeeded to his father's constituency in the north of Japan, his father having succeeded his grandfather, and his grandfather having succeeded his great-grandfather. That Nozawa had managed to attract a man with such a secure franchise was a testament to his political momentum.

"Did you enjoy the concert?" asked the Diet member Makino, sipping a glass of white wine.

"Very interesting," replied Martine.

"I suppose it must be impossible for a foreigner to understand Nozawa-sensei. He has the true Japanese spirit."

"Ah," said Martine. It was a sound that signified neither agreement nor disagreement, but agreement to avoid disagreement. Over the years she had got used to being told that such and such a phenomenon was "impossible for foreigners to understand." In the case of Nozawa, though, Martine wondered if Makino might not be right. Nozawa appealed to such a range of the Japanese population, regardless of sex, age, or level of education. Martine couldn't grasp how he had done it, what propelled him so far above the rest, but then she hadn't grown up with Nozawa. She hadn't heard her father singing his songs in the bath, seen his face on TV before she learned to talk, discussed the meaning of the lyrics with her school friends, or followed the rumors about his personal life in the weekly magazines. She had done none of these things because she wasn't Japanese. There were parts of the code that she would never be able to crack.

A former boyfriend, an investment banker whose hobby was writing haiku, had once told Martine that there were Japanese words that she would never really understand, no matter how hard she tried. These were not complicated words, but simple ones like "house" and "mist" and "mountain." When he used the word "mist" in a haiku, he had a particular picture in mind, an essence of all the "mists" that had appeared in Japanese literature and art throughout the ages. Martine's "mist" was bound to be different, blending traces of all the mists she had ever seen, from the highlands of Scotland to Cape Cod, from the paintings of Turner to Sherlock Holmes movies.

That relationship hadn't lasted long. Glimpsing a hostess's namecard in his wallet—a hostess from a transvestite club, at that—had been the final straw. But she took the point. There were things that could never be grasped from the outside. You had to live them to get the full message.

"The future of this country very much depends on Nozawa-sensei," Makino was saying. "He is the only one who can give us hope."

"What kind of hope?"

"Hope to go forward in our own way. We've been running to catch up with the West for one hundred and fifty years. Now it's time to stop running."

"So you support Nozawa-sensei's policies?"

Makino frowned. "It isn't that definite. But the current government is following bad policies, very damaging to our farming community. They're quite unacceptable."

Martine nodded sympathetically. The agricultural liberalization program, implemented under heavy US pressure, had wreaked havoc on the farmers of northern Japan. Homelessness, penury, family suicides, daughters forced into prostitution to pay off their parents' debts—the descent into misery had come astonishingly fast.

"In times of national crisis Japan needs a different kind of leadership, someone from outside the political establishment. That's what happened in the Meiji Revolution. Young samurai from remote areas seized power and changed the whole country, from top to bottom. We need the same thing now. We need a second Meiji Revolution."

"And is this one going to open up the country or close it?"

Makino chuckled. "My great-grandfather was involved in that struggle. He fought to expel the barbarians and keep Japan pure. But when his side was victorious, they westernized as fast as they could. The point is to clear out the old corrupt ways and bring in new blood, men of sincerity who will dedicate themselves to the nation."

"And you think it's the same this time?"

"That's right. We're not anti-Western. We're pro-Japan. That's a big difference."

Martine noted the "we." Makino had obviously made his decision already.

Glancing over his shoulder, Martine saw the female newscaster walking down the steps of Nozawa's trailer. There was something about the way she was patting down her hair, the dizzy look on her face—Martine guessed it hadn't been an ordinary interview.

"Meyer-san—there could be time for a quick interview, if you want one."

Shimizu was at her shoulder, radiating the odor of hair oil.

"That's a kind thought," said Martine politely. "But I don't think I'm properly prepared."

Shimizu shrugged and walked away. Martine finished her wine and headed for the exit. On the other side of the stage the huge crowd had melted into the night, and technicians were busily dismantling the banks of loudspeakers and video screens. Hundreds of pressmen were bunched in front of the VIP enclosure, straining to get a glimpse of the celebrities in the marquee. As Martine passed through the security zone, a volley of flashes exploded in her face. Instinctively she held up her hand as dozens of camera shutters whirred and buzzed.

Behind the press were clusters of fans, waiting patiently for a glimpse of their heroes. Many of them were Nozawa clones, kitted out in bellybands, baggy trousers, and split-toed sandals. If you went to Harajuku on a Sunday afternoon, you could see thousands of young people dressed like that, complete with "Certain Death" headbands and artificial eyebrows halfway up their foreheads. They might look like gangs of day laborers searching for work, but their outfits were designer brand versions that might cost a week's wages.

One of the clones ran up to Martine and tapped her on the shoulder.

"What do you want?" she snapped, nerves on edge.

"Excuse me. I don't mean to bother you… You attended the VIP party, didn't you?"

He was well spoken, painfully shy, only a few years older than Ichiro. Martine placed him as a student at one of the better universities, the kind who would have gone on to join a bank or insurance company in the old pre-crisis days. Now he would be lucky to get any kind of job. A group of his friends, all dressed the same way, were watching and grinning from a safe distance.

"Yes, that's right."

"Did you see Nozawa-sensei?"

Martine recalled the newscaster emerging from Nozawa's trailer, patting down her hair, walking away a little too fast. "He didn't appear. It seems he was caught up in some kind of discussion."

"So you didn't have a chance to meet him?"

"Not this time. But we did have a conversation last week."

"You actually spoke to him?"

"Yes, for about thirty minutes."

"Fantastic! Meeting Nozawa-sensei face-to-face, talking to him—that's the dream of my dreams! I mean, he's a genius, isn't he? What were your impressions? Was he everything you expected?"

The student was gazing at Martine with shining eyes. He reminded her of a puppy wagging its tail at the prospect of a biscuit. She paused, then nodded.

"Yes he was. Everything I expected, and more."

Which in a way was true. In today's Japan Nozawa was the main event. Of that she had no doubt.

Martine had a sudden desire to get away from the throng of Nozawa fans. She cut down a neon-lit alleyway reeking of stale fish, then turned into a shabby entertainment district. It was one of the less salubrious areas of Shinjuku, with homeless guys peering out of cardboard boxes and schoolgirl prostitutes hanging around street corners, but it was still safe, unlike the badlands around Kabuki-cho where gangsters of different nationalities regularly engaged in shoot-outs, sword attacks, and fire bombings.

The main street was lined with cardsharps, jugglers, monkey trainers, bear handlers and fortune-tellers, all calling out for custom. Some of these would have been ordinary salarymen until recently. Martine stopped to glance curiously at their faces, some straining with fake enthusiasm, others slack-mouthed and blank.

"Hey, foreigner-san. Don't you want to know your future?"

The voice, a wheezing croak, came from just behind her. Martine turned to face a fortune-teller hunched in the shadows of a doorway. The flickering candle on his trestle table lit up bloodshot eyes, a gap-toothed grin, a face as dark and wrinkled as an old prune.

"Not really," said Martine politely.

"What's the matter?" cackled the fortune-teller in a thick accent she could barely understand. "Are you scared of it?"

Martine caught the fetid smell of his clothes and winced. "Of course not. I haven't got time."

"For a beautiful woman like you there's a special discount. Why not try? Don't you want to be happy?"

"I'm happy enough already."

The gap-toothed grin widened. "I don't think so."

Martine turned away, then paused to consider. How many customers would this pathetic character attract tonight? Enough to buy a meal and a room in a flophouse? Probably not.

"All right," she sighed. "But let's be quick."

She sat down on the tiny stool and watched as he rattled the wooden sticks around the cup. He muttered a few words that Martine didn't catch, then tossed the sticks onto the table. For a moment he was motionless, the only sound the bronchial rasp of his breath.

"Well, what's the result?"

"You are too impatient," said the fortune-teller softly. "Impatient with yourself and impatient with others. This is one reason for your problems concerning men."

"I don't have problems concerning men. They have problems concerning me."

"You are a lonely person, I think. You haven't found a home in this world."

Martine crossed her arms over her breasts. "You're wrong there. I have a very pleasant apartment, facing south over Meguro Park."

The fortune-teller ignored her. His eyes were fixed on the clutter of divining sticks.

"Ho!" he croaked. "Here's something strange! A chance to change your life forever. Perhaps it has happened already, just recently. Is this possible?"

He glanced up, holding her in his watery gaze. "Yes—there it is. The traces are visible in your face."

"So you can read faces too?"

The old man gave a little snort of laughter. "Sometimes yes, sometimes no. But your face is like a book. Things are written there that you don't know yourself."

This time Martine said nothing. The yellow flame ducked and swayed, shooting shadows across the fortune-teller's grizzled cheeks.

"You must accept what you've been given," he murmured.

"But nobody has given me anything."

"Accept it. Don't think. Don't ask any questions at all."

"Wait a moment. I'm a journalist. Asking questions is my job."

The fortune-teller shook his head. "This time you must swim with the current. If you try and swim against it, you'll drown."

"What is that supposed to mean?"

"I'm saying nothing more. Your time is up."

With that he spat on his fingers and snuffed out the candle. Martine sighed with exasperation. Did the guy really expect to make a living out of such absolute bunkum? She got to her feet and took out her purse.

"How much?"

"The fee is two thousand yen."

"Two thousand yen? I thought you said there would be a special discount!"

He gave a cackle of laughter that turned into a cough, then back into laughter again. "Ah, but your fortune was a difficult one, the most surprising I've seen for a long time."

Martine held out two banknotes, which he grabbed and stuffed into the pocket of his shapeless trousers. She could still hear him laughing as he hobbled toward a woman in a schoolgirl's uniform standing at the street corner.

Kurokawa City, sixty miles from Tokyo, was in a region that had been hit hard by the crisis. The industrial base of small- and medium-scale manufacturers had been decimated, and dozens of small credit unions had folded. When the local bank finally went under, it was found that sixty percent of its loans were unrecoverable. In terms of unemployment, suicide, child abuse, and arson, Kurokawa was at the top of the national rankings. But there was another phenomenon for which it was even more famous—the road war.

Every Saturday night, thousands of teenagers congregated at a cluster of fast-food joints, pachinko parlors, and used car dealers facing the big Kurokawa intersection. This was where the trucks and other heavy traffic got onto the national road that led to Tokyo. It was also the start of the Kurokawa Skyline, a public works project started toward the end of the era of stagnation in a vain attempt to shore up the local economy. It was a fine road, thirty miles snaking up into the mountains, well lit and with a smooth, fast surface. The problem was that it led nowhere, and the toll booths had been taken down last year when the Road Corporation collapsed. Since then it had become a magnet for road racers from all over the country. They started with tests of speed, an unofficial Formula One for packs of souped-up stolen cars. But it wasn't long before the races turned violent. The purpose became not just to outspeed the others, but to force them off the road or send them skidding into a concrete pillar at one hundred miles an hour. The racers started taking along "soldiers," spaced-out young crazies who would hang out of the hurtling cars wielding chains, baseball bats, and crossbows. There were often ten or twelve victims a night, but the police made little effort to intervene. It was better to have the race gangs in one place where they wouldn't harm ordinary citizens, rather than causing mayhem in suburbs all over the Kanto region.

Tonight one of the local gangs, the Black Devils, was in their usual place in the parking lot of the Starjacks café. They were good customers, since the drugs they took gave them a craving for sweet cakes and gallons of soft drinks. Around twenty of them were standing around, joshing and preening themselves, listening to Nozawa's voice blaring from a smashed-out car window. The song was "Rainy Season Women," a thumping blues from his hard rock period. The boys had orange Mohican cuts, filed teeth, electroluminescent tattoos of death's-heads and dragons. The girls had their eyebrows shaved and teeth painted black, and were wearing skintight jumpsuits that turned translucent with changes in body temperature. Suddenly one of them dropped her cardboard cup and fell choking to the ground. The others gathered around in a circle, watching blankly as she curled up into the fetal position and started puking. Then one of the boys dropped his baseball bat and did the same. Then another. Then another.

"Stand up, you idiots!" roared the chief, a shaven-headed thug with red contact lenses and stretched earlobes that dangled down like little sausages.

"It's the drink," gurgled someone twitching on the ground.

"The orange juice!"

"There's something in the orange juice."

"What're you talking about?" screamed the chief, earlobes swinging. But then he too sank to the ground, hands clutching at his throat.

At the same time, in a Starjacks café in Tokyo's fashionable Daikanyama district, a miniskirted college student suddenly stood and threw up all over the middle-aged businessman who was paying for an evening of her company.

"What's the matter?" yelped the businessman, as she slumped forward, sending the table crashing to the ground.

On the next table, a real-estate salesman stood bolt upright and a stream of orange liquid gushed from his mouth.

"What's happening?"

"Quick—call an ambulance!"

"It's the orange juice."

"There's something wrong with the orange juice."

Over the next few hours the same cries were heard at Starjacks outlets all over eastern Japan.

TWELVE

Martine sat cross-legged in front of the TV, a cup of coffee cradled in her lap. Outside the window, a gang of crows was greeting the morning with a raucous chorus of squawks and caws, but Martine didn't hear them. What was happening on the split screen had her full attention.

On the INN side a blond-haired square-jawed man was furrowing his brows and flashing his perfect dentistry, trying to sound concerned and calm and decisive all at the same time. He was slim, tanned, and looked like a tennis pro or a surfer. In fact Kip Harper was in his mid-fifties, and thanks to the truckload of share options he had awarded himself, he was one of the most highly paid CEOs in America.

"Our sympathies are of course extended to the victims and their families. The causes of this unfortunate incident are still unclear, but we have total confidence in the quality of Starjacks products. Every day over one million consumers in ninety-three different countries eat at Starjacks cafés…"

Harper had probably rehearsed the speech half-a-dozen times already, under the expert tuition of his public relations team. They would have written the script that he was currently reading off the teleprompter. They would have told him what kind of shirt to wear (light blue denim, open-neck), which words to emphasize, when to smile, and when to frown. All this had been done in a couple of hours, an impressive feat of damage limitation.

On the other half of the screen, a Japanese reporter was standing in the forecourt of a hospital speaking excitedly into the microphone. Twelve people confirmed dead, he was saying, over fifty seriously ill. The names of the dead people scrolled down the screen, together with their ages and areas of residence. Martine noted that most were young, between the ages of sixteen and thirty. Then the screen cut to a female reporter interviewing the parents of one of the victims.

"So what are your feelings now?" asked the reporter, pushing her microphone into the shocked face of the mother.

"It's so sad … she was a such kind girl … she never did any harm to anyone…"

The woman broke into sobs. The camera zoomed in and lingered lovingly on her crumpled face and streaming eyes.

Back on the INN side of the screen, Harper was leaning forward slightly.

"Our mission is not just to supply food and drink. We also have a mission to spread positive human values. At Starjacks cafés people of all races, ages, and religions can gather together and enjoy super-tasty, great-value cakes and pizzas made with all-natural ingredients…"

On the NHK side, they were back at the hospital. Ambulances were swerving into the forecourt; stretchers carrying prone bodies were being wheeled through sliding doors. Then they cut to a senior doctor peering sternly through his glasses.

"What information can you give us?" asked the female reporter.

"It appears to be a new strain of the E. *coli* bacteria, never seen before in Japan. It is extremely dangerous, even to healthy adults…"

"And do we know how it was transmitted?"

"Investigations are not yet complete, but we can say that the bacteria was certainly present in the orange juice."

"So we should be careful about drinking imported orange juice?"

"Of course. That goes without saying."

Back on the INN side, Kip Harper was winding up his speech, as smooth and confident as ever.

"Now I have a special message for our Japanese customers," he said, his face filled with boyish enthusiasm. "Remember this, folks, Starjacks is super-fresh and super-tasty. Or as you folks over there say, Starjacks is totally *oishii*!"

At that point someone off-screen handed him a plate with a bagel on it. Harper gave a huge wink, picked it up, and sank his pearly white teeth into it. But Martine was no longer watching. The doctor's words were still echoing in her mind—"the bacteria was certainly present in the orange juice." Orange juice! Bad for your health! That was the second time her mystery e-mail admirer had forecast an upcoming disaster. Once might be a coincidence, but not twice. What on earth was going on?

Martine switched the screen to computer mode and logged onto her files in the office. She found the e-mail from her mystery admirer and read it again. Kimura's friend had asked her to establish a dialogue with the man. Apparently they needed greater data flow to have a chance of tracking him. That went against not just her natural instincts, but the guidance given by the *Tribune*'s own security department. Responding to an online stalker was positively discouraged—there was no saying where it would lead. On the other hand, she had a feeling that if she let this story slip she would regret it afterward. In Martine's thinking there were two kinds of regret. Positive regret—for things you shouldn't have done, but did—was unavoidable, part of growing older and wiser. Negative regret—for what you should have done, but didn't—was the kind that gnawed at your soul forever.

She typed in a two-line reply.

> Thank you for giving me such useful advice. Perhaps you could tell me who you are and how you know these things.

She gazed at it for a few moments, then clicked on "Send."

An hour later Martine walked into the nearly deserted restaurant of the Seikyu Tower Hotel. The Seikyu had once been one of the most fashionable places to have Sunday brunch, but today there were as many staff as customers. White-jacketed waiters with slicked-back hair and shiny shoes stood around gazing blankly into space. Martine guessed they were dead on their feet, having worked all night in bars and clubs. Most of them were in their late twenties, probably graduates of medium-grade universities. They would be living on the kind of wages that used to be paid to teenagers for holiday jobs.

Martine took a table by the window, no need to book. The last time she had sat here was for a casual lunch with Makoto. It had been two years ago, when they were just getting to know each other. She remembered Makoto explaining how he was going to get his beer into the major hotel chains, and the way his eyes lit up with enthusiasm. He had been irresistible. Somehow or other—they still argued about whose idea it was—they had ended up taking a room in the hotel and staying there until evening. Martine still found Makoto's enthusiasm irresistible. She only wished it was occasionally focused on something other than his beers.

This morning she was meeting not Makoto, but Gary Terashima of the US Embassy. As usual he was late. Martine gazed out the window at the bulk of Mount Fuji, which looked close enough to reach out and touch. Not so many years ago, you could see Mount Fuji only on public holidays, when the factories were closed and the air was free of pollutants. Now you could see it almost every day, one beneficial side effect of the collapse of the manufacturing sector.

"Can I offer you something?"

Martine looked up into the eyes of a tall young waiter, bending down to offer her a menu. He had a strong, smooth face, broad shoulders, and a wide, confident smile. Martine noted the outline of an electroplasma tattoo on the back of his hand. The plasma was deactivated, but the "nZw" logo was clearly visible.

"Coffee and fresh orange juice, please."

The waiter flicked a quiff of hair from his forehead. "I'm afraid we aren't serving orange juice. You know, the incident yesterday evening."

"Well, in that case I'll have grapefruit juice."

"No grapefruit juice either. That's also an imported product. How about some apple juice made from delicious Tohoku apples? It's good for your health."

The waiter was still looming over her, grinning in a slightly odd way. Martine remembered hearing that even in some of the best hotels the staff were providing unofficial sexual services these days. For the lonely businessman there were chambermaids and elevator girls keen to supplement their meager incomes. And for bored middle-aged housewives, there were pretty-boy waiters and masseurs.

"A glass of water, please."

"Plain or sparkling?"

"Plain." The waiter backed away, still grinning ingratiatingly. Martine took the *Nikkei Shimbun* out of her bag and started browsing through a long article on fiscal reform, the code word the government used to describe its program of tax hikes and benefit cuts. As usual, the *Nikkei* was parroting the government line about the need for national sacrifice, everyone pulling together, and Martine guessed that whole chunks of the article had actually been written by government officials. Nozawa, of course, was promising lower taxes and higher benefits. The shortfall, he claimed, would be made up by reducing foreign aid to zero and introducing a penalty tax on investment in overseas financial markets—the speculation tax. His numbers didn't add up, but then neither did the government's.

Martine gave up on the *Nikkei* article halfway through and looked around her. Three tables away a middle-aged couple were sitting down to a breakfast of croissants and coffee. The man was wearing a dark suit, and was occasionally fingering his collar in a way that suggested he didn't wear one very often. The woman was conservatively but elegantly dressed, in a blue dress and thick pantyhose. They were totally silent. Martine placed them as country people who had done well from the crisis, perhaps by keeping their wealth in gold bullion stashed under the floorboards. It was often the most conservative and unsophisticated people who survived best, whereas the risk takers were wiped out at an early stage. Anyway, the couple's relative position had been boosted to the extent that they could afford to stay at the famous Seikyu Tower. The only problem was that the Seikyu now was a different place from the glamorous hotel they remembered seeing in magazines and trendy TV dramas. So they sat there chewing their croissants in silence and trying to hide their disappointment.

Gary Terashima finally came rolling in with a heavy handshake and a string of loud pleasantries. He was a third-generation Japanese American, big-boned and athletic. The job title on his namecard was "economic analyst," though his information-gathering activities generally had little to do with economic data. The good thing about him was that he was completely frank about what he wanted and why. The less appealing thing was that he always wanted something in return.

"Gee, isn't it terrible about this poisoned orange juice? I eat at Starjacks all the time. It's the only place around here you can get a decent pastrami sand-wich, you know with rye bread and pickles..."

"Do you think this incident will affect US–Japan relations?"

Terashima looked puzzled. "Why should it? It was an accident, for God's sake, the kind of thing that happens all the time."

When the waiter came over, Terashima ordered doughnuts, coffee, and orange juice. He spoke Japanese haltingly, with a heavy American accent.

"Sorry, we aren't serving orange juice," said the waiter. "How about some apple juice made from delicious Tohoku apples?"

Terashima shook his head. "Uh-uh. I'll have a Coke instead."

"Sorry, but we don't have Coke either."

"Yes, you do. You have it in the bar downstairs. Now go down there and get me a Coke right away."

The waiter's smile froze, and he turned away without another word.

Terashima reached into his briefcase, pulled out a copy of yesterday's *Tribune*, and slapped it on the table. He jabbed a big square-tipped finger at the interview with Nozawa.

"Congratulations. You got good access there."

"Thank you," said Martine cautiously.

"Still, I think you were too sympathetic. The guy is a fruitcake, a putz, and a menace to global security."

"Because he opposes American interests?"

"Because he opposes everyone's interests. Japan needs the US, now more than ever. This world is a dangerous place, you know."

"The Japanese public believes that being allied with the US makes it even more dangerous. That's what the opinion polls say, anyway."

"Look, the public here changes its mood like my five-year-old daughter. That's why you need stable political leadership, the kind that gives people a sense of security and direction. If you don't have that, God knows what will happen."

Martine shrugged and took a sip of coffee. The problem was that the "stable political leadership" that Terashima's people had sponsored for decades had proved to be hopelessly corrupt. As the UNG scandal had shown, hardly a single senior politician was untainted by the rot.

"The same goes for journalists too," continued Terashima. "You're too happy to see any kind of turmoil. You should think more seriously about defending democratic values."

"You mean you want the Press to put the boot into Nozawa?"

"I didn't say that."

"Why don't you put the boot into him yourself? You people are pretty good at that sort of thing, aren't you?"

"Well, something will have to be done," muttered Terashima darkly.

Martine raised an eyebrow. "Something? Like what?"

"Martine, you need to understand—this Nozawa business has cropped up at a very bad time."

"Any time would be a bad time for you, wouldn't it?"

"This is a particularly bad time. As you know, the administration has just initiated a major foreign policy review. The word on the grapevine is that we could be looking at a one hundred and eighty degree shift, the kind that happens once a generation. This could be the big sayonara."

For once the mask of joviality had gone. Terashima was looking deadly serious.

"Sayonara to who?"

"To Japan, of course. We have these policy reviews every time there's a new administration, and it's always the same thing—the pro-Japan people against the pro-China people. Last time around, our team won big time, but this time we're in a position of real weakness. Let's face it, the pro-China guys have got some strong arguments, and of course they've got the president herself on their side."

"Strong arguments? I didn't expect that from you."

"Come on—look at Japan and what do you see? A total shambles. The economy keeps shrinking, our best friends are all screwed up with this UNG scandal, and the public has gone dancing with the Pied Piper of Hamelin."

"Not an easy sell, is it?"

Terashima shook his head sadly. "We're calling it a temporary adjustment, but that's what we said last time and the time before that. Frankly we never imagined the fundamentals could get this bad. It's been the most serious forecasting error since the collapse of the Soviet Union."

"Surely there are problems with China too—the massacres, the missile exports, the whole human rights issue."

"Yeah, but this is a pragmatic administration elected on a program of economic recovery and reducing foreign entanglements. Nobody likes the Chinese, but the reality is they're getting stronger and richer and we need them on our side. It's better to have them inside the tent pissing out than outside the tent pissing in—if you'll excuse the expression."

Martine wrinkled her nose, assailed by distant memories of camping holidays in the south of France.

"I see. And what happens to the Japanese when they get pushed out of this tent of yours?"

"They're gonna get wet, of course."

"They might prefer to build their own tent, as Nozawa suggests."

Terashima sucked his breath in through his teeth, one of the few Japanese traits passed down from his forbears.

"Nobody's got any patience for that kind of crap, believe me. We got the Indian situation, we got the Romanian situation, we got a new guy in Algeria that makes Gaddafi look like Tony Blair, we got the whole world spinning out of control. Now over in Japan—nice, polite Japan, where nothing unexpected is supposed to happen—suddenly we got this rabble-rousing fruitcake threatening our security interests."

"It must be pretty tiresome for you."

"No kidding. It'd be better for everyone if Nozawa goes."

The words were spoken with a quiet vehemence that surprised Martine.

"Goes where?" she asked lightly.

But Terashima was not to be drawn out any further. The Coke arrived on a silver tray and he grabbed it without a word and took a long suck on the straw. The waiter leaned against the wall watching, his face a mask of hostility.

After brunch Martine walked through Ginza. Once it would have been packed with shoppers, but now many of the stores had stopped opening on Sundays. The Matsukawa department store was still boarded up, and the ground floor of the old Mitsuya department store was now a pachinko parlor. On the other side of the street was a string of discount shops, money lenders, and fast-food outlets. Amongst them was a Starjacks outlet, supposedly the most profitable in Asia. Today it was totally empty.

Martine thought about what Terashima had told her. It made a certain kind of sense. Japan had been the wealthiest country in Asia for three hundred years, while China had lurched from disaster to disaster—internal collapse, colonization, civil war, communism. Now, though, the roles were being reversed. China was booming, while Japan was mired in stagnation. The Americans, beset by their own economic problems and keen to lighten up on global commitments, were just responding to that reality. There would be uproar from the Taiwanese, just as there was in the seventies when Nixon turned his back on them. And now, just as then, the support of big business and the labor unions would be decisive. Human rights, free Tibet, save the panda—those issues played well when the good times were rolling. In a global depression people had different priorities.

When Martine got home, there was a light flashing on her answering machine. The message was from Shimizu, complimenting her on the Nozawa interview and asking her to call him back. As she picked up the phone, Martine wondered how he had got her home number.

"Ah, Meyer-san, thank you for the prompt reply. The sensei was very pleased with your work. He is absolutely convinced you are the finest journalist in the world."

"That's nice to know."

"And he apologizes for cutting the interview short. Now he wants to go ahead with part two."

Martine paused to think. "Part two? Another piece would be rather unusual, coming so soon after the last one. I'd have to ask my editor whether he can find space."

"Why not do the interview first? When your editor sees the material, he'll find a space immediately. I can assure you of that." Shimizu gave a smug little laugh. He was certain of it.

"When do you want it?" asked Martine.

"The sooner the better. How about tomorrow at four?"

"Fine," said Martine dryly. She might have to accept being ordered around, but she didn't have to like it. No sooner had she put down the phone than it started ringing again. Would Nozawa never leave her alone? She scooped up the receiver.

"Yes?" she said, not bothering to disguise her impatience.

"What's the matter with you? Have you got a hangover or something?"

Martine heaved a sigh of relief. It was Makoto, now in Los Angeles. He was in a good mood, cautiously optimistic about the reception he was getting.

"I think these investors understand what I'm doing. They can see the potential..."

Martine thought about explaining what had been happening—the e-mail messages, the orange juice, the Nozawa concert. She decided against it. Makoto's mood was too precious to spoil. He sounded so relaxed, burbling away like a man fifteen years younger. Martine would have liked to have seen him when he *was* fifteen years younger. She would have liked to have known him when he was softer, dreamier, more willing to make mistakes. But that part of him had been given to another woman. And when Sachiko-san had gone, she had taken it with her.

"I've just been thinking," said Martine suddenly. "Maybe I'm in love."

She had no idea why those words popped into her head. But, there, she had said it.

Then came a pause in which she could almost hear Makoto's brain whirring.

"Who with?" he asked, tentatively.

"Who do you think, you silly man."

There was another pause, twice as long as the first.

"Thank you very much," said Makoto finally.

"What did you say?"

"I said thank you very much. I'm grateful."

"Grateful? Is that what you feel?"

"Yes. I'm really grateful."

A hot current surged through Martine's body, starting in her stomach and finishing behind her eyes. "In that case this conversation is over. Forget I ever said anything."

She slammed down the phone. When it started ringing again, she pulled out the jack. She was still fuming half an hour later when she walked into the karate dojo. Saya Miki, the tall cop, glanced at her curiously.

"What's the matter?" she asked. "Man trouble again?"

"Sort of."

"Maybe you should do like me and get a dog."

"Maybe I will," replied Martine, yanking off her T-shirt. "What breed do you recommend?"

Peng Yuan was in high spirits. It wasn't often that he could take time off from his work at the institute. Still rarer was the opportunity to enjoy some of the country's finest tourist spots in the company of a beautiful woman. The people in the guest house looked at him in envy when he came down from the bedroom with Ling-Mei following after him dutifully and correctly. She was tall and elegant, her hair as fine as silk, her eyes shining with devotion, and she showed everyone that Peng Yuan was a man of taste, just as the chauffeur-driven Mercedes outside showed that he was a man of power.

The benefits of success were such that they allowed men to develop interests that would otherwise have remained hidden. Peng Yuan had become a connoisseur of women late in life. In his younger days he had been shy, and too wrapped up in academic pursuits to waste time on female company. At the age of twenty-two he had married a fellow student, the daughter of a lecturer at Beijing University. Even then she had not been attractive—extremely unattractive in fact, with her squashed-up face and foul-smelling breath—but that hadn't mattered to Peng Yuan. His wife had satisfied his sexual needs in the same way as she had satisfied his stomach—quickly and efficiently, allowing him to focus his energies on his career. At that stage of his life he had never been close to a beautiful woman, let alone spoken to one or touched one.

After ten years of marriage Peng Yuan's wife was sent to teach political theory at a junior school near the Vietnamese border. Peng Yuan wasn't sorry to see her go. Her father had been dismissed after a series of ideological blunders, and anyway she had failed to provide him with a son. Instead there was a daughter who was the exact image of her mother—the same piggy little eyes, the same stubby legs, even the same rancid breath. For years Peng Yuan had rarely thought about women at all. Sometimes, close friends from the institute would return from overseas trips with forbidden videotapes, and they would watch them in the dead of night in the institute's screening room. That was a dangerous, thrilling activity. In those days betrayal would have meant the labor camp, perhaps even the death sentence. "Moral deviation," "bourgeois decadence"—these were crimes for which every year tens of thousands of men and women were hauled into sports stadiums and executed before jeering crowds. They even made your family pay for the bullet, just as with common thieves. But the images of these women—American, Japanese, European, black and white, in every type of position—were extraordinarily addictive. They stayed in your brain. They were there when you closed your eyes at night, or when you stared blankly into your computer screen. Peng Yuan soon started his own collection, and showed it to promising students whose loyalty he wanted to strengthen.

It was only after Peng Yuan had developed his connection with the old general that he felt secure enough to indulge himself with real women. Several attractive women came to work at the institute, and it wasn't difficult to persuade them to do the same as the women in the videotapes. All he had to do was offer promotions, better housing allowances, or job recommendations for their husbands. From there Peng Yuan expanded his interests to students, and actresses like Ling-Mei. Some of them he set up as mistresses, living in apartments paid for with money diverted from the institute's central budget. In the old days this would have been doubly dangerous, but with the old man's influence behind him Peng Yuan felt safe enough.

Ling-Mei was Peng Yuan's current favorite. Her skin was flawless, like the finest satin. Her breasts were high and heavy, and she had the poise of a trained actress. In her presence, Peng Yuan felt proud, strong, totally at ease. She held the door of the Mercedes open for him, and he stepped inside. In truth he wasn't all that interested in the schedule of tourist locations she had prepared, but it made a change from the daily routine at the institute. It was the old general's son who had suggested that Peng Yuan take a holiday in the mountains. He had even arranged for the car and chauffeur to be made available. That was the measure of Peng Yuan's rise in the world. He had become the trusted associate of a national hero, the recipient of personal favors that he had never even asked for.

"Where are we going now?" he asked, running his fingers through Ling-Mei's long flowing hair.

She turned and patted him lightly on the upper thigh.

"To the mountains. There is a famous place called the Dragon's Door."

"I've never heard of that."

"It's a crack in the mountain. You're supposed to shout your dreams into it, and if you hear the echo it means they will come true. Isn't that right, driver?"

The driver nodded, eyes fixed on the road ahead. He was a local man in his mid-forties, possibly an ex-soldier. He rarely spoke, and when he did the accent was so heavy that Peng Yuan could barely understand a word. Peng Yuan gazed out the window at the people working in the fields—hundreds of them bent over in the sunshine, from young children to wizened old women. This hadn't changed for two thousand years. Perhaps it would never change. Regardless of the regime or the ideology or the state of international relations, there would always be hundreds of millions of Chinese living and dying in places like this. There would always be the fields, the rice, the backbreaking work.

The car left the fields behind and began to climb the winding road that led up the mountainside. Progress was slow as the road was broken and rutted. Gradually the terrain became rougher and wilder. There were beds of baked mud, dead trees with their roots in the air, gulleys of bare rock where the topsoil had been washed away in landslides. The people were different too, leaner and darker. There were children sitting at the side of the road, their sunken cheeks smeared with dirt and dazed looks in their eyes. When the car passed they turned their faces away, as if frightened to be seen. Enormous buzzards, the biggest Peng Yuan had ever seen, were swooping over the scrubby ground, casting dark shadows.

"What happened here?" asked Peng Yuan, pointing at the blackened ruins of some huts. "It looks as if they were hit by an earthquake."

The driver made a low gurgling sound that was barely recognizable as a laugh. He muttered something incomprehensible underneath his breath, then swerved violently to avoid a deep crater in the center of the road.

"What did he say?"

"He said there was a kind of government earthquake," said Ling-Mei, who had a good ear for the man's accent.

"What does that mean?"

Ling-Mei shrugged. "I think it means trouble with party officials. The people here are very stubborn."

As they ground their way up the mountainside, they passed hundreds of burned-out huts. There were no animals, no crops. Peng Yuan couldn't help wondering how the people lived. There were grisly stories about what happened in these remote areas when food was short. In some villages, it was said, half the female population under the age of twelve would disappear during the winter months.

"From here we have to walk," said Ling-Mei, pointing to a pile of rubble that marked the end of the road. Again Peng Yuan was surprised at how well informed she was. She must have gone to great trouble to memorize the details of these tourists spots. It was another proof of her devotion to him.

"How far is it?"

"Not too far."

Peng Yuan was relieved to hear that. He was wearing one of his best pairs of shoes, made of supple brown leather with little tassels. It would be a shame to scuff them on the sharp stones that littered the ground. Ling-Mei held the door open for him, and then they walked arm in arm along the path, the chauffeur following a couple of yards behind. At first Peng Yuan had felt rather inhibited in the man's presence, but now he was used to it. He patted Ling-Mei on the buttocks and ran his fingers through her hair as if they were alone.

They were quite high on the mountain now, well above the last of the burned-out shacks. Being so far away from the eyes of other human beings was a strange feeling, liberating and also disturbing. There was so much silence. The path narrowed until they had to force their way between the bushes. Peng Yuan gave a cry of anger as a bramble snagged the sleeve of his silk shirt. Fortunately he managed to free it without any damage.

"We're almost there," said Ling-Mei, clutching his arm.

The path emerged onto a plateau of bare rock split by a jagged fissure, about fifteen feet wide. It was hard to imagine that the place was any kind of tourist spot. It was harsh, empty, ugly. The buzzards had followed them up the mountain and were wheeling overhead. They were low enough for their claws to be visible, curling downward like grappling hooks.

"What was the legend again?" asked Peng Yuan, taking out his camera.

"You have to stand on that rock and shout your dreams into the crevice." Ling-Mei was pointing to a rock right at the edge of the gorge.

"Oh yes—then there's supposed to be an echo."

"Yes, if you're lucky there should be an echo."

"You go first. I'll take a photo."

Ling-Mei giggled and tried to refuse, but Peng Yuan insisted. He wanted to hear her dream. The driver helped her scramble up onto the rock. She cupped her hands around her mouth and shouted out "Good marriage and long life!" Peng Yuan took a photo of her bending forward, buttocks in the air. A split second later a faint echo could be heard, then another, then another, as the sound waves bounced from side to side of the crevice.

"Now it's your turn."

Peng Yuan walked up to the rock, then stopped. The problem was that he couldn't decide what his dream should be. He wasn't sure he had one any more. Everything he wanted was already within his grasp. Status, connections, women, expensive clothes and food—what else was there to dream of?

"Go on," said Ling-Mei. There was a surprisingly harsh tone to her voice, usually so soft and sensual.

The driver gave Peng Yuan his large, rough hand. Peng Yuan mounted the rock and peered down. The crevice was dark, with sheer sides. Peng Yuan wondered how deep it was, and what lay at the bottom. He shivered, feeling a sudden compulsion to scramble back down from the rock and rush back to the car. But he couldn't do that—Ling-Mei would take him for an old fool. So instead he bent forward and cupped his hands around his mouth.

"Victory to the Chinese people!" he shouted, without much conviction. He waited for the echo, but none came.

"Let me try again," he said, turning to face Ling-Mei. Strangely, though, she was ignoring him, walking back toward the path. What was the matter with the girl? Was she deliberately trying to offend him? She should have realized by now that Peng Yuan was not the kind of man who could be insulted lightly.

"Come back here!" he yelled.

She didn't even turn her head. Peng Yuan let out a long sigh of anger. He held out his hand to the driver and hopped down from the rock. Except that his feet didn't touch the ground. For some reason the driver was hugging him tightly, turning him around to face the crevice.

"What do you think you're doing?" growled Peng Yuan impatiently.

The driver made the same gurgling sound he'd made in the car. He had a strange sense of humor, thought Peng Yuan. It wasn't at all funny to be so close to the edge of the crevice, hanging over it, looking down ...... and then rolling forward, clutching at the empty air, tumbling into the blackness, letting loose a yell that carried on bouncing between the crevice's rocky sides long after Peng Yuan had crashed to the bottom and was no more.

"Yaaah!"

Peng Yuan never heard the echo, but the mountains heard it and the bushes heard it. The buzzards heard it too. They tilted their wings and descended in slow, lazy circles.

THIRTEEN

Martine watched as Nozawa crept along the verandah, opening the sliding doors one by one. He was dressed in a loose black kimono, with a silk cloth covering the lower half of his face. His eyes were bulging with tension, and in the middle of his forehead a single bead of sweat glistened in the moonlight.

All the rooms were empty except the last, where a young geisha lay trussed up on the floor.

"Help me," she moaned, tossing her head from side to side.

Nozawa darted into the room, then stopped just in time. The floor panel between them had dropped away to reveal a pit of writhing snakes. Then another floor panel swung open. Underneath was an array of steel spikes, the points dripping with poison. The geisha started giggling hysterically. Nozawa whirled around just as the doorway burst into flames and the floor panels on either side of him fell away.

Trapped! No way out! But a huge leap took him clean over the geisha's head. Then he ran up the pillar at the far end of the room, scuttled upside down across the ceiling, and somersaulted through the tiny window into the garden outside. Three monstrous soldiers with scowling red faces, long noses, and straggly yellow hair were waiting for him, muskets at the ready. Nozawa disarmed them with a hail of throwing stars. The soldiers roared in comical panic as the razor-sharp metal went slicing into windpipes and lopped off fingers and ears, spattering gouts of crimson blood over the paper screens. Then he finished them off at close quarters with flashing sword and whirling chain.

With the bodies lying inert on the ground behind him, Nozawa pulled the black cloth from his mouth and picked up a shamisen leaning conveniently against a nearby barrel. He plinked out a scurry of notes, then the riff was picked up by a chorus of saxophones and Nozawa launched into the first verse of "Born to Sweat," his soulful lament for the unemployed.

The screen went dead, and the real Nozawa turned to Martine.

"What do you think?" he asked.

"The picture quality is excellent."

"Of course! Softjoy Corporation uses the world's finest imaging technology. That's why we always ask them to make our games. No other company could do it."

They were sitting in Nozawa's personal recording studio, a squat windowless building in Harajuku. Getting inside had been no easy matter. Martine had had to fight her way through the crush of fans surrounding the entrance, hoping for a glimpse of their hero. They would be lucky to get one, since Nozawa's people were adept in the uses of decoy and disguise. The hooded figure in the back of the accelerating limo could be anybody.

Nozawa was here to add the finishing touches to the soundtrack of the "National Regeneration" videogame. In a week's time the new game would be in the shops, and in two weeks it would be heading the popularity rankings, as had all his previous games. People would be playing it on home consoles, in virtual reality pods in Softjoy's high-tech amusement arcades, in handheld versions on trains, in a multiplayer version on the internet. Sales of five million units were expected in the first month. Nobody would be able to escape "National Regeneration."

Martine had spent the past hour watching the production team fiddle with the mix of "Born To Sweat," replacing the saxes with an accordion, speeding up the shamisen solo, and drenching the vocal track in echo to give it a karaoke feel. Nozawa himself had favored the basic version, but Yamazaki, his chief producer, was not satisfied. And it was Yamazaki's opinion that counted. Now they were taking a break while Yamazaki sat at the mixing desk with his headphones on, hands silently working the switches and dials.

Martine glanced over at Shimizu, who was sitting on a table swinging his legs and looking totally out of place among the scruffy sound engineers and musicians.

"When shall I start the interview?"

"Start when you like. This is all on the record, nothing to hide."

Shimizu was always relentlessly upbeat, but today he sounded as if he didn't have a care in the world.

"Very well," said Martine, turning to Nozawa. "First of all, let me express my gratitude for your cooperation. I'm sure our readers will find your views extremely interesting."

Nozawa's lips curled.

"Interesting? That's too weak, Meyer-san. I don't want to be interesting, like some little monkey riding a bicycle. I want to be taken seriously. I want this country to be taken seriously."

"You think you're not being taken seriously at the moment?"

"Of course not. The world is laughing at us. Foreigners buy our products and accept our money, but behind our backs they're laughing. Do you know why they're laughing?"

"Please tell me," said Martine, although she had a good idea what he was going to say.

"Because we can't defend ourselves, of course. A country that relies on another country for protection isn't a real country. A country that has no pride in its own history isn't a real country. It deserves to be laughed at!"

"And this is why you want to scrap the US bases?"

"It's one big reason, but it's not the only one. The fact is, we can't rely on the Americans anyway. They are unpredictable and actually very dangerous. They believe that what is good for them must be good for all human beings everywhere. We Japanese don't think like this. We believe that what is good for Japan is good for Japan only, not for others. Most of our economic problems come from obeying the Americans' demands. This was a big mistake for us."

Martine nodded. It was a view she was hearing everywhere these days—from young and old, reactionaries, progressives, and moderates. And it wasn't completely wrong.

"American people should do things the American way, the French should do them the French way, and the Japanese should do them the Japanese way. This is best for everyone, I think."

Martine flipped over a page in her notebook. When Nozawa got excited, the words came quickly.

"But what is the Japanese way? Who decides?"

"Nobody decides. That's a typical Western question, if I may say so. We don't need to decide. We all already know the Japanese way. It's encoded up here, in the left side of the brain."

He tapped a finger on his left temple.

"The Japanese way means respecting our ancestors and our parents. It means working hard, making excellent products at cheap prices. No more speculation, no more chasing profits, and no more wasting hard-earned money on stupid foreign luxuries. We must remember how to enjoy simple things. We must remember how to sweat."

Sweat was a key word in Nozawa's songs, denoting sincerity and self-sacrifice.

Martine wrote quickly. These days there were few politicians anywhere in the world who weren't blathering about a return to traditional values. To convince the editors, she would need something much meatier than that.

"Let's go back to the security question. You said that a country that relies on another country for protection is not a real country."

"That's right," growled Nozawa. "A real country defends itself with its own blood, not other people's. This is common sense, I think."

"But is Japan really capable of defending itself outside the alliance structure?"

"Really capable—what does that mean?"

"Well, as you pointed out, Japan has been dependent on the US alliance ever since the war. Upgrading your own forces would be a slow and immensely costly process, wouldn't it?"

Martine was fishing, not really expecting him to bite. But he did, without a second's hesitation.

"In terms of conventional forces, yes, you're right. That's why it will be necessary to equip ourselves with the most powerful weapons available."

Martine's heart skipped a beat. So Shimizu had been telling the truth. This really was going to be sensational material.

"The most powerful weapons available are nuclear. Are you suggesting Japan should start a nuclear weapons development program?"

"Development program? We aren't some third-world country full of peasants and oxen, you know. Japan has the highest-grade nuclear power industry in the world, with plutonium produced by our own fast-breeder reactors. As for missile technology, some of the guidance systems used by the US are actually made by Japanese electronics companies. If we want to have nuclear capability, we can prepare it in a matter of weeks."

Martine tried to look calm, but her pulse was racing. Never before had any Japanese politician made a public commitment to nuclear weapons. Nozawa wasn't just breaking a fifty-year taboo, he was gleefully tearing it to shreds and stamping them into the ground. She had once heard an aged right-winger mutter something similar late at night over whiskey and water. But that had been off the record, and the man had been half-drunk.

"Let me confirm this. Your political group will be campaigning for Japan to go nuclear?"

Martine shot a nervous glance at Shimizu. Would he step in and block the question? No, he didn't say a word, just sat there examining his manicure.

Nozawa leaned back in his chair, hands locked behind his head, eyes half-closed. "Look at the countries that have these weapons—the Americans, the French, the British, the Chinese. These are the countries that control the world. They attack whoever they want whenever they want. And if anyone fights back they call it an atrocity or a war crime."

"So you will be campaigning for Japan to go nuclear too?"

Nozawa held a long pause. Martine bit her lip. She knew that he was playing with her, enjoying the tension. Finally his long, rather feminine eyelashes flicked open.

"Not campaigning," he barked. "We will be insisting. After all, there is no other choice, is there?"

Martine let out a long, slow sigh of relief. There it was, safely in her grasp, the biggest story of her career.

Martine was still buzzing with triumph when she walked into the office, a plastic shopping bag swinging jauntily from her hand.

"So what's the matter with you?" queried Kyo-san, glancing over the top of her glasses. "You look as if you've won the lottery."

Martine put the bag down on the table in the center of the room and took out a box of bean-jam cakes, handmade at the best cake shop in Tokyo.

"That's more or less what happened. I've got a major scoop. It'll be on the front page the day after tomorrow."

"Really," said Kyo-san, eyes flicking back to the book she was reading. She knew all about the "major scoops" that got correspondents so excited and nobody even remembered a couple of weeks later.

"Well, aren't you going to ask me what it is?"

"All right, what is it then?"

"You mustn't tell anyone about it, not even your pet goldfish."

"Don't worry—I won't be telling him anything. He died last week."

Martine glanced from side to side, then leaned over Kyo-san's desk, low enough for her hair to brush the surface.

"He's going to campaign for Japan to go nuclear," she said in a loud whisper.

Kyo-san's head jerked backward. "What? Nozawa said that?"

"He certainly did," beamed Martine. "It's all on the record!"

But Kyo-san wasn't beaming. In fact she looked more shaken than Martine had ever seen her before.

"People are going crazy," she muttered, shaking her head. "Sometimes I don't want to live in this country any more."

Martine was furious with herself for misreading her reaction. Kyo-san was a fervent pacifist in a way that the younger generation could never be. Her father had been killed in Manchuria in the last days of the war, leaving behind a nineteen-year-old bride who was a widow before she realized she was even pregnant.

"So where would you go instead?"

"Any place where the news doesn't reach. I don't want to be informed about this stuff any more."

"You're too stressed out, Kyo-san. What you need is a massage."

Martine went behind Kyo-san's chair and started kneading the muscles of her neck. Calm, good-humored Kyo-san, a woman who had spent the best part of three decades working in news organizations, couldn't tolerate the news any longer. That was the effect the crisis was having. Sensible, moderate people were getting more and more frazzled. And the others—the ones who would say and do anything to have their names in the papers—their energy levels were rising all the time.

Kyo-san's muscles were as hard as a board, and there were several gristly nodes in the area between her left shoulder blade and spine. Martine worked on them slowly and methodically, the same as Makoto did for her when she was too tired to relax.

"By the way," said Kyo-san, head bobbing to the rhythm, "I've got some bad news about the Morikawa Leadership School. They don't want to see you."

"Really? Who did you speak to?"

"The head of the public relations department. He said they weren't accepting any requests from journalists. It's a top-level decision, apparently."

"That's interesting. Did you ask why?"

"He wouldn't give a reason. He was not at all polite, actually."

Martine blinked. A public relations department that didn't want any publicity. Perhaps that made sense for a school of leadership whose graduates preferred to remain in the shadows. She finished the massage with a flurry of little hand chops, then went to get some plates for the cakes. After laying them out, she sat down at her desk and called Shiina at the antique shop. She disliked herself for doing it, but this story couldn't be allowed to die.

"Thank you for the information you gave me last week. It was very useful."

"That can't be called information," wheezed Shiina. "It was just the personal opinion of a weak-brained old man."

There followed a crescendo of coughing at the other end of the phone. Shiina really did sound in bad shape.

"You mentioned the Morikawa School of Leadership."

"Yes, yes."

"I was thinking that might be a good subject for an in-depth article. I doubt if many of our readers have even heard of it."

"Yes, yes—a good idea. Many Japanese people are not aware of the Morikawa school either. Yes indeed—someone should write about it."

Another spasm of coughing, as rough and rasping as sandpaper. Martine pictured the state of his lungs and shuddered.

"It seems they are refusing to see any journalists," she prompted.

"Maybe that's wise. Journalists can cause a great deal of trouble."

"All we are doing is putting information in front of the public."

"And that is a dangerous thing. The public shouldn't have too much information, only what is necessary."

Shiina broke into another spasm of coughing, this time interspersed with laughter. They had had this conversation several times before.

"It's difficult to treat the subject properly without the school's cooperation."

"Yes, very difficult. Morikawa people don't like to cooperate with outsiders. They only cooperate with each other."

"So maybe I should drop the idea."

"And maybe you should not. Maybe you should show up there without an appointment and ask to see the deputy chief of the school. And maybe he will agree to see you."

"You think so?"

"Mmmm..." Shiina's next words were drowned in a gale of coughing. When he recovered, he started talking about a set of Genroku-era tea ceremony implements that had recently come into his possession. Martine made polite noises, but she wasn't really listening. She was thinking about a young French woman who lost her life in a car crash sixty years ago.

After putting down the phone, Martine prepared some coffee and sat chatting with Kyo-san about their favorite places in the world. Kyo-san, who was a keen golfer, dreamed of retiring to Hawaii. Martine talked about the grasslands of East Africa, which she'd last seen at the age of six. She still carried the images with her—the huge sky, the noise and color of the markets, the herds of animals. Occasionally she came across news items about the country of her birth, brief accounts of disease, violence, and political chaos. They barely registered with her. That was a different place entirely.

After their coffee break, Martine sat down at her desk and checked her messages. Two immediately caught her attention. The first one she opened was from her anonymous admirer.

> Dream angel,
> You do not need to know who I am. Just be sure that I am thinking of your beautiful golden body all the time. The next important thing is to avoid the Tachikawa area. There will be a big problem with falling objects.

Dream angel? Beautiful golden body? Stalkers were supposed to be wild and weird, their imaginations fired with perverse energy. This guy kept coming up with clichés, as if he were copying a bad translation of a nineteenth-century erotic novel. As for falling objects, what did that mean? With a sinking feeling, Martine recalled that Tachikawa was close to the American air base. She quickly typed her reply.

> Please tell me what is going to happen at Tachikawa.

After sending it, she opened the next message, which was from Makoto. It took her a while to focus on what he was saying. What with the Nozawa scoop, the leadership school interview, and now another prediction of disaster, she had completely forgotten about their little quarrel. How had it happened again? Oh yes—Makoto had displayed male insensitivity of the worst sort, humiliating her without even realizing it. "Thank you very much," indeed! The memory of his words set off another little surge of vexation. And now he had come up with some plodding apology.

Dear Martine,
I'm sorry I seem to have made you angry. I am doing my best to understand you, but sometimes it isn't easy. Don't you know that I care for you very much?
Very best regards,
Your Makoto

Martine didn't know whether to laugh, cry, or yell out in frustration. "Very best regards"—how pathetic could you get? It sounded like a bank manager calling in an overdraft. Martine wrote her reply quickly and stabbed the "Send" key, not even checking for typos.

Dear Makoto,
You can't apologize unless you understand what you're apologizing for.
Very best regards,
Your Martine

Kyo-san was staring at her, spectacles glinting. Sometimes she reminded Martine of her first Latin teacher, a kindly but strict methodist preacher.

"Is something wrong, Kyo-san?"

"I'm all right, but what about you? You've suddenly gone red in the face."

This was a problem that Martine had had since she was a teenager. Strong emotions—anger, pride, joy—showed up in her face straightaway. It was one of the reasons she was such a terrible bridge player.

"Oh—it's nothing. The stress is finally getting to me, I suppose."

"In that case it's your turn for a massage."

Kyo-san came over to Martine's chair. Martine quickly closed her mailbox. She dipped her head forward as Kyo-san's supple fingers dug into her clavicles.

"You poor thing," murmured Kyo-san. "The muscles here are all knotted up."

Not just the muscles, thought Martine. She closed her eyes and let the rhythm of Kyo-san's fingers work on her shoulders. But the tension wouldn't dissolve because she didn't want it to dissolve. It was a necessary part of being Martine Meyer, alive at this particular moment of history.

Mark Fletcher gazed down at the huge slab-like chest gently rising and falling—the only sign that his father was still alive. The eyelids were pale and waxy, the cheeks gray, the mouth slanting slackly to one side. Mark knelt down to the ruddy bacon-rasher of an ear.

"How are you doing there?" he whispered. "Can you hear me?"

There was no response but the bleep of the electrocardiogram and the twitching of the needles on the dials.

"What happened, Dad? You should have taken more care of yourself."

The wiry hairs inside his nostrils—silver-white, Mark noticed—quivered with the shallow breathing.

"You should have stayed with Mum. She was the only person who could keep you on the rails. Jenny could never do that for you."

There was a dry rattling sound from his father's throat, and one of the needles gave a sudden jump.

"That's a high-stress response," said David Liu, who had appeared in the doorway. "You'd better lay off for a while."

Mark followed Liu down the corridor to his office. Liu was a small, fussy man with a clammy handshake and a taste for gold jewelry. According to Mark's sources he had a growing reputation, though to say he was "the top man in his field," as Roger Mance had, was stretching it somewhat.

Liu's office was a spacious room with a picture window that framed central Los Angeles like a postcard—the skyscrapers glinting in the noonday sun, the blue sky scored by the vapor trails of a couple of jets. On the wall behind Liu's desk was a late-period de Kooning, the American flag bisected by a splash of red paint. Lining the interior wall was a display cabinet containing golf trophies, a photo of Liu with Tiger Woods, and another of him with the new president, who appeared to be giving him a kiss on the left cheek.

"Do you collect de Kooning?"

Liu smiled pleasantly. "Yes, I do. I think he's seriously undervalued."

"And you're politically active too?"

"Well, I had a modest role in the president's fund-raising activities here in LA. I'm a strong supporter of the president and everything she stands for."

"So are we, apparently."

"That's nice to hear."

David Liu hadn't caught the note of irony in Mark's voice. It was at Jenny's prompting that InfoCorp had swung its weight in favor of the president, making substantial contributions to her support groups and imposing a single cross-media editorial line. Previously, InfoCorp had always hedged its bets, but this time Jenny had insisted that there was only one possible winner. And she had been right.

"David, I'd like an honest appraisal of my father's condition. No bullshit, no false hopes. What's going to happen to him?"

Liu folded his fingers together under his chin. They were short, plump, well tended. He wore three rings, and a bracelet on each wrist.

"This is a complex condition, Mark. There's a whole range of potential outcomes, from quick recovery to long-term coma. Fortunately, your father has an immensely strong physique. On the other hand, the cerebral infarction was massive and there has certainly been brain damage."

"Enough to stop him working again?"

Liu leaned forward in his chair, still smiling pleasantly. "You said no false hopes, didn't you? Well, the reality is that your father is unlikely ever to talk again, and if he does talk he's not going to make any sense. Returning to work would be out of the question."

Mark's face felt as stiff as cardboard. An old man in a wheelchair sipping soup through a straw, unable to remember anything, unable to make himself understood—that wouldn't be his father. It would be someone else entirely.

The jet lag was just starting to hit when Mark arrived at the InfoCorp headquarters. This gigantic mirror-plated suppository had been the home of InfoCorp's American operations for the past three years. Before that InfoCorp had been based in New York. Under Jenny's influence, Warwick had decided that New York was too Atlanticist, too old economy, too Wall Street. The company needed to become more Asia-focused, more entertainment-driven, more tech-savvy. So, like an amoeba, the organization divided into two and, as Jenny put it, the twentieth-century businesses went to London and the twenty-first century businesses moved to Los Angeles.

Jenny was waiting for him in the club room, a recreation area designed to his father's specifications. It contained a long bar, billiard table, sauna, and a swimming pool with a glass side that looked out over the city from a height of two hundred feet. Last time Mark had been there his father had insisted on a race, the two of them splashing up and down the pool like a pair of kids. Mark, on the outside lane, had felt as if he were swimming across the sky. It had been a close race which Jenny, the judge, had scored to his father.

Today Jenny was wearing a black trouser suit bare at the shoulders. Her hair was shorter than Mark had ever seen it before, and she was wearing a pair of large thick-framed glasses which made her look like a studious, though intensely sexy, elf. That was one of the things about Jenny—every time you saw her she looked different. Her hair was different, her glasses were different, the lines on her face were different. Sometimes you could even swear her height was different. She could look small and demure or tall and domineering, depending on the look in her eye.

The look in Jenny's eye as she walked toward Mark, heels clicking on the parquet floor, was somber and self-possessed. She pressed her lips on his right cheek, leaving a trace of musky perfume.

"How was he?" she asked in her Mary Poppins British accent.

"According to the specialist, there's been no change in his condition. I don't know if that's good or bad."

"David said that? He's a good fellow, you know. Totally discreet."

Discretion had always been an important issue with Jenny. Although she had been jointly running one of the world's largest media companies for three years now, she had an intense distaste for media exposure. She rarely appeared at public events and would go to any lengths to avoid having her photo taken. There had been a minor scandal a few months ago when she had instructed her bodyguard to give an enterprising paparazzo a severe beating.

"I don't know how long you can keep this facade up, Jenny. The world is going to find out before too long."

"The world will be told what it needs to know, nothing more, nothing less. The markets are very volatile these days. We can't afford to panic them."

Mark nodded. He could guess what Jenny had in mind—persistent heart problems, a long period of recuperation, day-to-day responsibility handed over to deputy chairman Jenny Leung. And there was little he could do about it. The way the supervisory committee had been set up meant that Jenny and her stooges had complete discretion over top-level appointments. It would have to be approved by the group's shareholders, but serious opposition was unthinkable. Investors liked Jenny and her "look east" strategy. She was telling them what they wanted to hear.

"So what's happening with the spin-off and third-party placement that Dad was talking about?"

"Oh—it's coming along well."

"That's all you can say? It's coming along well?"

"Look, Mark, when it's finalized you'll be the first to know. That I promise."

Mark was about to say something about the quality of Jenny's promises— her promise not to dilute the family stake, her promise of joint ownership of the *Tribune*—but he checked himself. There was no point.

"How long are you planning to stay over here, Mark?"

"I haven't decided yet. My program's pretty flexible these days."

"How enviable!"

Now she was staring at him with ill-concealed hostility. She really did want him out of the way as soon as possible, thought Mark. She wanted to carry on unhindered with her carve-up of a business empire built by three generations of the Fletcher family. Well, he was not going to oblige her without a struggle. Now was the time to throw the dice.

"Jenny, I didn't come here to quarrel with you. I only want to do what's best for Dad. We both love him in our different ways, don't we?"

Mark imagined his father cackling with derision. He hated "soppy words" and sentimentality, whether in movies or in real life.

"Of course," said Jenny, suddenly doe-eyed and contrite. "After all, he's my husband."

Mark nodded. Her ability to switch moods never ceased to amaze him.

"You make a good couple. When I see you with him, I think of Daisy Buchanan."

Jenny's perfect brow creased into a frown. "Daisy who?"

"Oh, it doesn't matter. She's just a character in a movie."

"From our studio?"

"No, an old movie. I think it was black and white."

Jenny scrutinized him for a moment, then a smile of genuine amusement appeared on her face.

"Black-and-white movies, Mark? That's very good. That's very twentieth century. Next you'll be telling me you like New Orleans jazz!"

"Funny you should mention that. Not only do I like dixie, I used to play it at college."

"Did you now? What instrument?"

"Clarinet. They called me Hot Lips Fletcher."

"Hot Lips? That sounds intriguing."

The modest Jenny had now been replaced by the flirtatious, leg-crossing Jenny. This was the Jenny, guessed Mark, who had won his father's heart. She could turn on the sex appeal like turning on an electric light.

"Look, I'm only going to be around for a few more days. Why don't we have dinner one night? I'd like to clear the air with you in more relaxed circumstances. We've never had a chance to have a real heart-to-heart conversation."

"Well, Mark Fletcher, you're starting to surprise me. Does your dear wife allow you to have heart-to-heart conversations with strange women?"

"You're hardly a strange woman. You're my stepmother."

The electric light was on full blaze now. Jenny's eyes were suddenly shinier, her lips moister, her breasts as taut as a bowstring. "So your dear wife won't mind?"

Mark looked her straight in the eye. "What my wife thinks is irrelevant. I do what I want."

But Jenny really was a strange woman. There could be no doubt any longer. Fifteen years ago she had written a thesis on "The Construction of Identity in the Work of Scott Fitzgerald." But now she didn't even recognize the name of the heroine in Fitzgerald's most famous novel.

The conversation slid into easy small talk, and Mark left without even raising the subject of the third-party placement.

Thirty minutes later he walked through the hotel lobby like a zombie. The jet lag, the shock of seeing his father in the hospital, frustration with Jenny's scheming—all had hit him at the same time. He was barely aware of the man who got into the elevator with him, a heavily built Indian with a bandit moustache and a gleaming bald head. No sooner had the doors closed than the Indian swung around to face Mark. He looked even bulkier front-on, with immense forearms and a mountainous belly that drooped over his waistband.

"You're Mark Fletcher, aren't you?"

Mark backed away, measuring the distance between them. "Never mind about me. Who the hell are you?"

"I'm Ricky Patel."

"Ricky who?"

"Patel. I'm doing some research on your behalf. Don't you remember?"

It took Mark a few seconds to register the name of the detective who had been recommended by his friend at Kroll.

Patel raised the attaché case he was carrying. "Apologies for bothering you like this, but I've dug up something interesting. Of course if you'd rather discuss it another time..."

"Not at all," said Mark, suddenly re-energized. "There's no time like the present."

The elevator doors opened, and he led Patel down the corridor to his room.

FOURTEEN

There was another security alert at Tokyo Station and dozens of police with dogs were lined up at the ticket barriers. Martine gazed at the huge crowd of people waiting their turn to be searched and sniffed at and questioned. Most were sullenly obedient. They had been through these alerts many times, and they knew there would be many more to come.

Martine took her place in the crowd, which was shuffling forward at the pace of a yard every two minutes. The air was warm and fetid, filled with the hysterical blare of loudspeaker announcements. People were pressing in on all sides and you breathed their breath. You brushed against them and their sweat dried on your skin. It was the kind of situation that would drive you insane if you didn't know how to handle it. Japanese people were brought up to handle it, and Martine had learned the technique too. You had to let your consciousness dissolve and leave your body to shuffle through the sticky human density while your mind was somewhere else entirely.

A flick of the mental switch, and Martine was back at her desk, putting the finishing touches on the Nozawa interview. Then she was sitting on the train, preparing her questions for the deputy chief of the leadership school. Then she was talking to Makoto on the phone, explaining what a woman expected from a serious relationship. Then she was in her karate gear, facing off against the tall German. Then she was sketching, cooking, rollerblading, mapping out tactics for the next *shogi* game against Makoto...

And then suddenly she was at the ticket barrier. Twenty minutes had passed and she was standing there explaining what she was doing in Japan to a young cop fiddling inexpertly with a palmtop computer.

Martine's train eventually pulled out of the station an hour behind schedule and filled to two hundred percent capacity. Fortunately, Kyo-san had been able to get a reserved seat. Martine sat sipping coffee watching the crazed collage of Tokyo go rushing by her window.

It was a fine day, the kind of day when the world looks bright and clean and promising and it's hard to believe that anything could go wrong anywhere. She could make out children in a playground, a mother cycling along the sidewalk with a fat-faced baby in her front basket, diligent young salarymen hurrying to their next meeting. It was the same sort of scene that had greeted Martine's eyes when she came to Japan for the first time, almost twenty years ago. She had been a schoolgirl, here to spend the summer with Japanese friends of her mother. It had been the tail end of the era of growth, and everything she saw had delighted and fascinated her. Her next visit was six years later, to take a course in Asian political thought and brush up her language skills. By then the high growth era had given way to the period of stagnation, and the social mood had become more introverted and defensive. The next time Martine came was to take up the job with the *Tribune*. She was just in time to witness the brief flurry of optimism surrounding "structural reform," although it was strange to recall that now since it was those half-baked reforms that had plunged Japan into the crisis.

Since then the crisis had become so much an old friend that it was hard to imagine life without it. Financial crisis had spawned economic crisis which had spawned political crisis which had spawned social crisis. Manufacturing and agriculture, as well as the education, banking, pension, and health systems were all in a critical state. What's more, this was happening in the context of the steadily spreading global crisis. Martine had once read a book called *The Thirty Year Crisis*, about the period between the two world wars. What was happening now was something similar to the loss of coherence and collective nervous breakdown experienced during those years. Except that, thanks to technological progress, what once took thirty years could now be accomplished in five.

Martine finished her coffee and took her computer out of her bag. She needed to review her notes on the leadership school. First, though, she checked to see if there was a message from Makoto. He hadn't called or sent a message for more than a day now, and tomorrow he would be flying to London.

There was only one new message, and it wasn't from Makoto but someone called James Murphy. It took Martine a moment to recognize the name of her new boss. Murphy's message was short and to the point.

Dear Ms Meyer,
As you know I will be arriving in Tokyo at the end of the month to take up the position of bureau chief. My mission is to restructure the Tribune's coverage, giving our readers a focused, clearly defined message. It's no longer enough to tell people what is happening. We need to make them care about it. That means

having our own positions, controversial if need be, which we can present powerfully and consistently.

I have been reviewing the work you've done over the past year. You have managed to get hold of one or two quite interesting stories. Well done for that! It can't be easy for an inexperienced young woman operating more or less on her own. The trouble is, I don't get any sense of where the Tribune stands on the big issues. I hope you won't take this personally, but I feel your work needs a stronger intellectual framework. That is why I want you to send me all the stories you are intending to file for my prior approval and review. When I arrive in Tokyo, I will explain the changes to your role in the bureau. Yours,

J. J. Murphy

Martine gazed at the message in astonishment. "Well done for that!" "I hope you won't take this personally"—who on earth did the condescending bastard think he was? And he was seriously expecting her to send *her* stories—including the nuclear weapons scoop—for him to "review" and no doubt hack to pieces. He had to be joking! As for the changes to her role at the bureau, she didn't like the sound of that at all.

Martine deleted the message. It would be one of those unfortunate computer failures, a random error that caused a string of data to evaporate into thin air.

The Morikawa School of Leadership was located an hour and a half from Tokyo, in the foothills of the Japan Alps. From the train it looked like a huge flying saucer nestling in the forest. From the parking area where Martine was deposited by her taxi, it looked like a mausoleum of bone-white concrete. It was an impressive building, designed thirty years ago by Japan's most famous modern architect. According to the explanation on the website, the swooping curves of the roof were meant to symbolize "the synthesis of modern technology and traditional culture that is at the heart of the Morikawa philosophy."

The security guard at the gate squinted at Martine's namecard.

"You're a journalist? Have you got an appointment?"

Martine shook her head. "No appointment, but Professor Suematsu should be expecting me."

The guard looked suspicious, as well he might. Not for the first time, Martine wondered if this was really going to work. Did Shiina's influence stretch so far that he could get her into an organization that was refusing any contact with the press?

The answer was yes. Martine watched through the window as the security guard read the details of her namecard into a microphone. Then he nodded and gave a bow.

"Understood," she heard him say. He flipped a switch and the security gate swung skyward.

"Wait a minute," he grunted, leaning out the window. "Tell me, what size are you?"

Martine stared at him in amazement. "Size? What do you mean?"

"First you must put on a uniform. Everyone here must wear the Morikawa uniform."

"I see. Well, I'm medium size."

"Are you sure? You don't look medium."

"Medium will do fine," said Martine icily.

The security guard gave a gap-toothed grin. He turned to a wall cupboard and produced a neatly folded gray uniform and a locker key. "I hope it's not too tight," he said. Martine hastily put the uniform under her arm and walked quickly toward the changing room.

Inside was stiflingly hot, a reminder that old man Morikawa had been militantly opposed to air-conditioning, which he considered "wasteful" and "decadent." Martine had slipped off her blouse and was just unzipping her skirt when her eyes caught the video camera above the door. It was swinging toward her, red light blinking. Martine ducked under the line of vision, picked up a towel, and tossed it over the lens.

The uniform consisted of a peaked cap, belted tunic, and trousers made of a coarse linen that chafed her skin. On the back of the tunic was the Morikawa logo, and embroidered on the breast pocket were the letters DHD, which stood for the English words "Diligence, Harmony, and Duty." That had been old man Morikawa's favorite catchphrase, as well as the title of a magazine he had founded. Martine glanced at herself in the mirror. The uniform was indeed a little tight around the hips and breasts, and ringlets of blond hair were sprouting from the cap in all directions. She looked, and felt, like an actress in a lowbrow comic movie.

Professor Suematsu was waiting for her in the entrance hall, a dome-roofed sepulcher which was only slightly cooler than the changing room. Suematsu was a tall man of about sixty with piercing eyes and a shock of white hair. He was wearing blue overalls which hung loosely from his skinny body. Martine knew of him as an expert in bioelectronics and a tireless campaigner for lavish, government-financed research programs. His New Technology Institute in the north of Japan, celebrated for its work in bioelectronics, was funded partly by Morikawa Heavy Industries and partly by the government, though all patents were registered to Morikawa.

"Thank you for sparing the time to meet me," said Martine with a bow. "You must be very busy."

"Not so busy yet. The students won't be back for another two weeks."

"You mean they're on holiday?"

Suematsu gave a dry laugh. "There are no holidays here, Miss Meyer. It is the time of year when the students are away undergoing their life experience."

"Life experience?"

"Yes, it's a key part of our educational philosophy. The students don't just spend their time mastering theory, though of course that is essential. To become true leaders they must experience Japanese society directly, as a living, breathing organism. They must learn to understand it as a parent understands his own child. This is why we send them away for life experience three times a year."

Suematsu moved toward the elevator and pushed the call button.

"Interesting," said Martine, dabbing her brow with a handkerchief. "What kind of places do you send them to?"

"That depends on the personality of the individual. Usually we choose something that is as remote from their experience as possible. Last year there was a very shy and timid man whom we sent to join a gang of house-burglars. A tough judoka was sent to work as a hairstylist, and a very proper young lady, one who had been living with her parents all her life, was sent to a top-less bar in Roppongi. Others have become garbage collectors, fortune-tellers, factory workers, farmhands, every kind of occupation."

The elevator doors opened and Suematsu ushered her inside. Martine wondered how many leadership school students she had unknowingly encountered today. Maybe the homeless guy at the station had been one, or the taxi driver who brought her here, or even the security guy who had ogled her breasts so blatantly.

"By the way," said Suematsu, "this is all off the record, of course. We don't talk to journalists very often."

"Why not?"

"It's too much trouble. They don't understand what we are doing here."

"But don't some of your graduates go to work in the media?"

"Oh yes, many of them. Even so, they do not discuss the school. That's a matter of principle with us."

"But you don't mind talking to me?"

"In this case you're an exception."

An exception that—from his mournful tone of voice—Suematsu was far from happy to make. Martine wondered what wiles Shiina had used to set up an appointment that was so obviously unwelcome. Or to put it another way, what could have happened to put Professor Suematsu so much in Shiina's debt.

The doors of the elevator hissed open, and Suematsu led her down a corridor so gleaming white it looked as if it had been cleaned with toothpaste. At the end of the corridor was Suematsu's office, a large book-lined room looking out over the mountains. On the wall was a full-length portrait of old man

Morikawa, his wizened face glaring down fiercely at the increasingly undiligent and disharmonious world he had left behind.

Suematsu directed her to an armchair in front of the window, then disappeared into the next room. Martine heard him pick up a phone and bark an order for coffee. She gazed out the window at the thickly forested plain below. A couple of months ago Martine had done a story on that plain. It was a famous location for suicides, with dozens of bodies being discovered each year. In more romantic times the dead were usually heartbroken lovers; now they were unemployed salarymen, debtors on the run from loan sharks and even, increasingly, the sick and senile who had been led into the heart of the forest by their middle-aged children and left behind.

"So please tell me, Meyer-san—what is the purpose of your inquiries?"

Suematsu was back, holding a large paper fan bearing the DHD logo which he flapped vigorously in front of his glistening face.

"I'm here for some background research. I'm interested in the role of the Morikawa school in the current political turmoil."

"How do you know the school has any role?"

"It's common knowledge that many of Japan's most promising young politicians are graduates of the Morikawa school. Nobody pays much attention because they are spread across various different parties and factions and they have no record of working together. Until now, that is."

Suematsu's fan flapped a little more slowly. "Please continue."

"My information is that the Morikawa group of Diet members is preparing to join a distinct political unit—a new party led by a certain political celebrity."

Suematsu leaned back in his chair, his eyes narrowed to a glimmer. "You have some interesting information," he murmured.

"Thank you," said Martine, radiating humility. "Though I must say it struck me as rather a strange combination."

"Strange? Why strange?"

"Because Morikawa people are supposed to be elite technocrats, believers in economic efficiency and technological progress. This celebrity is a populist with fairly extreme, some would say unbalanced, ideas."

"In a time of national crisis all ideas must be considered, even the unbalanced ones."

"Even burning passports and taxing foreign luxury goods? Are those kind of measures going to create an economic recovery?"

A ghost of a smile passed over Suematsu's face. "Not by themselves of course, but that is not the purpose. You cannot have economic recovery without a recovery in national morale and self-respect."

"So that is Nozawa's role—to get the public excited while you technocrats do all the serious stuff?"

"That's one way of thinking about it."

"It isn't the way that Nozawa thinks."

"Perhaps not. But he is a sincere man who wants whatever is best for national recovery."

"Though what he thinks is best and what you think may be rather different."

"My views are well known to everyone. Japan needs to spend much more on technological research, according to clear guidelines set out by the government. We shouldn't be wasting money on luxury goods, whether foreign-made or homemade. We should be investing all we can in the future competitiveness of our industries. In that respect I can find many points of agreement with the views of Nozawa-sensei."

Martine nodded. The creation of an American-style military-industrial complex occupying a good-sized slice of GNP—no doubt Suematsu and Nozawa would see eye to eye on that too.

"Still, isn't it a rather risky strategy?"

"In what way?"

"Well, Nozawa isn't exactly a disciple of the Morikawa philosophy of harmony and discipline. What happens if you can't control him?"

Suematsu was fanning his face faster now, head cocked as the breeze ruffled his mop of white hair. "This is all hypothetical," he said. "Who knows what will happen anyway? There's a proverb that says, 'In the world of politics one step ahead is darkness.' Have you heard that one before?"

Martine nodded. She caught the change of tone at once. Suematsu had said all he was prepared to say, and the rest of the conversation would be on a different level of disclosure.

And so it proved. Suematsu went on to discuss the structure of research funding, the meaning of national pride, and old man Morikawa's views on excessive individuality. Martine tried to steer him back to the subject of Nozawa and his policy plans, but with no success. Suematsu had reverted to the role of a dedicated scientist with little interest in any other subject. The interview dragged on for another half an hour, but as far as Martine was concerned it was already over.

As Suematsu led her back down the pristine white corridor, Martine glanced at the photographs lining the wall. They commemorated the graduating classes of the last thirty years or so—ninety percent male, and one hundred percent fresh-faced, eager-eyed, and glowing with patriotic fervor. Suematsu appeared in most of them, standing with the other faculty members behind the rows of students on benches, his mournful features gazing owlishly at the camera. Martine paused to stare at the last photo in the series.

"What you see there is the future," said the real Suematsu from over her shoulder. "These youngsters will be the leaders forty, fifty years from now."

But Martine's eyes were not on the students. She was staring at the partially obscured face of the man standing next to Suematsu.

"Isn't that Yasuo Shimizu, the management consultant?"

Suematsu nodded. "Yes, that's right. He's a part-time lecturer here. He teaches a course on information technology and globalization."

There was something in Suematsu's voice that suggested that neither Shimizu nor the subjects he taught met with his approval.

"Is he a graduate of the school too?"

"He is not a graduate," said Suematsu brusquely. He turned toward the elevator and pressed the call button.

"So how did he come to be appointed to the faculty?"

"As I remember, he more or less appointed himself. After all, he is deputy chairman of the governing board."

Martine blinked in surprise. A slick-talking management consultant in his late forties lording it over a faculty of crusty old academics like Suematsu—that kind of generational leapfrog would be a surprise anywhere in Japan, let alone in a school dedicated to the values of social discipline and harmony.

"And how did Shimizu come to be appointed deputy chairman?"

Suematsu looked puzzled by the question. "How? Through family connections, of course."

The elevator doors opened, and Suematsu gestured for her to step inside. Martine stayed where she was, holding the door open with her hand.

"I'm sorry, I don't understand. Whose family connections?"

"Didn't you know? Shimizu is married to the great-granddaughter of Soichiro Morikawa. He is the family's representative here. Now I'm sorry, Meyer-san, but I have some examination papers to mark."

Martine stepped into the elevator and the doors closed on Suematsu's frowning face. So Shimizu was actually a member of the Morikawa family! That explained everything. Martine had always suspected he was a conduit for someone else's ideas. Now she was positive.

The senior Morikawa people must have been planning this for years. They had planted Shimizu in Nozawa's political office, and plugged him into the Morikawa network of bureaucrats, media people, and businessmen. Meanwhile, they would be busily fanning the fires of Nozawa's popularity. Then when the time was right—and that looked like now—their political representatives would come out into the open and join hands with Nozawa, professing great admiration and total agreement with everything he said. They would ride the wave all the way to political power, and then... And then what? And then they wouldn't need him any more. They would ally themselves with whichever of the mainstream factions accepted their terms, which would no doubt include a major share of the expanding defense budget for the Morikawa group. Forget about the stagnation of the market for consumer electronics. Here was a huge new opportunity that would continue growing for decades. It was neat. It was devious. It fitted together like a jigsaw.

It was mid-afternoon by the time her train rolled into the station. The security alert had been lifted—no nail bomb hidden in a trash bin, no beer bottle spewing out nerve gas—and everything was back to normal. That was typical of this crisis. It had a strange ability to switch itself on and off, to make you forget it even existed. You would be strolling through a prosperous part of the city, watching housewives shopping and school kids laughing, and the world would seem as orderly and benign as it had ever been and all thoughts of misery and damage would be like a bad dream that dissolves in the morning sunshine. Then you would see a homeless man slumped in a doorway, barking out a tubercular cough. Or a phone booth covered in stickers advertising child prostitutes. Or you would pick up a newspaper and get hit by the bad things happening everywhere, more and more each day—the stuff you didn't want to know but couldn't help absorbing, those fragments of crisis that lodged themselves deep in your soul.

Martine didn't go directly to the *Tribune* bureau; instead she stopped off at the office of McCallum, one of the best-known management consultancies in the world. Her contact there was the head of the Tokyo office, a jovial bear of a man called Haruki Kaneda. They had first met by chance in a karaoke bar in Nagoya. Kaneda loved singing karaoke, as well as guzzling whiskey, telling dirty jokes, playing pachinko, and slurping down spicy noodles, all of which they had both done to excess that night. Kaneda also had a doctorate in nuclear physics from MIT and was an accomplished classical violinist.

They met in his office, which was lined with pictures he had painted, photos of himself with various global leaders, and bookcases filled with his own books. Kaneda was not a modest man. He took a childlike delight in his own achievements that would have been intolerable in anyone who lacked his generosity, humor, and restless energy.

"Tell me what you want to know," said Kaneda, leaning back in his revolving chair, his huge hands wrapped behind his thick neck.

"What makes you think I want to know anything?"

"You journalists are one-pattern people. You're always after information that you're not supposed to have."

"It's our job. We can't help it."

"So what's the subject this time?"

"Management consultancy, actually. I thought that you'd be the best person to ask."

"I'm the only person to ask. Nobody else in this country really understands the dilemma of modern management. It's all analyzed in my latest book. Have you read it yet?"

Kaneda was waving a hand at a bookshelf containing copies of his latest book in half-a-dozen different languages.

"Of course," said Martine, as convincingly as she could. "It's fascinating stuff, the best management book in years. But the kind of analysis I'm looking for is not quite so theoretical. I need your professional opinion on a certain person."

"Which person?"

"Yasuo Shimizu."

"Hah!" Kaneda rocked forward on his chair, slapping the palms of his hands on his knees. Martine knew that the two men were arch rivals, as different in personality as they were in appearance. Kaneda was a bear, heavy-handed, gruff, and totally straightforward in everything he did and said. Shimizu was more like a Siamese cat, slender, elliptical, and impossible to read.

"First of all, how do you rate him as a management consultant?"

"Hmm ... that depends on your perspective. His writing is frankly banal, just a mixture of other people's concepts thrown together and spiced up with fashionable jargon. It's like a bowl of sukiyaki without any meat. On the other hand, he's a brilliant salesman, with a top-class record of bringing in business."

"Presumably he's got the companies in the Morikawa group locked up tight."

"Of course. His first big contract was developing an overseas production strategy for Morikawa Electric. That was when he was with Byrne and Company. When they saw the size of the contract, they had no choice but to make him a partner straightaway. Then a few months later he announced he was going to marry the granddaughter of old man Morikawa. That's what we call getting close to the customer!" Kaneda gave a throaty chuckle. It was obvious that he didn't take Shimizu too seriously.

"So his success was based on personal connections?"

"At first, yes. But soon he was winning new contracts from all sorts of companies outside the Morikawa group. Without him, Byrne and Company would never have gotten so big in Japan. You can see that now. As soon as he went independent, their share of the market collapsed."

Martine nodded. She couldn't help wondering what proportion of these new contracts had been allocated by anonymous graduates of the Morikawa school, occupying management positions across the industrial spectrum.

"And what do you think about this venture into politics? Do you think it will work?"

Kaneda shook his huge head. "From a theoretical point of view, I've got serious doubts. What Shimizu is attempting is a classic brand crossover, and nowadays this rarely works. Markets have become too dynamic. You may get a big short-term impact, but the brand value decreases as you lose focus. As a long-term strategy it doesn't make sense."

"So what would you suggest?"

"A brand overhaul, aimed at forging a new emotional bond with the market. Instead of just exploiting the old image of Nozawa the singer, I would make people respond to him in a completely different way. You have to be ruthless in marketing these days, Meyer-san. In order to build a new image, you have to kill the old one."

Kaneda's eyes were gleaming with enthusiasm. There was a serious risk that once he got onto this kind of subject you would never get him off.

"Very interesting," said Martine. "Thank you for all your help."

"All this is explained in detail in my new book. By the way, your review will be appearing soon in the *Tribune*, I suppose."

Martine smiled sweetly and rose to her feet. This was definitely the time to leave.

An ordinary day in an ordinary suburb of an ordinary town. A thick-necked young cop sat dozing in his police box, exhausted after a full night's work moonlighting as an enforcer for a loan-sharking company. A gaggle of middle school girls were squatting on the station steps, waiting for their customers to lead them to the cut-price love hotels lining the backstreets. A guy with a crewcut sat in his car, reading a manga magazine and listening to an old Nozawa song on the radio.

Outside the "50 yen" shop a man in a bow tie and tuxedo—stifling hot in this weather!—was yelling through a megaphone, frantically trying to drum up custom for the bargains on offer. At the bus stop an elderly man stood gazing into space, exactly as he had been for the past four hours. The electroluminescent tattoo on his forehead flashed brightly enough to be read from five yards away—"Noodle Heaven—all you can eat for ¥200!" Three steps closer and you'd be able to smell the alcohol, the only payment he got from Noodle Heaven for his work as a human advertisement.

On the other side of the street was a more expensive advertisement—a huge poster of Tsuyoshi Nozawa, three stories tall, wearing his headband and construction-worker trousers, his naked chest rippling as he held up a carton of fruit juice.

"Made with Tohoku's Most Delicious Apples," ran the slogan. "Not a Single Imported Drop!"

In a side street adjacent to the bankrupt Mitsukawa department store was parked a small white van. According to the logo on the side, it was the property of the maintenance division of NTKDI, the telecommunications monopoly that had recently been taken back into public ownership. A few hours ago two men in NTKDI uniforms had climbed the fire escape at the back of the department store, lugging a huge box of communications equipment. They had climbed all the way to the roof, host to an array of cellular base-stations. Without these base-stations, the cop would not be able to get his latest instructions from the loan-shark people, the middle school girls would not be able to communicate with their salarymen customers, and the guy with a crewcut sitting in his car would not be able to market his portfolio of designer drugs to the middle school girls. The proper maintenance of the base-stations was vital to the town's economy.

Suddenly the drowsy peace was broken by an ear-splitting roar. A silver arrow appeared in the sky, zooming directly toward the town. Nobody looked up. It happened almost every day at the same time, when the planes returned to base after a run over the Japan Sea. Strangers might have been disturbed by the noise, but the people of this town hardly even heard it any more.

Five hundred yards above ground level, Ray Rodriguez glanced out of his cockpit at the landscape below, the train tracks gleaming in the sunlight, the clusters of houses, the snub-nosed train disappearing into the tunnel like a snake sliding into a hole in a wall. It was like toyland down there, everything cute and clean and dinky. Rodriguez liked that about Japan. He liked the women too, and sometimes thought about marrying one and taking her back Stateside.

The shadow of the plane flitted across the field toward the town, beyond which lay the airfield with its runway stretching out to receive him. In a matter of seconds he would be on the ground, and then relaxing in a hot bath, getting ready for his Japanese language lesson. None of the other pilots bothered with these language lessons. They spent most of their free time on the base, and liked to hang out with English-speaking hookers. Rodriguez had different ideas. He wanted to travel around the countryside on his own, see what there was to see, and date ordinary girls with ordinary jobs, the kind who would take him home to meet their parents.

Rodriguez dipped a wing as he juddered through an air current. The voices of ground control were crackling in his ears, but he didn't need to listen. He had come in on this flight path dozens of times before. He could do it in his sleep.

He was about six miles from the town when he first realized something was wrong. The voices in his ears kept cutting up and disappearing under bursts of static. It was the kind of thing that might happen in stormy conditions, but not on a clear day like this. Then the emergency lights started flashing and his earphones went completely dead.

"We have a reception problem," he called into the mouthpiece. "Please shift to backup immediately."

There was no response. Then the head-up display vanished from in front of his eyes, and Rodriguez began to get scared. He glanced down at the instrument panel. Suddenly there was a fizzing noise, and then a blue flash.

"Holy shit!" he yelled. "I got system failure!"

Even if the ground people were listening, there was nothing they could do now. He was just a mile from the town, losing altitude fast. He was close enough to make out cars, and some billboard of a guy wearing a headband. He struggled with the instruments and tried to get the nose up. It was useless. The plane was out of control, homing in on the town like a missile. There was only one thing to do—eject.

Rodriguez crossed himself, closed his eyes, and hit the button. A blast of cold air knocked him backward, and his guts swapped places with his brains. For a moment he blacked out, then he heard the crump of the parachute opening and he was dangling in space, watching helplessly as his plane went hurtling toward the heart of the town.

"Please! Not there!"

There was a sound like a thunderclap as the plane smashed into the station and disappeared in a ball of orange flame. From his seat in the sky Rodriguez could hear the screams of the people below and see their tiny figures scurrying about.

"I'm so sorry. I'm so sorry."

Rodriguez was crying. Deep sobs convulsed his body as he slowly drifted down to earth.

Inside the station a curtain of fire was sweeping through the main shopping concourse, and clouds of toxic fumes were pouring into the underground passageways where the homeless were allowed to dwell. The entrance was a chaos of alarms and sirens and people with their hair and clothes on fire rushing screaming into the street.

Such was the confusion that nobody noticed the two NTKDI engineers climb down the fire escape of the Matsukawa department store, lugging their box of equipment. Nobody noticed them get into the little white van and drive away as if nothing had happened. Nobody bothered to call NTKDI and complain about the attitude of the company's staff. Even if such a complaint had been received, it wouldn't have been taken very seriously since, according to NTKDI's official records, those two engineers and their little white van didn't even exist.

FIFTEEN

Martine walked out of the karate dojo feeling like a squeezed dishcloth. The sparring session with the cop, Saya Miki, had been even more one-sided than usual. Saya was just too quick, too fit. She had such a wonderful figure too, not a pinch of flab on her waist. If she hadn't been such an all-round nice woman—friendly and intelligent, with a streak of dark humor—Martine might have suffered a few pangs of envy. Her own body was definitely losing flexibility, the muscle tone fading. And as for the sight of her bum in the mirror as she walked past—she hardly had the courage to take another look.

Outside, it was a sweltering midsummer morning. Already the sun was hammering down on the rush hour traffic, softening the tarmac and turning parked cars into ovens. Martine slipped on her sunglasses—white frames with big rectangular lenses that completely covered her cheekbones—and turned toward the subway station.

"Meyer-san! Meyer-san!"

Martine glanced across the street, where a tall guy in mirrored sunglasses was waving a long tanned arm. It took her a couple of seconds to recognize Ichiro, Makoto's son. In his jeans and cheesecloth shirt he looked more like a cool man-about-town than a fifteen-year-old studying for his exams.

"What's going on? Aren't you supposed to be at cram school?"

"I wanted to ask you something. Come and have a coffee."

Martine glanced at her watch. "All right. But I haven't got much time."

As she was crossing the road, she heard someone behind her call out, "See you on Sunday!" It was Saya, standing at the entrance of the dojo with a mischievous smile on her face. Martine smiled back, somewhat stiffly. It wasn't hard to guess what the dog-loving cop was thinking.

Ichiro pointed out a coffee bar, and they went inside. It was a fussily elegant sort of place, with a chandelier and circular glass tables and potted plants that had somehow adapted to the icy blast of the air-conditioning. All the other customers were female, mainly young office workers stopping for a sticky pastry and a browse of the gossip magazines before starting their day's work. The background music, hardly audible above the roar of the air-conditioning, was "One Hundred Million Dreams," one of Nozawa's chanson-style ballads. They took a table by the window and ordered iced coffee.

"So what do you want to know?" asked Martine. She was expecting another fiendishly complex question about European history.

Ichiro took off his sunglasses and slid them into the breast pocket of his shirt. He looked serious.

"I want to know if it's true," he muttered.

"If what's true?"

Ichiro's eyes flicked downward. "You know, about Dad and you."

"Dad and I what?" asked Martine, mystified.

"Dad and you getting married."

"Married!" exclaimed Martine, loud enough to be heard in the street outside. "Where on earth did you get that idea!"

"From Granny."

"It sounds as if your grandmother's imagination has been working too hard. There's no truth in it whatsoever, I assure you."

Just then the waiter brought the iced coffee. Out of the corner of her eye Martine caught him staring at her with a strange half-smile on his face. Everyone was smiling at her this morning, but they all had the wrong idea.

"Oh, I see," said Ichiro. He poured three spoonfuls of syrup into his coffee, then poked in his straw and took a long noisy suck. Disconcertingly, he had reverted to his schoolboy persona.

"So there's nothing at all to worry about," said Martine, patting him on the forearm.

"You don't understand. I wouldn't have been worried, I would have been happy."

Martine blinked at him in surprise. "Happy? Really? That's a very nice thing to say. Thank you very much."

"That's okay. But if Granny has got it wrong, then it doesn't matter. I just wanted to know the truth."

"Well, now you do," said Martine lightly. "Anyway, tell me about your history studies. Have you managed to sort out the difference between the ghibellines and the guelfs?"

For some reason she felt hot, despite the air-conditioning.

They sipped their coffee and discussed late medieval Italy. Martine caught a few sideways glances from people walking past the window. She couldn't blame then. A handsome adolescent having early morning coffee with a blond foreigner roughly twice his age—it was worth a closer look.

When they had finished their coffee—Ichiro's straw rootling amongst the ice cubes for the last drops of sweetness—Martine called for the bill. As they were leaving she asked the question that had been weighing on her mind all through the conversation.

"Tell me something. This strange idea that your grandmother had—where did it come from?"

Ichiro frowned, very serious again. His dark cheeks were as smooth as satin. Martine had an impulse to reach across the table and run her fingertips down them.

"I think it was when Dad told her about the move."

"The move?"

"Yes, Dad said he's looking for a bigger apartment. He said we're going to need more space, an extra bathroom and a room with plenty of light and big enough for lots more books."

"Oh," said Martine, suddenly at a loss for words.

"Why do we need an extra bathroom?" mused Ichiro, flicking a quiff of hair out of his eyes. When he was puzzled by something he looked so like Makoto— the same twist of the lips, the same jut of the jaw.

"I don't know," said Martine, getting up to leave. "You'd better ask your father."

Ichiro held the door open for her. As she walked through it, she was conscious of a dozen pairs of female eyes boring into her back.

Martine arrived in the office shortly after nine. Kyo-san was nibbling a rice cracker and watching the news on the wide-screen TV on the wall. A reporter was standing at the scene of yesterday's plane crash, interviewing a middle-aged man with his arm in a sling and a bandage covering the left side of his face.

"There was an incredible bang," he was gabbling. "Like a bomb exploding just above our heads."

"And where were you when it happened?"

"I was on the second floor, next to the ticket machines. I ran for the emergency exit, but flames were shooting out of the air vents. It was hell in there."

The scene shifted to the local hospital and an interview with the chief doctor, somber as he explained the technicalities of skin grafts and reconstructive surgery. Beside him the list of casualties scrolled down the screen—eight people dead, twenty-five seriously injured.

Martine's anonymous stalker had known this was going to happen. He had known the place and he had known the time. But how? How could anyone forecast a random event like a plane crash? The only plausible answer was that it wasn't a random event, that someone had made it happen.

Now the scene was the Diet building and an interview with the chief cabinet secretary, a wrinkle-faced veteran of innumerable factional squabbles and backroom deals. He mumbled a few words about "regrettable events," "full investigation," and "cooperation with the American authorities." The next interview was with Nozawa, a live link with the TV studio in his villa in the trendy Denenchofu district. He was dressed more conservatively than Martine had ever seen him before, in a dark suit and an immaculate silk shirt. The only trace of his showbiz persona was the "nZw" insignia on his tiepin. He was glowering with indignation, his eyes hard and bright.

"This kind of cowboy hooliganism cannot be tolerated. The pilot should be charged with murder, and the commanding officer of the base must take full responsibility."

"The US authorities have already expressed deep apologies. Do you think that is sufficient?"

"Absolutely not! This is Japan, not America. The Japanese people are demanding that the Americans apologize in the traditional Japanese way. The commanding officer must visit the houses of every single victim, get down on his hands and knees, and beg for forgiveness! This is the least he can do."

"And how do you see the future of the air base?"

"Future? It has no future! We the Japanese people demand that it be closed down as soon as possible. The Americans' real reason for keeping these bases is obvious to everybody. They talk about regional stability, but their real purpose is to stop Japan becoming an independent nation again. They want to keep those little yellow monkeys safely locked up!"

The next shot was an aerial view of the damaged station building. There was a huge hole in the glass frontage where the plane had smashed clean through. Martine picked up the remote control and switched off the volume.

"Unbelievable," muttered Kyo-san softly. "Just think of those poor people in the station, peacefully going about their daily business. Then suddenly the whole place goes up in flames, just like a war zone."

Martine didn't say anything. She could guess what was on Kyo-san's mind —the fire bombing that had burned Tokyo to a cinder in the summer of 1945. A baby at the time, she had been rushed to safety in a papoose on her mother's back. Kyo-san claimed to remember the huge orange flames dancing from building to building and the showers of cinders flying in the wind. Martine doubted whether those were real memories—more likely they were images from photos and books and the words of the grown-ups around her; but Kyo-san had made them part of her life story, and the emotions they excited were powerful enough. In that sense they were as authentic as any newsreel.

"All these fighter planes and bombs and weapons—we don't need them here in Japan. All we want to do is live in peace."

Kyo-san's unconditional pacifism was dying out with her generation, the last to have any personal experience of war. And the comfortable world of that generation was changing too. If Gary Terashima was right about the reorientation of US foreign policy—the big sayonara, as he called it—unconditional pacifism was going to be an untenable option. Nozawa had grasped this instinctively. He was riding with the tide of history.

Which reminded Martine that she hadn't checked the interview yet. The *Tribune*'s online edition should have appeared already. She switched on her monitor and went straight to the front page. There it was, in big, bold headlines that screamed out of the middle of the screen.

Japan's Nuclear Blackmail

Prominent Japanese politician Tsuyoshi Nozawa yesterday threatened the world with a new arms race. Nozawa, a radical right-winger committed to restoring Japan's prewar glory, revealed in an exclusive interview with our Tokyo correspondent that he plans...

The style was more sensational than she had expected—closer to tabloid than the *Tribune*'s usual stodgy prose. Still, she couldn't complain. It was a huge spread, the largest she had ever been given. And alongside was a four-column photo of Nozawa, scowling theatrically with arms crossed.

Martine clicked onto the features page and scanned the interview itself. Miraculously the copy editors had left it more or less intact. There were no misprints, no cuts, no jumbled grammar where three sentences had been squashed into one. She was basking in satisfaction when suddenly she noticed that something was missing. There was no byline at the head of the piece! In fact there was no mention of Martine Meyer anywhere.

Martine gave a little groan of disappointment. Of course everyone who mattered would know who had written the piece—there was no other correspondent, now that Charlie had gone—but even after five years on the paper Martine still got a buzz out of seeing her name on a story. And this was no ordinary story; it was by far the biggest of her career.

Out of habit she clicked through the letters section, then the editorial column. To her surprise, the Nozawa interview was the subject of the lead editorial, feebly entitled "Just Say No to Nozawa." That was strange, to say the least. Japan-related editorials were usually supplied by the Tokyo bureau. If for some reason that didn't happen, there would still be lengthy consultation between Martine and the editorial team. So who had written this piece? It certainly didn't read like the work of the gay Winchester-and-Oxford man who covered the Japanese economy.

It is high time that the international community woke up to the very real dangers of Japanese ultranationalism. The man who is now threatening the world with nuclear catastrophe is not some right-wing kook, but the most popular politician in Japan. It goes without saying that this outrageous show of aggression must be opposed with full vigor. We call on the UN, the G8, and the United States Congress to make it absolutely plain that the Japanese threat to regional stability will not be tolerated. The right response is to hit them where it hurts—through coordinated restrictions on Japanese exports and imports of raw materials. Major corporations have an important part to play also, and NGOs should organize a program of dramatic direct action. If history has taught us one thing, it is that the only sensible policy toward a rogue state is bold, uncompromising defiance...

Martine gazed at the screen in horror. "Rogue state"—what a ridiculous concept! The *Tribune* was putting Japan—which even after years of crisis was still one of the richest countries in the world—on the same level as places like Libya and North Korea. And as for the "program of dramatic direct action"— that was akin to an incitement to terrorism. Fire bombing fast-food restaurants, kidnapping scientists—these were some of the forms of direct action that had been in the news lately. Whoever had written this editorial must have been drunk at the time. And the worst thing of all, the thing that made her tremble with anger and humiliation, was that people would believe the person responsible was Martine Meyer!

"Is something the matter?" asked Kyo-san. "You've gone as red as a tomato."

"I'm fine, thanks."

"You need to be sensible, Martine. Too much stress can be harmful, particularly for a woman your age. You've got to take care of yourself, make sure your hormonal balance doesn't get upset."

"Hormonal balance?"

"It can happen," said Kyo-san grimly. "I had a friend who wasn't much older than you. She was working like a dog, day and night, trying to support her lousy husband."

"And then what?"

"And then nothing. She woke up in the morning one day, and it was all over. She knew it straightaway."

Martine nodded. She didn't need to ask the identity of the "friend."

"By the way," said Kyo-san. "There was a call just before you came in, some guy with an Irish name."

"You mean James Murphy, the new bureau chief?"

"Is he? Well, he didn't introduce himself, in fact he wasn't at all polite. He just said you need to check your mail receiver, and no mistakes this time."

Martine's eyes flicked back to the screen and the grotesque "No to Nozawa" editorial. Now she understood what had happened. It was Murphy in Washington who had written the editorial. It was Murphy who had removed her byline from the interview. As promised, he was "refocusing the *Tribune*'s coverage," providing the readership with "a strong and clear message about Japan." The fact that the message was ill-written, ill-informed, and absurdly wrongheaded was beside the point. At least it was strong and clear.

Martine opened the mail folder. As expected, there was a message from Murphy, received just half an hour ago.

Ms. Meyer,
It appears you ignored my instruction to send me all your stories for prior review. Fortunately I managed to catch this one just in time and exploit its potential. I warn you that as bureau chief I have full authority over all personnel matters in Tokyo. If you disobey an instruction again, the consequences will be severe.
Regards,
J. J. Murphy

Kyo-san's voice sounded from the other side of the room. "What's the matter, honey? You look terrible."

"Quite possible," answered Martine darkly. If history had taught her one thing, it was that the only sensible policy toward guys like James Murphy was uncompromising defiance.

She deleted his message and on impulse dashed off a couple of lines to Makoto.

Get back here, you silly man. I miss you terribly. I miss your touch and your taste.

She sent it off straightaway, deliberately giving herself no time to change her mind.

The press conference had been called for three o'clock in the afternoon, which would give the evening talk shows enough time to rewrite their scripts and get hold of the right kind of commentators. The venue was unusual for a major political event—not a hotel or lecture hall, but the Tokyo Dome. The press and TV people—from giggling female newscasters in microminis to silver-haired political editors—had to shove their way through the crush of Nozawa fans waiting for the evening concert. Many had been waiting since the morning, and some had brought sleeping bags and spent the night there. The word had gone out that something special was going to happen. There was a buzz of excitement amongst the press people too. The invitation had come at short notice, and nobody was sure what to expect.

Martine knew, though. It was the launch of the new political party, with Nozawa as the figurehead, graduates of the Morikawa leadership school supplying the organization, and grassroots support coming from every Japanese citizen who had ever hummed a Nozawa song. The "National Regeneration" tour was kicking off with five successive nights at the Tokyo Dome. As Nozawa had explained at the first interview, it was the optimum time for the official announcement.

The last time Martine had been inside the Dome was to cover the mass wedding of ten thousand couples who had never even met before their nuptials. That had been a strange event, but this was even stranger. In this huge artificial space, where the grass was always green though the rain never fell, where foreign rock groups had cavorted and baseball players had smashed home runs—here, for better or worse, a new chapter in Japanese history was about to open. This was a country that had played safe for so long, clinging to the status quo like a toddler to a blanket. Now it was getting ready to play risky. You didn't have to be of Kyo-san's generation to feel nervous about the consequences.

Martine made her way to the enclosure that had been prepared next to the main stage. Nozawa and his staff were already seated at a long trestle table equipped with microphones, bowls of fruit, and bouquets of red roses. Nobody was saying anything, but already the air was full of the flicker of strobes and the fizzing of camera shutters. Martine reckoned there were about three hundred media people present, including several dozen camera crews, who had elbowed their way to the front. Apart from the mainstream media, there were TV comedians, literary critics, music journalists, online data suppliers already tapping away at their tiny keyboards, correspondents from *Business Week*, the BBC, and *Le Globe*, France's most prestigious daily. It was an impressive turnout, testament to the fact that Nozawa was the biggest news in the Japanese political world for years.

Nozawa sat silently gazing into space. On his right was Shimizu, and on his left Yamazaki, who was just back from a digital son-et-lumière show in Venice. Martine recognized several of the others, including Professor Suzuki of Tokyo University and Yasutani, the manga writer with an uncanny knack for making sensational archaeological finds. She wondered how many of them had connections with the Morikawa school. According to Kyo-san's research, Suzuki had been a part-time lecturer there almost a quarter of a century ago, just before he got the professorship. As for Yasutani, both the producer of his TV show and the chief editor at his publishers were Morikawa graduates.

Shimizu stood up and called for silence. He spoke with the slick plausibility that was the defining characteristic of every management consultant Martine had ever met.

"Welcome everybody. It is a great honor to see all the most famous and important faces in the media world gathered here before us. The reason we have invited you is simple. We want you to celebrate a birth. The birth of a new political party, the birth of the new Japan."

That cued in the opening chords of "Also Sprach Zarathustra," overlaid with the squelchy trance-dub beat that Yamazaki had made famous. The black curtain at the back of the platform parted, revealing a long line of men in dark suits. They formed a row at the back of the stage and made a deep, perfectly synchronized bow. There was a murmur of surprise from the assembled journalists as they recognized so many of Japan's prominent young politicians together in one place. Conservatives and reformers, representatives of rural areas and depressed industrial suburbs, spokesmen for the Buddhists and the environmentalists and the trade unions and the bankers and the software industry—all standing in line, committing themselves to Nozawa.

Above them hung a giant video screen bearing the image of Nozawa dressed up as Ryoma Sakamoto, the samurai hero who inspired the Meiji Restoration and got assassinated for his pains. Nozawa/Sakomoto was holding a gleaming sword; strands of disorderly hair fell over his face; and his cherry-red lips were pursed in an expression of furious concentration. Underneath, written in blood-red characters, was the phrase "National Regeneration Party." Of course, thought Martine. What else would you call it?

Now it was the turn of the real Nozawa. He stood there smiling, microphone in hand, apparently surveying the audience one by one. When he spoke, it was in the husky half-whisper that had his young female fans squealing.

"Before I explain what we're going to do, let me explain why we need to do it. Let me take you back many decades, to a small fishing village looking out over the sparkling ocean, a young woman bending down in a rice field, a four-month-old baby on her back..."

Martine knew the story. She had read the manga, seen the movie, heard similar words sung over a lush orchestral backing, a pulsing reggae beat, and the thundering chords of thrash-metal. The baby was Nozawa. The village was his paradise of lost innocence and tranquillity, where human beings lived in harmony with each other and with nature, where the women were pure and beautiful and willing to wait forever, and the men were honest and strong and were sincerely sorry about breaking the women's hearts and moped about it ever after in big-city karaoke bars. Martine was sure that no such village had ever existed. It was beyond nostalgia, it was myth, and like all myth it felt more real than your own life. The boy standing on the beach, waiting for his father's boat to return, the cranes flying north under a silver moon, the stationmaster saluting the last train that would ever leave the station, a single tear glistening in the corner of his eye—these images were imprinted on the nation's consciousness in songs like "Mama's Miso Soup," "Where have all the fireflies gone?" and "This land is the land of the gods."

While Nozawa talked, Martine checked through the press pack that each journalist received at the entrance. It contained the three most recent CDs, each personally autographed on the cover, the new videogame, and a glossy brochure explaining "The Road to National Regeneration." This was a slick summary of Nozawa's pet themes—cultural pride, moral education, patriotic investment, industrial recovery, and so on. In each case there was a quotation from a Nozawa song, a glossy photo of a happy family engaging in a Nozawa-approved activity, and then a few paragraphs sketching out the new policies. "Agricultural Restoration" was a theme that Martine hadn't come across before. First came the quotation:

Every grain of rice is a treasure
Every grain of rice contains our ancestors' sweat
Every grain of rice contains Japan

Then underneath was a picture of a smiling mother teaching her daughter to make riceballs. The policy itself was typically radical and typically vague. Apparently, unused rice paddies were to be bought up by the government and distributed free to unemployed workers, who would then receive agricultural subsidies instead of social security payments. There were no targets, no numbers, no details at all.

Martine flicked through the brochure until she came to the page explaining the membership and structure of the National Regeneration Party. It was as she expected, with Nozawa as party leader and Morikawa graduates filling out the three key party positions of secretary general, chairman of the policy affairs council, and deputy leader. She was surprised to note that Shimizu had been appointed deputy leader of the party. That was strange since he was not even a Diet member.

On stage, Nozawa was moving into the most emotional part of his speech —his vision of the future. This too was familiar stuff. The nation was to be united like a huge family, everyone working together harmoniously, no more strife and greed, no more wasteful consumption, society as perfect and pure as described in his idealistic megahit ballad, "Remember."

When he had finished there was a moment of silence, then rapturous applause from the audience. Silver-haired editors, sexy young newscasters, pony-tailed cameramen, all were visibly moved. One thing was obvious straightaway—the National Regeneration Party was going to get a soft ride from the mass media.

Next it was time for the Diet members lined up behind Nozawa to have their moment in the spotlight. Each man stepped forward as Shimizu called his name, bowed, and muttered a few bland slogans—"I'll give my all for the future of Japan," "Let's build a better tomorrow," "The Japanese dream, one more time!" If the idea was not to upstage Nozawa, it worked superbly. They sounded sincere, pleasant, and deeply dull. Martine wondered how long it would take for the "Agricultural Restoration" and Nozawa's other pet schemes to be sidelined in favor of the Morikawa school's real agenda.

Only fifteen minutes were left for questions. The *Tribune* interview had hit the streets just a few hours before, but it was already the talk of the town. Inevitably, the first questions focused on the nuclear weapons issue, and just as inevitably Nozawa batted them away with clichés about "keeping all options open," and "responding flexibly to dynamic changes in the international environment." He had broken the taboo—for the moment that was enough. The questions moved on to the restoration of lifetime employment, the tax subsidies for filial piety, and the plan for a new military college.

Martine waited right until the end before standing up to ask her question. She was aware of every other journalist in the room scrutinizing her, probably wondering what she had got up to with Shimizu in order to earn the scoop.

"Shimizu-san, I see that you are taking up the position of deputy leader of the new party. First, let me offer my congratulations."

"Thank you very much, Meyer-san. And congratulations to you on your excellent work in today's *Tribune*."

They had already spoken about this. Surprisingly, Shimizu hadn't been at all upset by the hostile editorial.

"Please forgive my ignorance," continued Martine, "but how can a non-politician take on the role of deputy leader?"

"No problem," was Shimizu's suave answer. "The deputy leader has no specific area of responsibility. It's largely a ceremonial role."

"But how can you have even a ceremonial role if you're not a member of the Diet?"

"Ah, but I will be a member very soon. One of the gentlemen behind me has decided to retire for health reasons, and he has asked me to take over his constituency. The by-election will be held next month."

Martine made a bow of acknowledgment and sat down again. "Health reasons" indeed! It was a blatant fix, a way for Shimizu to surf to power in the shortest possible time. Once in the Diet he could keep a close watch on the party "leader," making sure he followed the Morikawa line at all times. And when the first Nozawa administration was formed, he could slot quite easily into a junior post—minister of culture, perhaps, or chief of the environment agency. Martine realized just how much she had been underestimating Shimizu. He wasn't just a mouthpiece for other people's ideas. He was the lynchpin of the whole project.

The press conference ended with a saké toast to the future of the new party, and everyone in the audience raised the little cup—emblazoned with "National Regeneration" on one side and "nZw" on the other—and shouted "*Kampai!*" Tickets for the evening concert had been handed around, but Martine decided not to stay.

Outside she met the correspondent of *Le Globe*, and they walked to the station together. During the ninety minutes of the press conference, the number of Nozawa fans waiting outside seemed to have doubled. Among them were dozens of look-alikes in headbands and construction-worker trousers, playing guitars, banging taiko drums, flying digital kites that dipped and swerved overhead, blaring out Nozawa songs and flashing images of his face.

"I was fascinated by your editorial," said Alain Lemaitre in his sternly courteous French. "Might I be forgiven for viewing it as a departure in certain ways from your established approach?"

Lemaitre was a dapper, handsome graduate of the Ecole Normale Supérieure with a well-developed taste for Japanese porcelain, noh theatre, and teenage boys. His dispatches from Tokyo were fact-free zones, tending instead to reflect at length on such topics as "Cultural self-definition in a hyper-capitalist social context."

"I had nothing to do with that," said Martine. "We have a new bureau chief who has some rather simple ideas."

"Ideas? I'm not sure I would call them ideas. Anyway, my own articles have taken a different line. I believe that Nozawa symbolizes the ascendancy of the cultural sphere over the economic sphere and the inevitable decay of the unipolar ultraliberal world view."

"You mean he annoys the Americans."

"Exactly. And this of course is to be celebrated. Even the problem of nuclear weapons that your editor makes such a fuss over—in my view, a Japanese *force de frappe* is not to be blindly opposed. The desire to defend one's cultural autonomy is rational and necessary. De Gaulle thought exactly the same way."

"It's going to create instability."

"Instability is something we must learn to embrace. It is an inevitable side effect of our evolution to a multipolar structure of values."

"As in Romania, I suppose."

Martine couldn't resist the jibe. Today's *Tribune* had carried stomach-churning reports of a new massacre, carried out by one of the rebel groups that the European forces had been sent to protect.

Lemaitre shrugged. "Romania is a messy business, but at least Europe is finally acting as an independent cultural entity. In historical terms this is a healthy development."

Martine raised an eyebrow, but said nothing. Only a French intellectual would be capable of describing a bloodbath as a healthy historical development.

"Getting back to Nozawa—are you really as enthusiastic as you sound?"

"Yes, indeed. Nozawa will be an important figure in Asia, and a natural ally of European interests. We must cultivate him carefully. Now that his party has been launched, he will be officially invited to Paris and Brussels in the near future. Also there is a high probability that the Académie Française will make him a *chevalier d'ordre des lettres.*"

"Don't you have to be a writer for that?"

Lemaitre frowned at her ignorance. "Not at all. Several foreign musicians and film directors have been made *chevaliers.* The honor is open to any artist willing to stand up for the values of cultural autonomy."

"I see. And who arranged the nomination?"

"I did," said Lemaitre, allowing himself a tiny sphinxlike smile.

They walked past a darkened Starjacks outlet that had been closed down pending investigation and crossed the street. The area around the station was seething with fans and ticket touts calling out prices. Martine was amazed to hear that the going rate for a ticket was more than a week's wages for an average worker. Shimizu's publicity offensive had been superbly effective.

Martine said good-bye to Lemaitre, who was off to make an early start on the Shinjuku nightlife. This crisis suited him fine, much better than the tedium of bourgeois prosperity. The best restaurants were always half empty, antique porcelain was getting cheaper and cheaper, and the rent boys were much better educated. The opportunities to "embrace instability" were frequent and cheap.

The train doors opened, and twenty Nozawa look-alikes spilled out onto the platform. Martine had never seen so many different Nozawas in one place. There were tall Nozawas swinging their bony arms, short square-hipped Nozawas, smooth-faced fifteen-year-old Nozawas, tough middle-aged Nozawa's with bulging biceps and hairy forearms, even one or two female Nozawas with their hair pinned up under rising sun headbands.

Nozawa was everywhere, Nozawa was everyone. He was a fruit-juice salesman, a rocker in a leather jacket, a crooner in a tuxedo, an idealistic folksinger holding hands with his girlfriend, an auto worker brandishing a welding tool, a farmer bent over in a rice paddy. He was your brother, your father, your lover. He was Charles de Gaulle or Ryoma Sakamoto or Saddam Hussein. He was whatever you wanted him to be.

Martine went straight back to her apartment and had a shower. She pulled on a new pair of denim shorts and a Tintin T-shirt that Makoto had bought for her at the Tintin museum in Brussels. It showed Tintin running with notebook in hand, Snowy yapping at his heels. "My favorite journalist—until I met you, that is," said Makoto. A double-edged compliment, but she was used to those by now.

She did some stretching exercises, then made herself a long glass of mint tea, and took it out onto the balcony.

It was her favorite time of day, the sun sliding toward the horizon, moving a little closer every time you looked away. The eastern half of the sky was indigo, with a sliver of moon already surprisingly high. One by one the neon signs were flickering into life, pulsing and twisting and fizzing, turning the city into a vast electronic book. It made you feel cooler somehow, though the temperature hadn't changed at all.

Only when the sun had gone did Martine go back inside, ready to face an evening's work. There were two messages waiting on her answering machine. The first was from Makoto, asking in rather hurt tones why she hadn't been in touch. He had obviously called before reading the provocative e-mail she'd sent him that morning. The second message was from Kyo-san, warning her not to come back to the office. Apparently the phone hadn't stopped ringing since she left. Amongst the dozens of people demanding to talk to her about the Nozawa interview were a senior official of the Defense Agency, a staffer from the Senate Foreign Relations Committee, Gary Terashima of the US Embassy, and the producer of InfoCorp Network News, calling in person from the command center in Los Angeles. Martine was in no mood to talk to any of them. She did try to get hold of Makoto—it would have been nice to give him the same message over the phone, and to listen to his embarrassed but secretly delighted struggle for words—but he had already left.

Martine poured herself another glass of mint tea and switched on the computer. There were dozens of messages, most of which she deleted unread. Just as she was about to close the mail folder a new message arrived. It had no title or name.

Sweet angel,
That was a brilliant piece about Nozawa in today's paper. All the same it is not worth wasting too much time on this story. Soon he will not be able to cause any more problems. Incidentally, those blue shorts suit you so well. What color panties are you wearing underneath?

An icy finger ran down Martine's spine. Blue shorts? She'd never worn them before in her life. Which meant one thing—he must be out there right now, watching her.

She rushed to the window and jerked the curtains shut. For a moment she stood there frozen to the spot. What should she do? Call the police? Call a security company? She made a little gap in the curtains and peered down at the street. There was the usual throng of people, a few standing outside the convenience store, a few more waiting at the bus stop. But he didn't have to be at ground level. He could be in that big office building, staring out of one of the windows. Or he could be further away, lying on a rooftop with a pair of infrared binoculars. After all, this man was no ordinary stalker. He foretold plane crashes and mass poisonings and explosions in chemical plants. And the only way he could possibly have foretold these things was if he was actually involved in making them happen.

The telephone rang, and Martine practically jumped out of her skin. She let it ring five times then, hands trembling, picked up the receiver. There was nobody at the other end, just clicks and buzzes.

"What do you want?" she whispered

"What's going on over there? Your voice sounds very strange."

It was Makoto, calling from London. Martine breathed a huge sigh of relief. For a moment she felt like spilling out everything, the stalker at the window, the plane crash, the predictions... The predictions! What about the new one? "Soon he will not be able to cause any more problems"—what was that supposed to mean?

"Martine, is something wrong? I can't hear you. Please say something."

Makoto's voice sounded strained, genuinely worried. At that moment Martine knew that she wasn't going tell him anything. If she did, he would want her to drop the story immediately, and then she would have to refuse because she couldn't drop a story with this potential. Every journalistic fiber of her being rebelled at the idea.

"Oh—I'm sorry. My mind was somewhere else."

"Work?"

"Yes, kind of."

"I see. Well, I was just calling to say that I miss you very much."

"Yes, I miss you very much too."

Martine was finding it hard to concentrate. The man watching her on the balcony—how long had he been watching her apartment? How many times had she passed him on the street without knowing?

"I want to get back as soon as possible. I've got important things to say, but it's difficult to talk on the phone."

"Yes, it's difficult."

Martine's eyes were fixed on the computer screen. She needed to answer the stalker immediately, draw him in closer, get him to give away more...

"I'm sorry if I'm clumsy with words sometimes. I was brought up to be

177

clumsy with words, just as you were brought up to be graceful..."

"Don't worry. It doesn't matter."

"It doesn't matter?"

"No, I understand you."

Now they were talking in clichés, saying nothing. Martine sensed his discomfort and ended the conversation as soon as she could. This really wasn't the moment.

She sat down at the computer and batted out a fast reply.

> Why are you following me around? And what else do you know about
> Nozawa?

The answer came immediately.

> I am interested in you because you are the most beautiful journalist in the
> world. As for the Nozawa situation, the key to everything is the Atami incident.

Martine got up and peered through the curtains again. There was a man at the bus stop fiddling with his mobile phone. That could be him. But what about the young guy squatting in front of the convenience store, also fiddling with a mobile, now raising his head and gazing straight at her apartment? That could be him too, as could the man in shirtsleeves at the window of the office building, or the driver of that parked van. He could be anywhere.

Martine sat down again. Her fingers flew over the keyboard.

> I want to know more. Why don't we meet somewhere and discuss it?

What would Makoto say if he was looking over her shoulder right now? Would he be appalled by her recklessness? She put the question out of her mind and sent the message before the guilt had time to settle.

Tonight demure Jenny Leung and stern businesslike Jenny Leung were nowhere to be found. It was raunchy Jenny all the way, right from the moment she opened the door of the Beverly Hills house and, in full view of the Filipina housemaid, slipped her arms around Mark's neck and her tongue into his ear. Then she broke away with a giggle.

"Isn't my stepson cute? He's so different from his father, it's unbelievable."

"What's so different?" asked Mark, stepping into the house.

"For one thing, you're a gentleman with women, whereas your father is a complete ruffian. He just takes what he wants whenever he wants it."

"I see."

Mark didn't see, and he didn't want to see. The thought of what his father got up to with Jenny was something he had learned to blank out of his mind.

"I invited some friends for dinner. I think you'll find them quite amusing."

This was unexpected. Mark had envisaged a lengthy, gently probing conversation with Jenny. Now he found that there were four other people seated around the pool waiting for him. Two were instantly recognizable—Flic Marsden and Candi di Lucci, the young stars of *Glory over the Pacific*, the biggest hit that InfoCorp's movie subsidiary had produced in years. There was even talk of an Oscar for Flic's portrayal of a heroic young pilot and another for Anthony Hopkins' portrayal of General MacArthur.

The other two were from the INN cable channel, a senior editor and a newscaster with pneumatic lips and breasts that defied the laws of gravity.

They drank cocktails by the side of the pool and chatted about movie people and TV people and who was on the way up and who was on the way down. Then Jenny arrived with a silver tray carrying a silver box. Mark lifted the lid and gazed dubiously at the white powder inside.

"What's the matter, darling stepson? I suppose your dear wife wouldn't approve."

"It's nothing to do with my wife. I need to have a clear head tomorrow."

"This stuff is excellent quality," said Jenny, ever the gracious hostess. "Tomorrow you'll be in top form, I assure you."

Mark shook his head, wondering if drugs on a tray had been a regular feature of his father's new lifestyle. It seemed incredible—after all, his father had been noted for his medieval views on the punishment of drug offenders. And yet Warwick had been determined to form close personal relations with the top people in the music and movie industries. His ambition had always been to transform InfoCorp from an information company into an entertainment company. Mark knew his father well enough to appreciate that whenever principles had clashed with business logic, business logic had always been the easy victor.

Suddenly Candi di Lucci stepped out of her backless, deep-cleavage dress, peeled off her thong, and dived into the swimming pool. The newscaster did the same, revealing a clean-shaven pubic mound, and then their two partners joined them in the pool, splashing and yelling.

Mark stood at the edge, sipping gin and tonic.

"No chickening out this time," hissed Jenny in his ear.

"What do you mean?"

"Don't be shy, Mark. I promise not to look."

"You can look if you want. It doesn't bother me."

Jenny took him at his word, sitting down a yard of front of him and staring as he kicked off his boxer shorts. "Not a bit like your father," she smirked.

Mark ignored her, and broke the surface of the water with a perfect swan dive. Jenny was the last to undress, turning away from the pool as she slipped off her panties. Was she shy, or just pretending?

"Horses and jockeys," she called out, once she had slipped into the water.

Before Mark had time to think, Candi di Lucci had clambered onto his back and wrapped her statuesque legs around his neck. Jenny had vaulted onto the news editor's shoulders, and the INN newscaster—a hefty woman whose buttocks alone would outweigh a good-sized sack of potatoes—was perched on the slender shoulders of the Oscar candidate, Flic Marsden. They rushed at each other, jousting with slaps and shoves, then switched partners. Next, Mark had the newscaster bouncing and yelling on his shoulders, her bare labia rubbing against the back of his neck. Then finally he was carrying Jenny, whose thigh muscles held him in a grip of steel.

"Come on, Mark," she growled. "Let's see what you can do." She spread her hands across the top of his head, massaging his scalp before suddenly grabbing a hank of hair in each hand.

"Yow!" shouted Mark.

"When I pull left you go left, and when I pull right you go right."

Mark jumped, twisted, sent her sailing over his head and crashing into the water face first. There was laughter from the others. Jenny came spluttering to the surface and stared at him with an expression of pure malice.

"Sorry about that."

"Not as much you will be, stepson"

The others laughed again. Jenny joined in, but her eyes didn't change at all.

Dinner was out on the patio, a "nouvelle asiatique" blend of French and Chinese cuisine prepared by the chef under Jenny's personal direction and served by a team of Filipino houseboys. Jenny treated them the same way she treated all social inferiors. She didn't so much ignore them as look straight through them. For her they simply didn't exist.

Flic Marsden talked about *Glory over the Pacific*, the biggest budget war movie ever made. Audiences all over the world were thrilling to the hologram technology used in the Battle of Midway sequence, the computer simulation of the bombing of Hiroshima, and the final scene when Flic parachutes into the Imperial Palace in Tokyo and defeats a whole division of Japanese troops single-handed.

Hot-tempered Jenny had been replaced by Jenny the far-sighted visionary. She talked technology, business theory, the need to swim with the tides of history, the need to destroy in order to create, the need to think visually not verbally.

"Chinese people are already visual thinkers because our writing system is made of pictures. But in Western writing the words have no relation to what they're supposed to be describing. They're like grey insects crawling across the page."

"What's wrong with that?" queried Mark, toying with a slice of stir-fried abalone set on a bed of Andalusian goat cheese.

"There's nothing particularly wrong with it," replied Jenny haughtily. "But it's inefficient and inappropriate for learning to think visually."

"Inefficient? How's that?"

"Well, the problem with verbal thinking is that words have different meanings for different people. In visual thinking, all people can be trained to see the same image. If I say the word 'Coca Cola,' we probably have the same thing in mind, but if I say the word 'tree' we all have different ideas. The merit of visual thinking is that all people will get to think the same 'tree,' just like we think the same 'Coca Cola.'"

"Cool," said Candi di Lucci, on her fourth glass of Chardonnay. "We'll all be turning Chinese."

"That's not what I meant at all."

Mark smiled at Jenny's irritation, but said nothing.

After dinner there was brandy, more white powder from the silver box, and another naked frolic in the swimming pool. The other guests took off shortly before midnight, leaving Mark and Jenny staring at each other in the main lounge. Outside, gas-flame torches flickered in the breeze, lighting up the faces of the Greek statues that decorated the long, rolling lawn.

"You don't like me very much, do you?" said Jenny, crossing her elegant legs.

"Whatever gave you that impression?"

"I can't say I blame you. I broke up your father's marriage and turned the company upside down, and now he's in hospital after having a stroke. Naturally you consider that my fault too."

"Well it certainly wouldn't have happened if he'd stayed with my mother."

Jenny shook her head slowly, like a teacher reprimanding a child. "Sometimes I think I know your father better than you do. Playing it safe is not in his nature. He has to be in motion, he has to be thinking ahead. I've never known anyone with so much male energy."

How many men had Jenny known, Mark wondered. How old was she really anyway? From her appearance she could be anywhere between twenty-five and forty-five.

"As I told you before, he takes whatever he wants. And one of the things he wanted was me."

"Did he know what he was getting into?"

"Of course. He understands women very well. Much better than his son does."

"Oh really?"

There was a moment of silence as their eyes locked.

"You see, that proves it," said Jenny with a sniff of contempt.

"Proves what?"

"Your father wouldn't just sit there staring at me. He would understand what the situation requires and act."

She crossed her legs the other way and gazed at him, glossy-lipped, pouting and mocking at the same time. Mark saw what the situation required. He acted. Jenny didn't resist as he picked her up and marched upstairs.

He pushed open the door of the master bedroom with his foot and tossed her onto the bed. She pulled him down on top of her, sinking her teeth into the side of his neck. Mark jammed his hand around the back of her neck, pulled her away, and kissed her roughly on the mouth.

"So you are a tough guy after all," she breathed, fingernails digging into his back.

Mark grabbed the neckline of her dress, twisted it around his fist.

"Hey, what are you doing? It's a Manuel Blani."

Mark twisted and pulled, and the dress tore right down the seam.

"Hey! You now owe me fifty thousand dollars."

"You owe me billions, bitch!" Mark shoved her down on the bed, and ripped off her panties one-handed.

"That's another two thousand, you ruffian."

"Shut up," snapped Mark. He had never done anything like this before, and was starting to enjoy it.

"Wait—I want to get something." Jenny slid across the bed and opened the top drawer of the dresser. From inside she fished out two sets of handcuffs. Mark experienced a sudden decline in ardor. For some reason he pictured his father lying prone on the hospital bed, tubes and wires snaking around his head and chest.

"I want you to put these on."

"No, you put them on," glowered Mark.

"All right, let's do the rock, paper, scissors game. The winner can decide."

They did the rock, paper, scissors game and Jenny won. She sat on the bed dangling the handcuffs and grinning like a cat.

"I'm looking forward to this, Hot Lips Fletcher."

Mark gazed at her, eyes narrowed. What would his father do in a situation like this, where principles were in conflict with business logic. No question— principles would go out the window. His father would take what he wanted.

Mark grabbed her by the wrist, and gave her a backhanded slap across the side of her face. It was harder than he'd intended, and sent her flying across the bed. Before she could recover, he was on top of her, wrenching the handcuffs from her grasp. She flailed with arms and legs, raking her fingernails across his left cheek, but in seconds she was pinned to the bed.

"Liar!" she spat.

"Not as big a liar as you."

Mark dropped the handcuff keys in his trouser pocket. Then he sat beside her on the bed, teasing her breasts, watching her nipples rise and harden.

She tossed her head from side to side, rattling the handcuffs. "Come on, Mark," she murmured. "You can do anything you want."

Mark brushed his fingers across her face and she took them into her mouth, nibbling and licking. Then suddenly she bit down hard, sinking her front teeth into the first joint of his forefinger.

"Yow! You really are vicious!"

Mark rolled on top of her, pinning her with his full weight. He used his knee to force her thighs apart, then slid down her body until his eyes were level with her pubic mound. There, on the inside of her left thigh, was a bluish-black star shape, about two inches wide. Through the water of the swimming pool it had looked like a bruise, but now he could see it was a birthmark. Ricky Patel had asked him to confirm it, and now he had.

"Aren't you going to punish me?" she murmured. "There are some other things in the drawer, if you want."

Mark fingered his cheek, where Jenny's nails had drawn a few drops of blood. Then he stood up and gazed around the room. On top of the dresser were a couple of Jeffrey Archer novels, a strange choice for an expert in American literature. In the cupboard he could see his father's suits and shirts. Hanging from the door was the monogrammed silk dressing gown that Mum had given him as a birthday present years ago.

"Next time, maybe."

"Next time? What do you mean?"

"Sorry, I've got a busy day tomorrow."

Jenny stared up at him, legs splayed apart, eyes blazing. "What's the matter with you? Aren't you man enough to fuck me?"

There was something about the aggrieved Mary Poppins voice that caused Mark to chuckle out loud.

"No, I don't think I am," he said, turning for the door.

Jenny was spitting obscenities, rattling the handcuffs against the bedframe. He wondered how she would treat her houseboys when they appeared in the morning. Looking right through them wouldn't be an option.

SIXTEEN

Martine spent the evening at her computer, nibbling chocolate cookies and running down information on the Atami incident. A number of sensational events had taken place in Atami over the years, including love suicides, battles between biker gangs, insurance murders, and the mysterious deaths of some construction company executives, but there was only one that the press consistently referred to as the Atami incident. This was something that had happened thirty years ago, when the student radicalism of the late sixties was declining into murderous factional rivalry.

Three members of the Workers Revolutionary Army had fled to Atami after a fire-bomb attack on the underground headquarters of the fanatical Red Core Faction. They were living under assumed names in a cheap guesthouse, staying inside during daylight hours and constantly on guard for police surveillance. Then one night, as they were strolling down a quiet residential side street on their way back from the local yakitori restaurant, a van drew up alongside them and out spilled half-a-dozen Red Core Faction members wielding steel pipes. According to witnesses they were wearing crash helmets and face masks and screaming like banshees. The operation had been well planned, as the police discovered. Telephone lines had been cut to prevent anyone calling for help, and the steel pipes had been taped at one end. They didn't want their hands to slip as they set to work crushing their enemies' skulls.

Two of the victims died instantly, the third suffered brain damage. The case was never solved, and no suspects were ever named. No surprise there, thought Martine. The police would not have been too troubled by the prospect of the radicals annihilating each other.

So that was the Atami incident, a minor outrage in a half-forgotten era of turmoil and blood-drenched psychosis. The question was how on earth it related to Nozawa here and now. Martine had no answer to that. She went through every reference she could find, but nothing fitted. If this was the key, where was the lock?

Martine went to bed, her head spinning with a jumble of messages, phone calls, interviews, headlines from an alternate universe, conversations with non-existent people. When she closed her eyes, lines of newsprint went scrolling across the inside of her eyelids.

In the summer Martine usually slept naked, but tonight she wore a light cotton kimono that Makoto had brought her from Kyoto. Her sleep was fitful. Once she woke up in a cold sweat, convinced that someone was in the room. She switched on the light and glimpsed a lizard scuttling behind an antique chest. She had nothing against lizards—they fought the good fight against mosquitoes and other insects—but all the same she got up and closed the bathroom window. On the way back she took a bottle of Makoto's new premium beer from the refrigerator and sat and drank it with slow relish. This was the nutty, foamy, eight-percent-alcohol beer. The taste was deeply relaxing. It made her want to stretch out on the sofa, gazing at the shadows on the ceiling, thinking about Makoto, the things they'd done together here on this sofa...

The next thing she knew the digital clock was winking six-thirty and sunshine was streaming through the gap in the curtains. Outside, the cicadas were fizzing and the crows were limbering up for their daily depredations. Martine rolled off the sofa, feeling as heavy-headed and blurred as if she had just flown around the world twice.

She made some coffee, did twenty minutes of yoga, then switched on the TV. The top story on NHK was the launch of the National Regeneration Party. There was a video clip of yesterday's press conference—first a close-up of Nozawa talking about his plans for agricultural subsidies, then a reaction shot of a blond woman in the audience nodding in silent agreement. Martine cringed. She always looked so big and clumsy on TV, an overgrown schoolgirl pretending to be serious. And this shot was spectacularly unflattering. The way they caught the line of her jaw, it almost looked as if she had a double chin!

Martine quickly switched channel to INN, just in time for the international news. The first story was Romania again, and the massacre of gypsies which all sides were blaming on each other. The second item was about Yamada Motor, now under concerted attack for the SUV rollovers. One of the victims' lawyers—a handsome young finger-wagger right out of a John Grisham novel—was explaining the class action suit.

"We want to send a clear message to Yamada Motors and all other irresponsible foreign corporations. No more will you be allowed to bring death and destruction to ordinary American families. No more will you get away with lies and cover-ups. No more will you trample on the values of freedom and democracy..."

The damages were being estimated at several billion dollars. Yamada was Japan's second-largest auto manufacturer, but that would blow its balance sheet to smithereens.

The third story concerned the diplomatic tremors caused by Nozawa's nukes comment. The Chinese and the Koreans had already registered "disquiet and anger." The Europeans were appealing for calm on all sides. The US was demanding an official clarification. So what did the experts think? Cut to a sharp-faced man making shapes with his hands as he talked rapidly into the camera.

"This is certainly the most serious threat to Asian stability for decades. In my view the only way to halt Japanese adventurism is through a new policy of containment. We need to draw a line in the sand right now."

The title at the bottom of the screen said "Jim Murphy, Tokyo bureau chief of the *Tribune*." So this was the obnoxious Murphy! Martine had been expecting an older man, someone with the presence to back up his domineering management style. But Murphy was no older than Martine herself, and he was wriggling around with the nervous energy of an eel.

Cut back to the anchor, the woman with saucer eyes and lips stretching to the edge of her face.

"So Jim—what do you make of this guy Nozawa? Is he for real?"

Murphy nodded vigorously. "He most surely is. Nozawa is the most popular politician in Japan. In fact, since the UNG scandal he's the only popular politician. In my view he will be the next prime minister."

Back to the rubber-mouthed anchor. Martine wondered if she did stretching exercises every morning, pulling her lips open with her fingers.

"And that was Jim Murphy, the man who broke the story of Japan's nuclear threat…"

"WHAT!" yelled Martine at the screen. "Say that again, you brainless bimbo!"

But the brainless bimbo was already on to the next story, the wave of strikes across Europe. Martine switched off the TV and went to get her karate gear. Suddenly she felt wide awake.

Murphy wanted her out, she was convinced of it. First that comment about "full authority over personnel matters." Now this theft—for that's what it was, outright larceny—of the Nozawa scoop. It was a deliberate insult to her professionalism. And to think that she had been glad to see the back of poor old Charlie! Clearly, Murphy had no intention of developing a working relationship. His game plan would probably be to demote her to "researcher" or some such menial job, pick up the contacts she had spent years cultivating, and then find some excuse to fire her. Well, she wasn't just going to roll over and let it happen. She would fight back, hard and dirty. It wouldn't be easy—the word was that Murphy had powerful friends in the InfoCorp organization—but Martine had some ammunition of her own. She would put the word out and make sure Murphy got not a sliver of cooperation anywhere where she had any influence.

Martine was still fuming when the doorbell rang. She glanced at the security monitor in the wall. A motorbike messenger was standing in the lobby, holding a package up to the camera. She let him in, wondering who on earth would request a delivery at this time of the morning.

The answer, from the label on the envelope, was Shimizu.

"Sign here, please," smirked the messenger, obviously delighted to meet a half-dressed blond woman in the course of his duties. His breath was heavy with the odor of pickled radish. Martine took a step back and signed without a word. The messenger strode down the corridor, his "DaiNippon Transport" bag swinging jauntily from his shoulder. Martine had a strong presentiment he would turn at the corner and give another gap-toothed smirk. He did, but by then Martine's door had slammed shut.

The label on the envelope said "photo." Martine remembered the unflattering profile that had just flashed across her TV screen and been viewed in millions of households all over Japan. If this was the publicity material from yesterday's press conference, she only hoped her own picture had not been included.

But the envelope did not contain publicity material of any sort. Instead there was just one photo inside, a grainy black-and-white image that looked as if it had been blown up several times. It showed a woman in jeans and black turtleneck sweater, arms folded, gazing down at two men sitting cross-legged on the floor. Her eyes were startlingly beautiful, and her hair fell in curtains over her shoulders. The men, both seen from the back, were wearing helmets. On the wall behind were revolutionary slogans, a poster of Che Guevara, and, dimly visible, a banner that read "Red Core Faction."

Martine gazed at the photo in bemusement. Why had Shimizu sent her this? Or—wait a moment—was Shimizu really the sender? The reference to the "Red Core Faction" was too much of a coincidence. She went back inside, picked up the phone, and called the number on the envelope.

The phone rang a dozen times before a surly voice answered.

"Yes? What do you want?"

"Is that DaiNippon Transport?"

"No. This is Shinjuku Police Station. What do you want?"

It must be a misprint, thought Martine as she put down the phone.

She called directory assistance and got the number for DaiNippon Transport. It bore no resemblance to the number printed on the outside of the envelope. This time the voice that answered was female, ecstatically polite, and on roughly the same frequency as a canary.

"DaiNippon Transport here. Thank you very much for your patronage. How may we be of service?"

"I'd like to check some information please."

"Yes, certainly. What would you like to know?"

"It's about a delivery you just made to my apartment."

"To your apartment?" twittered the woman in surprise. "But we don't make deliveries to people's apartments. Our company specializes in transporting cranes, bulldozers, and heavy construction equipment."

"Not documents?"

"Unfortunately not."

"Sincere apologies," cooed Martine, answering in the same register. "Could please tell me if there is another company called DaiNippon Transport in the Tokyo area?"

The woman put her hand over the phone and yelled out the question in a twenty-cigarettes-a-day voice with a strong Osaka accent.

"I have just checked with my colleagues," she said, returning to her saccharine squeak. "There is no such company. We have been in business for twenty years, and no such confusion has ever occurred before."

Martine slowly put down the phone. She remembered the messenger's leering face, his yellow teeth, the smell of radish on his breath. Could that have been the stalker at her door, staring over her shoulder into her apartment? If so, it was a violation, deliberate and mocking. The very idea made her shudder.

Today's matchup with the cop Saya Miki was closer than usual. Martine caught her off-balance several times and once sent her staggering backward with a reverse kick to the center of her face guard. Afterward they sat in the changing room, towels around their waists, and swilled cold green tea and chatted about men, dogs, and the condition of being a woman at this particular moment in history.

"I've always wanted to ask you this question," said Martine suddenly. "What's it like being a female detective?"

"What's it like? What part do you mean?

"Well, you're in the middle of a man's world. Most of your colleagues are male, the prosecutors are male, the criminals are male. How do you get on with all that?"

Saya Miki gave one of her enigmatic smiles. "Is this an interview?" she asked dryly.

Martine wrinkled her nose, annoyed with herself. Unconsciously she had slipped into her journalist's persona, something Makoto complained about from time to time. "Stop asking questions," he'd said once when they were lying in an outdoor hot-spring bath surrounded by snow. "This isn't supposed to be material for an article."

"Sorry, Saya-san."

"No problem. But if we're going to interview each other, let me go first."

"All right then. Go ahead."

Saya Miki pushed out her fist as if it held a microphone. "So tell me, Meyer-san, what does it feel like to be a female journalist in Japan?"

"What's it like? What part do you mean?"

Saya Miki's smile got a little wider and her fist a little closer. "Well, you're in the middle of a man's world. The people you interview, the politicians and businessmen and so on, they're nearly all male, and they nearly all have the same thing in mind."

"Which thing?"

"They want to take your clothes off and kiss your naked body."

"What?" exclaimed Martine, sitting bolt upright on the bench.

"You know it's true. You know what men are like, worse than dogs after bones."

"Are they?"

"Sure," said Saya Miki, eyes twinkling. "Every single one. Looking the way you do, it really can't be helped."

"Well, I'm not going to argue with you. But as for being a female journalist—actually there are some serious disadvantages."

"Like what?"

"You really want to know?"

"Yes."

Martine closed her hands around Saya Miki's fist. "All right then, let's put away the microphone."

Before she knew what she was doing, Martine was spilling out the story of the stalker, the delivery man, the mysterious e-mails. She wasn't sure why she was revealing these things—after all, she hadn't breathed a word to Makoto—but there was something about Saya Miki that was comforting, instantly trustworthy in a way a man could never be. It was like talking to her big sister, except that Martine didn't have a big sister.

"Weird stuff," said Saya thoughtfully. "And what was inside this envelope?"

Here Martine hesitated. Going further would mean giving away the story, potentially a much bigger scoop than the nukes interview.

"It's hard to explain," said Martine. "You're a cop after all."

"Not if you don't want me to be," said Saya, giving her a squeeze on the forearm. "I'm an ordinary human being too, you know."

She sat there smiling, wet hair hanging down over her breasts. The nipples, peeking through the strands of hair, were semierect after the cold shower. Not for the first time, Martine felt a tinge of envy as she glanced at her. This woman was five years older than Martine, ate and drank what she wanted when she wanted, and nowhere on her body was there an unwanted bulge or suspicious dimple. She never wore makeup, hardly even bothered to comb her hair, and yet there were Hollywood actresses spending billions of dollars to look like Saya Miki.

"All right, ordinary human being. Let me show you what I've got."

Martine took the envelope from her bag and shook out the photo.

Saya studied it closely, lips pursed, her large eyes suddenly serious and alert. "Do you know who this is?" she murmured, tapping a fingernail on the figure in the dark polo-neck sweater.

"I believe she's some kind of student radical. At least she was thirty years ago."

"Not just any student radical. That woman is Reiko Matsubara, leader of the Red Core Faction. You can find her picture on the wall of every police station in Japan."

"What did she do to earn that?"

"Hijacking, kidnapping, assassinations, almost anything you can think of. She's personally responsible for dozens of deaths in Europe, the Middle East, and Japan. It's said that she ordered the execution of her first husband."

"Really? What did he do?"

"Apparently he'd been conducting secret negotiations with one of the rival groups. Matsubara couldn't tolerate that. So she decided to show that her devotion to the cause was pure, untainted by even the tiniest blemish of personal sentiment. Her group was staying in Syria at the time, being treated like heroes after the attack on that Israeli airport. The guy was strangled in the middle of an ideology session. They wrapped a rope around his neck, and everyone there helped to pull it tight."

"That's horrible."

"For people like you and me it's horrible. But if you've already killed twenty or thirty people, I guess another one doesn't make much difference."

"Even your own husband?"

Saya shrugged. "Husbands and wives are always killing each other. It's the most common form of murder in the world."

They were silent for a moment, both aware of the gap between the world view of a female cop and the world view of a female journalist. An idea came into Martine's head, a question that would be a mistake to ask unless they had reached a certain level of openness and intimacy. They had hardly spoken before, but Martine decided it had been reached.

"Can I ask you a favor?"

"What kind of favor?"

"One that needs you to be cop and a friend at the same time. I think Nozawa is connected to this Matsubara woman somehow."

Saya Miki's large, lustrous eyes got a little larger. "Tsuyoshi Nozawa? What a strange idea!"

"Well, they're almost the same age, aren't they? And Nozawa used to be pretty radical, back in his folk-rock period."

"But Nozawa mixed up with a crazy woman like Matsubara—it hardly seems possible."

"Even the sane people went a little crazy in those days, or so I'm told." Martine was picturing Makoto with long hair and an Afghan coat.

"Maybe so. I was in junior school at the time. So what do you want me to do?"

"I'd like to know if there's any mention of Nozawa in this woman's police file."

Now Saya the cop was genuinely shocked. "Wait a moment. This is serious stuff you're asking. Revealing police data is a criminal offense."

"It's serious all the way, Saya-san. Nozawa could be the next prime minister. Don't you think the world should know what kind of person he really is?"

Saya shook her head, sending a drop of moisture flying against Martine's cheek. "You're talking like a journalist again. People could lose their jobs helping you."

"You're right. I am talking like a journalist. But I believe in what I'm doing, just as much as you do. If Nozawa goes any further, there'll be much more to worry about than lost jobs. You understand that, don't you?"

Saya Miki turned to face her and their eyes locked. Saya had big, liquid eyes, friendly and funny most of the time, but hardcore scary when you were facing her in a karate match. Now she was giving Martine her toughest, most menacing karate stare. Martine held the stare, absorbing it just as she had the first time they faced off.

"What's the matter, Saya? Don't you trust me?"

Saya Miki paused, holding her gaze, then nodded slowly. "All right" she said, getting to her feet. "I'll see what I can do."

She walked over to her locker, letting the towel drop to the floor. Martine sat there admiring her high, shapely breasts, the smooth strength of her legs, the way she moved, back straight, no bullshit, no apologies. If it ever occurred to Martine to feel attracted toward a woman—although it never had, not once, not even in the days when a lot of unusual things occurred to her— then this was definitely the kind of woman she would choose.

191

In mid-morning Martine called Kimura and arranged to meet him and his computer expert friend in the grounds of a shrine dedicated to scholarship and literacy. Outside the exam season it was a secluded spot.

The stone staircase leading up to the shrine was half hidden behind a pachinko parlor and a Starjacks café, now closed "pending investigation" like every other Starjacks outlet in the Kanto region. Kimura and his friend were already there, tossing a Frisbee between the thick red pillars of the shrine gate. The only others present were a homeless man sprawled under a pine tree and a one-eared cat watching the Frisbee spin through the air with supercilious indifference. From their hiding place in the bushes, the cicadas were screeching out a long chorus.

Kimura moved stiffly, grimacing with effort whenever he had to bend his knees. His friend was as lithe as a dancer, every movement precise and balanced. He would have been a natural at karate, thought Martine. Kimura flicked the Frisbee at Martine in a wobbly parabola that ended at ankle height and she made a one-handed catch and sent it whirring back toward his head in a twisting, ducking curve. Kimura missed his catch, and the Frisbee smacked into the old shrine gate, knocking off flakes of red paint.

"Ouch!" he yelled, clutching his fingertips. "Where did you learn that?"

The answer was from her father, on a beach in Greece twenty years ago, the summer her mother's drunken outbursts finally drove him away for good. She didn't say anything, however, and just laughed.

They sat down on a stone bench at the side of the shrine. Kimura produced a big plastic bottle of green tea and offered it around. Martine took a swig, then stared in amazement at the label.

National Regeneration Tea
Cool, refreshing, packed with vitamins to help you strive for Japan's future.

Underneath was a cartoon picture of Nozawa wearing his "certain death" headband, his hand balled into a fist almost as large as his head.

"So which one of you is the Nozawa fan?" asked Martine, handing the bottle back to Kimura's friend.

Kimura grinned. "Neither of us. I went to the convenience store at the corner, and this was the only brand available. Apparently it's a new product, with huge marketing muscle behind it. You know how the system works, don't you?"

Martine nodded. She knew how the system worked because Makoto had complained about it so many times. The simplest way for manufacturers to ensure the success of a key product was to persuade the retailers to take competitors' products off the shelves. The favored means were kickbacks posing as "discounts" and threats of across-the-board supply cuts. Illegal, of course, but nobody cared. One aspect of the crisis was that the strong got stronger and the weak got weaker, and meddlesome rules like this were only applied to the latter.

"So what about my stalker?" asked Martine, dabbing her face with a handkerchief. "Any progress with tracking him down yet?"

"You need to be patient," said Kimura's friend. "These things always take time."

The sweat was beading Kimura's forehead, glistening from the pores on his nose, and running down his hairy forearms in tiny rivulets. His friend was as cool and unruffled as if he were sitting in an air-conditioned office.

"I understand that. It's just that I've been getting a little nervous lately."

"So what's making you nervous?"

Martine wrinkled her nose in irritation. Everything that came through to her computer was automatically bounced through to Kimura's friend. Surely he had seen that comment about the color of her underwear.

"Well, it's obvious, isn't it? The guy's a pervert. He's probably dangerous."

"I don't think so," said Kimura's friend. He picked up the Frisbee and started twirling it around on the end of his finger.

Martine sighed. It would be impossible for a man to understand how she felt about the situation.

"What makes you so certain?" she retorted.

"Simple. This person is no ordinary stalker. Everything he does is carefully planned. He never repeats a pattern. He never uses your name. He always varies the way he addresses you—"blond goddess," "favorite beauty," and so on. This makes him very difficult to trace."

"But what about the personal comments?"

"I think he planted those as attention grabbers, to make sure you didn't ignore the messages. And it worked, right?"

"It certainly did," said Martine tightly. "If I ever come face-to-face with this guy..."

Kimura's pal shrugged, eyes fixed on the spinning Frisbee. "Of course we don't even know it is a guy."

"What? You think it's a woman?"

"That's always possible, I suppose. More likely it's a computer program, instructed to generate information strings that are hard to trace and highly likely to be read."

Martine gazed at him in amazement. A machine in an empty room generating lewd thoughts about her panties and breasts. The idea was bizarre, even by the standards of all the other bizarreness she had been encountering recently.

She reached out and lifted the Frisbee off his finger. "Look, a real human being was watching me yesterday. He saw me on my balcony wearing a brand-new pair of shorts."

Kimura's friend nodded. "Okay," he said nonchalantly, "but a sophisticated program would have requested exactly that kind of input. It would have said, 'Find item of clothing worn only at home,' and someone would have gone to check."

"You think that's likely?"

"It's only a theory. At the moment everything is only a theory."

Martine handed him the Frisbee. What she had just learned was both reassuring and disturbing. Reassuring because the mystery messages were not coming from an ordinary pervert, the kind whose fantasies can do terrible damage to other people's realities. Disturbing because she now had even less idea of what was happening around her.

When Martine passed through the shrine gate, the homeless guy was sitting with his back against the pine tree. She glanced at him, and his eyes shifted to the ground. His hands, she noted, were strangely clean.

At the bottom of the stone steps, a baked yam seller had parked his van at the curb. He was staring at Martine through the grubby window. A potbellied salaryman stood outside a pachinko parlor, watching her out of the corner of his eye. A woman in a bookstore glanced at her over the top of the magazine she was reading.

Who were these people? Why were they watching her? Could they be students of the Morikawa school, following her around as part of their life experience? Or data-gatherers sent by a computer program? Or just ordinary people curious at the sight of a tense-looking blond woman walking away from the shrine with unnatural haste?

Reiko Matsubara sat in her hotel room in Macao waiting for the man from Shanghai. He was late again, which annoyed her. Right from the start Matsubara had distrusted him. Whenever someone made a comment, he always watched how the others responded before making a response himself. If they smiled, he smiled. If they looked stern, he looked stern. It was only a split-second glance—usually directed at the young general, or some other powerful person—but Matsubara had trained herself to notice these things. That was how she had survived the past thirty years.

For the moment there was no choice but to take his instructions. The man from Shanghai had the young general's total confidence, and the latter was crucial to Reiko Matsubara's plans. Backed by the young general, there was no limit to what she could accomplish. The opportunity for revolution in Japan, a wave of terror that would destabilize the ruling clique and dissolve the false attitudes of the masses, was closer than ever before.

For years it had seemed like a distant dream, but not any longer. All around the world, the dispossessed of the earth were finally rising up against their oppressors, toppling the glittering towers of capitalism with the sheer force of their revolutionary spirit. A new generation of activist no longer willing merely to wave placards and chant slogans was targeting greedy bankers, pollution-spewing oil companies, and pharmaceutical companies that maximized profits while millions of children were dying. Farmers were torching supermarkets. Animal liberation guerrillas were kidnapping scientists and giving them a taste of their own experiments. And this was only the beginning. You couldn't expect the masses to attain true consciousness during an economic upwave. Only in the depths of an economic downwave, when the gaps in wealth between the oppressors and the oppressed became too wide to endure—only then would ordinary people be ready to rise up and join the struggle. She had known this as a teenager reading Adorno, Marcuse, and Fanon, and all these years she had been waiting for the downwave to arrive. Now at last it was here, tearing through whole regions, and shattering the false promises of capitalism with gratifying ease.

Over the past quarter of a century she'd traveled under hundreds of different passports from dozens of different countries. She'd been expelled from Syria, Bulgaria, Afghanistan, Cambodia, Cuba, and Venezuela. She'd spent two years in the Andes with the Shining Path, watching as they rounded up villages of government sympathizers, flayed the headmen alive, and threw their women into tubs of boiling oil, and she'd survived an Israeli rocket attack in the Bekaa valley. But always she had known that she would return to Japan. That was where her struggle had started, and that was where it would end.

There was a knock on the door. Matsubara opened it a bit and put her eye to the crack. The man from Shanghai was standing there, and next to him was someone with hollow cheeks and the narrow eyes of a fox.

"Who's that?" queried Matsubara in English.

"He's the man I told you about."

Matsubara opened the door. The fox-eyed man walked inside. He was carrying a calfskin attaché case which he placed carefully on the table. He said nothing, and didn't give Reiko Matsubara even a sideways glance.

She frowned. "What's his name?"

"He's called Li. He's one of our top men, certainly the best for your purposes."

"How do I know that?"

"He'll show you."

The man from Shanghai nodded at Li, who sat down at the table. He clicked open the briefcase and began to assemble the rifle that was inside. He moved quickly and methodically, using a superfine white cloth to rub down every joint and screw before engaging it.

Matsubara watched his every move closely. He looked young, probably in his mid-twenties, and he had a prominent Adam's apple which bobbed up and down as he worked.

"What has he done?"

"Many things. He has just returned from Kansu, where there were disturbances caused by antipatriotic elements. Li was part of a squad that tracked down the leaders and eliminated them. He has also done special work in Tibet and Nepal."

Li finished assembling the rifle, then fitted the sight and the silencer. He spent several minutes lying flat on the bed, fiddling with the sight. When he was satisfied, he walked over to the window and eased it open. They were high up—on the twenty-fifth floor—but the roar of the traffic was loud enough to make them raise their voices.

"The bird," said Li, with good English pronunciation.

Matsubara squinted in the direction he was pointing. "What bird?"

"The one on that satellite dish."

The satellite dish was jutting out from a building about five hundred yards away. Surely it would be impossible for the human eye to make out a bird at that distance.

"Here, take these."

Li handed her a pair of binoculars. Matsubara scanned the satellite dish, and sure enough there was a straggly seagull perched on the top lip.

Li got into position, leaning forward, with the barrel of the rifle protruding through the window. There was a dry crack, like the sound of a stick breaking, and suddenly the bird wasn't there any more.

"Not bad," said Matsubara, putting down the binoculars.

"You can rely on Li," said the man from Shanghai with a smug smile. "Show him your bird, and he will do the rest."

Li closed the window and carefully placed the rifle on the table. Matsubara frowned. She had no grounds for rejecting Li, but was conscious of the way the man from Shanghai was scrutinizing her out of the corner of his eye.

"What if I asked for someone else?"

The man from Shanghai shrugged. "As you like. But time is so short now. I don't know what the others would say..."

He left the comment hanging in the air, but the meaning was clear. The young general would not be happy if her stubbornness put the project at risk. He might reduce his support for her plans. He might even reconsider entirely.

"Okay. I suppose he'll have to do."

The man from Shanghai glanced over at Li, who didn't even look up from his work with the rifle.

SEVENTEEN

"So what shall I do with Plato?" asked Saya, leaning into Martine's entrance hall.

Martine glanced down at the dog by her side. It was a short-haired, sandy-colored creature, about the height of Saya's knees, with friendly eyes and a floppy pink tongue.

"He's bigger than I expected. What breed is he?"

"Mongrel. Half Akita, half spaniel."

"Is he going to pee on my carpet?"

Saya looked aghast at the idea. "Of course not. He's got excellent manners. These mongrels are difficult to train, but once you've done it they're totally trustworthy."

"Different from human males, right?"

"The exact opposite. Those will promise you the whole world, then piss on the carpet when your back's turned."

Martine gave a noncommittal smile. On the subject of men Saya's sense of humor was always particularly dark. Not for the first time Martine wondered what kind of experience had molded it.

They went inside. Martine got coffee and rice crackers for Saya, and put a bowl of water out on the balcony for Plato.

"Great place you've got here," said Saya, gazing around Martine's living room. "It's like something out of a TV commercial."

"You're joking."

"Not at all. My entire apartment would fit into your kitchen. A cop's salary doesn't buy much space, you know, not these days."

Martine nodded sympathetically. All public sector workers were being hit hard by the fiscal crisis. The police, already swamped by the surge in crime, were taking hefty salary cuts.

"Anyway, I thought it would be best to drop in. I did some digging around on that subject you mentioned."

"Really? That was quick work."

"I have a good friend working over at the records department. He used to be my boss, but got transferred there about a year ago. The poor guy made a mistake, raided the wrong yakuza office."

"I see," said Martine, not seeing at all. "So have you found out anything about the terrorist woman?"

"It's like you said. She was suspected of being behind the Atami incident. She was pulled in for questioning several times, but her alibi was completely watertight."

"So she wasn't involved?"

"Not directly. The top commanders of the Red Core Faction preferred to save themselves for true revolutionary actions, like planting bombs on buses and so on. These interfactional disputes were considered low-priority affairs. The actual attacks were carried out by sympathizers, usually younger men keen to prove their fitness for membership. According to the files, Matsubara provided a special reward for the ones who showed the most zeal."

Martine blinked. "You mean sex?"

"That's right. In her writings she claimed that sexual revolution would be a tool of the global class revolution. It seems she practiced what she preached with great enthusiasm."

"Hmm... And what about Nozawa?"

"There was no mention of Nozawa in the files. That doesn't mean he wasn't involved, of course. We never came up with any other suspects for the Atami incident. In fact, the identities of most of the Red Core Faction sympathizers were never uncovered."

"Is that right?" said Martine, unable to keep the disappointment out of her voice. Saya's research was intriguing, but completely lacking in hard facts. Unless there was some way of tying Nozawa to Reiko Matsubara, Martine didn't have a story.

At that moment the balcony door creaked open and Plato nosed his way into the living room. He walked over to Saya, gave her a long, lolloping lick on the knee, then flopped down on the floor, gazing at her out of half-closed eyes. Adoration, trust, respect—it was all there, just as she'd said.

"There's one other thing," said Saya, leaning over to tickle Plato under the chin.

"Yes?"

"After checking Matsubara's file, I thought it might be interesting to check Nozawa's file too."

Martine sat bolt upright on the sofa. "Nozawa has a police file?"

"Well, that's what I was wondering. Unlikely, of course, but worth having a look. So I made another call to my ex-boyfriend, my ex-boss I mean."

"Go on."

Martine was so excited that she barely noticed Saya's verbal slip.

"Well, the first strange thing was that Nozawa does have a file. It was opened eighteen months after the Atami incident."

"So what does it say?"

Saya broke a rice cracker in two. One half she popped in her mouth, the other she held out for Plato, who jumped up to snatch it.

"That's the second strange thing. The file was empty."

"Empty?" echoed Martine. "How can a police file be empty?"

"I don't know. It must have happened when the records were computerized. The existence of the file got registered, but not the contents."

Martine nibbled her lower lip. Now disappointment had been replaced by frustration. She was on the right track, she was sure of it. Nozawa had been in trouble with the police, and someone had airbrushed away the details.

"Was there any other information?"

"Just the date, and the name of the police station. It's somewhere outside Nagasaki."

"You're sure there's nothing else?"

"Nothing. Sorry." Saya seemed taken aback by the directness of Martine's questions.

"Saya, I'm the one who should say sorry. You've done a fantastic job, breaking the rules like this. I've been thinking like a journalist again."

"Don't worry about it. If there's anything you need, please call me—as a journalist, as a karate opponent, whatever you like."

"Thanks," said Martine. Plato glanced up at her, nostrils quivering. Martine held out a whole cracker and he wolfed it down, tail thumping the carpet.

Martine left her apartment in mid-morning. It was another sticky day, with humidity in the nineties. She didn't hurry, nor did she glance nervously at the people around her. It was time to calm down and try to put everything that had happened into a sensible framework. There was no point in being paranoid, and imagining that she was being followed down the street by that orange taxi or that the potbellied salaryman at the station was the same potbellied salaryman she had noticed near the shrine yesterday.

Except that this plump salaryman followed her down to the platform and got into the next car of the train. He got out at the same station too, staying a dozen yards behind on the escalator. When Martine dropped into a convenience store to buy some crackers for Kyo-san, he stopped half a block behind, pretending to be absorbed by the window display of a shop selling cut-price Buddhist reliquaries. Martine didn't go straight to the *Tribune* building. Instead she turned into an alley lined with empty yakitori bars and shuttered pawn-shops and ducked into a narrow passageway opposite a couple of overflowing trash cans.

First she heard the footsteps, then the heavy breathing. Martine waited until he was level with the first trash can, then came flying out of the passageway and planted her foot in the side of his belly.

"Aagh!" The man went sprawling against the trash can, sending the lid clattering to the ground. He tried to push himself upright, but Martine jabbed a fist into his kidneys, then swept away his legs.

"Stop, stop!" The man was on his hands and knees in the trash, looking up at her imploringly.

"Who are you?" snapped Martine. "Why have you been following me for the last two days?"

"Please let me explain." The plump man sat back on his haunches and reached inside his jacket pocket. Martine took a half-step back and steadied herself. The first flash of a knife blade and she would launch a flick-kick at his head, full power. It was a move she had practiced hundreds of times at the dojo. The man took a namecard from his pocket and held it up for her to read.

"My name is Kato, I'm a researcher for Global Executive Search. At your service."

Martine stared at him incredulously. "You mean you're a *headhunter*?"

"Yes, yes. I help to find top-class executives for challenging employment opportunities."

"By following them around?"

"Our clients require detailed personal information to make their decisions."

Martine wrinkled her nose with distaste. "Please stand up. You're covered in trash. Now tell me what's going on."

Kato got to his feet, puffing for breath. There were dark stains all over his trousers, and a half-chewed yakitori stick caught in his cuffs.

"It's the truth," he said, taking out a handkerchief and wiping specks of soy sauce from his face. "I'm doing background research on you for a client."

"What client?"

"I'm not supposed to tell you that."

Martine's eyes narrowed. "You're not supposed to get caught either. One complaint from me, and you could lose your job."

A shadow of panic passed over Kato's fleshy features. Clearly this was the most respectable job he had ever had or was ever likely to have.

"All right, all right. It's for Silverman Brothers. They're looking for someone to handle government relations. It's an excellent job, with an attractive remuneration package and the opportunity to contribute to international understanding. I do hope you'll consider it, Meyer-san."

"Shut up."

"Sorry," said Kato, grinning apologetically.

"Now tell me why I'm on your list."

"It's because we heard you're looking for a new job."

"What you heard was wrong. I'm not looking for a new job."

Now Kato was picking fishbones out of his hair. "Not yet. But—oh, you're not supposed to know about that."

Martine fixed him with her hardest gaze. "What is it? Out with it, or I'll stick that trash can over your head."

Kato glanced at the can, glanced back at Martine, and licked his lips nervously. "Okay," he croaked. "You see, Meyer-san, the thing is this. We have information that your replacement has already been recruited."

"My replacement? As correspondent at the *Tribune*?"

"Yes. It happened about a month ago, or so I'm told. I'm just a humble investigator. All that high-level stuff has nothing to do with me..."

Kato carried on mumbling, but Martine wasn't listening. She was thinking how telegenic Jim Murphy had already decided to fire her before they had even exchanged a word.

"Good morning, Kyo-san. Everything under control?"

"More or less. The phone hasn't stopped ringing, of course. That nuclear weapons piece of yours is the biggest story for years."

"My piece—I'm glad you said that, Kyo-san."

Martine slung her bag onto the table. The devious embezzlement of her scoop was already enough to make her blood boil. Now there was the outright robbery of her job too!

"This new guy Murphy sounds like a real piece of work."

"Let's be more precise, Kyo-san. He's a real piece of shit."

"Oh-kay," said Kyo-san, using a rising intonation that came from years of dealing with short-tempered journalists and husbands.

Martine took the crackers from her bag and shook them onto a plate. She put it in the middle of the table, where they could both reach it. How long would Kyo-san last under the new Murphy regime? Not long. First he had got rid of Charlie, then he had starting maneuvering behind Martine's back. No doubt he was planning a clean sweep, bringing in a new team that would owe him total loyalty. There would be nobody to stand in the way of his "clearly defined, passionately felt" blatherings, nobody to correct his prejudices and banal simplifications. And what would Martine be doing then? Promoting smooth governmental relations for Silverman Brothers, the global investment bank which had made billions out of the crisis by exploiting its high-level political connections? That was impossible to imagine. She would never be able to look Makoto in the eye again. She wouldn't even be able to look at herself in the mirror again.

Martine switched on her computer and gazed dully at her messages. There were pages and pages of them, messages from diplomats, politicians, businessmen, and other journalists, as well as hundreds from readers all over the world, male and female, crazy and sane. One near the top, with no header or sender's name, immediately caught her eye.

> Woman of my dreams,
> Do not waste time worrying about this man Nozawa. By the end of next week he will be dead, and then nothing can come between us.

Martine sat bolt upright, staring at the computer screen. So far the stalker—or team of stalkers, or computer program, or whatever he was—had been proved right every time. Which could only mean one thing: that Nozawa was in danger of being murdered. Martine sent her reply straightaway.

> When and where is this going to happen?

Martine's mouth felt as dry as paper. Nozawa murdered. What would that mean? Just think what the murder of Mari-chan had meant, and multiply it many times over. What you got was a nationwide collective nervous breakdown. An entire equilibrium—political, social, and emotional—would be shattered. It would be like the death of JFK. In an instant the world would become a different place.

"Are you all right?" asked Kyo-san. "You've gone very pale again."

"It's my natural complexion," Martine muttered feebly.

"I don't think so. I'm sure working on that computer all the time is bad for a person's health."

"You know something, Kyo-san? Sometimes you sound just like my mother."

"Thank you. I'll take that as a compliment."

But Martine wasn't listening. She was gazing at the screen, where a new message had just appeared.

> Be patient, blond queen. You will not have to wait long.

Ricky Patel's Audi eased to a halt outside the dilapidated clapboard house. It was the only one on the block with a "For Sale" sign outside.

"Is that the one?" asked Mark, gazing dubiously at the overgrown garden.

"Sure," said Patel in his lilting Indian accent. "Can't you see his name on the mailbox?"

Mark hadn't noticed the mailbox, which was half hidden behind a tangle of creeper that had spilled over the fence. The "A" and the "D" of "ANDERSEN" were missing, and the mailbox itself was a discolored white that matched the shabby fence.

"This doesn't look like the sort of place an insurance executive would live in," mused Mark.

"Like I said, the guy's up to his neck in credit card debt. He's had to sell half his furniture already."

Mark flicked through the file on his lap. Patel had done an excellent job in a short time. Not only had he located Andersen, he had also dug up enough information to make the approach worthwhile. In the file were copies of bank statements and credit card bills and a summary of his wife's divorce filing. Fortunately, Andersen was a man of many problems.

"You sure you don't want me to come with you?"

"I can manage," said Mark, opening the car door. Patel might be a skilled investigator, but with his immense bulk and smooth-shaven scalp he had an intimidating presence. The whole idea was to put Andersen at ease, to create an atmosphere of trust.

Mark rang the doorbell. The man who answered was tall and balding, with pale blue eyes peering through wire-rimmed spectacles.

"You've come to see the house?" he muttered.

"Yes, I have. I hope you don't mind me coming direct like this."

Mark's accent and appearance made him an unlikely purchaser of this piece of real estate, but Andersen didn't seem to care.

"What do you want to see first?"

"Well, how about the kitchen?"

The kitchen was a mess. The sink was stacked with greasy plates, and a half-eaten pizza was sitting on the table between baskets of clothes ready for washing. The air was laden with the odors of sour milk and cat piss. Mark examined the plumbing and asked a few obvious questions, anxious to move on as quickly as possible. Andersen answered with a numb politeness that made Mark wonder whether he was on mood stabilizers.

"That building through the trees—I understand it's some kind of prison."

"It's a daycare institute for female offenders. They're no trouble at all, really. The other day I got one to come and fix up my garden."

Andersen nodded at the tangled mass of shrubbery in the yard. If that had been fixed, Mark wondered what it must have looked like before.

"You're English, aren't you?"

"Australian, actually," replied Mark with his best friendly-guy smile.

"English, Australian, whatever. You're probably wondering if this is the right kind of area for you, what with the female offenders and the black guys on the next block. Well, let me tell you something—this is a great little neighborhood and this is a great little house. I've had a great time here."

Andersen spoke with jerky passion, as if he were worried about being contradicted. Mark thought back to Patel's file. Andersen was on the verge of declaring personal bankruptcy. His wife had walked out, complaining of spousal abuse. His children had gone with her. He had lost his job with the insurance company. And yet everything was great. How could it be otherwise?

They walked into the lounge and Mark sat down on the only remaining armchair.

"Don't you want to see upstairs?"

Mark looked him straight in the eye. "Mr. Andersen, how much are you asking for this place?"

Andersen leaned back against the smudgy wallpaper. He thrust his hands in his pockets and tried to sound casual. "Uh, well—uh, around two hundred, I guess."

"Two hundred thousand dollars?"

"Well, uh, that's a kind of target, I guess—but if you want to talk further…"

"I think it's too cheap," said Mark soberly.

Andersen's pale blue eyes blinked in surprise "Too cheap? How do you mean?"

"This is a two-eighty house. If I were going to buy it, I would expect to pay two-eighty."

"You would?"

"Yes. But I've got to be honest with you, Mr. Andersen. The main reason I'm here today is not to look at the house. I've come to ask for your help."

Andersen looked totally bewildered. "Help? What kind of help?"

"This is going to sound a little strange, I know, but I'm a businessman in the global media industry. We're thinking of recruiting a senior executive, and I'm running a background check on her personal history."

"And you think I can help? Are you nuts? I'm just an insurance salesman."

"Fifteen years ago, I believe you were friendly with a lady named Jenny Leung."

"With who?"

"Perhaps you've forgotten. A lady you met at the Asian-American Friendship Foundation."

A flicker of recognition passed across Andersen's face. "You don't mean Chen Leung, do you?"

Chen Leung—that was the name used in Patel's file. Mark nodded. "These days she calls herself Jenny. Have you heard from her recently?"

"No, I haven't heard anything since then. Wait a moment—you're not telling me Chen Leung's a high-flying media executive?"

Now there was a huge grin on Andersen's face.

Mark gazed at him intently. "Does that sound strange to you?"

"Strange? It's the craziest thing I ever heard! Chen Leung knew nothing about business. She was only interested in literature and writers."

"Like Scott Fitzgerald?"

"Sure. Fitzgerald was her absolute favorite. She once told me that everything you need to know about America is in *The Great Gatsby*!"

The robotic politeness had gone, and for the first time Andersen was sounding like a living human being.

"You had some good times together."

"Yes, we certainly did. Jeez, I was devastated when it ended."

Andersen raised his hands to shoulder height, then let them fall.

"So why did it end?"

"It was the darndest thing," sighed Andersen. "One day she just upped and left, cleared her room without a word to anyone."

Mark pursed his lips. "I see. And what kind of woman was she in those days?"

"Her personality? Kind of quiet, kind of funny. Very intelligent of course. And a great cook."

Andersen was almost glowing with nostalgia. It was a shame to shake him out of it.

"I believe you two had a sexual relationship?"

"What kind of question is that, for God's sake? You've really got a nerve coming in here, pretending to be interested in my house, and then asking these personal questions. Who the hell do you think you are, you English fuck!"

Mark held up his hands, palms forward. "Actually, I'm Australian," he said mildly.

"Then go suck a kangaroo dick!"

"Hold on, hold on—it seems we've got a misunderstanding here. I'm not just pretending to be interested in this house. I really am interested. In my view, it's definitely worth two-eighty."

Mark opened his attaché case, took out five wads of banknotes, and laid them on the table. Andersen stared at them as if hypnotized.

"What do you want to know?" he mumbled.

"It's a very personal question. You may not want to answer."

"I'll answer, goddammit."

"Good. First of all, did you ever see Chen Leung without her clothes on?"

"Of course I did. We were fucking for a year." Andersen gave a nervous chuckle.

"Did you ever notice anything unusual on the inside of her left thigh, right at the top?"

"On the inside of the thigh? Like what?"

"Like a birthmark."

Andersen closed his eyes for a moment, let some happy memories flicker through his mind.

"Chen Leung had no birthmark," he said finally. "Her thighs were as smooth as satin, every part of them."

Mark nodded. It was time to go. He had everything he needed. Ricky Patel's suspicions, unlikely as they had seemed at first, had been totally confirmed.

At the door Andersen's handshake was twice as strong as it had been when Mark arrived, and the tremble had gone from his voice. The evaporation of his credit card debt had done him a world of good.

"Thank you for your help," said Mark politely.

"No problem. By the way, Chen Leung's not in any trouble, is she?"

"Chen Leung? No, she's doing just fine."

Mark turned to the car, the smile withering on his face. He hoped Andersen never found out what had really happened to Chen Leung.

"Good result?" asked Ricky Patel as Mark slid into the passenger seat.

"Excellent result," said Mark grimly. "Now I've got another job for you, not a very pleasant one I'm afraid."

"They rarely are," sighed Patel, swinging the big car out into the road.

EIGHTEEN

From the outside it looked like any other grimly functional apartment in a grimly functional tower block sprouting out of a grimly functional suburb on the edge of the giant city. There was a small window that had never been opened and never would be, a gray wall webbed with cracks, and a metal door with a heavy lock and a tiny nameplate in the middle. It was just the kind of place you would expect an unemployed cram school teacher to live. On the other side of that door, though, was something else entirely—a shrine to Tsuyoshi Nozawa.

Everywhere you looked in the tiny apartment you saw Nozawa. The walls were covered with Nozawa posters: Nozawa the bodybuilder, Nozawa in kabuki makeup, Nozawa straddling his 850cc Yamada Shogun. The bookcases were filled with Nozawa biographies, essays, memoirs, comic books, photo collections, and post-structuralist critical interpretations. The ashtrays, plates, cushions, towels, and lamp shades all bore his image. There were Nozawa dolls on the shelves, Nozawa shoehorns in the entrance hall, Nozawa wind chimes tinkling in the breeze of the electric fan.

Martine knelt at a low table in the center of the room sipping coffee from a Nozawa mug and nibbling at dried squid from a Nozawa bowl. On the other side of the table sat a man who didn't look like Nozawa at all. Ken Tabuchi was stubby-legged and heavy-hipped, with a broad, shiny face. Apart from being an unemployed teacher, he was the chairman of the unofficial Nozawa fan club, operator of the most popular Nozawa website, and editor of a long-running monthly magazine dedicated to the words and deeds of Tsuyoshi Nozawa. He had attended every Nozawa concert in the past decade, cataloged every song that Nozawa had ever sung, interviewed band members, recording engineers, even women who had slept with him once a quarter of a century ago. He owned tapes of the sixteen-year-old Nozawa strumming a guitar at a school festival. He had copies of his first wife's divorce filing. If Nozawa fans had the same ranking as judoka, Tabuchi would be a black-belt tenth dan, undefeated for his entire career.

Which was why Martine needed to talk to him. There was no person in the world—no family member, friend, or lover—who knew more about Nozawa than Tabuchi did. And nobody else enjoyed talking about Nozawa so much. You only had to prompt him, and out came a flood of information.

"You ask if Nozawa was sympathetic to student radicals? The answer is yes, of course. At that time nearly all musicians and writers supported them. The thinking was that these people might be extreme, but their hearts were pure. They were staking their lives for a better society, not for their own benefit."

"Staking their lives? Nozawa uses that phrase a lot. 'I want to be a burning dharma, I want to stake my life.' Isn't that how the song goes?"

Tabuchi's eyes lit up. "You obviously know his music well. If you like, I can check how many times he's used that phrase, when and where—whatever you want to know. My database contains all his songs and speeches, plus all the other information I've gathered about him too."

Martine glanced at the personal computer on his desk. The screen-saver was a manga picture of Nozawa in ninja garb riding across the ocean on a giant turtle.

"That's quite an achievement," she said gently.

"Thank you, thank you. It's my lifework, actually. There's more and more information about Nozawa these days, but I gather up everything I can find and put it all in there. My goal is to create a complete knowledge base. I want more information to be available about Nozawa than about any other human being who has ever lived."

"Amazing."

"You're in there too, Meyer-san. You've had two face-to-face interviews with him and you've written about him in five different articles. Don't think I don't know! Don't think you can escape me!"

Martine gave a feeble smile. Not long ago she would have found someone like Tabuchi amusing. Now she saw something frightening in his obsessiveness. He had such a weak attachment to reality, it wouldn't take much for it to wither away completely.

"Now what were we talking about?" asked Tabuchi.

"We were talking about radical students. Was Nozawa just sympathetic to their cause, or did it go further than that? Did he give them any direct support?"

Tabuchi grinned delightedly. "Yes, yes! He denies it now, but I have the evidence."

"Go on."

Tabuchi leaned forward and spoke in a conspiratorial half-whisper. "He participated in two fund-raising concerts in aid of the defense for some radicals who'd been arrested."

"That's interesting. And was he close to any of the radical leaders?"

"What leaders?"

"Well, Reiko Matsubara, for example?"

Tabuchi looked genuinely surprised. "Reiko Matsubara? That's impossible."

"Are you sure?"

"Of course, I'm sure. I have a comprehensive record of Nozawa's early years. I know the kind of people he met, the places he visited, even what he ate and drank. Friendly relations with a person like Reiko Matsubara certainly wouldn't slip through my fingers. What a weird idea!"

Tabuchi was not used to having his knowledge questioned, and he didn't like it. The respect that Martine had won by remembering the words to "Dharma on Fire" had evaporated. She decided to change the subject.

"Would it be possible for me to look at your database?"

"Of course. What would you like to know?"

"Hmmm ... could it tell me how many times Nozawa has played in a particular city?"

"That's easy. What city do you want to try?"

"How about Nagasaki, for example?"

"No problem," said Tabuchi, his mood lightening again.

They moved over to the computer, which was perched precariously on a trestle table loaded with bundles of Nozawa magazines and comic books. Tabuchi clicked on the rising sun motif on Nozawa's headband. The speakers twanged out a familiar riff on the shamisen as the database menu appeared.

"Here we go," said Tabuchi proudly. "Just type the question, double click here, and there's the answer straightaway. All the concerts that Nozawa has ever played in Nagasaki, starting with his first national tour."

Martine examined the list. In the early days Nozawa had played Nagasaki frequently, but over the past two decades hardly at all. That was strange, since it had become more accessible with the opening of the bullet train line. The year after the Atami incident, Nozawa had played there on three successive nights. For some reason, the third concert had a flashing red star next to it.

"What does that mean?" asked Martine, tapping the screen with her finger.

Tabuchi peered at the flashing red star. "I don't remember exactly."

"Can we check it?"

"It won't be anything important."

"I'd like to see, please."

Tabuchi gave a grunt of annoyance and clicked on the star. Above it, a box appeared containing a few lines of text.

"The third Nagasaki concert was cancelled at the last minute due to bad health. No further details were ever given. According to rumors, Nozawa was drinking heavily during this tour. Afterward he took a three-month break from professional activities."

"So what exactly happened?" persisted Martine.

"How do you mean?"

"Come on—you must have a theory. What happened that night?"

Tabuchi shrugged. "Probably as it says—too much drink. The doctors were telling him to cool down."

"That's all?"

"It's such a long time ago. What does it matter now, anyway?"

Tabuchi closed down the database. Martine sat down and drank the rest of her coffee in silence. It was that last remark, so utterly out of character, that convinced Martine he was lying.

The train back to central Tokyo was jam-packed. Martine had to stand the whole way, unable to move her arms or legs and barely able to breathe. She felt strangely weak, dizzy from the juddering of the train, tingling hot and cold with the blasts from the air-conditioner. Was the stress finally getting to her? Or maybe she was coming down with the mystery bug that was raging through western Japan. Fifty people had already died of it, half of them adults in the prime of life.

Martine closed her eyes and submitted to the rhythms of the train. She switched off her personal force field, merging into the crush of flesh around her. Some of her friends complained about sexual harassment, but at this level of human density how could you tell whether you were being harassed? Several times Martine had felt something hard pressing up against her buttocks, and craned around to see a housewife clutching an umbrella or a shopping bag. Once her own hand had gotten trapped against the groin of a long-haired male student. He'd kept on staring out the window, but the growing pressure against her fingers was unmistakable. In a situation like that, who was harassing who?

Forty minutes later the train pulled into Tokyo Station. Martine called Kyo-san from the platform.

"I won't be back in the office this afternoon. There's some research I need to do, and anyway I'm feeling really washed out."

"Take care of yourself now. No sitting in front of a computer screen all day long. That's no way to stay young and beautiful."

Kyo-san sounded concerned, as well she might. Martine had never before taken any sick leave.

"Okay. Were there any important messages?"

"Not really. Though there was one from the complete shit."

Martine frowned. "James Murphy? What does he want now?"

"He's coming to Japan in two weeks' time, and he wants us to arrange interviews with major political figures and business leaders. He says he's planning a special supplement on 'the Japanese threat to global stability,' focusing on the National Regeneration movement."

"Oh really? And I suppose he wants a list of my contacts too."

"That's right. How did you know?"

"It figures," said Martine grimly.

"So what do you want me to do?"

"Nothing. Just say I'm taking care of it personally."

"I see," said Kyo-san dubiously. "And what are you going to do?"

"Absolutely nothing."

This latest example of Murphy's deviousness was enough to banish Martine's torpor. She walked briskly across the station concourse, lips squeezed tight, heels stabbing the concrete.

An hour later she was sitting in the National Library browsing through, microfiche files of thirty-year-old regional newspapers. It was a slow, frustrating process. The records were in poor condition and badly cataloged. Not many regional newspapers had survived the crisis and few had survived the past thirty years without mergers, name changes, and long periods in which publication was suspended.

The *Nagasaki News* was in particularly bad shape. For the dates that interested Martine, half the pages were missing or too spoiled to read. In the case of the *West Kyushu Times*, the entire month's worth of issues was missing. The only intact publication was the *Nagasaki Weekly*, a long-defunct English language paper. It was produced on a tiny print run for the foreign community, and the only space allotted to local news was a couple of paragraphs obviously translated from the local press by someone with a shaky command of English.

Martine glanced through the issue covering the week of Nozawa's concerts. There was no mention of them, which was unsurprising. In those days Nozawa would have been an up-and-coming folk-rocker, hardly famous enough to compete with the local production of *The Mousetrap* or the recipe column.

There was just one item that caught Martine's attention, no more than a few lines in the local news section.

> Police still have no clues regarding the hit-and-run killing of twelve-year-old Junko Kawaguchi. A man was briefly held for questioning but not charged. Anyone in the area shortly after midnight on the 17th is requested to come forward and contact the police.

Nozawa's concert on the eighteenth was canceled at the last minute. In the early hours of the morning a twelve-year-old girl had died in a hit-and-run accident. Coincidence, or something more? Martine flashed back to Nozawa singing the "Lonesome Death of Mari-chan" in Shinjuku Park, his voice cracking up with the strain. She remembered the head of the unofficial Nozawa fan club, a man who had dedicated his entire life to gathering information about his hero, saying that whatever had happened in Nagasaki was too long ago to matter. Her reporter's instincts were yelling out "no coincidence," but her instincts were not enough. She needed a clincher. Where was she going to find it?

Martine called Saya. They arranged to meet in a manga coffee bar not far from the police station. Saya walked in wearing her cop face, tough and unimpressed. With her hair pulled back in a bun, she looked harder and sharper than usual. You wouldn't want to be handcuffed by this woman. You wouldn't want to be alone with her in the interrogation room.

"Thanks for coming out. You must be busy."

Saya sat down at the table. "It's the end of the month. We always get more customers after pay day."

"Really?"

"Yes. Especially for robberies and rapes."

"That's interesting. Robberies I can understand, but why more rapes?"

"Use your imagination. It's the time when men get drunk together and go to hostess bars and pink salons. Then maybe they don't have quite enough money for what they want. So later on they're walking home and they see some woman on her own and they decide to grab what they couldn't pay for. It can't be helped, I suppose."

Martine was shocked. "It can't be helped? Why not?"

"It's an instinct, isn't it? Thanks to the crisis, there are more and more men who can't get women. And when men can't get women, they behave like cats. You know what cats do? The male cat bites the female cat on the back of her neck. That paralyzes her and then he takes what he wants. Female cats spend their lives getting raped over and over again."

"How awful! What about dogs?"

"Dogs are much better behaved. Plato is a good example. He's very gentle with all his girlfriends."

They both laughed. Saya had loosened up now, and her cop face had gone. Martine touched her on her arm.

"Saya-san, I'm sorry to ask, but I need another favor."

"Meaning you want me to break the law again."

"Exactly. There was a young girl called Junko Kawaguchi who was killed in a hit-and-run accident in Nagasaki. I'd like to know what's in the file."

"When was that?"

"Way back, the year after the Atami incident."

Saya nodded thoughtfully. "All right. I'll do what I can."

"Thanks. You're a good friend, Saya."

"I'm not doing this for friendship. There's too much weird stuff happening in this country, and what you're doing could make a difference. I really believe that."

She took Martine's hand, and for a moment they looked into each others' eyes. Saya had beautiful eyes, large and deep and sparkling with life. Martine managed to pull her gaze away before it got embarrassing.

When Martine got home, there was a message from Makoto on the answering machine. An important potential investor had asked for a second presentation, which meant he would have to stay in London for a few more days.

It was good news about the investor, but Martine noticed how reserved he sounded, as if he were holding something back. But then Makoto was always holding something back. That was his character. At least that's how he was these days. The more Martine had discovered about his past—which wasn't much, since he preferred to keep it locked up inside his head—the more she realized how his wife's death had changed him. You could see it in the old photos—the way he'd smiled then was uninhibited, filled with enjoyment of life's possibilities. Now he had a different smile, careful and controlled.

The number of times Martine had seen the old smile were few and far between. Once in the early days, they had gone to a hot-spring resort in the mountains and got superbly drunk on saké and beer. Makoto had been soaking in the outdoor bath, along with half-a-dozen young salarymen on a company trip, when Martine came walking down the path, coolly slipped off her kimono, and stepped into the water. For a moment there had been silence, then Makoto stood up and started applauding. Within seconds all the salarymen had joined in, as red as prawns in the steaming water. That had brought out the old smile on his face, and afterward he'd been like a man in his twenties. He enjoyed being outraged, or pretending to be outraged. It broke down his inhibitions, physical and mental. In fact their few really important conversations, the ones where feelings were deliberately laid open and explored, had all taken place when they were naked or drunk or both.

It was late afternoon, Martine's favorite time of day. The heat was fading, the metabolism of the giant city slowing down. She considered rollerblading to the park and doing some yoga or sketching or just sitting there and reading Proust—all sensible stress-reducing activities that Kyo-san would surely approve of. In the end she decided to do something almost as relaxing as yoga: she would make a fruit gateau, a thank-you present for Saya. Martine rarely did any serious cooking—not for herself, not even for Makoto—but for some reason the idea of a fruit gateau was particularly appealing. She could picture it quite clearly, with moist sponge cake soaked in sherry, a row of gleaming cherries. It was going to be scrumptious.

She found what she was looking for on the internet, downloaded the recipe, then cycled over to a top-of-the-line supermarket where expatriate wives did their shopping. She was out of place there, amidst the overpriced vegetables and jewelry-draped housewives. When they peered at her out of the corner of their eyes, what did they see? They saw a blond in jeans and T-shirt, an obvious non-housewife, wandering inexpertly up and down the aisles. They saw the kind of woman they wouldn't trust their husbands anywhere near. And what did Martine see, when she looked at them? She saw emptiness, disappointment, an overpowering boredom that would have invaded her soul, snuffing out every spark of Martine-ness until there was nothing left.

It was nearly dark by the time Martine got home. She parked her bicycle and walked into the lobby of the building. There was a copy of the *Tribune* sticking out of her mailbox. The delivery boy must have made a mistake, since she had already received her copy in the morning. Martine rolled the paper under her arm and got into the elevator. It was only when she tossed it onto the kitchen table that she noticed the headline on the front page.

"Japanese Politician Assassinated by Drug-Crazed US Citizen."

The shopping bag hit the ground with a thud, sending black cherries rolling in all directions. Martine ignored them. She flattened the paper on the table and stared at it in astonishment. Under the headline was her own byline— "by Martine Meyer in Tokyo"—then two short paragraphs of text.

> Japan was today plunged into a state of shock by the assassination of Tsuyoshi Nozawa, the leader of the radical National Regeneration Party. Nozawa, also one of Japan's most popular singers, was shot dead while making a speech in front of Shibuya Station. The lone gunman, believed to be an American citizen, shot himself in the head and is currently in critical condition. According to initial police reports, the man has a long history of substance abuse.
>
> Spokesmen from all across the political spectrum have been paying tribute to Mr. Nozawa's courage and integrity. "He was a true Japanese patriot," said Yasuo Shimizu, acting leader of the National Regeneration Party. "We will redouble our efforts and carry his vision forward into the future.

Martine checked the rest of the paper. Every other story—every photo, every detail, from the weather report to the stockmarket numbers—was the same as in the copy she had received that morning. How difficult would it be to fabricate something like this? Not difficult at all. Martine was no computer expert, but she had often used page layout programs. All you would need to do is scan the front page, then blank out the story and replace it with something of equivalent size. The last message from the stalker had been a warning that Nozawa was going to be killed. She had responded by asking for details and now she had her answer. Nozawa was going to be shot dead while making a speech in front of Shibuya Station.

And somehow this was related to Reiko Matsubara and the Atami incident. The orange juice poisoning, the sabotage at the chemical plant, and the plane crash were all related to Matsubara. That wasn't hard to believe—the woman was notorious for murder and mayhem. So what did that make Martine's cyberstalker? An acquaintance of Matsubara's group, probably a member of the group. Somebody eager to make a claim of responsibility in advance.

Martine knelt down and started putting the scattered cherries back in the bag. Suddenly she was no longer in the mood for cake-making.

In the backstreets of Shimokitazawa stood a wooden two-story building half-covered with ivy. The ground floor boasted a small shop specializing in "ethnic goods"—African masks, incense burners from Thailand, leather goods from South America, silver jewelry and blankets and wood carvings from all over the world. The floor above contained the tiny apartment where the shop's proprietor had been living for the past twenty years.

The proprietor was a soft-spoken man with shaggy gray hair. His elderly neighbors felt sorry for him since he had no family or friends. He was such a pleasant man—well educated and courteous—that nobody liked to inquire too closely about the state of his business. It was obvious that conditions were difficult because hardly anyone visited the shop, apart from a few students on Sunday afternoon. Still he remained cheerful and diligent. Often he traveled abroad to find new suppliers, leaving the shop closed for weeks on end. On his return, he always brought his neighbors little gifts—cookies or handkerchiefs or bath salts.

Today, though, if anyone had been watching, they would have noticed an unusual level of activity in the shop. Half-a-dozen different people dropped by in the course of the afternoon. One looked like a high school teacher, in a shabby jacket and shoes with trodden-down backs. As he left, he glanced up and down the little alley as if he were emerging from a porno theater not a trinket shop. The next looked like a wealthy doctor, the kind that might buy up all the display items in one go. Unfortunately for the proprietor, however, he bought nothing, though he lingered inside for a long time. Three other men appeared, nondescript types who might have been salarymen at mid-ranking companies.

The last to arrive were two women, a young one with a figure like a movie star, and a stout middle-aged one. They stayed the longest, well over an hour, but at least they did make a purchase. The middle-aged lady came out clutching a calfskin attaché case.

NINETEEN

Martine watched Kawamoto emerge from the Nozawa headquarters—ringed, as usual, by a crowd of look-alike fans—and walk across the street to the coffee bar. From a distance she looked like any other fashionable young woman hurrying to work, though dressed rather plainly in her black cotton trouser suit. Only when she pushed the door open could you see the lapel badge and collapsible baton that identified her as a security guard.

"I supposed you've had breakfast already."

"Two hours ago," said Kawamoto, unsmiling. "After the traditional ethics class."

"You're studying traditional ethics?"

"I'm teaching it."

Kawamoto sat down and asked for a cup of green tea. Martine ordered a morning set, with iced coffee and toast with strawberry jam.

"Thanks for coming out at such short notice."

"I came because you said you had important information about Nozawa-sensei."

"That's right. Remember when we met in Shinjuku a couple of weeks ago? You told me about all the threats he was getting."

The security guard gave a little shudder. "Yes, there are so many people who want to harm him. The bright light of his genius fills them with hatred and jealousy."

"Have there been any particularly serious threats recently?"

"Serious? What do you mean?"

"An assassination threat, for example."

"We get several of those every week, mostly from crazy people who never leave their rooms. But if you've heard about one, please tell me. I'll make sure it's thoroughly investigated."

Martine waited until the drinks arrived before continuing. "I did hear about a threat to kill Nozawa, and the people behind it don't sound crazy. They sound clever and well organized."

Kawamoto took a notebook from her inside pocket. "Go on," she said calmly.

"It's going to happen soon. They're planning to shoot him while he's making a speech in front of Shibuya Station."

Kawamoto's pencil clattered to the table. Suddenly she looked as if she'd seen a ghost.

"What's the matter?" asked Martine curiously.

"Nothing. I mean, it's just such an upsetting idea, isn't it? The sensei means so much to everyone…"

Whatever skills Kawamoto had learned under Shimizu's tutelage, they did not include deceit. Rarely had Martine come across so clumsy an attempt to withhold information. Kawamoto tried to get up from the table, but Martine took her wrist and firmly pulled her back down.

"I thought you said he got these assassination threats all the time."

"He does. It's just that—I don't know, I shouldn't really say anything. I'll get into so much trouble…"

Kawamoto looked utterly lost. She had reverted to the confused, naïve young woman who had arrived in Tokyo from the countryside.

"Go on. You can tell me," coaxed Martine, despising herself as she spoke. Tell all your secrets to a journalist—what a recipe for peace of mind that was!

Kawamoto took a deep breath. "The thing you just told me—it shouldn't be possible."

"Why not? There would be plenty of opportunities for a clear shot, wouldn't there?"

"No, I don't mean that. It shouldn't be possible because nobody should know about it yet—the speech in Shibuya, I mean."

Now it was Martine's turn to be confused. "Nobody should know? You mean the speech in Shibuya has already been scheduled?"

Kawamoto's voice fell to a whisper. "It's for tomorrow. But nobody outside our organization is supposed to know about it. It's supposed to be a surprise event."

For a moment they stared at each other in silence, digesting the implications of what they had discovered.

"I think you'd better cancel it," said Martine quietly.

Kawamoto nodded. She looked on the brink of tears. When she stood up this time, Martine didn't try and stop her.

When Martine got to the *Tribune*'s office, Kyo-san was watching the INN news on the flat-screen TV. The picture showed a middle-aged Japanese man, being led out of a building by two burly cops, head bowed, jacket folded over his arms. He stumbled at the curb and the jacket fell to the ground, revealing the handcuffs underneath.

The voiceover was by the big-haired newscaster with the rubber mouth.

"Today top executives of Japan's Yamada Motors were facing charges of criminal negligence relating to thousands of deaths and injuries caused by the best-selling Yamada Ninja sports utility vehicle. Investigations carried out by INN reporters have shown that Yamada executives took no measures to remedy the Ninja's tendency to roll over when cornering at speed..."

Martine made a face, and Kyo-san turned down the sound.

"Is there anything else happening?" asked Martine wearily.

"The usual stuff. The trade talks are stalled. The peace talks are stalled. The environmental talks are stalled. Oh—and a present arrived from one of your admirers."

On the table was a package wrapped in extravagant red paper. Martine opened it and took out a box of chocolates and a note from Shimizu that read "Thank you for your excellent work."

Martine opened the lid to find twenty-four chocolate figures of Nozawa, each representing a different activity—Nozawa riding his motorbike, Nozawa playing the guitar, Nozawa planting rice seeds, and so on. She handed the box to Kyo-san, who took out a figure of Nozawa in judo gear and vindictively bit its head off.

"Go on, have one," said Kyo-san. "Chocolate is good for you apparently. It gives you energy and combats stress."

"Really? Who says so?"

"Scientists say so. The *Tribune*'s health column reported it a few weeks back."

The health column was the first part of the newspaper that Kyo-san read. After that came the book reviews, then the sports page, and finally the cross-word puzzle.

"Did these scientists also point out that chocolate gives you pimples and cellulite?"

"Relax, Martine-san. You're so tense these days. You really need those chocolates."

Martine picked out a chocolate Nozawa posing with a sword. She examined it critically, then nibbled at it cautiously. It was surprisingly good, filled with a dark, gooey sweetness.

Kyo-san was right, of course. She was too tense. The Nozawa story was bigger, uglier, and more dangerous than she had thought. It came after you, followed you around, and grabbed you when you weren't looking. Before you knew it, you were no longer sitting there reporting the news. You had been pulled inside the news, and there was no way out.

The phone rang. It was Saya. In the background Martine heard sirens whooping and a woman screeching out obscenities in an Osaka accent.

"What's all that noise?" said Martine. "I can hardly heard you."

Saya sounded as calm as ever. "I'm standing outside a pink salon in Roppongi. We just made an arrest for robbery and assault with a baseball bat."

"That woman was beaten with a baseball bat?"

"She's the one who did the beating. The client wouldn't pay so she whacked him over the head and took his wallet."

"Ah. It can't be helped, right?"

"I can understand her point of view. Unfortunately she went a little too far and the guy's in a coma."

Martine gazed over at Kyo-san, who was already working on the crossword. She doubted whether Kyo-san would approve of Saya.

"What about the hit-and-run incident? Did you manage to find anything?"

"That's why I'm calling, Martine-san. It's strange, but this file is empty too."

"Empty? But the girl was killed! There must have been a lengthy investigation, witness reports, statements from her parents. All that information can't have just disappeared!"

"That's what I told my friend in the records department. He said they'd been having all sorts of problems with the computer system. He blames the budget cuts."

The woman from Osaka was growling out blood-curdling threats at close range. It dawned on Martine that the object of her anger was Saya.

"I don't think budget cuts are responsible for this particular problem."

Saya had to raise her voice over the gravel-throated cursing. "Neither do I," she said tightly.

Martine put the phone down. The outlines of the story were getting clearer. A young folk-rocker—not well known yet, but with obvious talent and charisma—gets involved in a hit-and-run incident. The police take him in for questioning, but a powerful person intervenes. The singer gets released without charge and all records of the incident are conveniently lost. Many years later, when the singer has become the biggest star in the Japanese music industry, the powerful person calls in the debt. The singer is steered toward right-wing nationalism and a whole movement is fashioned around him. Then, when the plan is complete, they get rid of him and the political professionals take over.

She glanced over at Kyo-san, who was still absorbed in the crossword.

"Kyo-san, could you do some research for me? I'm interested in the educational backgrounds of the major political figures in the Nagasaki area. I'd like to know if any of them are graduates of the Morikawa school."

"That shouldn't be a problem. I've got a friend working in the Diet library."

"Thanks."

It didn't take long, and the answer was just as Martine had suspected. The Diet member for the Nagasaki region was a graduate of the Morikawa school. Meaning that he had been one of the silent men in dark suits who had lined up behind Nozawa at the press conference in the Dome.

The jigsaw pieces fitted together nicely, but there was still a gaping hole in the middle of the picture. What did this have to do with the Atami incident, supposedly the key to the whole puzzle? What was the link between Nozawa and Reiko Matsubara?

Martine spent the rest of the morning searching the internet and calling radical lawyers, music business sources, and tabloid writers. Nobody had any idea what she was talking about. The last resort would be to call Gary Terashima at the US Embassy. Terashima's people had detailed information on every significant political figure in every significant country in the world. They had financed the creation of Japan's governing party half a century ago and had carefully nurtured the politicians who supported their interests and destroyed the ones who didn't. But asking Terashima for a favor was a risky business. He would certainly demand favors in return, the kind of favors that were incompatible with journalistic independence.

Martine was deep in thought when her phone rang. It was the security guard, Kawamoto, sounding even more nervous than she had earlier.

"Meyer-san, I must talk with you as soon as possible."

"Did you tell them about the assassination threat?"

"Yes, of course."

"Are they going to cancel the speech in Shibuya tomorrow?"

"I can't talk now. Please come to our building right away."

The phone went dead. Strange behavior, thought Martine. Earlier Kawamoto had insisted on meeting outside, where none of her colleagues would see them together. Now she was asking Martine to come right into Nozawa's headquarters, previously off-limits to all journalists, even to the tame "Nozawa press club" of writers from the mainstream Japanese media.

Most Japanese politicians situated their offices within a convenient distance of the Diet building. That way they could snooze through debates in the daytime, then entertain powerful backers in Ginza nightclubs or scheme against rivals in the traditional restaurants of Akasaka. Nozawa, who rarely attended any Diet sessions and whose backers preferred to remain anonymous, had set up his office in the heart of the Harajuku fashion district. His recording studio was next door, linked by an underground passageway, and there was a helicopter pad on the roof. The street outside was always thronged with fans and stalls selling Nozawa kites, full-face Nozawa masks, and pint-sized Nozawa dolls that walked around strumming tiny guitars.

Martine squeezed her way through the crowd. The security people were obviously expecting her, and after a quick sweep of the metal detector they led her into an empty waiting room on the ground floor. Martine was not surprised by what happened next. The door opened and in walked Shimizu. Kawamoto was nowhere to be seen.

"Thank you for the chocolates," said Martine, bowing.

But Shimizu was not smiling. In fact his face was like thunder.

"It seems that your journalistic researches have exceeded the bounds of common sense, Meyer-san."

"I'm not sure I know what you mean," said Martine innocently.

"Yes, you do. Where did you get this information about the sensei's speech tomorrow?"

"I can't reveal my source, I'm afraid. But you should take the warning seriously. You must cancel the speech."

"Certainly not. If we canceled the sensei's activities every time some lunatic threatened him, we would never get anywhere."

"This isn't a lunatic. This is a person who means exactly what he says."

"Let me be the judge of that. Give me the name of your source."

Martine stared at him in fascination. She had never seen Shimizu lose his cool before. She had never imagined he could lose his cool. Yet here he was, practically shaking with rage.

"I can't do that, as you of all people should know."

"In that case you should know what can happen to you. Bad things, Meyer-san, bad things. I have friends at InfoCorp, people in important positions. I could have you fired in a matter of days."

"Is that all?" asked Martine. With James Murphy on the scene, that was hardly a serious threat.

Shimizu started talking fast, almost spluttering as the words rushed out of his mouth. "No, that's not all! I know plenty of things about your life, far more than you realize. That boyfriend of yours who owns the brewery—did you know he signed a loan guarantee for one of his suppliers? If that supplier went bankrupt, he would be personally liable for everything. It would wipe out his entire net worth, which in itself is far less than you might think."

"Really," said Martine evenly. She knew that the financial stresses were greater than Makoto let on. They had to be. In these economic conditions, just staying in business was a triumph.

"And that son of his. He's got some bad friends, you know, the kind that go places they shouldn't and buy things they shouldn't. Just imagine—if the police stopped him in the street and found something on him, what would happen? No exams, no university, nothing. All his life plans destroyed, before he even gets started."

Shimizu paused to examine her reaction. Martine said nothing. Could Shimizu really arrange something like that, she wondered. Yes, of course he could. With Morikawa people working in the background, it would be easy. The thought was devastating. Ichiro was the most important thing in Makoto's life, the one bright thing he had carried away safely from his marriage. If anything serious happened to Ichiro, Makoto would be crushed. It would turn him into an old man overnight.

"You don't believe me, Meyer-san? You don't think I can do these things?"

"Yes, I believe you."

"So are you going to tell me your source?"

"No, I'm not," said Martine, without a moment's hesitation.

They stared at each other across the table. Shimizu's smirk was hardening into something closer to a sneer.

"You don't really mean that," he rasped.

"Of course I do. By the way, my source gave me some other interesting information. It concerns a hit-and-run incident in Nagasaki."

The reaction exceeded all of Martine's expectations. Shimizu jerked upright in his chair, squeaking the legs against the polished wooden floor.

"What are you talking about?"

"I'm talking about a twelve-year-old girl left to die at the side of the road. Maybe Nozawa's next song should be called 'The Lonesome Death of Junko Kawaguchi.'"

Martine smiled brightly. Shimizu's eyes bulged and he opened his mouth to say something, but no sound emerged. Martine got up and walked out of the door without a backward glance.

She was sitting in a taxi checking the news on her palmtop computer when the message came through.

> Sweet angel,
> Tomorrow you must be ready to receive many important messages. Please keep your palmtop computer with you all the time, even when your golden body is naked in the bath.

Sweet angel? Golden body, yet again? It looked as if her mystery admirer was running out of clichés.

Ikebukuro in the evening. The safe daytime world of offices and shops and ordinary people going about their ordinary lives has faded from sight. In its place is a shimmering neon labyrinth where you can lose yourself for a night or forever.

This is not part of Japan. It is not part of anywhere. The currency is yen, dollars, rubles, drugs, sex, and weapons. The street vendors gabble away in a mixture of Japanese, Malay, and English impenetrable to outsiders. In the smoky back alleys you can watch snake-charmers and fire-eaters and real sword fights in which the ground is soaked in the losers' blood. You can buy forged passports and credit cards, ten-year-old refugee girls, a contract on the life of anyone you choose. Everything is available, at the lowest prices possible.

Jake McCloskey moved purposefully through the seething crowd. A street vendor thrust a lamp made out of a human skull right in front of his face, but he ignored it. A transvestite double-act tried to hustle him into a salon, one grabbing each wrist. "Special service tonight," crooned the voice in his ear. McCloskey replied with a vicious elbow jab, not even turning his head. He knew exactly where he was going. It was the same place he went every Tuesday evening.

McCloskey had been in Japan a long time, though he'd never planned it that way. Originally he'd come for a few weeks, a tousle-headed Midwesterner keen to experience a different culture. Then he got a job in an English language conversation school, and decided to stay longer. After all, speaking English was the only activity he was qualified to perform, and this was the only place on God's earth where people would pay him such good money for it. And then you had the women. Back home Jake had never had much luck with women, they had always made him feel clumsy and tongue-tied. In comparison, Japan was a paradise. The women laughed at his jokes even if they didn't understand them and told him he looked like a movie star. There was no need to say anything interesting. He just took them back to his tiny apartment, two at a time, three at a time, junior high school girls, twin sisters, whatever he wanted. They never complained, never mocked, never made him feel stupid and ugly.

The years slipped by, until Jake no longer bothered counting. Paradise was getting stale, but there was nowhere else he fitted in, nowhere else he could pick up a good-looking woman with a few simple phrases. He married three times—all mistakes—drank too much and started snorting, smoking, and injecting anything that gave him a buzz. When he looked in the mirror he saw a different person, a paunchy middle-aged man with sallow cheeks and empty eyes. So he stopped looking in the mirror.

Tonight Jake was in a hurry. He took a shortcut through the warren of alleys, coming out onto a major road whizzing with traffic. He turned left and trotted up the steps of a pedestrian bridge. There was the familiar figure standing in the middle of the bridge, elbows resting on the rail.

Jake trotted up the steps, then stopped and gaped at the man in surprise. He was the same build as Mo, and was even wearing the same kind of baggy combat trousers as Mo, but Jake had never seen him before in his life.

"Who are you?"

"Mo couldn't make it tonight," said the stranger, turning to face Jake.

"But I just called him an hour ago."

"Something came up. He sent me instead."

Jake examined the man closely. He had been doing business with Mo for several months now, always the same place and same time. Mo was the best dealer he had ever used.

"How do I know you're not a cop?"

"There are no cops round here. You should know that."

"All right. What have you got?"

"Buddha Kiss, one hundred percent pure. That's what you want, right?"

"How much?"

"Five thousand yen a gram."

Jake nodded. It was the usual product at the usual price. For ten thousand yen he could turn the world into a three-dimensional manga and himself into a superhero. Nothing he could do with a woman could ever compare to that sensation.

"It's down in the van. Come and check it out."

The stranger was pointing at a white van parked under the bridge on the other side of the road. Jake followed him down the stairs and climbed into the passenger seat. The stranger laid an attaché case on his lap and clicked it open.

"You want a test, right?"

The stranger gave him a straw, then took out a sachet and sprinkled some powder onto a piece of paper. Jake glanced nervously out the window. What they were doing was illegal, though the police would never dream of making an arrest in this area.

"Go ahead."

Jake bent down and took a sniff. It was good-quality stuff, no mistake. Already, a dull warmth was spreading through his body, and the neon lights were pulsing slower and fuzzier.

"Here, try some of this too."

The stranger was holding up a polythene bag with a black nozzle protruding from it. Before Jake had time to say anything, the stranger had squeezed the nozzle and an acrid spray went shooting into Jake's nose.

Jake pulled his head away. "Hey!" he yelled at the stranger. "What do you think you're doing?"

At least he wanted to yell, but something had happened to his throat. The muscles seemed to have locked tight, turning his voice into a strangulated croak. The stranger put the nozzle under Jake's nose and squeezed again. Then he opened the van door and stepped outside. His face was against the window now, watching calmly as Jake's mouth made strange shapes and his arms and legs started to thrash about as if he were drowning.

Jake McCloskey plunged though red water and black, through tunnels of pain and whirlpools of blinding light. The water thundered in his ears, ripped the hair from his scalp, sucked the marrow from his bones. He was down there for days, weeks, lifetimes, rolling and screaming, dying and being reborn. Then finally he glimpsed a face above him, a woman peering down at him with motherly concern.

"He's waking up," he heard her say.

"What shall we do?" There was a man standing just outside his field of vision.

Help me, Jake wanted to shout, what you should do is help me! But he couldn't shout because there was a cloth stuffed into his mouth and he couldn't move because he was tied to a chair. His head felt heavy with pain.

The woman's face loomed in front of him again. She was wearing gold-rimmed glasses, and the eyes behind them were calm and serious.

"He's sweating too much. Turn down the temperature."

She reached out with a cloth and mopped Jake's face and neck.

"I'd better check the heartbeat," said the male voice.

Jake gasped as the cold metal of the stethoscope pressed against his chest. Any sensation was pain. Looking over the woman's shoulder he saw a closed door, a concrete wall, a bare lightbulb hanging from a tangle of wires. He heard traffic rumbling somewhere overhead. Who were these people? Why had they brought him here?

"It's normal."

The woman glanced at her watch. "It's time to give him another shot. Be careful with the needle."

The man stepped forward. Jake watched, fascinated, as the gleaming hypodermic slid into his arm. He didn't feel a thing. They must be doctors, he thought as the black waters rushed over him and his eyelids fluttered shut.

TWENTY

Martine was woken by the ringing of the phone. She glanced blearily at the clock. Five-thirty. Who on earth would call at this time? It was Kawamoto, just about to start her traditional ethics class. Her voice was trembling with indignation.

"He refused, Meyer-san! Can you believe it? I begged him to listen, but he just sat there smiling."

"Calm down, calm down. Who refused what?"

"I mean Shimizu-san. He refused to cancel the Shibuya speech. He said he couldn't because it was the starting point of the political campaign."

"Really?"

It had been obvious from yesterday's confrontation that Shimizu had no intention of canceling the speech. The protests of a junior security guard were hardly likely to disrupt a plan in which so much was invested.

"I wonder if he cares about the sensei at all," wailed Kawamoto. "He's not a true believer. He's just using the sensei to further his own ambitions."

If only she knew, thought Martine. The reality was much worse. With Nozawa out of the way, Shimizu would become head of the National Regeneration Party, which would become nothing more than the political arm of the Morikawa school.

"You did your best."

"My best wasn't good enough. If anything happens to the sensei today, my life will be worthless."

"Don't say that."

"It's true. Without Nozawa-sensei, I'm nothing. This whole world is nothing. Who would want to live in such a place?"

Kawamoto's voice dissolved into sobs and the line went dead. Martine put down the phone, now totally awake and totally depressed. This girl was the kind who really would kill herself. And how many others like her were there? Thousands, probably tens of thousands—all ordinary, decent people on the surface, but with a strange vacuum at the core of their being. In former times that emptiness would have been filled by a religion or an ideology. In today's world there was only Nozawa.

And even after Nozawa himself was dead, the Nozawa brand would still be there. Martine recalled Kaneda, Shimizu's rival management consultant, pointing out the flaws in the brand crossover strategy. There would be a short-term benefit, he had explained, but without a new emotional bond with the public it would quickly fade away. Well, Nozawa's death would instantly solve that problem. A new emotional bond would be created that was far more intense than the old one. Nozawa would be like Elvis Presley, JFK, and Yukio Mishima all rolled into one—a martyr, a god, a brand beyond comparison. Then whatever the Morikawa school wanted—a Japanese Star Wars program, bioweapons research, robot warfare capability—could be presented as part of Nozawa's dream. Nobody would dare oppose it.

Martine went to the window and peered through the curtains. The tints of dawn had almost disappeared. The last of the late-night girls were trooping toward the subway station, already anomalous in their microskirts, hot pants, and full-body tattoos. Cicadas, crows, taxi drivers, delivery boys, joggers, school kids on their way to cram school—all were well into their early morning routine. It was hard to imagine that by the time the sun set that evening the city would be a different place, the minds of its inhabitants irreversibly transformed by a single terrible event.

Twenty minutes of yoga, a shower, some coffee and muesli. Only then did Martine switch on her computer and check her messages. There was nothing that caught her attention, except a few lines from Makoto.

> I will be back in Tokyo late tomorrow. Please meet me at the usual place as I
> have important things to tell you.

Martine gazed guiltily at the screen. For the past few days she had been too busy to spare a thought for Makoto. And in fact she had something important to tell him too, something she certainly wasn't going to discuss by phone or e-mail.

She was just about to log off when another message appeared.

> Glamorous goddess,
> You must be in Shibuya at two o'clock this afternoon. I would prefer you to
> wear silky white panties with see-through panels.

Pathetic, thought Martine. The guy really was stuck for ideas.

How many people do you need to start a revolution? A million? A hundred thousand? Ten thousand? No, the answer was around thirty. Reiko Matsubara had known this right from the start, when she was still a high school student attending demonstrations, throwing herself against the wall of riot police unarmed save for her nails and her teeth. In those days there were many who talked revolution in lectures and debates, who wrote revolution in magazines, who fucked revolution in grubby boarding house rooms. But so few were ready to live revolution, to die for revolution, to kill for revolution! Thirty people—that's all you needed. Thirty who had ice in their blood and iron in their souls. Thirty who were so committed that they would spend decades working as doctors, teachers, and businessmen, and yet be ready for the call at any moment. Thirty who would never give up on the revolution, even if they had to wait until they were a hundred years old.

Matsubara had tested hundreds, had tested them until they broke and ran back to the security of ordinary bourgeois lives. She had kept on testing until she found the comrades she needed. After that it had been a question of patience and survival. The tides of history would turn in the end, of that she had been certain.

There were times when her dream had seemed like a distant ship disappearing into the night. Then she had thought of Lenin drifting through Europe, an exile with no resources except his pure revolutionary spirit. And that had been enough to turn the whole world upside down, to spread a new consciousness through the oppressed masses for generations to come. Sometimes she had conversations with Lenin in her head. She told him everything and he encouraged her, smiling like a father.

There were other times when her dream had felt close enough to reach out and touch. But never had it been as close as today. This was the day for which Reiko Matsubara had been waiting all her life.

Matsubara stowed the car in an automatic parking lot a few hundred yards from Shimbashi Station. Her daughter would travel by the Ginza line, and one of the others would be there too, wandering amongst the homeless with ragged clothes and a dirt-streaked face. That would be enough for security. Matsubara believed in simple, well-planned operations. The problems she had experienced always came from overelaboration, too many people doing too many things.

Matsubara walked through the crowded station without a sideways glance. Only when she got to the noodle stand did her eyes stray over to the homeless man slumped against the wall, a jar of cheap saké in his trembling hand. The homeless man raised the jar to his mouth, a sign that he had seen nothing unusual. Matsubara glanced at the cluster of young women standing next to the newspaper kiosk, students and young office workers waiting for their boyfriends. In the middle was a tall, frizzy-haired girl, wearing the same style of cut-off jeans and fluorescent T-shirt as the others. She had a phone pressed to her ear and was nodding her head—also a sign that nothing unusual had been sighted.

Matsubara ordered a bowl of her favorite noodles, pork with chopped leeks. As she tilted the bowl to her mouth, she noticed a man approaching the noodle stand from the other side. He was thin, hollow-cheeked, and had the eyes of a fox.

Mid-morning in Shibuya. The air was filled with the ever-present karaoke of the city—the wail of sirens, the blare of announcements and advertisements and warnings, bleeps and squawks from game arcades, jingles from fast-food joints, crazed marches from pachinko parlors. Huge crowds swept across the multiflow crossings, surged across the elevated walkways, disappeared into underground passages like iron filings pulled by a hidden magnet. Orange and green trains rattled across the bridges, windows packed with faces.

Into this seething cauldron of human activity came word of the afternoon's special event. Tsuyoshi Nozawa was to give his first public speech of the year, right here, in front of the station. The information was blaring from loud-speakers, and flashing up on giant video screens. Nozawa balloons were being handed out to children, and Nozawa fans and tissue packs to adults.

Soon the police arrived, blocking off the traffic and yelling at people through megaphones. Banners were put up, spaces roped off. The noise got a little noisier, the heat a little hotter. Shibuya was buzzing with anticipation.

With all the activity in front of the station, nobody had eyes for the happenings in a narrow backstreet a few hundred yards away. Nobody paid attention when a van drew up outside a shaky-looking, pencil-shaped building filled with nightclubs, pink salons, and mah-jongg clubs. Nobody gave a second thought when three workmen in overalls got out of the van and hauled a heavy box of equipment out of the back. Nobody thought it strange when they took the elevator to the top floor, which contained a massage salon that had gone bankrupt three months ago. And nobody thought it strange that when they reappeared fifteen minutes later only two men were carrying the box, which they swung one-handed into the back of the truck.

Meanwhile, not far away, Tsuyoshi Nozawa sat gazing at himself in the mirror. On one side of his chair a makeup woman was rubbing linseed oil into his cheeks, giving them that special gloss that looked so good on camera. On the other side, a manicurist was adding the last touch of varnish to his nails. Already they had trimmed his eyebrows, extended his eyelashes, buffed up his lips with the cherry paste they used for kabuki actors. Before that,

Nozawa had spent two hours with his hairdresser, slicking his hair tight against his skull, creating a quiff that would flip down onto his forehead at the right moment in the speech. Before that, he had spent time with the acupuncturist, the aromatherapist, and his speech trainer. Today everything had to be perfect.

Nozawa watched the man in the mirror lift his chin and narrow his gaze. No question, he looked handsome, strong, dynamic, scared of nothing, eager to embrace his destiny.

And who was that man in the mirror? Nozawa saw him every day, and yet the man was still mysterious to him. The things he said and did were often baffling, aimed only at pleasing people he had never met and never would. The man in the mirror lived his whole life in the minds of others. In that sense he was unreal, a kind of ghost.

Shimizu appeared beside him, also with slicked-back hair and glossy cheeks. He was wearing a dark suit with a yellow polka-dot tie.

"How do you feel, sensei?"

"Excellent," said the man in the mirror. "Though I'm still not satisfied with the choice of costume."

"That's a shame."

The man in the mirror tightened his jaw, copying the expression of grim determination used on the cover of the most recent CD.

"Yes, it is. I still think my idea of a simple blue kimono with a brown belt is more appropriate. This outfit—it's totally the wrong color for the occasion."

Nozawa turned and nodded at the white suit and white silk shirt hanging from a rail.

Shimizu dropped his hands onto Nozawa's shoulders and started to massage his neck muscles.

"Don't worry, sensei. For an occasion like today, the color white will suit you better than anything."

Martine took the Yamanote line to Shibuya. Squashed up in one corner, with a shopping bag rapping her knees and a rolled-up magazine pressed into her back, she checked her palmtop computer every two minutes. There was no message. At Shibuya Station the platform was more crowded than she had ever seen it before. People from all over the city—office-workers, housewives, students—were congregating to hear Nozawa speak.

The crowd moved toward the exit like a slow viscous liquid. The mood was cheerful, politely excited. Martine wondered what would happen if there was a panic. How many people would die, crushed in the stampede down the steps. She moved with the flow through the central passageway and out through the Hachiko exit, which was already packed with bodies. The police had sealed off the main road in front of the station and were directing people into the cordoned-off areas on either side. Up in the sky half-a-dozen press helicopters were buzzing around in circles.

"Move along!" bellowed a young cop with a megaphone. "Get over to the other side."

Martine let herself be carried across the road to an area that had been cordoned off by the police. She was standing in a group of around eighty people, including mothers with bellowing babies, school kids in uniform, and the ever-present Nozawa look-alikes. She checked her palmtop computer. There was one new message.

Blond queen,
When you see this message, raise your left arm in the air.

She raised her left arm in the air. The next message appeared within a matter of seconds.

Goddess,
Cross the street, turn left at the pachinko parlor, then find the building with
the adult goods shop on the ground floor. Go to the mah-jongg club on the
second floor. There is a present waiting for you on the table by the window.

Martine spun around, scanning the sea of faces. There were people pouring out of the station, jamming the pedestrian walkways, filling up the roped-off areas. Any one of them could be a terrorist sympathizer enjoying his game of deception.

Another message arrived on her screen.

Do not delay.

No "goddess" this time, nothing about her underwear. He was finally getting serious.

———

Reiko Matsubara parked the van around the back of the fast-food restaurant off the No. 7 bypass. They went inside and ordered iced coffee and hamburgers. The fox-eyed man ate and drank ravenously, slurping his drink and licking the gravy off his knife. As usual, he was uncommunicative. Matsubara watched him with irritation. He had obviously been instructed to give away nothing. He wouldn't reveal how he had arrived in Japan, or even where he had stayed last night. This, she suspected, was the doing of the man from Shanghai. He was obsessed with keeping the different elements of the project separate. That way if anything went wrong the damage could be contained. As per his instructions, only Matsubara herself was allowed to report to him, and only Matsubara herself was allowed to accompany the fox-eyed man. The others—her trusted comrades for over three decades—had to keep in the background.

When the fox-eyed man had guzzled the last of his ice cream, Matsubara paid the bill and they left. The van had gone and in its place were two brand-new motorbikes, helmets dangling from the handlebars. Matsubara eased herself into the saddle. The engine started the first time. She pulled down the visor, and let out the clutch.

Riding a motorbike, feeling the rumble of the engine and the breeze tugging at her clothes, reminded Matsubara of her younger days. In Lebanon they had ridden motorbikes all the time. Her second husband had been blown to pieces on a motorbike, hit by a bazooka shell in a Mossad ambush. At his funeral she had sworn to continue the struggle as long as there was breath in her body. She had carried out that promise, never faltering once, no matter how many setbacks she endured, no matter how many colleagues she left behind on the way.

Terrorists—that was what the capitalists called those who dedicated their lives to the revolutionary cause. It was a description that even now Matsubara found grimly amusing. What did they know of terror, the politicians who condemned it in press conferences, the writers who pontificated about it, the rich and comfortable who wagged their fingers and shook their heads? Could they even imagine the terror of a child prostitute living like a rat in the sewers of Ulan Bator, or a pollution-choked mother in Dacca giving birth to a deformed baby? Of course not! And yet they were happy to rain down destruction on the cities of the oppressed, to smash their poor ramshackle houses and hospitals and schools. This they did not call terror. They called it collateral damage, and the men responsible were feted as military heroes.

But, as Matsubara had always known, the true heroes were the revolutionaries. There would be no parades for them, no medals—just hatred and contempt, even from their own families. Their whole lives would be spent on the run, not a moment of real peace, always on the lookout for a government agent with a gun in his pocket.

That was the life that Matsubara had chosen. And she had chosen it not from hate, but from love. Love of the hundreds of millions who lived and died in darkness, love of justice and freedom for all, not just the privileged minority. When she was a child her father had said she was too softhearted. She couldn't bear to see living creatures in pain, not even insects. As a teenager the amount of suffering she heard about made her dizzy, driving her to the brink of suicide. She couldn't bear the world as it was and so she dedicated herself to changing it.

Never had she borne malice to anyone, not even to those she had killed—not even the arrogant young cop who had stumbled upon their training ground in 1971, nor the thuggish American marines dancing in the Hamburg disco, nor the CIA man in Greece, nor the Israeli consul in Holland. And so it would be in the case of the man to be killed today. Reiko Matsubara felt no hatred toward him, no emotion at all. In a world of so much human suffering his death would mean no more than the tears of a sparrow.

She leaned forward over the handlebars. The two motorbikes thundered toward Shibuya.

T W E N T Y - O N E

Martine followed the instructions. She crossed the road, turned at the pachinko parlor, and found the adult goods shop. In the window was an inflatable doll, a blond woman on all fours wearing a leather G-string and an ecstatic expression. A stream of people passed by, hurrying toward the station, several glancing curiously at Martine. From the adult shop came the sound of a woozy cassette player. The music was "Typhoon of Love" by Tsuyoshi Nozawa.

Martine passed through the beaded curtain hanging over the entrance and took the elevator to the second floor. The door of the mah-jongg club stood slightly ajar: inside was silence and darkness. She knocked once, then pushed the door open. The air-conditioner was chugging away, but the room was empty. Tenuous shafts of light filtering through the blinds revealed dust dancing in spirals, magazine racks, a couple of battered sofas. Over by the window was a table, on it a cup of coffee, still steaming, and a plate of her favorite brand of shortbread. Under the plate was a large foolscap envelope.

Martine sat down and opened the envelope. A single black-and-white photo slid out onto the table. It was the same scene as that in the photo delivered by the bogus courier—the room with the Red Core Faction posters, the witchy woman in jeans and black turtleneck, the two men in helmets sitting cross-legged in front of her. Except this time the photo had been taken from a different angle. The woman was shown side on, and the face of one of the men was clearly visible beneath his helmet. He had a thin moustache and bangs flopping down to his eyebrows, but the facial expression was familiar. Martine held the photo to the light to be sure. Yes, there was no room for doubt. The man gazing at Reiko Matsubara with that expression of puppyish devotion was none other than Yasuo Shimizu.

So that was it! The key really was the Atami incident, as she had been told.

She had assumed that Nozawa was involved in the incident somehow, that his involvement had been used against him by Shimizu and the rest of the Morikawa group. How wrong she had been: it was Shimizu who had been involved in the Atami incident. Follow it through, and what did one get? The probability that he had kept up secret contact with Matsubara's group and that he had decided to use her to get rid of Nozawa. Martine felt like kicking herself for underestimating the man. In reality he was the fulcrum of everything. He had close links with the Morikawa group. He had close links with the terrorists. And in a few hours' time, he would be the acting leader of a political movement riding on an unstoppable wave of popular emotion.

Martine checked her computer again. Another message had appeared.

Princess,
I hope the cookies are satisfactory. You must not move from there. You should watch the building exactly opposite. The biggest story of your life is about to unfold before your eyes.

Martine stared through the gap in the curtain. On the other side of the street was a shaky-looking, pencil-shaped building, filled with pink salons, money lenders, and cheap karaoke clubs. Martine pulled up a chair and settled down to watch.

She didn't have to wait long. Fifteen minutes later a stocky middle-aged woman turned into the building. A few minutes later came a painfully skinny guy in a white shirt and jeans. Martine glanced at her watch. Nozawa's speech was due to start in half an hour. These people were planning to assassinate him. There could no longer be any doubt.

The enormity of the idea hit her all over again. But what could she do? Call the police? Martine had enough experience with the police to know that wouldn't work, not at this late stage. There was no way she'd be able to convince them over the phone. There must be *something* she could do. Martine gazed at the wall, racking her brains for inspiration. And then she saw the alarm in the corner and the smoke detector in the ceiling. That was it! All these buildings had to have a fire alarm on every floor. If she could find out where they were and set them off, that would do the trick. The fire brigade would be there within ten minutes, and the assassins would have got cold feet by then. If she moved fast enough, there would be time to stop the assassination.

On the table in the middle of the room was a cut-glass cigarette box and a heavy lighter in the shape of the Statue of Liberty. Martine grabbed the lighter and made for the door.

Outside on the street the flow of people had increased. Martine dodged through them into the lobby of the pencil-shaped building. The elevator was waiting on the twelfth floor, the top floor. Martine's finger stabbed the button repeatedly, but nothing happened. They've jammed it, she thought. She glanced at her watch again—twenty-five minutes to go—then raced up the staircase.

What she was doing was dangerous, no question of that. But that last message had infuriated her: "The biggest story of your life is about to unfold before your eyes." So she was supposed to just sit and watch while Nozawa was killed, and then go back to her office and dutifully file a report for tomorrow's paper. She just couldn't see herself doing that. They had got the wrong person.

Martine moved swiftly, stealthily. The staircase was dimly lit, strewn with used tissue papers and hand towels. Most floors contained two or three businesses—money lenders, pink salons, costume clubs, video booths, karaoke bars. A few were open, but she didn't see any activity. On every floor there was a smoke detector in the ceiling, just in front of the elevator door.

On the eleventh floor there was a single door, which had been left a few inches open. Martine peered inside, but there was darkness, no movement. According to the sign, this office belonged to a trading company specializing in herbal medicines, although the management didn't seem particularly health conscious, having left a plastic bin overflowing with trash just outside the door. Martine took what she needed—a few handfuls of wastepaper, used chopsticks, dried-out hand towels, polythene wrappers, rolled-up magazines—and stuffed them into a cardboard box, then crept up the staircase to the top floor.

The twelfth floor also contained just one business establishment. It was a massage parlor called "Joy Campus." There was a signboard with a range of tariffs and some Polaroid snaps of naked girls grinning stupidly for the camera. The door was closed, and the lights were off inside. Through a panel of opaque glass she glimpsed a movement inside, a white patch appearing then fading away. Martine stepped back from the door. The skinny guy had been wearing a white shirt. They were in there, she felt sure. She checked her watch again. Fifteen minutes until the speech started. She bent down, laid the box on the ground directly under the smoke detector. Then she took out the lighter and flicked the statue's head once, twice, three times. On the fourth try a blue-orange flame sprouted from the figurine's mouth. Martine applied it to the ball of wastepaper.

"What the hell are you doing?"

Martine swiveled around on her haunches, heart thumping like a drum. A woman was standing at the top of the staircase. She bore a striking resemblance to the young Reiko Matsubara, tall with witchy eyes and long frizzy hair falling onto her shoulders. And in her hand was a gun.

The closer to Shibuya, the heavier the traffic. The two motorbikes had weaved between lines of cars, zipped through winding backstreets, edged around junctions and across tiny crossroads. There was no need to hurry. Matsubara's comrades had rehearsed the whole operation many times over. Everything had been taken into account.

They parked the motorbikes at the back of an empty love hotel, then walked three hundred yards to the shaky-looking, pencil-shaped building. There were a few passersby, none of whom gave them a second glance. That was one advantage of Tokyo—nobody ever looked at anybody else. They took the elevator to the top floor, and Matsubara unlocked the door to the massage parlor. Inside was dust, darkness, a sharp antiseptic smell. By the light of the window a stack of chairs and a leather couch were visible. On the couch was the prone figure of a man, his head wrapped in a towel.

The fox-eyed man glanced at her. "You'd better check him."

"If there was a problem, I would have heard already."

All the same, Matsubara went to the sofa and unwrapped the towel. The man's eyes were open, rolling wildly, and he was making squeaking noises though the masking tape that covered his mouth. Matsubara put back the towel.

"Are you sure he's all right?" asked the fox-eyed man.

"The drug's wearing off, but he's still flying. That's just what we want."

The attaché case was leaning against the sofa. The fox-eyed man knelt down and clicked it open.

"Have you touched this?"

"We confirmed the contents, that's all. It's been treated with care."

The fox-eyed man made a clicking sound in the side of his mouth. Matsubara wasn't sure if it signified approval or irritation or just bad teeth. He went to the window, slid open the hasp, and made the clicking sound again. Matsubara followed his gaze down to the area in front of Shibuya Station.

"What's the matter? Is the distance too far?"

"Not too far. It's a comfortable distance."

It was certainly no further than the seagull in Macao. The fox-eyed man was a perfect marksman, as Matsubara had seen for herself.

"How about the position?"

"It's okay."

Matsubara nodded. The position was excellent, as it should be after the work put into finding it. They had bought the massage parlor through a dummy company, and had operated it for three months before putting it out of business. Nothing had been left to chance.

The fox-eyed man placed the attaché case on the table next to the window and carefully lifted out the gun. Reiko Matsubara watched him lift it onto the windowsill. He spent several minutes fiddling with the sight, all the while making those clicking noises in the side of his mouth. He was totally concentrated, oblivious to her presence.

"Hurry up," said Matsubara. "It's time to get the fingerprints."

"I will do that."

"No. You're here to shoot, that's all."

"The gun needs careful handling. Let me do it."

He turned, frowning as if something had puzzled him. Reiko Matsubara stared back into his sharp, narrow eyes. This man meant nothing to her. He was not a revolutionary, just a technician obeying instructions. His work would soon be over, and then he would melt back to wherever he came from. After today Matsubara would never have to speak to him again, or listen to him clicking his teeth.

"Okay, here's a good idea. Let's do it together."

She didn't bother to keep the sarcasm out of her voice, but he didn't seem to notice. They went to the sofa and Matsubara unwound the sheet from the body of the prone man. She undid his hands and pressed them onto the rifle —the barrel, the lock, the sight—ignoring his muffled groans.

"Once more."

The fox-eyed man shook his head. "That's enough. The gun is delicate."

"Once more, I said."

This time he relented. Matsubara pressed the American's hands around the stock. That would do for fingerprints. Everything else had been wiped clean, and they were both wearing super-thin plastic gloves. Matsubara retied his hands and covered his body with the sheet. They wouldn't be needing him for another ten minutes. And then it would be for something less complicated—a single shot through the underside of the jaw.

The fox-eyed man was back at the window, using his binoculars to scan the area.

"Is anything happening?"

"The truck is coming. It just turned the corner."

"Let me see."

He handed her the binoculars and Matsubara gazed out of the window. The truck was moving slowly toward the station, flanked by police cars. The roar of the crowd was almost as loud as the sirens.

"Nozawa, Nozawa!"

The white figure on top of the truck raised both hands in the air, and the roar of the crowd rose a few decibels higher. There were two others alongside him, Shimizu in his dark suit and a younger staffer talking into a microphone.

The fox-eyed man tapped Matsubara's arm.

"I can hear a noise."

"What do you mean? The crowd noise?"

"Not the crowd noise. Outside the door!"

Matsubara wheeled round. She too had heard a voice. Then there was a knock on the door.

"Open quickly. There's a problem."

It was her daughter's voice, low and urgent. She was supposed to be on the floor below, watching the staircase. The fox-eyed man was facing the door, the rifle raised to his shoulder.

"Put that down," Matsubara hissed. "It's my daughter."

"What's she doing here?"

Matsubara didn't answer. The marksman wasn't going to like this. Mai wasn't supposed to be there at all.

She went to the door and opened it. A blond woman walked into the room. Mai was behind her, holding a gun to her head.

Martine watched as the middle-aged woman emptied her bag on the ground and went through her possessions.

"You say you're a journalist?" she queried in Japanese.

"That's right."

"Who do you work for?"

"The *Tribune*."

"And who else? Who sent you?"

"I came by myself," said Martine quietly.

"That's a lie! Mai, give me the gun."

The frizzy-haired girl handed her the gun, and she pushed the barrel against Martine's throat. The metal was icy cold on her skin.

"You can't do that now!" The skinny guy with the rifle turned from the window. He spoke English with a harsh staccato accent.

"This woman's a spy," said Mai, her eyes flashing fire. "She must be executed!"

The skinny guy shook his head. "That would spoil everything. I'll deal with her afterward, the same way as him."

He nodded at the human figure lying trussed upon the sofa.

"Come on, there's no time now. Please get him ready."

Martine glanced at her watch. Another two minutes to go before the speech began. The skinny guy was back at the window, his head tilted over the rifle, his body tensed like a spring.

The truck carrying Tsuyoshi Nozawa moved slowly along Meiji Road, two police cars leading the way. There were crowds on both sides of the road cheering, yelling his name, and throwing streamers in the air. Dressed in his white suit, Nozawa waved to his fans from his platform on the roof of the truck.

"What do you think?" murmured Shimizu, standing beside him on the platform.

"It's fantastic."

"No other politician could get this kind of response. It's unprecedented."

"You've done an excellent job. It won't be forgotten."

"Thank you, sensei."

Shimizu turned to wave at the people on the other side of the street. Nozawa leaned out of the truck, beaming at the crowd. He could see their eyes, tens of thousands of eyes, filled with hope and yearning. They wanted him. They needed him. Their adoration was like a force field, reaching out to engulf him. Nozawa lifted his face to the sun. Today his spirit was dancing. Today he felt superhuman.

Nozawa basked in the energy of the crowd, the hope, the yearning, the love. There were so many of them, so many spirits for him to reach out and touch. Never before had he felt his own power so keenly. Never before had he felt so real. He was sharing himself amongst all those people, becoming a part of them. And at the same time they were becoming a part of him. Oneness, many identities fusing into a single whole. Gazing into the sea of faces, he wondered if this was what Jesus Christ had seen when he gazed down the mountainside, or what Buddha had seen while he meditated under the banyan tree.

Someone handed him a microphone and he started to speak. He didn't have to plan his thoughts. He didn't have to think at all. The words would come tumbling out, held together by pure emotions. His memories, his pride and sorrow and anger, his dreams for the future—he wanted them to have it all. This would be no ordinary speech. It would be a song without music, forged in the depths of his soul.

He lifted his face skyward, felt the warmth of the sun on his brow. Today Shibuya was like a valley, the surrounding buildings like cliffs. And from one of these cliffs—far away, almost too far to see—there was a glint of light and then a sound like a firecracker going off. Suddenly Nozawa was down on the ground, rolling on the floor. He was shocked to see blood splattered across his shirt and trousers. A single scream rose from the crowd and then suddenly the whole world was screaming and he knew that the Oneness was broken, gone forever.

TWENTY-TWO

The crowd's screams were getting louder and wilder. Nozawa covered his ears with his hands and rolled up into a ball. It was a horrible noise, the noise of dreams being smashed to pieces and hope being trampled underfoot.

Someone grabbed Nozawa by the arm and hauled him to his feet.

"What's going on?" he groaned. "Shimizu, can't you explain what's happening?"

But the man who had hold of his arm was one of the security guards. Shimizu was sitting slumped on the ground, blood pouring from a wound in his head.

"Shimizu, please do something!" wailed Tsuyoshi Nozawa. "What's wrong with you? Make them calm down! I'll do whatever you want, just tell me..."

He carried on yelling for several minutes, until they lifted him down from the truck.

Reiko Matsubara sat on the table, watching the fox-eyed man standing motionless at the window. Nozawa had been speaking for several minutes already. When was he going to pull the trigger? There was no time for delay. Matsubara felt strangely agitated, almost nauseous. It made her recall her first revolutionary action, fire bombing the house of a Narita Airport official. There had been reason for nervousness then—she had been only seventeen—but why now? One reason was the presence of the blond spy. Matsubara had no idea who she was and what she was doing. Worse, there would be no chance to interrogate her. From now on everything had to be done exactly as scheduled.

The fox-eyed man still hadn't moved. It was hard to tell whether he was even breathing. Then there was a lull in Nozawa's speech, as he waited for applause. And slowly, very slowly, the fox-eyed man's finger squeezed the trigger.

The noise of the gun filled the room. Matsubara ran to the window and raised the binoculars. Then they clattered to the floor between her feet.

"You fool!" she yelled. "You've shot the wrong man!"

The marksman turned to face her. Wordlessly he raised the barrel of the rifle. She edged backward, eyes fixed on the gun.

"Wait, I think we should discuss this..."

Suddenly she made a snatching movement with her hand, but the skinny guy was quicker. There was a deafening crack and her head bounced back against the wall. She made a gurgling sound, then slid to the ground, leaving a broad trail of blood on the wall.

Mai screamed and ran for the door. The skinny guy swung around and there was another dry crack. Mai fell to her knees, and somehow managed to push the door open. The skinny guy shot her again. She fell flat on her face, bucked her legs once, then lay still. Martine stood rooted to the spot, heart beating wildly. The skinny guy turned to face her.

"What are you doing here?"

"I'm a journalist," Martine stammered. "You can't shoot journalists."

The man's eyes narrowed to coin-slots. "Why not?"

"Big trouble. It'd be an international incident."

The skinny guy raised the gun again, uncertain this time. This wasn't in the plan. The sound of sirens was getting closer. He glanced at his watch, then at the human shape on the sofa. Then he dropped the gun in Matsubara's lap, leaped over her daughter's body, and raced through the open doors of the elevator. Martine waited until the elevator doors had closed on him before dashing for the stairs. She took them four at a time, stumbling, reeling, slamming against the walls, not stopping to catch her breath until she reached ground level.

Down on the street the air was filled with the sound of sirens, helicopters buzzing low, blaring loudspeakers, hysterical voices shouting, sobbing, yelling out Nozawa's name. Martine slipped into the stream of people moving toward the station. Ten yards away, half-a-dozen men in black helmets and uniforms came pouring out of the back of a parked van. They jogged toward the pencil-shaped building, shoving aside anyone in their way. Martine squeezed past them, chanting "Nozawa! Nozawa!" at the top of her voice.

TWENTY-THREE

The young general rolled the malt whiskey around his mouth, relishing the harsh-but-sweet taste. How much better the real thing was than the bootleg product that his factories used to churn out. Once more he gazed at the news flash that had just zipped across his stock price terminal.

"Tokyo shooting—one reported dead at political rally."

The warm glow of the whiskey spread through his chest. That was it—the culmination of years of planning. He had finally proven that he was a warrior too, not just a man of business. He had shown that he had inherited his father's brilliant sense of strategy. And he had performed an act of great filial piety, presenting his father, right at the end of his life, with the revenge that he had always craved. The Japanese devils, as the old general liked to call them, were about to have their complacency ripped to shreds. Never again would they preen themselves as the lords of Asia. Their short period of hegemony, born from the bloody oppression of the Chinese people, was over.

Of course the story was not yet complete. He was still waiting for the operations in the United States to deliver the planned result. But that shouldn't be long in coming. Just last night he had received a message from his daughter telling him to expect good news in a matter of days. Truly he was proud of what she had achieved over there. It was evidence that the family's strategic genius had been handed down to another generation.

At first he had been dubious. Her courage was beyond question, but did she have the strength of will, the sheer patience to follow the plan through to its conclusion? He needn't have worried. She had plunged into her role with enthusiasm, enjoyment even. The new identity had been her own idea. She had even located the ideal candidate—a fellow student at the American university she had briefly attended, a quiet girl with no friends or family. The young general had provided the resources, but the operation had been supervised by his daughter herself and she had acted fast and boldly, never ceasing to surprise him with her resolve. And thanks to her efforts, a communications empire that spanned the globe, reaching deep into the dreams of the masses, had now been captured without battle even being joined.

The American side could look after itself. After today's triumph in Japan, it could wind down its activities for a few years, if necessary. What that scholar-fool Peng Yuan had called the flux point had already been passed. There was no going back. From now on, Japan would be like a child's spinning top that had decelerated too much to hold its equilibrium. It would break away from its former path, dipping and lurching crazily from side to side. And at the lightest of touches it would topple over, never to rise again.

He knocked back the last of the whiskey, and immediately poured himself another inch. Then he reached for the phone and called his father. Strangely, there was no reply, so he called the man from Shanghai instead.

"I just saw the news. You've done well, Comrade."

"Thank you, General. It has been a great honor to carry out this work."

"Have you received confirmation from our people yet?"

"Not yet, General, but I have sensitive information to discuss with you urgently."

The man from Shanghai sounded as stiff and cautious as ever. That was his way. He was a good soldier, but totally lacking in strategic vision.

"Come over to my office. We can drink whiskey together."

"This is a difficult time, General. There are many details that still have to be dealt with."

"Understood, understood. In that case I'll come over to your place. And I insist that you drink whiskey with me."

The young general put down the phone, grabbed the bottle of whiskey, and called for his chauffeur. As he got ready to leave, he noticed the headline on the stock price terminal.

"Tokyo killing—chaos reported at political rally"

It was a fifteen-minute drive across Zhongnanhai to the offices of the *Asian Peace Journal* where the man from Shanghai had been installed as editor. The young general sipped whiskey from the bottle and contemplated the bustling street scene. His father always said that there was too much prosperity, that the Chinese people were going soft. But how could you march forward without prosperity? How could you develop the weapons and technology? Another of his father's sayings was that every country needs an enemy, and that losing an enemy was worse than losing a friend. Well, now China was about to find a new enemy, or rather an old enemy that had been lost for half a century. America was a useful enemy, arrogant and interfering, but it would never have a deep effect on the passions of the masses. It was too far away, too abstract, too different. Japan was another story. It had usurped China's rightful place in the world, grown rich and arrogant while the Chinese people suffered. This was an enemy to treasure, as perfect a match as a childhood sweetheart. With Japan to confront, the Chinese people would never go soft.

The young general's Mercedes eased to a halt in front of the *Journal*'s offices. He got out and marched through the door, swinging the half-empty bottle in his hand. He went up the stairs and entered the man from Shanghai's office without knocking. The latter was sitting at his desk, and there were three men sitting on the sofa in front of him.

"Who are you?" growled the general. They had hard, bitter faces, the kind that never show a glimmer of respect for their betters. Just breathing the same air as them had dampened his good spirits.

The three men stood up and saluted. The oldest one held out his ID card. "As you can see, we are officers from the political crimes division of the security police."

"What? Get out at once, or I'll have you arrested."

"No, General. We are here to arrest you on the grounds of bribery, illicit use of state resources, and treasonous political activity."

The young general rocked backward as if he had been thumped in the chest.

"Are you mad? Do you know who I am? One word from my father, and you would be executed tomorrow!"

A gloating sneer spread across the officer's face. "I doubt that. You see, your father has just been arrested on the same charges."

"That's impossible! My father is a great hero of the Chinese people!" He glanced at the man from Shanghai, who was sitting quietly at his desk as if nothing unusual were happening. "This is your office. Tell these idiots to leave at once. We have important matters to discuss."

Just then the man from Shanghai looked up, and the young general saw an expression on his face that he'd never seen before. Not cautious any longer, but cunning. Not stiff, but exultant. And as if a strobe light had exploded in his brain, the general understood what was happening.

"You must come with us now," said the officer, grabbing his arm. The general tried to shake him off, but the man was surprisingly powerful. One of the others grabbed his left arm, twisting and squeezing with vindictive force, and together they marched him toward the door.

"Just a moment," barked the man from Shanghai. He stepped forward and lifted the bottle of malt whiskey from the other's grasp.

"You'll pay for this with your life!" screamed the young general, as they bundled him into the corridor.

The man from Shanghai sat down at his desk and poured himself a generous slug. It was finally over, all the long years of patient scheming, the secret meetings, the strain of constant duplicity. What mattered was this—he had chosen the right side, the side that had won. The enemies of the old general had seen the opportunity. They had waited until the time was exactly right. Then they had pounced, as a mongoose pounces on an ancient, slow-blooded snake. Everything had gone perfectly. The sharpshooter Li had performed according to his reputation. Matsubara and her friends had never suspected a thing. The Japanese authorities had been as discreet and efficient as ever, providing all the resources requested then arranging a suitable cover story. Undoubtedly there would be many other opportunities for cooperation in the years to come, which he would exploit from his new position of power and influence.

Outside there was the noise of a car engine starting. The man from Shanghai stood up, raised his whiskey glass to the window, and knocked it back in a single satisfying gulp.

It was late in the afternoon when Martine got back to her apartment. She locked and bolted the door, closed the blinds and the curtains, and unplugged the phone. Thoughts and images were buzzing around her head like a swarm of bees. She tried yoga, but it was no good. Her nerves were too scrambled. She took a bottle of Makoto's premium beer from the refrigerator and drank it. That worked better. Creamy, cool, with a dark, slightly bitter taste—it was like Makoto himself in liquid form.

She went into the bedroom and sat on the bed, sipping beer from the bottle. She had six hours to put her thoughts together before the *Tribune*'s deadline. But what could she write? She had seen a man kill three people, shoot them with a rifle right in front of her nose. But who was he, and why had he done it? She had no more idea now than when she was racing down the litter-strewn staircase of the pencil-shaped building, hardly daring to believe that she was still alive. She didn't have a story. She had half a story, maybe less.

And what about the police? Should she go to them and report what she had seen? Almost certainly they wouldn't believe her. Almost certainly she would be stuck in a police station for the next twenty-four hours, answering the same questions over and over again, trying to come up with a convincing explanation of what she'd been doing there in the first place.

She finished the bottle and lay back on the bed. Suddenly she felt more exhausted than she had ever felt before in her entire life. A short doze was what she needed. It would refresh her mind, put her in the right mood to do the article.

Martine closed her eyes. There were noises inside her head, of Nozawa ranting, people yelling and shouting, gunshots. There were images drifting across the inside of her eyelids, of the middle-aged woman falling backward, blood speckling the wall, the skinny guy staring at her, completely expressionless.

Gradually the noises and images faded. The world turned darker and warmer and she was floating upward, as if she were being slowly lifted in a giant hand. Where was she being taken? Somewhere strange, but safe. For the first time in her life she would have a home.

And there was someone else there waiting for her. A man. She saw him smile in the darkness, welcoming her. He was above her, below her, behind her, surrounding her. She knew this man. She knew his scent and his taste. She knew the stroke of his hand and the touch of his tongue and the rough gentleness as he held her and the slow strength as he filled her. She knew everything about him, except one thing. She had forgotten his name. It was in a language that she didn't understand. How could she learn the man's name? How could she have him for her own if she couldn't say his name?

The thought rose within her like a wave as he moved faster, harder, abandoning restraint. She threw her hands to each side and gripped the sheets, bit her lip to summon concentration. She had to remember! It was almost too late. What was his name? It was there in the back of her mind. What was his name? What was his name? Here it was. Now!

"Makoto!" she screamed, and the sound of her voice woke her up.

She was lying on the bed, trembling, covered in sweat. And the clock told her it was six o'clock in the morning.

The way the NHK newscaster furrowed his brow told the world that unpleasant things were happening, but that the damage had been successfully contained. No need to worry, citizens. You can go to work secure in the knowledge that the authorities have the situation under control.

There was a short clip of the panicky scenes in front of the station—Shimizu being lifted onto a stretcher, Nozawa with blood on his shirt, wild-eyed and shaking, bellowing at the crowd not to go away. Then the newscaster returned, eyes narrowed and mouth pursed in an unmistakable expression of disapproval. Be careful citizens, his eyes were saying. This is what happens when we allow unruly elements to disturb our social harmony. Then there was a press conference at which a senior policeman explained how the notorious international terrorist Reiko Matsubara and her daughter had been killed while attempting to escape.

INN had given the story a different tweak. The big-haired female newsreader could hardly contain her joy as she announced the good news.

"Yesterday, Japanese police stormed a terrorist hideaway, saving the life of an American hostage and killing two of the world's most-wanted criminals in a shoot-out. The American ambassador in Tokyo has delivered a personal message from the president of the United States, thanking the Japanese police for their prompt and courageous action. Earlier today we spoke to Jake McCloskey, the freed American hostage."

The screen showed a balding, podgy-faced man blinking unhappily at the camera.

"So Jake McCloskey—how does it feel to be a free man?"

"Aw, it's great, Shelley. First of all, let me say that the Japanese police did a fantastic job. These terrorists were very bad people. They definitely deserved to die."

"Do you remember much about what happened?"

McCloskey looked uneasy, his eyes shifting from side to side.

"Not really. You see, these terrorists pumped me with drugs to keep me from escaping. I just remember the police coming in, a lot of shouting and shooting. Then they took the tape off my face and, man, was I glad to be alive!"

"I'll bet you were. Now we understand that you'll be leaving Japan next week and returning to your hometown in Minnesota."

"That's right."

The newscaster's rubbery lips stretched toward her ears. "And what's the first thing you're going to do when you get there?"

"Go to my favorite restaurant and have a double cheeseburger, followed by a chocolate sundae with whipped cream."

"Sounds good, Jake. And if your mom is watching now, do you have a message for her?"

The podgy gray face assumed an expression of puppylike sincerity.

"I love you, Mom," said Martine, sitting in front of her TV, a cup of coffee balanced on her knee.

"I love you, Mom," cooed Jake McCloskey on the screen.

The newsreader's smile was so wide now that her mouth was occupying the entire bottom third of her face. Martine, hit by a spasm of nausea, switched off the TV.

Ninety minutes later she walked into the office with a spring in her step and presented Kyo-san with a large box of her favorite rice crackers. She sat down at her computer and checked her messages. There was nothing from James Murphy, nothing from Gary Terashima, not a peep from her terrorist stalker. She had a strong suspicion that his interest in her was now finished.

"My, you're looking healthy today," said Kyo-san, gazing at her keenly over the top of her glasses.

"Well, thanks. You make it sound so unusual."

"No, seriously. You've got a glow in your face, looks like the stress has all gone."

Martine shrugged. "It must be my new diet—tofu and chocolate cookies, in equal quantities."

"Hmmm…" Kyo-san's gaze returned to the newspaper on her desk which, unusually, was not the *Tribune*. "So what do you think about these rumors?"

"Which rumors? There are so many these days I can't keep track."

Kyo-san tapped the paper with a bright red nail. "The changes at InfoCorp. There's a piece here in the gossip column of the *Journal*."

The *Journal* was the *Tribune*'s great rival, smarmy and tediously ideological but with a good reputation for accuracy.

"Go on, then. What's the story?"

"Jenny Leung is on her way out, and Mark Fletcher is going to take over the entire organization, Asia and the US included."

"Wow!"

"That's not all. Apparently he's planning a major restructuring of the *Tribune*, including a shake-up of the editorial team and distribution of half the equity to employees."

"Wow again!"

That was the kind of information that could have come from only one source—Mark Fletcher himself. Leaking it to the *Journal* would be as good as telling the *Tribune*'s editorial team that they were finished. No wonder James Murphy had gone quiet. With a bit of luck, his stint as Tokyo bureau chief would be over before it started.

Martine celebrated with a couple of rice crackers, then a couple more.

She spent the next hour stringing together a piece on the political reaction to the Shibuya incident. She got official reactions from a couple of politicians, and some bland quotations from political analysts and academics. From the National Regeneration Party, there was nothing but a terse "No comment." Did they already sense that their momentum was waning? Probably. In the words of the antique dealer, Shiina, the storm had passed. She had read it in Nozawa's panic-stricken face as he yelled for the crowd to come back, and in the disapproving frown of the NHK newscaster.

And after Martine's next article there would be no doubt. "Leading Politician in Hit-and-Run Cover-up"—this piece had to appear as soon as possible. She owed it to Kyo-san, to Saya, to Makoto, to Ichiro, to all the good people she knew. She even owed it to Nozawa himself. The Morikawa school had manipulated him like a puppet, but now he could turn his back on it, just as the crowd would turn its back on him. The statute of limitations would keep him out of jail, but his popularity would blow away like cherry blossom. Tsuyoshi Nozawa would become a curiosity, an embarrassment, and then, eventually, a forgotten face from the past, a fit subject for a "Where are they now?" profile. Maybe he would go back to playing tiny clubs in regional towns.

Maybe he would start writing some decent songs again.

In mid-morning there was a call from Kimura's friend. He sounded unusually nervous.

"Martine-san, I have some important information for you."

"Yes?"

"It can't wait.'

"Well, go on then."

Kimura's friend's voice dropped to a whisper. "Not over the phone. It's too risky."

So they arranged to meet at the most discreet location Martine knew—on the topmost viewing platform of Tokyo Tower, two hundred feet above the ground.

When Martine arrived, the only others present were a group of junior high school children on an outing and a courting couple gazing wordlessly at each other. There was a gusting northern breeze that tugged at her hair and made her dress billow out like a sail. Martine rested her elbows on the railing and gazed out at the hazy sprawl of the giant city, stretching to the north and the east as far as the eye could see, the mighty tangle of bridges and roads and train tracks, the chaos of signs and messages, the dizzying density of human events.

From this angle Tokyo didn't look like a city in crisis; it looked prosperous and peaceful, comfortably settled in its ways. Perhaps, thought Martine, this crisis really was ending. Or—a strange thought—perhaps the crisis had never existed. Perhaps it had been a mental state, a trauma that had built up over time and then suddenly erupted. There was a gap between the city that people lived and worked in, and the city they had built in their minds between the city of needs and the city of desires. The second of those cities was crumbling fast. The first was changeless, unending.

Kimura's friend appeared a few minutes later, his floppy hair bouncing in the wind. His usual calm had evaporated.

"Martine-san, please understand. I'm just an ordinary computer guy, I don't know anything about high-level political matters. It's too dangerous for someone like me."

He was waving his hands around like an actor on a stage. Martine grabbed him by both wrists.

"Calm down," she said sternly. "Now tell me what's happened. Have you managed to identify my stalker yet?"

"Not exactly."

"So what have you found?"

"I've found the computer the messages were sent from."

"And?"

Kimura's friend glanced at the courting couple, now busily taking photos of each other. Then he continued in a voice so low it was hardly audible in the gusting wind. "You won't believe this—it's one of the computers in the building where I work."

Martine let go of his wrists. "What? Are you sure?"

"Absolutely certain. It's used by the special operations people."

"Special operations? What does that mean?"

"It's a completely separate unit. They work for the public security department of the police."

Martine gazed at him, hands on hips, hair flying around her face. "Then I want to talk to whoever's in charge."

"That's impossible."

"Hmmm… They must have telephones in there, right?"

"I suppose so," Kimura's friend muttered unhappily.

"Come on," coaxed Martine. "You'd be able to find a phone number for me, wouldn't you?"

"Wait a minute! You can't just call these people up and ask for an appointment!"

"Why not?" asked Martine brightly. "It's more polite than barging in uninvited."

T W E N T Y - F O U R

They were waiting for her in a reception room on the fifteenth floor, three ordinary-looking men in plain dark suits and ties. They could have been section chiefs in a trading house, or hardworking officials at one of the less important ministries.

Martine bowed to the senior man and handed over her namecard.

"I'm Meyer of the *Tribune*. Thank you for sparing your valuable time."

The man bowed with studied politeness. No namecard was offered in return. They took their seats around a plain glass table. The senior man took out a cigarette and lit it.

"How can we help you, Meyer-san?" he said, exhaling a cloud of blue smoke.

"First of all, you can tell me your names. Then at least I'll know who to sue."

"Sue?" The senior man spoke as if he had never heard the word before.

"Yes. Sexual harassment is a criminal offense, even in Japan."

"I think there must be a misunderstanding. We are civil servants working hard to carry out government policy."

Martine waved away a curl of cigarette smoke. "Does that include sending out obscene messages? If so, the readers of my newspaper would be very interested in hearing about it."

"Ah." The senior man's eyes narrowed to a glimmer.

"I was there in that room, you know. I saw what really happened. You allowed that man to kill Shimizu, just as you allowed all those people to die from food poisoning and in that plane accident. Reiko Matsubara was behind it, but you people knew it was happening and you didn't stop it."

"Ah," said the senior man, more softly. The two juniors sat watching him intently, hardly moving a muscle.

"You thought I was just going to stay outside and watch as the police rushed in. Then you would get your international coverage, a big scoop on

255

how the terrorist plot was foiled. That was the idea, wasn't it?"

The senior man leaned back in his chair, eyes half closed. "I'm afraid you journalists have a weakness for outrageous conspiracy theories. They are usually unsupported by any hard evidence."

"I have evidence," said Martine coldly. "I have the messages you sent, the dummy newspaper too."

"Messages? Dummy newspaper? I don't believe such things exist."

"They do exist. They're stored in my computer."

"Are you sure of that? When did you last look?" His eyes blinked open, and a self-satisfied smile crept across his face. The two juniors noted it, and started smiling too.

Martine winced as the realization hit her. It would be too late now. They would have hacked into her computer, searched her apartment, done whatever was needed. "Look, you're not dealing with a reporter from the *Nikkei* or the *Yomiuri* here. This story is going to go global. It's too late to stop it."

The senior man made an "O" with his mouth, and a jet of blue smoke shot into the air. "Of course a famous journalist like you can write what you like. But you should be aware of the consequences. If you were indeed present at the crime scene, then perhaps you should be treated as a suspect."

"A suspect? That's ridiculous."

"Yes, it does sound ridiculous, doesn't it? But you yourself are claiming foreknowledge of several terrorist outrages. A sympathizer in the media, an ambitious journalist getting a little too involved with the story—it wouldn't be the first time such a thing had happened. What do you think, Kato?"

The senior man turned to the junior on his right, who nodded earnestly. Martine guessed that this piece of theater had been well rehearsed.

"In my opinion, no possibility should be ruled out," said Kato. "Obviously the testimony of the American witness would be crucial."

"Ah, the American witness. It seems his testimony was rather confused. Perhaps another interview is needed to clarify what happened."

Martine stared at them through the haze of smoke—the tired, bloodshot eyes, the ordinary faces of ordinary government employees. Were they really that ruthless? Of course they were! They would do anything to keep this information under wraps.

The senior man paused to take another long drag. "You're a journalist. The job of a journalist is to report the facts. But in this case you don't know the facts. Believe me, this is true. You do not know the facts. If you write a story that has no facts and no evidence, just rumors and suppositions—well, in that case you would merely be writing fiction. Don't you agree Kato?"

Again Kato nodded like a clockwork dog. They sounded confident, but in reality they had to be nervous. They were mid-ranking bureaucrats dealing with a situation that had slipped beyond their control. And there was no precedent to guide them.

"Look, this story is going to appear. It's too late to stop it now. If I don't know the facts, why not give them to me? At least you'll have a chance to give your version of what happened."

The senior man frowned. "But there is only one version of what happened. It was announced at the press conference given by the police last night."

Martine felt a wave of frustration welling up inside her. These men were going to continue performing their assigned role right to the bitter end. They had no other way of looking at the world.

"And that's your final position?"

"Meyer-san, please try and think in a more flexible way. We are always ready to cooperate with journalists of the highest quality."

"What does that mean?"

"In Japan there are sometimes incidents that are puzzling or mysterious, certain individuals hiding inconvenient facts. Naturally we have access to a good deal of special information of this nature. Some of it is of great interest, enough to keep a journalist in scoops for decades."

"So you leak these stories to favored journalists, I suppose?"

"A select few. Those who have demonstrated a keen sense of responsibility."

Martine said nothing. After the threats came the bribes. Their position was obviously weaker than they were letting on.

"Perhaps you, Meyer-san, have such a sense of responsibility. What do you think, Kato?"

Kato smiled encouragingly. "I think she's a true professional. I think she understands the value of information."

"Well, Meyer-san. Is Kato correct in his judgment?"

Martine waved away another wisp of smoke. "Certainly information is the lifeblood of journalism. I'll give serious consideration to what you've said."

The senior man stubbed his half-smoked cigarette into the ashtray. It lay in a twisted heap, still giving off a thin plume of smoke.

"That's good to hear. We have always had a high regard for your potential."

They led her to the elevator, the senior man making small talk about the weather, his juniors at his shoulders listening respectfully.

"Thank you very much for visiting us, Meyer-san. It was a pleasure to be of service."

The senior man bowed politely, and Martine bowed in response. "Thank you for giving me your valuable time."

Then the doors closed, and the elevator took Martine down to the lobby.

Only when she was alone in the back of a taxi did she unfasten the micro-recorder from her waist and check the tape.

Mark gazed down at the huge cinder block of a head lying on the pillow. Warwick Fletcher looked more peaceful dead than he ever had in life. The deep furrows had gone from his forehead, and his mouth was relaxed into a quizzical half-smile. It reminded Mark of the old photos, his father on the beach with his laughing wife or kicking a soccer ball at a somber little boy in shorts. He looked free of cares, which was how it was supposed to be.

David Liu patted Mark on the shoulder. He was standing too close, his face radiating bogus solemnity. "We're sorry you couldn't be here in time. It happened so fast, much faster than we expected."

Mark shrugged. "My father never liked to do what people expected. I guess he just got bored of lying there in a coma all day long."

"We did our best. You understand that, don't you?"

"Of course. When did you call Jenny?"

"Just before we called you. She should be here any minute."

Mark glanced out the window at the Los Angeles night, the streams of headlights, the glimmering neon. This anonymous, rootless place of hotels and highways and shopping malls was where his father ended his life, under hard, bright lighting, without friends or family, without myth or magic, without a touch of human kindness to console him. It was the logical end of the choice he made six years ago when he left the family home. Mark respected his single-mindedness, his drive to keep moving forward, but it wasn't for him. Human beings weren't like sharks. They couldn't keep moving forward forever. At some point they had to stop and connect.

Down at street level a white Mercedes stretch limousine with smoked windows swung through the security gate of the clinic. It parked outside the main entrance and Jenny appeared from the passenger side. She was wearing a black minidress with glossy patent leather boots, and her head was wrapped in a black scarf. To round off the picture, she slipped on a pair of dark glasses as she trotted up the steps. Jenny liked to wear dark glasses, even at midnight. Jenny didn't like to be surprised by paparazzi. She hated to be seen.

A few minutes later she marched into the intensive care unit, her face pale and pinched. She leaned forward to kiss him frostily on the cheek. Mark couldn't help flinching.

"Hello, Mark," she said. "Where on earth have you been? I've been trying to get hold of you for the past two days."

"I've been busy."

"Obviously."

She darted a glance at David Liu who muttered some unctuous words of regret and left the room.

"And how are you feeling?"

Mark gave her a blank stare. "My father just died an hour ago. That makes me sad. How does it make you feel?"

"Don't be insulting." She stretched out a hand to touch Warwick's cheek. Mark noted that she'd taken the trouble to wear black nail varnish too. Jenny the mourning widow was a polished act.

Jenny glanced sharply at Mark. "You and I need to talk, my darling son-in-law."

"If you've got something to say, then go ahead and say it now."

"What, here?"

"Why not? I'm sure Dad wouldn't mind. In fact he'd probably enjoy it."

There was a pause as they both stared down at Warwick's heavy body, as still as anything could be. The lips still held their color, the hair was as thick and springy as ever. It wasn't hard to believe that he was lying there listening to them.

For the first time in Mark's experience, Jenny looked disconcerted. Maybe somewhere underneath that armor-plating was a soft core of elemental dread. She turned away from the bed and moved toward the window.

"Well then," he pressed. "What is it you want to talk about?"

Jenny ran her fingers through her hair. "About that rather silly story in the *Journal*, the one about the new restructuring plan. I don't suppose you had anything to do with it?"

Mark beamed back at her. "As a matter of fact I did. I've been working on the idea for a while, and I thought it was a good time to test the waters."

"You've been working on a restructuring plan? On whose authority?"

"On my own authority. Of course I will be presenting it to the shareholders in due course."

Jenny gazed at him incredulously. "Aren't you forgetting something? As of an hour ago I am the chairman of the supervisory committee. If you oppose me, you will be removed from your current position in double-quick time."

"You're threatening to sack me? You can't do that. I'm the CEO of a major public company."

"Don't be childish. I control enough institutional votes to do exactly what I want."

"You think you can do what you want with a business that my father and my grandfather spent their whole lives building up? Just who the hell do you think you are?"

Jenny scowled, which gave her the appearance of an angry cat. "I'm fulfilling your father's dream, which is more than you could ever do. You were a great disappointment to him, Mark."

"You're trying to steal my father's dream. And it's not going to happen."

Jenny turned away as he approached. She'd sensed the change in his mood and realized that something was coming. Mark grabbed her by the arm and dragged her back to the bed.

"What are you doing?" she squealed, raking at his face. Mark spun her around and forced her head down to the pillow.

"Why don't you kiss him good-bye!" snarled Mark. "You won't be seeing him again."

He was vaguely aware of David Liu's panic-stricken face in the doorway.

"What's the matter with you?" panted Jenny, struggling to free herself. "You've gone completely mad!"

"Go on, kiss him. And after that you can tell him your real name."

Jenny suddenly went limp. She lay there on the bed, sucking in air. Mark removed his hand from her neck.

David Liu walked into the room, ignoring Mark's presence. "Are you all right, Jenny? Do you need any help?"

Jenny stood up gingerly, stroked the creases from her dress. "No thanks, David. Please leave us alone."

Mark tapped him on the shoulder. "Why not stay, mate?" he said grimly. "I'd like to introduce you to someone."

David Liu looked puzzled. Mark took a black-and-white photo from his pocket and threw it on the bed. It showed the naked body of a young Asian woman. She had two gunshot wounds in her left breast.

"Is this some kind of sick joke?" asked David Liu queasily.

"No joke," snapped Mark. "That is the real Jenny Leung."

TWENTY-FIVE

Martine had some spare time before meeting Makoto so she dropped by the antique shop in Ginza. Shiina was in his room upstairs inspecting a collection of Genroku-era tea ceremony implements. He rose shakily to his feet and greeted Martine with a long, rasping cough that was almost convincing.

They sat at a low table and discussed the weather, the properties of different kinds of lacquer, the best place to get early season persimmons. It was Shiina who nudged the conversation toward more pressing topics.

"I hear you have been very active recently," he wheezed. "For a young person that's good for the spirit. I wish I had enough energy to go out and find out what is really happening in the world."

It was one of Shiina's personal myths that he rarely left the musty atmosphere of the antique shop. In fact Martine knew that he was to be found in Ginza bars and Kagurazaka restaurants several times a week.

"Your advice was extremely valuable," said Martine. "Without your introduction to the Morikawa school, I would never have understood recent political developments."

Shiina used a paper handkerchief to dab at a rheumy eye. "Ah, it was nothing. I'm just a weak-brained old man who can hardly remember his own name."

"Even so, there are many questions remaining to be answered."

"Please remember the proverb—behind the back is another back. You will never find a single answer to events like these. There are many answers, all different according to how you ask the question."

Martine nodded. "But in this case some voices have said that questions shouldn't even be asked. They have said that looking for answers would be dangerous."

"Dangerous for whom?"

"Dangerous for everybody, they say. And especially dangerous for me."

"Ah." Shiina coughed again, a series of hollow barks that left his chest heaving. He took a long draft of barley tea before continuing. "Generally speaking, the public should not be burdened by excessive information. That's a sound principle, I think. However, it's also true that our way of thinking must change. These recent political disturbances could not have happened under the old system. Unfortunately, the old system has outlived its usefulness. This is a new era of turbulence and change. We mustn't let that fact be forgotten in all the jubilation and feelings of relief. It's certainly time to reform and rebuild."

"So you think these questions should be asked?"

"Yes, of course."

"And you think the results should be published, even if they are incomplete?"

"Perhaps I could help to improve them. Of course a feeble old man can have little idea of the true course of these complicated events. But there are several people who could provide a clearer picture. If you want, I will make the necessary introductions."

Martine looked at him in surprise. Shiina was offering his support in a way that was uncharacteristically direct. And the support of Shiina would outweigh the opposition of squadrons of mid-ranking bureaucrats.

"Thank you very much, sensei. That's a very generous offer."

"Perhaps you are wondering about the reason?" said Shiina, the leathery skin around his eyes crinkling with amusement.

"The reason for what?"

"The reason I provide you with information."

Martine fixed her gaze on a spot on the floor between them. "Yes, sometimes I do wonder."

'It's nothing to do with any French girl, you know. That's just a stupid story I made up to justify my actions to a couple of low-grade politicians. That's the kind of thing they understand."

Shiina gave a cackle of laughter that modulated into a long, racking cough.

"Are you feeling all right, sensei?"

"Yes, yes," Shiina wheezed. "I'm not ready to die yet. Now what were we talking about?"

"The French girl."

"Ah, the nonexistent French girl. Such pretenses are no longer necessary, I think. The real reason is that you are the most objective journalist I know. You're only interested in the story, not in what benefit you can get from it. That's a rare thing these days."

"Those are kind words."

"Not at all. This story must be told, for the good of the nation. I know you'll tell it well, without distortion or prejudice. You have the advantage of looking in from outside. You see things that nobody else can see."

"Not even you, sensei?"

Shiina smiled. "I am Japanese." At that he embarked on a series of deep, wheezing coughs that signaled that the conversation was over. Martine trotted down the creaky wooden staircase, her mind bubbling with ideas and plans. This was the kind of story that needed more than a few columns of newsprint; it needed a whole book. But how would she do that? Take a year's sabbatical? Quit completely? Suddenly there was so much going on. In Shiina's words, it was a time of turbulence and change—for the world, and for Martine Meyer too.

⎯⎯⎯⎯

The place where Martine and Makoto usually met after work was a yakitori bar under the railway tracks in Shimbashi. They had gone there on the first evening they spent together, and had been dropping by several times a month ever since. It was cramped and steamy, and when the trains thundered overhead the plates skipped on the little counter and the windows buzzed in their frames. It had suffered no discernible impact from the crisis, or indeed from anything else that had happened over the past quarter of a century. The menu was unchanged. The battered tables and benches were unchanged. Most of the clientele was unchanged. Martine had never tasted better yakitori anywhere else.

She poked her head through the sliding door, and the cook roared out a greeting. Makoto was sitting in the far corner nibbling on a stick of chicken gizzard. Today the place seemed livelier than usual. Or maybe it was Martine herself. Maybe her own high spirits were swirling around the smoky little restaurant, suffusing everything with a warm, soft energy.

Makoto stood up when he saw her coming. He looked younger than she remembered, and astonishingly attractive. Somehow he seemed to be made of a denser, stronger material than anyone else in the room. Martine made a move toward him, then suddenly it hit her. She felt short of breath, dizzy. One hand grasped the top of a chair, the other dropped to her belly.

Had the signs been right? Yes, for the first time she felt sure. Her body had known for several days, but now her mind was convinced of it too. There, deep inside her, was a tiny cluster of cells that would soon become shape and movement, then cries in the night, a real human presence. The hugeness of the idea turned her legs to jelly. That's what they had done, she and Makoto: they had planted the future.

He was still standing there smiling at her. She smiled back and gave a little shrug. He responded with a shrug of his own. She knew that she didn't understand this man, and probably never would. But he was the right man. A strange man in a strange country, but for a strange woman like Martine there could be no other. Light-headed with exhilaration, laughing at herself and at him and at everything else, she crossed the room toward him.

EPILOGUE

BEIJING 2008

W hen the bearer of the Olympic flame came loping into the stadium, the crowd erupted in a single wordless roar. Rather than dying away, the noise steadily increased as more and more people joined in, bellowing, clapping, stamping their feet, waving flags, hurling streamers, lifting their faces to the heavens and adding their voices to the mighty roar.

The man from Shanghai had heard nothing like it since the rally in Tienanmen Square forty years ago, when he, like tens of thousands of other schoolchildren, had stood with tears in his eyes and screamed out his devotion to the Great Helmsman, Mao Tse Tung.

But the world was a different place now. The force creating this tidal wave of noise was not ideological hysteria, but legitimate national pride. Everyone present—from high party officials to the humblest factory worker—knew what was being celebrated. The long march was finally over. Two hundred years after the Western colonialists began their depredations, China had recovered its status as a great nation and the undisputed leader of Asia.

The man from Shanghai smiled at the memory of Peng Yuan, the idiot scholar who had liked to sneer at "evolutionists." Well, the evolutionists had been proven right. The world system had already shifted to accommodate China's presence, and it would continue shifting for a long time to come. This was in accordance with the Way, the deep nature of things described by the sage Lao-tzu over two and a half thousand years ago, when Western Europe was the home of primitive barbarians and the ancient Greeks were amusing themselves with the first Olympic games.

"The best course is the course of no action," said Lao-tzu. The old general and that jumped-up son of his—what a pair of fools they had been not to understand this! It was an error that had cost them everything. The old general had died within a week of his arrest, shriveled up like a baked frog once his medicine was stopped. The young general was still alive, coughing his lungs out in a prison camp close to the Mongolian border, stripped of all dignity and honor. The others who had aided them had been dealt with more swiftly.

He watched as the torchbearer trotted around the track, the orange flame billowing above his head. How many gold medals was China going to win at these games? More than any other nation, that much was certain. As a member of the International Friendship Committee, he knew all about the "special diet" the athletes had been undergoing for the past five years. The results would be spectacular, setting the seal on the whole triumphant occasion.

As the man from Shanghai listened to the noise of the crowd—now closer to screaming than cheering—another phrase of Lao-tzu's popped into his head: "The wise man in the exercise of government empties the people's minds, fills their bellies, weakens their will, and strengthens their bones."

Lao-tzu would have greatly approved of the Beijing Olympics of 2008.

（英文版）カミの震撼する日
DRAGON DANCE

2002 年 12 月 6 日　第 1 刷発行

著　者　　ピーター・タスカ
発行者　　畑野文夫
発行所　　講談社インターナショナル株式会社
　　　　　〒112−8652　東京都文京区音羽 1−17−14
　　　　　電話　03−3944−6493（編集部）
　　　　　　　　03−3944−6492（営業部・業務部）
　　　　　ホームページ　http://www.kodansha-intl.co.jp
印刷所　　大日本印刷株式会社
製本所　　大日本印刷株式会社